noLi me TÁNGEYE

José Rizal

The last studio portrait, Madrid 1890, aged 29.

NOLI me TÁNGERE

JOSÉ RIZAL

Translated by Ma. Soledad Lacson-Locsin

Edited by Raul L. Locsin

Bookmark

ISBN – 971-569-188-9

Published by Bookmark, Inc.
264-A Pablo Ocampo Sr. Ave.
Makati City, Philippines
☎ 895-80-61 to 65
E-mail: bookmark@info.com.ph
Website: www.bookmark.com.ph

Printed in the Philippines by Island Graphics

The National Library Cataloguing-in-Publication Data

Recommended entry:

Rizal, Jose.
    Noli Me Tangere / Jose Rizal ;
translated by Ma. Soledad Lacson–
Locsin ; edited by Raul L. Locsin. –
Makati City : Bookmark, c1996. –
1 v 619 p.

    I. Locsin, Ma. Soledad L.
II. Locsin, Raul L. III. Title

PL5546 1996 899.21'03 P961000362
ISBN 971-569-188-9
ISBN 971-569-187-0 (cb)

04 03 02 01   00 99   2 3 4 5 6 7 8 9

What! No Caesar upon your boards, no mighty Achilles?
'Is Andromache gone? Does not Orestes appear?'

'No! But there are priests and shrewd commercial attachés,
'Subalterns and scribes, majors enough of hussars.'

'But, I pray you, my friend, what can such a laughable medley
'Do that is really great; greatness how can they achieve?'

Schiller: Shakespeare's Ghost
(Arnold-Forster Translation)

To My Motherland

In the annals of human adversity, there is etched a cancer, of a breed so malignant that the least contact exacerbates it and stirs in it the sharpest of pains. And thus, many times amidst modern cultures I have wanted to evoke you, sometimes for memories of you to keep me company, other times, to compare you with other nations— many times your beloved image appears to me afflicted with a social cancer of similar malignancy.

Desiring your well-being, which is our own, and searching for the best cure, I will do with you as the ancients of old did with their afflicted: expose them on the steps of the temple so that each one who would come to invoke the Divine, would propose a cure for them.

And to this end, I will attempt to faithfully reproduce your condition without much ado. I will lift part of the shroud that conceals your illness, sacrificing to the truth everything, even my own self-respect, for, as your son, I also suffer in your defects and failings.

The Author
Europe 1886

Introduction

When I was first asked if I could do a translation of Dr. Jose Rizal's *Noli me Tangere*, I felt that it could be superfluous in the light of the many English versions of our national hero's first social novel.

My introduction to the *Noli* was in its original—as its author had written it. I belong to that generation that came about at the turn of the 20th century when Spanish was still *the* language. And, although the Americans had already been here for a few years, the perceptions and mores of my early childhood were still largely influenced by the backwash of four centuries of Castilian rule and Catholicism. Thus, although the thoughts of Rizal were at that time radical, his manner of saying them, and what he wanted to say were closer and more familiar to most of us encased in the value traps of our generation.

I have subsequently read other fine English translations. Somehow I had the uneasy feeling that there was a greater pursuit to depict the political and social thoughts of Rizal's time in the context of the translator's milieu rather than simply to tell the story of a different world in a different time. Although translations have to be in tandem with the semantics of the age in which they are read to be appreciated, my own personal view is that they should, as much as possible, capture much of the nuances and cadence of the period in which they had been written; even at the risk of sounding awkward or stilted. I would imagine that there would be no pleasure, even though it be in the same language, of reading a translation of Shakespeare in modern American.

It is understandably difficult to thrust the mind into altogether faraway worlds and times with customs and social environments faintly remembered only by scholars and some ancients. Perhaps one of the ironies today is that few still relate to the subtleties of the historical past, except for a momentary and hazy glimpse blipped by the rhetoric of Independence Day celebrations.

It is also my view that the heart and mind need to understand and touch the past close to its pristine form, to sense the pulse of national heritage. If the Filipino cannot truly grasp his own past he may not value his present nor ascertain his future. For those who would like to view our passage across time under more comfortable auspices; that is, measured in the equivalent words of their own epoch, there are other excellent translations.

My own misgivings influenced the other options for this translation. Is it to hew closer to the original, to the way Rizal wrote it? Or, should it be freer and closer to the semantics of today? Spanish is a beautiful language; but translated into English literally, it becomes florid and clumsy with its long periodic sentences, shifting tenses and wandering modifiers and, therefore, less comprehensible. On the other hand, the sparse clarity of English often robs translated Spanish of its original ambience and precision.

In a sense this was the difficulty not only of the author but also of the translator who would like to live the best world in different tongues and have the best tongue in different worlds. The only work I can remember which faithfully recaptures the Iberian setting and aura in another language is Ernest Hemingway's *For Whom the Bell Tolls*. But, of course, the author wrote it in English. Otherwise, you could have thought of it as coming from the pen of Vicente Blasco Ybañez.

Whenever possible I have taken the liberty of cutting the long sentences by just converting them into more, but shorter ones; and of rearranging some of the adjectives and adverbs to bring them closer to the words they modify; adding or cutting words here and there but taking care not to enlarge or diminish the original, but to attempt to preserve the cadence of Spanish in the English translation. I must apologize to the reader if I have inadvertently made slips in this balancing act.

Some words have modern equivalents in English but do not have connotations similar to those endowed them by the social and political structures then. I have retained some of these in the original Spanish. Many of these words are still used in the Philippine national language with the same gist. For those who have a faint recollection of Philippine history, some of the annotations of the *Noli* as compiled by the National Commission on the Centenary of Jose Rizal from various sources and editions already published are appended and, at times, elaborated upon.

Since the *Noli* is a historical fact, and in fact read by

many as history as well as fiction, I referred to the facsimile edition of the original manuscript as well as the Berlin first edition for this translation, restoring some text omitted by Rizal in the first printing, such as the chapter on Elias and Salome. This is, therefore, a translation of the complete *Noli*.

It is my hope that the reader will enjoy this translation of the *Noli* with as much pleasure as I had doing it.

The Translator

Dedicated to my sons and daughters,

to my grandchildren,

and to Doreen Gamboa Fernandez,

whose trusting faith and active encouragement

motivated my translations of Noli Me Tangere

and El Filibusterismo.

Ma. Soledad Lacson vda. de Locsin

Contents

- 1 -

A Gathering

Towards the end of October, Don Santiago de los Santos, popularly known as Capitan Tiago[1], was hosting a dinner which, in spite of its having been announced only that afternoon, against his wont, was already the theme of all conversation in Binondo, in the neighboring districts, and even in Intramuros.[2] Capitan Tiago was reputed to be a most generous man, and it was known that his home, like his country, never closed its door to anything, as long as it was not business, or any new or bold idea.

Like an electric jolt the news circulated around the world of social parasites: the pests or dregs which God in His infinite goodness created and very fondly breeds in Manila. Some went in search of shoe polish for their boots, others for buttons and cravats, but all were preoccupied with the manner in which to greet with familiarity the master of the house, and thus pretend that they were old friends, or to make excuses, if the need arose, for not having been able to come much earlier.

This dinner was being given in a house on Anloague Street[3], and since we can no longer recall its number, we will try to describe it in such a way as to make it still recognizable—that is, if earthquakes have not ruined it. We do not believe that its owner would have had it pulled down, this task being ordinarily taken care of by God, or Nature, with whom our government also has many projects under contract.[4]

It is a sufficiently large building, of the style prevalent in many parts of the country, situated towards a bend of the Pasig river, called by many the Binondo creek[5], which plays, as do all rivers in Manila, the multiple roles of bathing place, drainage and sewage, laundering area, fishing ground, means of transport and communication, and even source of potable water, if the Chinese water hauler or peddler finds it convenient. It is noteworthy that this dynamic artery of the district where the traffic is heavy and entangled, a distance of almost one kilometer, relies only on a one-way wooden bridge rickety for a stretch of six months, and impassable the rest of the year, so much so that during the dry season horses take advantage of this permanent status quo to jump from the bridge into the water below, to the great surprise of the distracted mortals inside the coach who are either dozing or contemplating the progress of the times.

The house we allude to is somewhat low and misaligned—perhaps the architect who designed it could not see well, or this could have been the effect of earthquakes and hurricanes—no one can rightly say.

A wide stairway with green balustrades and rug-covered steps leads to the house from an entrance hall overlaid with painted glazed tiles, amidst potted green plants and baskets of flowers atop porcelain pedestals of motley colors and fantastic designs.

Since no porters or servants ask for the invitation cards, let us go up. You who read me, friend or foe, if you are attracted to the sounds of the orchestra, to the bright lights, or by the unmistakable tinkling of glass and silverware, and wish to see how parties are in the Pearl of the Orient[6]—I would find it more pleasurable and convenient to spare you the description of the house, but this is just as important. Generally speaking, we mortals are like tortoises: we are valued and classified according to our shells; for this and for other qualities as well, the mortals of the Philippines are the same as tortoises.

Once up we immediately find ourselves in a spacious living room, dubbed a *caida*[7], I don't know why, which this evening is being utilized as the dining room and at the same time as the orchestra hall.

At the center is a long table, profusely and elegantly decorated, which seems to wink temptingly at the freeloaders with sweet promises; and to threaten the timid youth or the unsophisticated lass with two mortal hours in the company of strangers whose language and conversation tend to have a jargon all their own.

In contrast to these earthly preparations we have before us a motley parade of picture frames aligned on the wall, representing religious themes such as *Purgatory, Hell, The Last Judgment, Death of the Just Man* and *Death of the Sinner*. In the background, encased in an elegant and splendid Renaissance-style frame by Arevalo[8], is a curious piece of canvas of wide proportions depicting two old women. The inscription reads: "Our Lady of Peace and Good Voyage[9], venerated in Antipolo, in the guise of a beggar who visits the pious and well-known Capitana Ines[10] in her sick bed." If the canvas does not reveal much taste or art, it has, however, extreme realism: the sick woman already appears like a cadaver in a stage of decomposition, with yellowish and bluish tints in her features; the glasses, objects and other utensils speak of a long history of illness. They are depicted so minutely and accurately to the last detail that the onlooker is able to catch a glimpse of their contents. Contemplating these paintings which excite the appetite and inspire bucolic thoughts, sets one to thinking that perhaps the cunning owner of the house knew the character of most of those who would be seated at the table, and to partly disguise his thoughts, caused precious Chinese lamps to hang from the platform, also bird cages without their occupants, crystal balls of quicksilver, red, green and blue colors, wilting orchids, desiccated puffer fish called *botetes*, and so forth, hiding completely the view on the other side of the river with ornately carved wooden arches, semi-Chinese and semi-European in style; leaving a view of the big *azotea* or terrace with lots of greenery; *emparrados* or green bowers made with the branches of propped vines and half-lighted by small multi-colored paper lanterns.

Those who are to partake of the meal are gathered in the living room surrounded by colossal mirrors and sparkling chandeliers. Over there on a pine platform is the magnificent grand piano purchased at an exorbitant price, and rendered still more costly this evening since nobody is playing it. In the living room is a giant-sized painting in oil of a handsome man in full dress suit, stiff, erect and very correct down to the gold tasseled cane which he holds in his bejewelled fingers. The picture seems to say: "Hm! Look at how much I have on! See how serious I am!"

The furniture is elegant, but somewhat uncomfortable

and unhealthy: the owner of the house is more concerned with the luxury of his household than with any hygienic consideration for the well-being of his guests.

It is as if he were telling them: "Dysentery is such a terrible thing, but you are seated on chairs imported from Europe. It is not every day that one can sit on a chair like this."

The living room is almost full of people: the men separated from the women, as they are in Roman Catholic churches and Jewish synagogues. The ladies, a few young Filipinas and Spaniards, open their mouths to suppress yawns, but cover their faces instantly with their fans, scarcely making a sound. Whatever attempts at conversation are ventured dwindle into monosyllables, like the sounds one hears at night, caused by rats and lizards. Is it, perhaps, the different images of Our Lady hanging from the wall between the mirrors, which makes them silent and assume a religious composure; or are the women here an exception?

The only woman receiving the ladies was Capitan Tiago's old cousin, she of kindly features, who speaks quite bad Spanish. All her manners and urbanity were reduced to offering the Spaniards a tray of cigars and a compound of betel nut, leaves and lime for chewing[11]; and to giving her hand to be kissed by the Filipinas exactly as the friars did. The poor ancient ended in boredom and, taking advantage of the sound of a plate breaking, left the living room in haste, muttering:

"Jesus! You wait, vile despicable creatures...!" and never reappeared.

As to the men, they are already making more noise. Some cadets are talking animatedly but in hushed tones in one corner of the living room, looking at everyone now and then, and pointing their fingers at various persons, laughing among themselves more or less quietly. On the other hand, two foreigners attired in white, with hands crossed behind their backs, and without saying a word, are pacing back and forth across the living room like bored passengers on board a ship. All the great excitement and heightened interest emanates from a group of two religious friars, two civilians and a military man around a small table with bottles of wine and English biscuits.

The soldier is a veteran Teniente, tall and with sullen features, looking like a duke of Alba, a straggler in the ranks of the *Guardia Civil*[12]; he talks little, but is brief and harsh. One of the friars, a young Dominican handsome to the point of prettiness, the epitome of pulchritude, and brilliant as his gold-mounted eyeglasses, is possessed of an early maturity. He was the parish priest of Binondo, and had been in previous years a university professor at San Juan de Letran.[13] He was reputed to be a consummate dialectician, so much so that in those times when the Dominicans dared to cross wits in subtleties with the seculars, the very capable commentator, B. de Luna, was never able to embroil nor catch him: the disputations of Padre Sibyla left him like an angler attempting to catch eels with ropes. The Dominican speaks little, but appears to weigh his words.

In contrast, the other friar, a Franciscan, is talking much and gesticulating more. In spite of his hair starting to turn gray, he seems to have conserved well his vigor and robustness. His features are correct, his glance not very reassuring; his wide jaws and his herculean build give him the appearance of a Roman patrician in disguise. Against your will you find yourself reminded of one of the three monks described by Heine in his book *Gods in*

Exile, who in the September Equinox somewhere in the Tyrol were cruising a lake in a boat at midnight and deposited each time on the palm of the poor boatman a silver coin as cold as ice, which filled him with fear.[14] However, Padre Damaso is not mysterious like those monks; he is jolly and if the sound of his voice is brusque like that of a man who has never bitten his tongue and who believes everything he utters is sacrosanct and cannot be improved upon, his gay and frank laughter erases this disagreeable impression, even to the extent that one feels bound to forgive him his sockless feet and a pair of hairy legs which would fetch the fortune of a Mendieta[15] in the Quiapo fair.

One of the civilians, a small man with dark whiskers, is notable for his nose, which, judging from its dimensions, should not have been his; the other, a blond youth, has the appearance of a newcomer to the country. The Franciscan was keeping up a lively discussion with this young man:

"You will see," the former was saying, "when you have been in this country for a few months you will become convinced about what I am telling you: it is one thing to govern in Madrid and another to stay in the Philippines."

"But ..."

"I, for instance," continued Padre Damaso, raising his voice a bit more in order not to allow the other to reply, "I who have been for twenty-three years thriving on bananas and rice in this country, I can speak with authority about it. Don't give me theories or rhetoric. I know the *indio*. You must take into account the fact that when I arrived in this country I was assigned to a town, small, it is true, but highly dedicated to agriculture. I did not understand the Tagalog dialect well then, but the women made their confessions to me, and we understood each other. And they became so fond of me that three years later, when I was being transferred to a bigger town made vacant by the death of the *indio* parish priest, all of them wept to see me go and gave me a send-off with gifts and music."

"But that only shows..."

"Wait! wait! Don't be too quick! My successor stayed for less time than I, and when he left town, had more people saying goodbye, more tears and more music despite the fact that he flogged them more, and had raised parish fees to almost double."

"But you will allow me..."

"Even more so, in the town of San Diego where I stayed 20 years, and which I...left only a few months ago. (He seems much disgusted.) Twenty years, no one can deny it, are more than sufficient to get to know a town. San Diego had six thousand souls and I knew every inhabitant as if I had given him birth and nourished him. I knew which one was lame; which side of his shoe pinched his foot; which one was making love to which *dalaga*; how many indiscretions this one had and with whom; who was the real father of the boy, etc. All made their confessions to me; they took good care to fulfill their duties. Let Santiago, the master of the house, bear me out. He has many properties in San Diego and it is in San Diego that we became friends. Well, you will see what the *indio*[16] is like: when I left, only some old women and some tertiary sisters[17] saw me off. And I had stayed there for 20 years!"

"But I do not see what this has to do with taking away the monopoly of tobacco[18]," answered the blond man, taking advantage of a pause in the conversation while the friar was sipping a glass of sherry.

Padre Damaso, taken by surprise, almost dropped

his wine glass. For a moment he looked at the young man squarely face to face and...

"What? How come?" he exclaimed with great surprise. "But is it possible that you do not see that which is clear as daylight? Don't you see, son of God, that this is palpable proof that the reforms of the ministries are irrational?"[19]

This time it was the blond man who was left perplexed; the Teniente knitted his eyebrows further; the diminutive man was shaking his head either in approval of Padre Damaso, or in disagreement with him. The Dominican then started to turn his back to them.

"Do you believe so?" the young man finally was able to ask seriously, looking at the friar curiously.

"Do I believe it? As I believe in the Gospel. The *indio* is so indolent!"[20]

"Oh! Forgive me for interrupting," said the young man, lowering his voice and moving his chair slightly closer. "You have uttered a word which evokes all my interest. Is such indolence naturally inherent in the native, or do we, as a foreign traveler has said, justify with this indolence our own, our failings and our colonial system? He was speaking of the other colonies whose inhabitants are of the same race..."

"Oh no, just envy. Ask Señor Laruja who also knows the country, ask him if the ignorance and indolence of the *indio* have any equal."

"Actually," replied the small man who had been alluded to, "nowhere in the world can be found another more indolent than the *indio,* nowhere in the world."

"Nor one as vicious and as ungrateful!"

"Nor one so uncouth!"

The blond man began to look uneasily at everybody.

"Gentlemen," he said in a low voice, "I believe we are

in the home of an *indio*... those young ladies..."

"Bah! Don't be so apprehensive! Santiago does not consider himself a native, and besides he is not present and even if he were...those are the foolish statements of newcomers. Let a few months pass and you will change opinion after you have frequented many fiestas and their *bailujan*, slept in many beds and eaten plenty of *tinola*."[21]

"What you call *tinola*, is it a fruit of the lotus variety which causes some men to be sort of forgetful?"

"What lotus or what lottery!" answered Padre Damaso laughing.

"You must have bells in your head. *Tinola* is a *gulay* of chicken and squash. How long has it been since you arrived?"

"Four days," answered the youth, somewhat piqued.

"Did you come as an employee?"

"No sir! I came on my own to get to know the country."

"Man, what a rare bird you are," exclaimed Padre Damaso regarding the other with curiosity. "Coming on your own and for nonsensical notions! What a phenomenon! There being so many books...just by having two finger-widths of forehead...many have written such great books! Just having two finger-widths of forehead..."

"Your Reverence, Padre Damaso, you were saying," the Dominican brusquely interrupted, cutting into the conversation, "that you spent 20 years in the town of San Diego and you left it...was not your Reverence contented...with the town?"[22]

At this question, asked so casually and almost carelessly, Padre Damaso suddenly lost his aplomb and laughter.

"No!" he growled brusquely, and let his full weight

fall hard against the back of the chair.

The Dominican went on in an indifferent tone: "It must be painful to leave a town where one has stayed 20 years and which one knows as well as the habit one wears. I, at least, felt deeply when leaving Camiling[23], and I had been there only a few months...but my superiors did that for the good of the community...it was also for my own good."

For the first time that evening Padre Damaso seemed much preoccupied. Suddenly he banged his fist against the arm of the chair and, breathing forcefully, exclaimed: "Oh! Is there religion or not, that is, are the parish priests free or not? The country is being lost...it is lost!"

And again, he pounded with his fist.

All those in the living room, startled, turned towards the group. The Dominican, much surprised, raised his head to peer at the Franciscan from beneath his glasses. The two foreigners who were strolling stopped for a moment, looked at each other, slightly agape, and continued their walk.

"He is in a bad humor because you did not address him as Your Reverence," murmured the blond youth to Señor Laruja.

"What does Your Reverence mean? What is the matter?" asked both the Dominican and the military man in different tones.

"That is why many calamities come! The government supports the heretics against the ministers of God!" continued the Franciscan, raising his fists vigorously.

"What do you mean?" the sullen Teniente asked, half rising.

"What do I mean?" Padre Damaso repeated, raising his voice and confronting the Teniente. "I say what I want to say! I mean that when the parish priest throws out of the cemetery the corpse of a heretic, nobody, not even the King himself, has the right to interfere, much less impose punishments. That little general...a calamity of a little general..."[24]

"Padre! His Excellency is Vice-Royal Patron!" shouted the Teniente, getting up.[25]

"Some excellency or Vice-Royal Patron!" answered the Franciscan, also getting up.

"In other times he would have been dragged down the stairs as the religious orders did one time to the impious Governor Bustamante.[26] Those were really days of faith!"

"I am warning you that I will not allow...His Excellency represents His Majesty, the King..."

"What King! What nobody? For us there is no King but the legitimate..."[27]

"Halt!" shouted the Teniente threateningly, as if he were addressing his soldiers. "You take back what you have said, or tomorrow, promptly, I will report to His Excellency!"

"Go ahead—this very moment, go ahead!" replied Padre Damaso with sarcasm, approaching the Teniente with doubled fists. "Do you think that because I wear a habit I lack...Go ahead! I will even lend you my carriage!"

The matter was taking a comical turn; fortunately the Dominican intervened.

"Gentlemen," he said in an authoritative tone and with that nasal twang that is so becoming to all friars:

"Do not confuse matters, or look for offenses where there are none. We should distinguish in the words of Padre Damaso two things: the words of the man, and those of the priest. The words of the latter as such, per se, can never offend because they come from the absolute truth. In those of the man a subdistinction has to be made: those which are said *ab irato* and those which are said *ab ore* but not *in corde;* and those which are said *ex corde.* These last are the only ones that can offend; and that is, accordingly: if already *in mente*, pre-existing for a motive, or only coming *per accidens*, in the heat of argument, if there is..."

"Well, I—*per accidens* and for myself—know the motives, Padre Sibyla!" interrupted the soldier, seeing himself embroiled in so many distinctions, and fearing that if these continued he would not come out of it guiltless. "I know the motives, and Your Reverence will make the distinctions. During the absence of Padre Damaso from San Diego, his assistant buried the body of a very worthy person—yes, Sir, a highly worthy person. I had met him many times in his home; he had honored me with his hospitality. That he had never gone to confession, so what? I myself do not confess either; but to claim that he committed suicide is a lie, a calumny! A man like him, having a son in whom he had placed all his affection and hopes; a man who had faith in God; who was cognizant of his duties towards society; a man who was honest and just, does not commit suicide. Thus I speak, and am silent as to other things, with which I bid for Your Reverence's grateful acknowledgement."

And, turning his back on the Franciscan, he proceeded:

"Well, this priest upon his return to the town, after maltreating the poor assistant priest, made him exhume the body, and remove it from the cemetery to bury it—I don't know where. The town of San Diego had the cowardice not to protest; the deceased had no relatives and his only son is in Europe, but His Excellency learned about it, and since he is a man of righteous heart, asked for the punishment; and Padre Damaso was transferred to another town. This is the whole story. Now let Your Reverence make your distinctions."

And having said this he left the group.

"I regret very much having touched a subject so delicate without any previous knowledge," said Padre Sibyla with compunction. "But finally the people got the advantage of the exchange..."

"That it has gained. And what about the losses in the transfer...and the papers...and all that have been misplaced..." interrupted Padre Damaso, blurting out, scarcely able to contain his fury.[28]

Gradually the gathering settled down to its former tranquil state.

Some guests had arrived, among them an old hobbled Spaniard, with gentle and harmless features, leaning on the arm of an aged Filipina, heavily curled and made-up, attired in European costume.

The group greeted the couple amiably. Doctor de Espadaña and his wife, the *doctora* Doña Victorina, joined the group we have already met.[29] There were some journalists, store owners or keepers, mutually greeting each other, conversing on one side and another, not knowing what to do.

"But can you tell me, Señor Laruja, how fares the owner of the house?" asked the blond young man. "I have not yet been introduced to him."

"They say he has gone out. I too have not seen him."

"Here there is no need for introductions," Padre Damaso interpolated, "Santiago is a good sort."

"A man who did not invent gunpowder," added Laruja.

"Señor Laruja, you also," exclaimed Doña Victorina with mild reproach, fanning herself. "How can the poor man invent gunpowder which, according to what they say, was invented by the Chinese long ago?"

"The Chinese? Are you mad?" exclaimed Padre Damaso. "Forget it. It was invented by a Franciscan, one of my order, by a Padre I don't recall, a certain Savalls, in the 7th century."

"A Franciscan! Well, this one could have been a missionary in China, this Padre Savalls," replied the lady who did not easily give up on her own views.

"Madam, you must be meaning Schwartz," replied Padre Sibyla without looking at her.

"I don't know. Padre Damaso said Savalls. I can do no less than repeat."

"Well! Savalls or Chevas—what does it matter? One letter does not make him Chinese," replied the Franciscan with ill humor.[30]

"And it was in the 14th century and not in the 7th," added the Dominican in a condescending tone, as if to mortify the other's pride.

"Well! a century more or a century less will not make him a Dominican!"

"Man! Don't be upset, Your Reverence!" said Padre Sibyla, smiling.[31] "All the better that he invented it. Thus he has saved his brothers that much labor."

"And Padre Sibyla, you say that it was done in the 14th century?" asked Doña Victorina with great interest. "Before or after Christ?"

- 2 -

Crisostomo Ibarra

Happily for the one being asked the question, two persons entered the living room.

These were neither beautiful nor well dressed youths to call the attention of everyone, even that of Padre Sibyla; it was not His Excellency, the *Capitan General* with his aides, to draw the Teniente out of his reverie. He took a step forward. Padre Damaso reacted as if petrified: it was simply the original of the painting in the full-dress suit, leading by the arm a young man clad in deep mourning.

"Good evening, gentlemen. Good evening, Padre," were the first words uttered by Capitan Tiago, kissing the hands of the friars, who forgot to give him the usual blessing. The Dominican had removed his glasses in order to look at the young newcomer and Padre Damaso was livid, with eyes bulging out of their sockets.

"I have the honor of introducing to you Don Crisostomo Ibarra, son of my deceased friend," continued

Capitan Tiago. "The gentleman has recently arrived from Europe and I want you to meet him."

There were some exclamations at the mention of the name; the Teniente forgot to greet the host, drew near to the young man and examined him from head to foot. The latter was exchanging the customary greetings with everyone in the group.

There was nothing striking about him other than his black suit in the midst of that gathering. His commanding height, his features, his movements, exuded an aura of wholesome youthfulness in which body and soul had developed and blended equally well. One could see in his frank and pleasant visage some slight traces of Spanish blood through a beautiful tan, somewhat roseate on the cheeks, perhaps the effects of an extensive stay in cold countries.

"You don't say," he exclaimed with some surprise, "the parish priest of my town! Padre Damaso, my father's close friend!"

All eyes looked towards the Franciscan. The man remained immobile.

"Do forgive me; I have made a mistake," added Ibarra, confused.

"You have not made a mistake," the friar finally was able to answer in an altered tone, "but your father was never a close friend of mine!"

Ibarra gradually withdrew the hand he had extended, regarding the friar with extreme surprise. He turned and found himself facing the gloomy figure of the officer, who continued to observe him.

"Young man, are you the son of Don Rafael Ibarra?"

Ibarra bowed in acknowledgment.

Padre Damaso half-raised himself from his seat and looked at the Teniente squarely in the face.

"Welcome to your own country, and may you be happier here than your father was!" said the soldier in a trembling voice. "I met and knew him, and I can say that he was one of the Philippines' most worthy and honorable."

"Sir," answered Ibarra deeply moved, "the eulogy you give my father wipes away my doubts concerning his fate of which I, his son, am still in the dark."

The eyes of the older man filled with tears; he half turned and hurriedly left.

The young man found himself alone in the room. The owner of the house had disappeared and there was no one to introduce him to the ladies, many of whom were regarding him with great interest. After vacillating for a few seconds, and with simple and natural grace, he directed himself to them:

"Allow me," he said, "to bypass the rules of strict etiquette. I have been out of my country these last seven years, and on my return I cannot help but greet her most precious adornment—her women."

Since none ventured a reply, the young man was obliged to withdraw. He headed towards a group of some young men, who, upon seeing him coming, formed a semi-circle.

"Gentlemen," he told them, "there exists a custom in Germany, that when a stranger comes to a gathering and there is no one to introduce him to the others, he gives his own name and introduces himself, and the others do the same. Allow me to do this, not to introduce foreign customs, because ours are also beautiful, but because I am compelled to do so. I have already greeted the skies and the women of my country. Now I want to greet the citizens and my fellow countrymen. Gentlemen, my name is Juan Crisostomo Ibarra y Magsalin."

The others gave their names which were more or less insignificant, more or less unknown.

"My name is A—, ah," said one young man wryly, scarcely bowing his head.

"Do I perchance have the honor of meeting the poet whose writings have kept alive my enthusiasm for my Motherland? I was told that you no longer write, but they failed to tell me the reasons..."

"The reasons? Because I do not call upon inspiration to drag itself down and to tell lies. One had a case against him for putting into verse a truism so common. They have called me a poet, but I will not be called a mad man!"

"And may I know what truism that was?"

"He said that the cub of a lion was a lion.[1] He was almost exiled for that."

And the strange young man left the group.

Almost running, a man with a smiling countenance arrived, attired like the citizens of the country, with buttons of brilliant stones on his vest. He approached Ibarra and gave him his hand, saying:

"Señor Ibarra, I have been wanting to meet you. Capitan Tiago is my good friend...I knew your worthy father...my name is Capitan Tinong; I live in Tondo, where my house is also yours.[2] I hope you will honor us with a visit. Will you come tomorrow and have lunch with us?"

Ibarra was delighted with so much amiability. Capitan Tinong smiled, gleefully rubbing his hands.

"Thank you!" Ibarra replied with feeling, "but tomorrow I leave for San Diego."

"What a pity! Well, when you come back then."

"Dinner is served!" announced the attendant from the Cafe La Campana.[3] The guests started filing past towards the dining hall, not without some prodding by the women, particularly the Filipinas.

- 3 -

The Dinner

(Jele-jele bago quiere)[1]

Padre Sibyla appeared gratified: he was dignified and calm, and his thin pursed lips reflected no disdain. He even condescended to speak with the cripple, Dr. de Espadaña, who answered him in monosyllables because of a speech defect. The Franciscan was in a foul humor. He kicked the chairs which were in his way, and even elbowed a cadet. The Teniente was serious. The others were talking animatedly, praising the magnificence of the table. Doña Victorina, however, deprecatingly puckered her nose, but immediately turned furiously like a viper that had been stepped on: in effect, the Teniente had stepped on the train of her dress.

"Don't you have eyes?" she said.

"Yes, madam, I have two eyes better than yours, but I was staring at your curls," answered the ungallant gentleman, moving away.

Instinctively the two friars proceeded towards the

head of the table, perhaps by force of habit. And there took place what is expected of contenders for a professorial chair: they praised with words the merits and the superiority of the opponents but subtly hinted at quite the contrary, and then grumbled and murmured when they did not obtain the prize.

"After you, Padre Damaso!"

"After you, Padre Sibyla!"

"Oldest friend of the house...father confessor of the deceased lady of the house...age, dignity and rulership."[2]

"Rather too old, shall we say, eh?...On the other hand, you are the parish priest of the district," replied Padre Damaso in peevish tones, without, however, letting go of the chair.

"Since you are in command I shall obey," conceded Padre Sibyla and prepared to seat himself.

"I do not command you!" protested the Franciscan, "I am not commanding you!"

Padre Sibyla was about to sit down, not minding the protest, when his glance crossed that of the Teniente. The highest official is, according to religious opinion in the Philippines, inferior to the position of a lay brother cook. *Cedant arma togae*, said Cicero in the Senate; *cedant arma cottoe*, say the friars in the Philippines.[3] But Padre Sibyla was a cultured person and he answered:

"Señor Teniente, here we are in the world and not in the church...the seat is due you!"

But judging by the tone of his voice, even in the world the seat belonged to him. The Teniente briefly refused, either not wishing to be bothered, or to escape the ordeal of sitting between the two friars.

None of the contenders remembered the owner of the house. Ibarra saw Capitan Tiago contemplating the scene with satisfaction, smiling.

"Why, Don Santiago, you are not joining us?"

But all the seats were already taken: Lucullus was not dining at home with Lucullus.[4]

"Don't move! Don't get up!" said Capitan Tiago, placing his hand on Ibarra's shoulder. This feast is in thanksgiving to the Virgin for your arrival. Oh! let them bring in the *tinola*[5]. I had it made for you because you have not tasted it for a long time." They brought in a huge tureen of the steaming dish. The Dominican, after muttering the *Benedicite*[6], to which almost nobody knew how to answer, started to distribute its contents.

Due to neglect or for some other reason, Padre Damaso got the dish where swam a bare neck and hard chicken wing among plenty of white squash and broth, while the others had legs and breasts, especially Ibarra, who was lucky enough to be given the choice bits. The Franciscan saw it all; he mashed the squash, took a little broth, let his spoon drop noisily and pushed his plate forward rudely. The Dominican was busy talking to the blond young man.

"How long have you been away from the motherland?" asked Laruja of Ibarra.

"Almost seven years."

"Come! You must have already forgotten her!"

"On the contrary; and even if my country seemed to have forgotten me, I have always thought of her."

"What do you mean?" asked the blond young man.

"I mean that it has been two years that I have failed to receive news of my country, so much so that I find myself like a stranger, who does not even know when and how my father died!"

"Ah!" exclaimed the Teniente.

"And where were you that you were not notified by telegraph?" asked Doña Victorina. "When we married we wired the *peñinsula.*" [7]

"Madam, during these last two years I was in Northern Europe, in Germany and in Russian Poland."

Doctor de Espadaña, who till then had not dared to say anything, thought it convenient to say something.

"I...I met in Spain a Polack from Va...Varsovia by the name of Stadtnitzki, if my memory does not fail. Have you by chance met him?" he asked timidly, almost blushing.

"Quite possibly," answered Ibarra amiably, "but at this moment I do not recall him."

"But you cannot mistake him for another," added the doctor, encouraged, "he was blond like gold and spoke very bad Spanish."

"Those are good identifications, but unfortunately over there no word of Spanish is spoken except in some consulates."

"And how did you manage?" Doña Victorina asked admiringly.

"The language of the country was useful to me, Madam."

"Do you also speak English?" asked the Dominican, who had stayed in Hong Kong and spoke well pidgin English, that adulteration of Shakespeare's language by the sons of the Celestial Empire.

"I stayed a year in England among people who spoke only English."

"And what is the country in Europe that you like the most?" the blond young man asked.

"After Spain, my second homeland, any country in free Europe."

"And you who seem to have travelled so much, come, what is the most noteworthy thing that you have seen?" asked Laruja.

Ibarra seemed thoughtful.

"Noteworthy...in what sense?"

"For example, with reference to the life of the people...social life, political, religious...in general in its essence...in its totality...!"

Ibarra reflected for a long while.

"Speaking frankly, what is surprising in those peoples, laying aside the national pride of each one...before I visit a country I endeavor to study its history, its exodus[8]—if I may call it that—and after that I would find it understandable. I always found that the prosperity or the misery of a people is in direct proportion to its liberties or concerns, and consequently to the sacrifices or selfishness of its ancestors."

"And you have not seen more than that?" asked, with sarcastic laughter, the Franciscan, who since the supper began had not uttered a single word, busy perhaps with the meal. "It is not worth squandering your fortune in order to learn so little. Any schoolchild knows that!"

Ibarra found himself not knowing what to say; the others, taken by surprise, looked at each other and feared a scandalous confrontation. "The supper is about to end, and his Reverence is fed up," the young man was about to say, but he controlled himself, and only said the following:

"Gentlemen, do not be surprised at the familiarity with which our friend and former parish priest treats me; he treated me thus when I was a young boy, so for his Reverence the years pass lightly, but I am grateful to him for it, because I remember too vividly the days when his

Reverence frequented our home and honored the table of my father."

The Dominican was looking furtively at the Franciscan, who was shaking. Ibarra continued, getting up:

"Please allow me to retire, because I have recently arrived and I have to leave tomorrow. I have many matters to attend to. The main course of the dinner is finished and I take very little wine. I hardly partake of liquor. Here's to Spain and the Philippines, notwithstanding!" And he drank from a glass which until then he had not touched. The old Teniente followed suit, but without saying a word.

"Don't leave yet," Capitan Tiago was cajoling Ibarra in a low voice. Maria Clara is coming. Isabel has gone to fetch her. The new parish priest of your town, a saintly man, is coming too."

"I will come tomorrow, before leaving! Now I have to make a very important visit."

And he left. Meanwhile, the Franciscan was giving vent to his feeling.

"You saw it?" the religious was telling the blond young man, gesticulating with his dessert knife. "That is out of sheer pride! They cannot stand being corrected by the priest. They presume to be decent persons! That is the evil consequence of sending young people to Europe. The government should prohibit it."

"And the Teniente?" Doña Victorina was saying, making common cause with the Franciscan.

"Knitted brows all throughout the evening! He has done well in leaving. So old and still...only a Teniente!"

The lady could not forget the allusion to her curls and the damage to her train.

That night the blond young man was writing, among other things, the next chapter of his "Colonial Studies": "On how a chicken wing and neck in a friar's dish of *tinola* can disturb the joy of a feast." And among his observations were these: "In the Philippines the most useless person in a supper or feast is the one giving it: to begin with, the master of the house can be thrown out into the street and everything will proceed as usual. In the actual state of things it is almost for the good of the Filipinos not to be allowed to leave the country or to be taught to read..."

- 4 -

A Heretic
and a Subversive

I barra was undecided. The night breeze which, at this
time of the year in Manila, is usually cool, seemed to
erase from his mind the cloud which had darkened it.
He uncovered his head and took a deep breath.

Passing him were carriages like flashes of lightning,
snail-paced calesas[1] for hire, passersby of different
nationalities. With the measured steps of one whose mind
was somewhere else, or of one who had nothing else to
do, the young man started on his way towards the Binondo
plaza[2], looking around him as if trying to recall a memory.
They were the same streets, with the same houses painted
white and blue, the white-washed walls painted in fresco
in bad imitation of granite. The church tower still displayed
its clock with the translucent face; the same Chinese stores
with their dirty old curtains and their iron grills, one of
which, as a boy, he had twisted one night, following the
example of the ill-bred brats of Manila. It had not been
straightened.

"Everything moves slowly," he murmured as he turned to Sacristía Street.

The ice cream vendors were shouting: *Sorbetes!" Huepes* or small torches still lighted the stalls of Chinese vendors and the women selling food and fruits.

"It is surprising!" he exclaimed. "It is the same Chinese of seven years ago, and the same old women. I could say this evening that I have dreamt for seven years of Europe; and Holy God! the stone in the pavement is still out of place, just as when I left it!" In fact, the stone lay still detached from its foundation in the pavement which formed the junction of San Jacinto and Sacristía streets.[3]

While he was pondering this wonder of urban stability in the country of the unstable, a hand was softly laid on his shoulder. He raised his face and found himself confronting the old Teniente who was gazing at him almost smiling. The man had shed the hard look and sullen brows which were so characteristic of him.

"Young man, be careful! Learn from your father!" he told the former.

"Do forgive me, but it seems to me that you have known my father... Can you tell me how and when he died?"

"That, you do not know?" asked the officer, stopping.

"I have asked Don Santiago, but he promised to tell me only tomorrow. Do you, perhaps, know?"

"I believe, as everybody else does, that he died in jail!" The young man took a step backward and gazed squarely at the Teniente.

"In jail! Who died in jail?" he asked.

"Man, your father, who was imprisoned," answered the Teniente, somewhat surprised.

"My father, jailed...! in prison? What are you saying?

Do you know who my father was? Are you..." countered the young man, grasping the soldier by the arm.

"I do not think I have made a mistake. Your father was Don Rafael Ibarra."

"Yes, Don Rafael Ibarra," weakly replied the younger man.

"But I thought that you knew about it!" murmured the Teniente in a tone full of compassion, contemplating what the young man was undergoing in his soul. "I supposed that you...but take courage. Here no one can be honorable without having gone to prison."

"I believe that you are not playing games with me," answered Ibarra in a weak voice after a brief silence. "Can you tell me why he was in prison?"

The old man paused to reflect. "To me it is very surprising that you were not cognizant of matters and the business of your family."

"In the last letter I received a year ago he told me he was not writing to me again for he would be very busy; he urged me to continue my studies...he blessed me..."

"Well then, he wrote that letter before he died... Soon it will be one year since we buried him in the town."

"Can you tell me the reason for his being in prison?"

"For a very honorable reason. But follow me, for I have to go to headquarters. I will tell you as we go along; lean on my arm."

They walked in silence for some time. The old man seemed to be in deep thought, seeking inspiration by stroking his goatee.

"As you very well know," he finally started, "your father was the richest man in the province, and even as he was loved and respected by many, there was someone who, on the contrary, hated and envied him. We Spaniards who have come to the Philippines are unfortunately not as we ought to be. I say this for one of your grandfathers as well as for his enemies. The continual changes, the state of demoralization in the higher spheres, favoritism, the shortness and the cheapness of travel are responsible for everything. To this country come the dregs of the peninsula and if one arrives a good man, soon he is corrupted in the country. Well, your father, if he seemed to be on good terms with the priest and with many other persons, had among the natives and the Spaniards many enemies."

He paused briefly.

"Months after you left, the troubles started with Padre Damaso, for what motive I cannot explain. Padre Damaso accused him of not going to confession. Before this he had not gone to confession either, and despite this they were friends, as you will remember. Besides, Don Rafael was an honorable man and more just than the many who regularly took to confession. He had his own rigid code of morality, and was wont to tell me when he was speaking to me of these troubles: 'Señor Guevarra, do you believe that God forgives a crime, a murder, for example, just by telling it to a priest, who in the end is a man like us, who has the duty to keep it secret, and fears to burn in hell, which is an act of attrition? Despite being a coward, a shameless cad and assured of salvation? I have a different idea of God,' he said. 'For me an evil is not corrected by another evil, neither forgiven with empty weepings nor alms given to the church.' And he gave this example: 'If I, for instance, have murdered a family man, if I have made of a woman a hapless widow and turned happy children into helpless orphans, will I really satisfy God's eternal justice by being hanged, by confiding the secret to one who would keep it, by giving alms to the priest who needs them the least, or by weeping day and night? And the widow? And the orphans? My conscience tells me that I should make restitution where and if possible to the person I have murdered; consecrate all of myself and for all my life to the good of the family to whom I caused so much harm; and even then, even then, who can replace the love of the husband and father?' Thus reasoned your father and he acted always according to this severe morality. It can be truly said of him that he never offended anyone.

"Quite the contrary, he endeavored to efface with good deeds certain injustices which he said had been committed by his grandparents. But, going back to his troubles with the priest, these were taking an evil turn. Padre Damaso was alluding to him from the pulpit, and if he did not clearly mention your father's name, it was indeed a miracle. Anything can be expected from such an individual as Padre Damaso. I foresaw that sooner or later matters would take a turn for the worse."

And the Teniente made another pause. "At the time, doing the rounds in the province, was an ex-artillery man expelled from the rank and file for being too brutal and ignorant," he continued. "Since the man had to live and was not allowed to do physical jobs that would damage our prestige[4], he obtained—from I don't know where—the job of collecting duties on vehicles. The hapless man had not received any education at all, and the *indios* soon got to know him well enough. For them a Spaniard who does not know how to read and write is quite a phenomenon. He was an object of derision and paid with blushes for the duties he collected: he knew he was despised and derided, which soured his already rude and evil nature even more. They intentionally gave him papers written upside down. He made a pretense of reading them and signing the blank spaces with some scrawls representing his signature. The *indios* paid, but made fun of him. He swallowed it all, but he collected, and in such a mood did not respect anyone, and with your father had an exchange of harsh words.

"It so happened that one day while he kept turning over and over a document given to him at a shop, trying to position the paper properly, a schoolboy made signs to his companions and, laughing, pointed to the man. The latter heard the laughter and saw the derision etched on the serious faces of those present. He lost his patience and ran after the boys, who fled, shouting *ba be bi bo bu*.[5] Blinded by anger and unable to catch up with them, he threw his cane, wounding the head of one of those who were deriding him, caught up with him and gave him a kick; and none of those present had the courage to intervene. Unfortunately, your father happened to pass by. Indignantly he turned to the collector, took hold of the latter's arm and rebuked him severely. The man, without doubt, saw red. He raised his hand, but your father gave him no chance and, with the strength characteristic of the descendants of the Basques...some say he hit the collector; others that he just pushed the man away. What happened was that the man tottered and fell some steps away, hitting his head against a stone. Don Rafael calmly raised the wounded child and took him to the courthouse. The ex-artillery man was bleeding from the mouth, and did not revive. He died some minutes later.

"Naturally, justice intervened and your father was put in prison. All the hidden enemies came out then and rained calumnies on him.

"He was accused of being a subversive[6] and a heretic. To be accused of heresy is everywhere a great disgrace especially in that period when the province had as *alcalde* a man who showed himself devout, who, together with his servants, loudly recited the rosary in church, perhaps to be heard by everyone who would pray with him. But to be a subversive is even worse than being a heretic and killing three tax collectors who know how to read and write and to discern. Everyone deserted him. They collected his papers and his books. He was accused of subscribing to the *Correo de Ultramar*[7], and to newspapers from Madrid; of having sent you to Swiss Germany; of having in his possession papers, letters and the photograph of a priest sentenced to death[8], and I don't know of what other things. There were condemnatory conclusions for everything, even for his usage of the *barong*[9] while being a descendant of peninsulars. If your father had been other than himself perhaps he would have been released soon enough, because a physician attributed the death of the unfortunate collector to congestion...but his fortune, his confidence in justice and his hatred of everything that was not lawful lost him his cause. I myself, despite my repugnance of imploring mercy from anyone, I approached the *Capitan General*, predecessor of the present one; I made representations to him that one could not be subversive who was hospitable to all Spaniards, whether poor or emigrant, giving them shelter and board, and in whose veins still ran generous Spanish blood. It was useless for me to guarantee your father's freedom with my own head; I swore on my poverty and on my honor as a soldier. And all I was able to achieve was a poor reception, a worse dismissal, and the name of *chiflado* or swellhead... Ah! those were sad days!"

The old man stopped to recover his breath and, perceiving the silence of Ibarra, who was listening without looking at him, continued: "I took care of all the requisites of the trial upon your father's request. I approached the well-known young Filipino lawyer, A—, but he refused to handle the case.[10] 'I would lose it for him,' he told me. 'My defense would motivate another foul accusation against him and perhaps against me. Go to Señor M—, who is a vehement orator of eloquence, a peninsular who enjoys the highest prestige.'[11]

"And so I thus proceeded, and the famed lawyer took charge of the case which he masterfully and brilliantly defended. But the enemies were greater in number and some, hidden and unknown. There were many false witnesses, and their calumnies, which elsewhere would have dissipated at a single ironic and sarcastic word from the defender, in this trial acquired consistency and substance. If the lawyer was able to annul them by pointing out their contradictions, there would be other accusations. They accused him of having unjustly appropriated large tracts of land; they demanded indemnification for damages and losses; they said he was in touch and maintained rapport with *tulisanes* for the protection of his crops and animals. In the end the matter was becoming embroiled in such a way that at the close of the year no one understood each other. The *alcalde* had to leave his post; another one came to replace him who was reputed to be righteous, but unfortunately stayed only one month, and his successor loved good horses too much.

"The sufferings, the frustrations, the discomforts of prison and the pain of seeing so many ingrates corroded his health of steel, made him ill with that sickness which only death can heal. And when all was about to come to a close, when he was about to be acquitted of the accusation of being an enemy to the Motherland and of having caused the collector's death, he died alone with no one to attend to him. I arrived to see him draw his last breath."

The old man was silent. Ibarra did not utter a single word.

In the meantime they had reached the door of the headquarters. The soldier stopped and, giving Ibarra his hand, said: "Young man, ask Capitan Tiago for the details. Now, good night to you! I need to see if anything has happened here."

Ibarra effusively grasped the thin gnarled hands of the soldier in silence, and followed him with his glance until the latter disappeared from view.

He slowly turned away and saw a passing carriage stop. He made a sign to the driver.

"To the Fonda de Lala[12]," he said with a scarcely intelligible accent.

"This one must have come from prison," mused the driver to himself, raising the whip to his horses.

- 5 -

A Star in the Dark Night

Ibarra went up to his room, which had a view of the river.[1] He dropped into an armchair, gazing at the space which was wide before him through the open window.

The house in front, on the other bank, was profusely illuminated and the gay sounds—of string instruments for the greater part—reached his ears. If the young man had been less preoccupied and more curious, he would have wanted to see with the aid of opera glasses what was taking place in that atmosphere of light. He would have admired one of those fantastic visions, one of those magical apparitions which at times are seen in the great theaters of Europe, in which to the muted sounds of an orchestra, in a shower of light and a cascade of diamonds and gold, in an oriental setting, and enveloped in transparent gauze, can be seen to appear a deity, a sylph, advancing without touching the floor, circled and surrounded by a luminous halo. At her presence the flowers bloom, the dance frolics, melodies awaken, and a choir of devils, nymphs, satyrs, genii, maidens, angels and shepherds, dance, shaking tambourines, gyrate and at the feet of the goddess, deposit, each one, a tribute. Ibarra would have seen a young and most beautiful maiden, svelte, attired in the picturesque costume of the daughters of the Philippines in the center of the semi-circle formed by all sorts of persons, talking and gesticulating with animation. There were Chinese, Spaniards, Filipinos, soldiers, priests, old women, young ones etc. Padre Damaso was beside that beauty; he was smiling the smile of the blessed. Padre Sibyla—the same Padre Sibyla, was addressing her; and Doña Victorina was arranging on the young girl's magnificent tresses a string of pearls and diamonds which reflected the colors of the rainbow. She was fair—too fair; her eyes, which were almost always downcast, revealed a pure soul when she raised them; and when she smiled and showed her small white teeth one could almost say that the rose is simply a plant; and ivory the tusk of an elephant. Between the transparent texture of the piña[2] and around her well-turned white neck winked, as the Tagalogs say, the bright eyes of a diamond necklace. One single man seemed oblivious to her luminous influence, one might say. This was a young Franciscan, thin, pale, emaciated, who was contemplating her, motionless at a distance, unbreathing, like a statue.

But Ibarra saw nothing of this, his eyes saw something else: four dirty bare walls enclosing a small space. In one of these, high above, were grills; on the dirty loathsome floor a pallet; and on the pallet lay an old man in the throes of death. He was breathing with difficulty. His gaze was directed everywhere around him and he was calling a name. The old man was alone. Every now and then could be heard the clanging of a chain or a groan behind the walls...then from a distance the gay echoes of a party, almost a bacchanalia. A young man laughs, shouts, and pours wine over the flowers amidst the others' applause and drunken laughter... The old man has the features of his father, the young man looks like him and the name the old man is tearfully calling is his, that of his son.

This is what the unhappy young man sees before him. The lights in the house in front have gone out, the noise and the sounds of the music have stopped, but Ibarra still hears the anguished cries of his father looking for a son in his final hour.

The silence had blown its hollow breath over Manila and everything seemed to slumber within the arms of nothingness: one could hear the cockcrow alternating with the chimes of the tower clocks and with the melancholy alarm of the bored sentinel. A piece of the moon showed its face; all seemed at rest. Ibarra himself was sleeping, exhausted by his sad thoughts, or by the trip.

But the young Franciscan, whom we recently saw immobile and silent amidst the general animation in the living room, was not sleeping—he was standing watch with elbows resting on the window sill of his room, his pale and emaciated face resting on the palm of his hand. He was gazing silently far away at a star in the sky in the darkness of night.

The star waned and was eclipsed; the moon lost its brilliance as it waned, but the friar did not budge from his place. He was gazing at the horizon, which was vanishing with the morning mist, in the direction of the Field of Bagumbayan[3], towards the sea which was still asleep.

The servant who came to knock at the door to awaken him so he could say early morning mass, drew him from his meditation.

- 6 -

Capitan Tiago

"Your will be done on earth."

While our personages are sleeping or having breakfast, let us concern ourselves with Capitan Tiago. We have never been his guest, so we have no right or duty to hold him in contempt, summarily dismissing him even in important circumstances.

Low of stature and fair-complexioned, corpulent of body and features thanks to an abundance of fat which, according to his admirers, came from heaven, or, according to his enemies, from the blood of the poor, Capitan Tiago looked actually younger than he was in reality. He could have been taken for a man of 30 to 35 years of age. At the time we refer to in our narrative, he had a constant beatific expression on his face. His round skull, small and covered with ebony black hair, long in front and short in the back, contained many things—so they say—within its cavity. His small but not "chinified" eyes never varied in expression; the nose was thin and not flat; and, if his mouth had not been disfigured by the excessive abuse of tobacco and *buyo*, the *sapá* of which he gathered within one cheek, thus altering the symmetry of his features, we would say that he did well in believing and advertising himself as a good-looking man. However, despite tobacco and *buyo* abuse, he kept his own teeth white, as well as the two false teeth lent him by the dentist for twelve *duros* apiece.

He was considered one of the most affluent property owners in Binondo, and one of the most important plantation owners because of his land holdings in Pampanga and Laguna, especially in the town of San Diego, sold to him or surrendered by his debtors. San Diego was his favorite town for its agreeable baths, its famous cockpits and the memories that he had of the town. He was wont to spend there at least two months of the year.

Capitan Tiago had many real estate properties in Sto. Cristo, Anloague and Rosario streets; he and a Chinaman ran an opium trade; and it is superfluous to say that he obtained from thence the greatest benefits. He fed the inmates of Bilibid prison and supplied *zacate*[1] to the principal houses in Manila through contracts, it is understood. In good terms with the authorities, gifted with a mercantile spirit, cunning, flexible and even bold in speculating on the needs of others, he was the only feared competitor of a certain Perez in all that pertained to leases of and biddings for positions and employments which the government of the Philippines always entrusts to private enterprise. Thus, in the time of these events, Capitan Tiago was a happy man as far as such a man of small mind can be happy in these lands: he was rich, he was at peace with God, with the government and with his fellowmen.

That he was at peace with God was undoubtable,

almost dogmatic. One has no reason to be on bad terms with the good God when you are well off on earth; when you had never communicated with Him, or ever lent Him money. He had never approached God in his prayers, not even in the hour of his serious difficulties; he was rich and his gold prayed for him: for masses and prayers God had created powerful and arrogant priests; for making novenas and rosaries, God, in His infinite goodness, had created the poor for the benefit of the rich; the poor who, for a peso, are able to pray the fifteen mysteries and read all the holy books, even the Hebrew Bible if the fee is raised; and if sometimes a great difficulty required celestial aid and there was none on hand, nor a single red Chinese candle available, the saints of one's devotion were invoked, promising them many things to oblige them and convince them of the worthiness of the petitions.

But the one to whom he promised the most, and for whom he complied with the most pledges was the Virgin of Antipolo, Our Lady of Peace and Safe Voyage. With certain lesser saints the man was neither very punctual nor decent; once he got what he wished for, he forgot to call on them again; the truth is that he never bothered them anymore even if there was occasion to do so. Capitan Tiago knew that there were many saints in the calendar who were not occupied and who perhaps had nothing to do in heaven. Besides, he attributed greater power and efficacy to the Virgin of Antipolo, more than that of any other of the Virgins who carry silver sceptres, sometimes a naked child Jesus or a dressed one, sometimes scapulars, rosaries or leather belts. Perhaps this was due to her fame as a very severe and strict lady, very careful of her name, hostile to photography, according to the senior *sacristan* of Antipolo; and who turned black as ebony when she was angry; and because the other Virgins were more soft-hearted, more indulgent. It is a well-known fact that certain souls have more love for an absolute monarch than for a constitutional one. Ask Louis XIV, Louis XVI, Philip II and Amadeus I. This perhaps explains why in this famous sanctuary can be seen walking on their knees Chinese infidels, and even Spaniards, except that it cannot be explained why the priests escape with the money of this forbidding icon; they go to America and get married there.

The door of the sala hidden by a silken curtain led to a small chapel or oratory that should never be absent from any Filipino home. Here are the house-gods of Capitan Tiago, and we call them house-gods because this gentleman had a preference for polytheism rather than monotheism, which he never understood.[2] Here are seen images of the Holy Family with busts and extremities of ivory, eyes of crystal, long eyelashes and blond curled ringlets, masterpieces of Sta. Cruz sculpture[3]; paintings in oil by the artists of Paco and Ermita[4] representing the martyrdom of saints, miracles of the Virgin, etc.; Saint Lucia looking upwards and carrying on a plate another pair of eyes with brows and lashes like that painted in the triangle of the Trinity or on Egyptian sarcophaguses; Saint Pascual Baylon, Saint Anthony of Padua in cotton habits contemplating, teary-eyed, a child Jesus dressed as a *Capitan General*, with a three-cornered hat, saber and boots as in the dance of the children in Madrid. This signified for Capitan Tiago that even if God adds to His power that of a *Capitan General* of the Philippines, the Franciscans would still play with Him like a doll.

There is also a Saint Anthony, abbot, with a pig by his side, a pig which for the worthy Capitan Tiago was just as miraculous as the saint himself; and for which reason he dared not call it a pig but a creature of the saint, Saint Anthony; a Saint Francis of Assissi with seven wings and a coffee-colored habit, placed over a Saint Vincent who has only two, but, on the other hand, carries a bugle; a Saint Peter, martyr, with his head parted by the *talibong*[5] blade of a malefactor, clutched by an infidel on his knees beside a Saint Peter cutting off the ear of a Moor, undoubtedly Malchus[6], who is biting his lips and contorting with pain, while a fighting cock crows and beats its wings against a Doric column. From this Capitan Tiago concluded that to be a saint it was the same not to cut as to be cut.

Who can enumerate that army of images and detail the qualities and perfections stored in them? One chapter will not suffice. However, we will not pass up in silence a beautiful wooden Saint Michael, painted and gold-plated and almost one meter high: the archangel biting his lower lip had glowing eyes, a knitted brow, rosy cheeks, and was holding close a Greek shield and brandishing in his right hand a *kris*[7] or Muslim sword from Jolo, ready to wound the devout or he who came near (judging from his attitude and looks), rather than the devil with a tail and horns sinking teeth in his maiden-like leg.

Capitan Tiago never came near the statue, fearing a miracle. How many times had more than one image, not as well made as those from the woodcarvers of Paete[8], come to life to the confusion and punishment of unbelieving sinners? It is well-known that a certain Christ of Spanish make, invoked as a witness to a promise of love, assented with a movement of his head before the judge; that another Christ detached its right arm to embrace Saint Lutgarde? And had he not read a recently published booklet about a sermon in mime preached by an image of

Saint Dominic in Soriano? The saint said not a word but, from its gestures, the author of the booklet concluded that he was announcing the end of the world.

Was it not also revealed that the Virgin of Luta, of the town of Lipa, had one cheek more swollen than the other, and the border of her dress dirtied with mud? Does this not logically prove that the sacred images also take walks without raising their skirts, and even suffer toothaches, perchance on our account? Had he not seen with his small eyes all the Christs in the Sermon of the Seven Last Words, move and bow their heads three times in unison, moving to tears and groans all the women and the sensitive souls destined for heaven?

And more: we ourselves have seen the preacher show the public at the moment of descent from the cross a handkerchief soaked in blood, and we were ready to weep with piety, when, unfortunately for our souls, the *sacristan* assured us that it was only a joke: the blood of a chicken butchered and roasted and incontinently consumed notwithstanding the fact that it was Good Friday...the *sacristan* was fat! Capitan Tiago, being a prudent man and pious, avoided getting close to Saint Michael's *kris.* "Let us avoid the occasion," he said to himself, "I know he is an archangel, but I do not trust him, I don't!"

Not a year passes that he does not attend the opulent pilgrimage to Antipolo with an orchestra: at that time he pays for two thanksgiving masses of the many that are part of the three novena series, and those for ordinary days when there are no novenas. After that he bathes in the renowned *batis* or spring, where the same sacred image would bathe. The devout still see traces of her feet and hair on the hard stone where she wet her hair with coconut oil like any other woman, as if her hair were of steel or of diamonds, weighing a thousand tons. We wish the terrible image would shake its sacred tresses in the sight of these devout persons, and stamp its foot on their tongue or head.

There beside that same spring, Capitan Tiago usually ate roasted lechon, *dalag sinigang* with *alibangbang* leaves[9], and other dishes more or less appetizing. The two masses came to cost him something more than four hundred pesos, but came out cheap if one considered the glory that the Mother of God acquired with the wheels of fire, rockets, firecrackers and mortars or *bersos* as they are called there, and if one calculated the great profits which, thanks to these masses, he would gain the rest of the year.

But Antipolo was not the only theater of Capitan Tiago's sonorous devotions. In Binondo, in Pampanga, and in the town of San Diego when he had to fight his cocks with huge bets, he would send to the priest gold coins for propitiatory masses. And, like the Romans of old who consulted their augurers on the eve of battle, giving food to the sacred cocks, Capitan Tiago also consulted with his, but made modifications proper to the times and the new truths.

He would observe the flames of the candles, the incense smoke, the priest's voice, etc., and from these proceed to deduce his future luck. It is an admitted fact that Capitan Tiago lost few bets, and this would be due to the official having a sore throat; there being few lights; the candles having too much grease; or the inadvertent mixing of a false coin with the genuine, etc., etc.; the guardian of a brotherhood[10] comforted the Capitan that those disappointments were trials imposed on him by heaven to strengthen his faith and devotion.

Beloved by the friars, respected by the *sacristans*, spoiled by the Chinese waxmakers and by the pyrotechnicians and toll-gatherers, the man was happy in the religion of this world. Persons of integrity and piety also attributed to him great influence with the celestial court.

That he was at peace with the government, there was no doubt, difficult as that might seem. Incapable of imagining a new idea, and content with his *modus vivendi*, he was always ready to give obedience to the last fifth official[11] or duty imposed by any of the offices; to give gifts of legs of hams, capons, turkeys, fruits from China of any season of the year. If he heard ill talk about the natives, he, who did not consider himself one, joined in the criticism and said even worse things; if the mestizos, half-breed Sangleys[12], or Spaniards were being criticized, he criticized as well, obviously because he believed himself to be of pure Iberian stock. He was the first to applaud any imposition of duty or tax, much more so when it smelled of a contract or a lease. He always had orchestras on hand to greet and serenade from the streets all kinds of governors, mayors, fiscals, etc. etc. on their feastdays, birthdays, the births or deaths of relatives, on any occasion, in fact, that altered the habitual monotony. He would have laudatory verses prepared for these occasions, hymns, in which the gentle loving governor or brave and bold mayor, awaits in heaven the palm of the just (or slap on the palm) and other things besides.

He was a *gobernadorcillo*[13] of the rich association of mestizos or half-breeds, despite the protests of many who did not consider him genuine. During the two years of his leadership he wore out ten dress suits and the same number of tophats and half a dozen canes; some dress suits, a couple of the tophats at the Ayuntamiento[14], in Malacañang and at headquarters; other tophats and dress suits at the cockpit, in the market, in the processions, in the Chinese shops. Underneath the hat and inside the suit Capitan Tiago sweated while handling his tasselled swagger stick, disposing, fixing, altering everything in an astonishing frenzy of activity and in all seriousness, which was even more astonishing. Even if the authorities considered him a good man with the best of wills, peaceful, submissive, obedient, hospitable, who did not read any book or journal from Spain although he spoke good Spanish, they looked down on him the same way a poor student regards the worn-out soles of his old shoes, twisted due to his manner of walking.

Of him phrases both Christian and profane could be said in truth: *"Beati pauperes spiritu y beati possidentes,* Blessed are the poor in spirit and blessed are the possessors."* And to him could very well be applied that phrase which according to some is a mistranslation from the Greek: "Glory to God in the highest and on earth peace to men of good will," for, as we will see later on, it is not enough for men to have good will in order to live peaceably. The impious took him for a fool; the poor, for a pitiless, cruel, exploiter of misery; his inferiors, for a despot and a tyrant. And the women?

Ah! the women! Slanderous rumors buzz in the miserable nipa huts, and it is bruited about that they have heard laments, and weeping, mixed with the cries of an infant. Many a young woman is pointed at by the malicious fingers of the neighbors: "She has a passive look and withered bosoms!" But these things do not deprive him of sleep; no young woman disturbs his peace. One old woman it is who makes him suffer; one who gives him competition in his devotions, and who has merited from the priests more approval and praise than he in his times was ever accorded.

Between Capitan Tiago and this widow, an heiress

of brothers and nephews, exists a holy emulation which redounds to the benefit of the church, like the competition between the steamships of Pampanga which benefits the public. Does Capitan Tiago give a sceptre with emeralds and topazes to any of the Virgins? Well, Doña Patrocinio orders another sceptre of gold and diamonds from Gaudinez, the goldsmith.[15] If in the procession of the Virgin of la Naval[16], Capitan Tiago builds an arch with two gates adorned with embossed fabric, with mirrors, crystal globes, lamps, and chandeliers, Doña Patrocinio will have another with four entrances, two arm-lengths taller and with more hangings and trimmings. But then Capitan Tiago resorts to his forte, his specialty: to masses with rockets and fireworks, and Doña Patrocinio has to bite her lips with her gums; being of an excessively nervous temperament she cannot stand the ringing of bells and even less, the detonations. While he smiles, she is thinking of getting even, and hires with other people's money the best orators of the five orders in Manila, the most reputed canonists of the cathedral, and even the Paulists, to preach during the solemn celebrations on profound theological themes to the sinners who understand only the language of the marketplace. The partisans of Capitan Tiago have observed that the old woman dozes during the sermon, but those of Doña Patrocinio claim that the sermon has already been paid for, and for her, in all things, to pay is the primordial.

Lately she humbled him by gifting a church with three biers of silver with gildings, each one of which cost her more than three thousand pesos. Capitan Tiago hopes this old woman would one blessed day cease to breathe, or lose five or six of her litigations in court in order to serve God only, but unfortunately these are handled by the best lawyers of the *Audiencia Real*.[17] As to her death, there is no way for disease to lay hold of her: she is like a steel wire, dauntless for the edification of souls, and she holds on to this vale of tears with the tenacity of a tumor. Her partisans are supremely confident that she would be canonized after her death and that Capitan Tiago himself would be venerating her even at the altars, which he concedes and promises as long as she dies soon.

Thus is Capitan Tiago in these days. As to the past, he was the only son of a sugar merchant of Malabon, sufficiently affluent, but so avaricious he did not want to spend a *cuarto* for the education of his son. For this reason little Santiago became the servant of a good Dominican, a virtuous man, who endeavored to teach the boy all the good that he knew and could. When he was about to have the honor of being called *logico* by his acquaintances, that is, when he was going to become a student of logic, his protector died, followed by his own father, and this put an end to his education. He therefore had to dedicate himself to business.

He married a beautiful young woman from Sta. Cruz, who helped him make his fortune and gave him social status. Doña Pia Alba was not content with buying sugar, coffee and indigo. She sought to plant and to harvest, and she bought the new conjugal property in San Diego, starting here their friendships with Padre Damaso and Don Rafael Ibarra, the richest capitalist in town.

The lack of an heir in the first six years of marriage made their eagerness for acquiring wealth almost a censurable ambition, and yet Doña Pia was svelte, robust and well-formed. In vain did she pray novenas; she made pilgrimages, upon the advice of the devotees of San Diego, to the Virgin of Caysasay in Taal[18]; gave alms, danced in the procession under the hot May sun before the Virgin of Turumba in Pakil.[18] All was in vain, until Padre Damaso advised her to go to Obando; there she danced during the feast of Saint Pascual Bailon and asked for a son.[19] It is a known fact that in Obando there is a Trinity which grants sons and daughters by choice: Our Lady of Salambau, Saint Clare and Saint Pascual. Thanks to this wise counsel Doña Pia felt a quickening in her womb...ah, like the fisherman alluded to by Shakespeare in Macbeth, who stopped singing when he found a treasure, she lost her joy, became sad and was not seen to smile again. "Caprices of pregnancy," everybody said, including Capitan Tiago.

A puerperal fever put an end to her woes, leaving motherless a beautiful baby whom Padre Damaso himself baptized. And because Saint Pascual failed to give the son asked of him, she was named Maria Clara in honor of the Virgin of Salambau and Saint Clare, punishing Saint Pascual Bailon with silence.

The child grew up in the care of her aunt Isabel, that good old woman of friar-like urbanity whom we met earlier. Because of its healthy climate, she resided for the greater part of the year in San Diego, where Padre Damaso, besides, made up many feasts for her.

Maria Clara did not have the small eyes of her father: like her mother she had them large and black, beneath long lashes; gay and smiling when she played, sad and soulful and pensive when she was not laughing. Since childhood her hair had an almost golden hue; her nose, of a correct profile, was neither sharp nor flat; her mouth reminded one of her mother's, small and perfect, with two beautiful dimples on her cheeks. Her skin had the fine texture of an onion layer, the whiteness of cotton, according to her enthusiastic relatives. They saw traces of Capitan Tiago's paternity in the small and well-rounded ears of Maria Clara.

Tía Isabel attributed those semi-European features to the pregnancy whimsies of Doña Pia, whom she saw many times during the first months of her conception, weeping before Saint Anthony. Another cousin of Capitan Tiago's was of the same opinion, except that she differed in the choice of the saint; for her it was the Virgin or Saint Michael. A famed philosopher, a cousin of Capitan Tinong's who knew the Amat from memory[20], sought for the explanation in planetary influences.

Maria Clara, everybody's idol, grew up among smiles and loves. The friars themselves celebrated her when in processions they dressed her in white, her curled and abundant ringlets interwoven with sampaguitas and day lilies, with two little wings of silver and gold pinned at the back of her dress and two white doves tied with blue ribbons in her hand. She was so gay, her childish chatter so innocent and guileless, that Capitan Tiago, deeply enamored, could do nothing but bless the saints of Obando and counsel everyone to acquire beautiful statues.

In warm countries, girls at the age of thirteen or fourteen become women, like the bud in the night turning into full bloom the following day. In this transition period, full of mystery and romance, she entered the convent of Saint Catalina upon the advice of the parish priest of Binondo, to receive from the nuns the rigorous training of a religious education.[21]

Tearfully Maria Clara bid farewell to Padre Damaso, and to the only friend she had played with as a child, Crisostomo Ibarra, who later left for Europe. There, in that convent, where communication with the outer world was carried on across a double grill and under the vigilance of a mother-eavesdropper, she lived for seven years.[22]

Each with his particular concern, and perceiving the mutual inclinations of the young, Don Rafael and Capitan Tiago agreed on the union of their children and made a social covenant. This event, which took place some years after the departure of the young Ibarra, was celebrated with the same jubilation by two hearts, each one at one end of the world, and in very different circumstances.

- 7 -

Idyll in an Azotea

The Song of Songs[1]

That morning, Tía Isabel and Maria Clara went to hear mass early, the latter elegantly attired, a rosary of blue beads around her wrist serving as a bracelet; the former with her glasses on, in order to read her "Anchor of Salvation" during the Holy Sacrifice.

Hardly had the priest left the altar when the young woman expressed a desire to go home, to the great surprise and disappointment of the good aunt who believed her niece to be pious and partial to prayer, like a nun at the very least. Grumbling and making signs of the cross, the old woman stood up. "Bah! the good God will forgive me, he who must know the hearts of maidens better than you do, Tia Isabel," she could have said, to cut short the severe but truly maternal reproaches.

Now that they have had breakfast, Maria Clara

distracts her impatience by knitting a silken bag, while her aunt attempts to eradicate the traces of the previous evening's feast with a duster. Capitan Tiago examines and reviews some documents.

Each sound from the street, each carriage that passes by causes the maiden's bosom to throb, and makes her tremble. Ah! now she wishes she were back in her quiet and peaceful convent among her friends. There she would be able to see him without trembling, without feeling disturbed. But, was he not your childhood friend; did you not play many games together, and even quarrel sometimes? If you who read this have loved, you will understand; if not, it is useless for me to tell you; the profane cannot comprehend these mysteries.

"I believe, Maria, that the doctor is right," said Capitan Tiago, "you should go to the provinces; you are very pale, you need fresh air. What do you say? Malabon or San Diego?"

At the sound of this last name Maria Clara reddened like a poppy and could not answer.

"Now, Isabel and you will go to the cloister to collect your clothes, and say goodbye to your friends," continued Capitan Tiago without raising his head. "You will no longer return there."

Maria Clara felt that vague melancholy which grips the soul when one leaves forever a place where one had been happy, but another thought assuaged that grief.

"Within four or five days, when you have new clothes, we will go to Malabon. Your godfather is no longer in San Diego; the priest you met last night, that young priest who is the new curate we have there, is a saint."

"Cousin, San Diego suits her better," observed Tía Isabel. "Besides, our house there is better, and the *fiesta* is near."

Maria Clara wanted to hug her aunt, but she heard a carriage stop and she paled.

"Ah! it is true," answered Capitan Tiago, and changing the tone of his voice added, "Don Crisostomo!"

Maria Clara let her knitting drop. She wanted to move but could not. A nervous trembling seized her body. Steps were heard along the stairs and soon after, a virile resonant voice. As if there was magic in the sound, the young woman let go of her emotions and fled to the oratory to hide herself among the religious icons. The cousins broke into laughter as Ibarra heard the sound of a door closing.

Pale and breathing rapidly, the maiden pressed her heaving bosom and sought to listen. She heard the voice, that voice so dear to her, which for a long time she had heard only in her dreams: he was asking for her. Mad with happiness she kissed the nearby image of Saint Anthony, abbot, a saint who had been happy in his life amid temptations. Then she took to the keyhole to peep through and contemplate him. She was smiling, and when her aunt pulled her out from her reverie, she hugged the old woman's neck and filled her with kisses.

"Silly! what is the matter with you?" the old woman finally was able to say, a tear falling from her withered eyes.

Maria Clara was embarrassed; she cradled her head in a shapely arm.

"Come! Fix yourself up, come!" prodded the old woman, lovingly leading her niece by the hand. "While he is talking to your father about your....you come and do not make him wait."

The maiden allowed herself to be led like a little child. They closeted themselves in her room.

Capitan Tiago and Ibarra were talking animatedly when Tía Isabel appeared, practically dragging forward her niece who was looking everywhere in the room except at those present. What were those two souls saying who were communicating in the language of the eyes, more perfectly than with the lips, a language given by the soul so that sound does not disturb the ecstasy of feeling? In those moments, when the thoughts of two happy beings are blended into one through the eyes, the word is gross, slow and weak; it is like the rude and dull sound of thunder, before the blinding flash and speed of lightning; it expresses an already known feeling, an idea already understood; and if we make use of it, it is because of the heart's ambition, which dominates all of one's being, and which overflows with happiness, wishing that all of the human organism with all its faculties, physical and psychic, would manifest the symphony of happiness intoned by the spirit. To a query of love by a glance, brilliant or veiled, the word has no answer: only the smile, the kiss or the sigh.

And afterwards, when the enamored pair, fleeing from the dust scattered by Tía Isabel's duster, went to the balcony to converse with more freedom amidst the tiny bowers of vine branches, what were they recounting in gentle murmurs that make you tremble, little red flowers of *cabello-de-angel*? Tell us, you who exude fragrance from your breath and hues on your lips! You, fresh breeze, who learned rare harmonies from the secrecy of the dark night and from the mystery of our virgin forest! Tell us, you sunlight-brilliant reflection of the eternal on earth, the only immaterial element in a world of matter; you tell us, for I only know how to recount prosaic madness!

But since you refuse to do so, I will myself endeavor to do it.

The sky was blue: a cool breeze, which did not have

the fragrance of a rose, agitated the leaves and the flowers of the vines—hence the trembling of the angel-wing tresses—the orchids, the dried desiccated fishes and the China lamps. The sound of boat paddles disturbing the murky waters of the river, the passing of carriages and carts over the Binondo bridge, reached them distinctly. But not what the aunt was muttering.

"All the better, there you will be watched by all the neighborhood," she was saying.

In the beginning they said nothing but nonsensical trivialities, those sweet nothings which are very similar to the vaunting of European nations. They delight and taste like honey to the natives, but they make foreigners laugh or knit their brows.

She, like a sister of Cain, is jealous, and asks her lover: "Did you always think of me? Did you not forget me on so many trips? So many big cities, with so many beautiful women!"

He too, another relative of Cain, knows how to ward off the questions, and is a bit of a fibber on that account: "Can I forget you?" looking enraptured at her large dark eyes. "Would I be faithless to a vow, a sacred vow? Do you remember that night, that stormy night when, seeing me lonely and weeping by my mother's deathbed, you came close, placed your hand on my arm—your hand which for a long time now you have not allowed me to hold—and said to me: 'You have lost your mother; I never had one'—and you wept with me. You loved her and she loved you like a daughter.

"It was raining outside and emitting flashes of lightning, but I seemed to hear music, to see a smile in the pale features of the corpse. Oh! if my parents were only alive to behold you. Then I took hold of your hand and that of my dead mother, I swore to love you, to make you happy no matter what fate Heaven had in store for me; and this oath I have never regretted. Now I am renewing it. Can I forget you? Your memory has always kept me company; it has saved me from dangers along the way; it has been my comfort in the solitude of my soul in foreign countries; your memory has negated the effect of the European lotus of forgetfulness[2], which effaces from the remembrance of many of our countrymen the hopes and the sorrows of the Motherland.

"In my dreams I saw you standing by the shores of Manila gazing at the distant horizon, wrapped in the warm light of early dawn; I listened to the languid and melancholic song which aroused in me slumbering feelings, and evoked in my heart's memory the first years of my childhood, our joys, our games, all the happy past which you enlivened while you were in town.

"You seemed to me the nymph, the spirit, the poetic incarnation of my country: lovely, simple, amiable, full of candor, daughter of the Philippines, of this beautiful country which unites with the great virtues of Mother Spain the lovely qualities of a young nation—just as all that is lovely and fair and adorns both races is united in your being. Hence my love for you and that which I profess for my Motherland are blended into a single love.

"Can I forget you? Many times I seemed to hear the sound of your piano, and the accents of your voice. Always in Germany in the late afternoon when I roamed through the thick forests peopled with the fantastic creations of her poets and the mysterious legends of her past generations, I recalled your name, and seemed to see you in the mists arising from the bottom of the valley; seemed to hear your voice in the murmur of the leaves; and when the villagers, returning from the fields in the distance, would sing their popular songs, to me they seemed to harmonize with my inner voices singing for you and giving reality and substance to my illusions and dreams.

"Sometimes I would get lost among the mountain trails, and night would gradually descend. I would find myself still wandering, looking for the trail amidst pines, beech trees and oaks. Some moonlight would filter through the clearing made by the thick branches; I seemed to visualize you in the heart of the woods like a hazy dear shadow between the light and shadows of the dense thickets. If perchance I heard the rising warble of the nightingale it was because I saw you and you were inspiring it to sing!

"Yes, I have thought of you. The ardor of your love not only enlightened my sight to see through fog, and set ice on fire. Italy's lovely skies spoke to me of your eyes in their limpid depths; its smiling landscapes, of your smile, just as the landscape of Andalucia with its fragrant air, populated with Oriental reminiscences, full of poetry and color told me of your love. Cruising on the Rhine on evenings lit by a slumbering moon, I asked myself if perhaps you were deceiving my fantasies, so that I saw you between the elms on the river bank, on the rock of the Lorelei, or amidst the water ripples, singing in the silence of the night, like the young fairy of consolation, in order to enliven the solitude and sadness of those ruined castles."

"I have not travelled as you have, nor do I know a town other than your own, Manila and Antipolo," she answered, smiling at Ibarra, for she believed everything that he said. "But since I bade you farewell and entered the convent I have always recalled and not forgotten you, even if my confessor commanded me to do so, imposing many penances. I remembered our games, our bickerings when we were children. You chose the best *sigüeyes* with which to play *siklot;* you searched in the rivers for the roundest and smallest stones of different colors with which to play *sintak*. You were very slow; you always lost, and as penalty I gave you the *bantil* on the back of your hand, but tried not to hit you too hard. I was sorry for you. You cheated in the *chonka* game more than I did, and so we often ended up in scuffles.[3]

"Do you remember that time when you got really angry? You made me suffer then, but afterwards, when I recalled it in the cloister, I smiled. I missed having you to pick a quarrel with, and to make peace with immediately after. We were so young!

"We went with your mother to bathe in that stream under the shade of the bamboo clumps. Along the bank grew many flowers and plants with strange-sounding names that you kept teaching me in Spanish and Latin, because by then you were studying at the Ateneo.[4] I did not pay you much attention. I was at times occupied chasing butterflies and dragonflies that fluttered around with pin-like bodies and all the colors of the rainbow, reflecting the light of mother-of-pearl, and chasing each other among the flowers. Sometimes I wanted to surprise with my hands the little fishes gliding rapidly through the moss and little stones along the bank.

"Suddenly you disappeared and came back bringing a wreath of leaves and orange blossoms which you placed upon my head, calling me Chloe. I plaited a circle of vines for you, but your mother took my crown and mashed it with a stone, mixing it with the *gogo* shampoo with which to wash our hair.[5] Tears filled your eyes and you told her that she had no understanding of mythology. 'Silly!'

answered your mother, 'you will see how good your hair will smell afterwards.' I laughed; you were offended and did not want to speak to me. The rest of the day you were very serious. I, in turn, wanted to cry.

"On our way back to the town, with the sun shining hot, I gathered the leaves of the sage plant growing alongside the path, for you to place under your hat to keep away headaches. You smiled then; I took hold of your hand and we made peace."

Ibarra was smiling to himself with happiness; he opened his wallet and took out of a piece of paper some blackish withered aromatic leaves.

"Your sage leaves," he replied to the questioning look on her face. "This is all of what you have given me."

She rapidly removed from her bosom a packet of white satin. "Psss," she said, giving him a flip with the palm of her hand: "You may not touch—it is a farewell letter."

"Is that what I wrote you before I left?"

"Has your lordship ever written to me again?"

"And what did I tell you then?"

"Many pleasant quibbles, alibis of a bad debtor," she said smiling, giving him to understand how agreeable to her were those fibs. "Quiet! I will read it to you but will suppress your gallantries to spare you an ordeal."

Raising the paper to the level of her eyes so that the other would not see her face, she began:

"'*My...*'—I will not read this part to you because it is a falsehood!—and she ran her eyes across a few lines. '*My father wants me to leave despite my supplications. You are a man, he told me, and you should give thought to the future and your duties. Learn the science of life, what your father cannot give you, in order one day to become useful. If you stay by my*

side, under my shadow, in this atmosphere of worries, you will
not learn to look farther; and on the day I will no longer be
around, you will find yourself like a plant alluded to by our poet
Baltazar[6]: grown in the water, its leaves when not watered,
wither after a moment's exposure to heat. Do you see? You are
almost a young man and you still cry.

'I was hit by this reproach, and confessed to him that I
loved you. My father was silent. He reflected, and then,
laying his hand on my shoulder, said to me in a voice that
shook: "Do you think that you are the only one who knows
how to love? That your father does not love you nor feel
keenly a separation from you? Only lately we lost your
mother. I journey towards old age, to that stage in which
one seeks the comfort and support of youth, yet I accept my
solitude; I do not know if I will see you again. But I must
think of other, greater things... The future opens for you,
but closes for me; your loves are born, mine are dying; fire
burns hot in your blood, the cold invades mine. And yet
you weep and do not know how to sacrifice the present for
a useful tomorrow, for you and your country!" My father's
eyes filled with tears. I fell on my knees at his feet, embraced
him, asked for his forgiveness, and told him that I was
ready to leave..."

Ibarra's agitation put an end to the reading of the
letter. The young man was pale, and paced back and forth.

"What is wrong? What is happening to you?" she
asked him.

"You have made me forget that I have my duties, and
that I must leave for the town at this very moment!
Tomorrow is the feast of the dead."

Maria Clara was silent; she fixed her large and
dreamy eyes on him for some time, and gathering some
flowers, told him with feeling:

"Go, I will not keep you any longer; in a few days we will see each other again. Put this flower on your parents' tomb."

A few minutes later the young man descended the stairs accompanied by Capitan Tiago and by Tía Isabel while Maria Clara closeted herself once again in the oratory.

"Do me the favor of telling Andeng to prepare the house for the arrival of Maria and Isabel. Have a good voyage!" said Capitan Tiago as Ibarra ascended the carriage which soon headed towards the plaza of St. Gabriel.[7]

Then, to comfort Maria Clara, who was weeping beside an image of the Virgin: "Go and light two candles at two reales each: one to Señor San Roque and another to Senor San Rafael, patron of travellers. Light the lamp of Our Lady of Peace and Good Voyage, for there are many brigands. It is worth spending four reales on wax and six cuartos on oil and not having to pay a heavy ransom later."

- 8 -

Memories

Ibarra's carriage traversed part of Manila's busiest suburb. Whatever it was that had made him sad the night before, by daylight made him smile despite himself.

The bustle he saw everywhere, so many carriages coming and going swiftly by; the *carromatas¹*, the *calesas;* the Europeans, Chinese, natives, each one in their particular attire; the fruit vendors, brokers, shirtless porters; the food stalls, lodging houses, restaurants, shops; even the bullcarts drawn by the impassive and indifferent carabao which seemed absorbed in dragging heavy loads while philosophizing——all the noise, movement, even the sun itself, a particular odor, the motley colors, awakened in his memory a world of sleeping remembrances.

The streets were still unpaved. When the sun shone for two consecutive days they turned into dust which covered everything, made passersby cough, and blinded them. One day of rain brought pools of stagnant water which at night reflected the lights of the carriages, spattering with mud from five meters away, the pedestrians on the wide sidewalks. How many women have left their embroidered slippers in those waves of mud! Then you see the streets being tamped down by a chain gang of prisoners with shaved heads, clad in short-sleeved shirts and drawers reaching to the knees, with numbers and letters in blue; chains around their legs, half-wrapped in dirty rags to reduce the abrasion, or perhaps the coldness of the iron; joined in pairs, sunburnt, prostrate from heat and fatigue, given lashes, and beaten with a club by another prisoner who perhaps found comfort in ill-treating others.

They were tall men with gloomy features which had never been seen to soften with the light of a smile. Nevertheless the pupils of their eyes glittered when the whistling lash fell on their shoulders, or when a transient threw them the stub of a cigar, half-moist and disintegrating. The one closest would catch it and hide it under his *salakot*[2]; the others were left looking at the other transients with strange expressions on their faces. It seemed to Ibarra that he was still hearing the crumbling noise of the stones being crushed to fill up the holes; and the clanging of the heavy chains around their swollen ankles.

Ibarra remembered, still shuddering, a scene which had wounded his imagination as a child: it was siesta time and the sun's rays were falling like molten lead. In the shadow of an open wooden cart lay one of those men, lifeless. His eyes were half-open. Two other men were fixing a bamboo litter, silent, without anger, without sorrow, without impatience, just as the native character is believed to be. "You today; we tomorrow," they might have been saying among themselves.

The people moved about hurriedly, oblivious to what was happening. The women passed by, looked and proceeded on their way: it was an everyday scene, which had hardened their hearts. The carriages continued on their way, reflecting on their varnished bodies the brilliant rays of the sun in a cloudless sky. Only he, an eleven-year-old new to the city, had been moved. Only he had a nightmare the following night.

The good and respectable pontoon bridge of barges was no longer there, that good Filipino bridge which did its best to serve, notwithstanding its natural imperfections, which rose and lowered according to the whim of the Pasig, and which this river had many times ill-treated and destroyed.

The almond trees of the Plaza San Gabriel had not grown: they were still emaciated.

The Escolta seemed less lovely to him despite the fact that a great building with caryatid columns occupied the site of the old warehouses.[3] The new *Puente de España*[4] attracted Ibarra's attention: the houses on the right bank amidst trees and clumps of bamboo, there where the Escolta ends and the Isla Romero[5] begins, reminded him of the cool mornings when in a *banca*[6] he had rowed through to go to the Baths of *Ulî-ulî*.

He saw many carriages drawn by magnificent teams of little horses: inside the carriages, employees half-asleep, on their way to the office; soldiers, Chinese, in fatuous and ridiculous postures; serious-faced friars, canons, etc. In an elegant *victoria* he thought he saw a serious Padre Damaso with knitted brows, but it had passed, and now, he is gaily greeted from his carriage by Capitan Tinong, accompanied by his wife and two daughters.

At the foot of the bridge the horses started to trot,

heading for the Paseo de la Sabana. To the left, from the Arroceros Tobacco Factory could be heard the noise of the cigarette girls beating tobacco leaves. Ibarra could not help smiling at the remembrance of the strong odor which at five o'clock in the afternoon saturated the pontoon bridge and made him dizzy as a boy. The animated conversations, the jokes automatically drew his imagination towards the barrio of *Lavapies* in Madrid, with its riots by cigarette girls so fatal to the ill-fated policemen and so forth.

The sight of the botanical garden drove away his gay reminiscences: the devil of comparisons placed him before the botanical gardens of Europe, in the countries where much effort and much gold are needed to make a leaf bloom or a bud open; and even more, to those of the colonies, rich and well-tended, and all open to the public. Ibarra removed his gaze, looked right, and there saw old Manila, still surrounded by its walls and moats, like an anemic young woman in a dress from her grandmother's best times.

The view of the sea vanishing in the distance!...

"On the other side is Europe," thought the young man, "Europe with her beautiful nations in constant agitation, searching for happiness, dreaming at dawn and full of disappointment with the advent of night...happy in the midst of its catastrophes. Yes, on the other shore of the infinite sea are the spiritual nations; although they do not condemn matter, they remain even more spiritual than those who claim they adore the spirit."

But these thoughts fled his imagination when his gaze turned in the direction of a small promontory on the field of Bagumbayan. The isolated little hill near the Luneta now called his attention and made him meditative.

He was thinking of the man who had opened the

eyes of his intellect, and made him understand what was good and just. True, the ideas inspired in him were few, but they were not vain repetitions: they were convictions which did not pale before the brightest focusing lights of progress. That man was an old priest, and the words he told Ibarra when he said goodbye, still resounded in his ears.

"Do not forget that if knowledge is the patrimony of humanity, it is inherited only by those who have the heart," the old man reminded him. "I have tried to transmit to you what I have received from my teachers; the riches I have endeavored to augment as much as I could, and I am passing it on to the following generation. You will do the same with those who come after you, and you can triple it, for you are going to very rich countries." He added, smiling: "They come in search of gold; go to their country to look for that other gold which we lack. Remember, however, that all that glitters is not gold." That man had died in Bagumbayan.

To these memories he replies, murmuring in a low voice: "No, despite everything, the country first; first the Philippines, Spain's daughter; first the Spanish nation! No, that which is fated does not tarnish the Motherland. No!"

Ermita does not call his attention, a phoenix of nipa which rose from its ashes in the form of white and blue painted houses, zinc roofing in red. Neither is he attracted to Malate, nor to the Cavalry headquarters with its trees in front, nor the inhabitants, nor the little nipa-roofed houses more or less pyramidal or prismatic, hidden among banana plants and betelnut trees, built like nests by each family man.[7]

The carriage kept rolling. It encountered a *carromata* drawn by one or two horses whose abaca harnesses betrayed their provincial origins. The carriage driver peered at the traveller in the bright carriage, and passed without exchanging a word, without a single greeting. At times a cart pulled by a carabao of slow and indifferent pace enlivened the wide and dusty highway bathed by the brilliance of a tropical sun. The melancholic and monotonous song of the driver, mounted on the back of the animal, accompanies the strident squeak of the heavy conveyance's dry wheels with unwieldy axles; at times it is the sound of the dull worn-out runners of a *paragos*, the native sled, dragging itself heavily over the dust or over the puddles of mud on the way. The cattle graze peacefully in the fields and in the open spaces among the white herons perched quietly on the loins of the carabao chewing and savoring the meadow grass with half-closed eyes. In the distance the breeding mares frolic, run and jump pursued by a quick-tempered colt with long tail and luxuriant mane; the colt neighs and beats the earth with its powerful hooves.

Let us leave the young man to continue his journey meditating or half-dozing: the sad or lively poetry of the landscape does not call his attention. That sun that makes the tops of trees shine and sets to running the peasants whose feet burn with the heat of the ground despite their calloused covering, that sun that keeps the village girl in the shade of the almond tree or of the reeds, causing her to dwell on vague or inexplicable things—that sun has no attraction for our young traveller.

Let us return to Manila while the carriage rolls like a drunk on the casual road, crossing a bamboo bridge, going swiftly up and down an incline.

- 9 -

Some Country Matters

I barra was not mistaken: in the victoria was indeed Padre Damaso, and he was headed in the direction which Ibarra had just left.

"Where are you going?" the friar asked Maria Clara and Tía Isabel, who were climbing into their silver-trimmed carriage. Padre Damaso, despite his calling, caressed the young woman's cheeks.

"To the cloister to fetch my things," she replied.

"Aha! aha! Let us see who will prevail, let us see," he murmured distractedly, leaving the two women somewhat aghast. Head down, he climbed the stairs slowly. "He must be committing to memory the sermon he is going to preach," said Tía Isabel to Maria Clara. "Get in; we will be late."

Whether Padre Damaso had a sermon to prepare or not, we cannot say; more important things must have absorbed his attention, for he did not extend his hand to

Capitan Tiago, who had to bend his knees slightly to kiss the friar's hand.

"Santiago," was the first thing he said. "We have to talk of very important things; let us go to your office."

Capitan Tiago became disquieted; he was at a loss for words. But he obeyed, and followed the corpulent priest, who closed the door behind him.

While they confer in secret, let us find out what happened to Padre Sibyla.

The wise Dominican was not in the parochial house. Very early, after saying his mass, he went to the convent of his order, situated at the entrance of Puerta de Isabel II or Magallanes, depending on which family was reigning in Madrid.

Unmindful of the rich flavor of the chocolate or the sound of the boxes and money which came from tithes, and hardly returning the brother collector's respectful greeting, Padre Sibyla crossed some corridors and rapped on a door with his knuckles.

"Come in!" sighed a voice.

"God restore health to Your Reverence," was the young man's greeting upon entering.

Seated on a big armchair one could see an old priest, emaciated, somewhat yellowish like the saints painted by Rivera.[1] His eyes were sunken in their hollow sockets under very thick eyebrows which, being always contracted, augmented the glassy stare of his tired eyes.

Padre Sibyla stared at him, contemplating the crossed arms under the venerable scapular of St. Dominic. He bent his head without saying anything, and seemed to be waiting for the other to speak.

"Ah! they advise me to undergo the operation, Hernando, at my age. This country, this terrible country!

Be warned at my expense, Hernando."

Padre Sibyla gradually raised his eyes and looked fixedly at the old man.

"And what has Your Reverence decided?" he asked.

"To die! Ay! Is there anything else left for me? I suffered much; I have made many suffer; I settle my debts. And you? How are you? What brings you here?"

"I came to give an account of the assignment you gave me."

"Ah! and what of it?"

"Psh!" answered the young one with disgust, seating himself and turning contemptuously to face the other way. "We have been fed with fables; the young Ibarra is a prudent young man. He does not seem to be a fool, but I think he is a good sort."

"Do you think so?"

"Last night the hostilities began."

"Already, and how?"

Padre Sibyla briefly recounted what had happened between Padre Damaso and Crisostomo Ibarra.

"Besides," he added, "the young man is marrying Capitan Tiago's daughter, who was educated in the convent of our sisters. He is rich and would not want to make enemies if that would mean the loss of his happiness and fortune."

The sick man nodded his head.

"Yes, I think as you do...With such a wife and that kind of a father-in-law we will own him body and soul. If not, it is better that he declare himself our enemy."

Padre Sibyla looked at the old man with surprise.

"For the good of our holy order, it is understood," he added, breathing with difficulty. "I prefer attacks to the silly praises and adulation of friends...of course, they are being paid."

"Does Your Reverence think so?"

The old man looked at him sadly.

"Take this into account," he answered, breathing heavily, "our power will last as long as people believe in it. If they attack us, the government says: 'They are being attacked because their enemies see in them an obstacle to their liberty,'—so then, let us preserve our power."

"And if it should listen to them? The government at times..."

"It will not!"

"However, if, impelled by avarice, they should want to appropriate what we collect...if there were someone bold and fearless..."

"Then woe unto him!"

Both men kept silent.

"Furthermore," continued the sick man, "we need to be assailed, to be awakened. This will reveal to us our weaknesses and will improve us. The exaggerated encomium tends to deceive us, lulls us into feeling secure, when out there we are held in ridicule; and the day we are ridiculed, we will fall as we fell in Europe. Money will no longer find its way to our churches; no one will buy our scapulars or leather belts, and when we are no longer rich we will not be able to hold sway over consciences."

"But we will always have our *haciendas* and our real estate."

"All will be lost as we lost them in Europe! And worse still is that we are working for our own ruin. For example: that boundless drive to arbitrarily raise each year the fees on our lands, that eagerness which I have in vain opposed in all our chapters, this eagerness will be our own undoing! The *indio* finds himself bound to acquire by purchase lands somewhere else, which are good or better than ours. I fear we are beginning to decline: *Quos vult perdere Jupiter dementat prius*, Whom the Gods seek to destroy they first make mad. That is why we do not increase our burden; already the people grumble. You have reasoned well. Let us leave the others to settle their own accounts; let us keep what is left of our prestige and since we will soon be appearing before God, let us cleanse our hands. May the God of mercy have compassion on our weaknesses."

"So Your Reverence believes that the tax or tribute..."

"Let us not talk any more about money," interrupted the old man with some disgust. "You were saying that the Teniente had promised Padre Damaso..."

"Yes Father," replied Padre Sibyla, half smiling, "but this morning I saw him and he told me he regretted what had transpired the other night; that the sherry had gone to his head and he thought Padre Damaso was in the same condition. And the promise? I asked him in jest. 'Padre Cura,' he answered, 'I know how to keep my word when with it I do not stain my honor: I am not nor have I ever been an informer. That is why I have only two stars.'"

After discussing other matters of less import, Padre Sibyla left.

The Teniente in fact did not go to Malacañang[2], but the *Capitan General* knew of the incident.

Talking to his aides about allusions in the Manila journals which they called comets or celestial apparitions, one of them referred to the matter of Padre Damaso with some intentional coloring but with more accuracy.

"From whom did you obtain that?" asked His Excellency smiling.

"From Laruja, who recounted it at the newspaper office."

The *Capitan General* again smiled and added: "Women and friars do not cause affronts. I intend to live in peace the time allotted me, and I do not want more complications with men wearing skirts. Furthermore, I also know that the father provincial has made fun of my orders. I asked for that friar's transfer as punishment, and he was transferred to a much better town. Friar business, as we say in Spain!"

But when His Excellency was left alone he was no longer smiling.

"Ah! if these people were not so stupid, they would trim my Reverences down to size!" he sighed. "But each deserves his lot. And we do as the rest of the world!"

In the meantime, Capitan Tiago had finished conferring with Padre Damaso, or better said, the latter with him.

"So now you have been warned," said the Franciscan on leaving. "All this would have been avoided had you just consulted me, or not lied when I questioned you. Try not to commit more foolishness! And trust your patron more!"

Capitan Tiago made two or three rounds in the sala, sighing and in a meditative mood. All of a sudden, as if a good idea had quickly crossed his mind, he ran to the oratory and quickly put out the candles and the lamp which he had ordered lighted for Ibarra's safety.

He muttered: "There is still time, and the journey is long."

- 10 -
The Town

The town of San Diego lies on the shores of the lake, amidst tracts of flat arable lands and rice fields. It exports sugar, rice, coffee and fruits which are sold cheap to the Chinese who exploit the naiveté or the vices of the laborers.

When, on a serene day, the youth climb to the top of the church tower, covered with moss and trailing vines, they break out in joyful exclamations, inspired by the beauty of the panorama before them.

In that cluster of nipa, zinc and *cabonegro roofs* separated by gardens and orchards, each one knows how to locate his small house, his little nest.[1] Everything serves as a sign post: a tree, the tamarind of sparse foliage; the coconut palm loaded with nuts like unto an Astarte, the goddess of fertility; or the Diana of Ephesus, with its multiple breasts; a pliant bamboo; a betelnut *palm*; a cross. Over there is the river, a monstrous crystal snake, asleep on a green carpet. Between distances, its current ripples on pieces of rock dispersed on a sandy bottom. There the river bed stretches between two elevated banks, to which tenaciously cling the gnarled roots of ancient trees. Here there is a gentle incline and the river widens and meanders.

Further beyond is a small house built precariously on its edge, defying the height, the winds and the abyss with thin supports, seeming like a monstrous mosquito waiting to strike a reptile. Trunks of palms or trees with still green bark, loose and unstable, span both banks, and if they are bad bridges they are, on the other hand, magnificent gymnastic equipment to balance on and not to be disdained. The children enjoy themselves in the river in which they bathe; a woman crosses with a basket on her head; an old man goes, trembling, and drops his cane into the water.

What always attracts attention is what one would call an island of forest in a sea of cultivated soil. There are century-old trees with hollow trunks which die only when their tops are struck by a lightning bolt that sets them on fire. It is said then that the fire encloses itself and dies on the spot. There are huge boulders which time and nature keep dressing in a velvet carpet of moss. The dust is deposited layer after layer in their hollows; the rain moistens the dust and the birds sow the seed. The tropical vegetation thrives freely: brambles and briars, curtains of intertwining tangled plants, extending from one tree to another, hang from the branches, holding on to the roots, to the ground, as if the goddess Flora in discontent had planted these on top of the other vegetation. Moss and mushrooms flourish in the rugged crevices, and aerial plants, those gracious guests, confusing their embraces with the leaves of the hospitable tree.

The forest is dreaded. Strange legends are woven around it, but the most credible and, for the same reason the one least known and believed in, seems to be the following:

When the town was just a miserable heap of huts on what passed for streets, the grass grew unchecked. In those times, when deer and wild boar still made nightly appearances, an old Spaniard with deep-set eyes, who spoke Tagalog fluently, arrived in San Diego. After visiting and making a survey of the lands in all their aspects, he asked the owners of the forest where the thermal waters flowed. Pretending to be one of the owners, the old man acquired the property in exchange for clothing, jewelry and some cash. Then he disappeared—no one knew how—but the folk believed him to be already enchanted, when a fetid odor emitted from the neighboring forest called the attention of some shepherds. They followed its trail and found the old man in a state of decomposition, hanging from the branch of a balete tree.[2] In life, his appearance had inspired fear because of his deep cavernous voice, his sunken eyes, his soundless laughter; but now dead by suicide, he disturbed the sleep of the women. Some threw his jewelry into the river and burnt his clothing, and ever since his body was buried at the foot of the balete tree, not a single person would venture into the forest.

A shepherd in search of his animals recounted that he saw lights. The young men went to see, and they heard laments. A hapless lover, trying to draw the attention of his disdainful lady-love, promised to spend the night under the tree wrapping around his body a long weave of reeds. He died of a high fever which he caught the night following his bet. Many tales and legends about this place soon spread.

Before some months passed, there came a young Spanish *mestizo* who claimed to be the son of the deceased. He established himself in that corner of the property, dedicated himself to agriculture, especially to the planting of indigo. Don Saturnino was a taciturn youth, of a character violent and at times even cruel. He was, however, active and industrious. He built a wall around his father's grave, which he visited, alone, from time to time. When somewhat advanced in age, he married a young woman from Manila who bore him Rafael, the father of Crisostomo.

Don Rafael, ever since his youth, made himself well-loved by the peasants. The agriculture introduced and encouraged by his father developed rapidly; new inhabitants poured in; many Chinese came. The hamlet soon became a village with a native priest. Later it evolved into a town. The priest died, and Padre Damaso came, but the grave and the surrounding territory were respected.

The neighborhood children at times ventured to roam around the place armed with clubs and stones, to pick guavas, papayas, *lomboi*. While they were so occupied, or while contemplating in silence the rope hanging from a branch, some stones were thrown at them, coming from nowhere. Shouting "The old man, the old man!" they dropped their fruits and their clubs, jumped from the trees, ran across the rocks and underbrush and did not stop until they had left the forest behind them, pale, some breathless, others weeping and laughing no longer.

- 11 -

The Sovereigns Divide and Rule

Who were the chieftains of the town?

It was not Don Rafael while he was alive, even if he was the richest, had more lands, and had almost everyone in his debt. Since he was modest and given to depreciating the importance of what he was doing, a following never formed behind him; we saw how they rose against him when they saw him falter.

Could it be Capitan Tiago? When the latter arrived, he was, in truth, welcomed by his debtors with a band. They feted him with a banquet and loaded him with gifts; the best fruits covered his table. If a deer or wild boar was bagged in the hunt, he had a fourth of it; if he found handsome a horse belonging to one of his debtors, half an hour later the horse appeared in his stables. All this is true, but they laugh at him and call him in secret "*Sacristan* Tiago."

Perhaps the *Gobernadorcillo*?

This was a hapless man who did not command; he

obeyed. He took no one to task, but was taken to task; he did not direct, but was directed. Instead he had to answer to the *Alcalde Mayor* for all that he was commanded, ordered, and directed to do, as if it had all come from his own head. However, it can be said to his credit that he had not stolen or usurped this privilege: it had cost him five thousand pesos and many humiliations which, for all it earned him, seemed very cheap.

Come! well then, can it be God?

Ah! the good God does not disturb the consciences or the sleep of the inhabitants. At least he does not cause them to tremble, and if they spoke of Him by chance in some sermon, they surely thought with a sigh: "If only there were a God!"...Few occupied themselves with the good Lord; they had enough to do, giving to the saints, male and female. God, for those people, had come to be like those poor kings who surround themselves with male and female favorites: the people only did obeisance to the latter.

San Diego was something akin to a Rome, but not the Rome whose boundaries the rogue Romulus marked out with a plow; nor the later Rome which, bathed in its own and alien blood, dictated laws to the world. No, it was like contemporary Rome, with the difference that instead of monuments of marble and coliseums, she had monuments of *sawali* and a cockpit of nipa. The parish priest was the Pope in the Vatican, the *Alferez* of the *Guardia Civil*, the King of Italy in the Quirinal, we must understand—all in proportion to the *sawali* huts and the cockpit of nipa. Here, as it is there, are many conflicts, each one wishing to be master, and considering the other superfluous. Let us explain and describe the qualities of both.

Padre Bernardo Salvi is that young and silent

Franciscan whom we have mentioned earlier. His habits and ways are distinct, and different from those of his brothers, and even more from those of his predecessor, the violent Padre Damaso. He is thin and sickly, almost completely pensive, strict in the fulfillment of his religious duties and careful of his good name.

A month after his arrival, almost all became brothers of the Franciscan tertiary order, to the great sorrow of its rival, the Confraternity of the Holy Rosary. His soul overflowed with joy upon seeing each neck decorated with four or five scapulars and around each waist a rope with knots, and those processions of cadavers or specters in coarse cotton habits.

The *sacristan mayor* became a little capitalist, selling—or giving as alms, as it is more rightly said—all those objects needed to save the soul and fight the devil. It is a known fact that this spirit, who once was bold enough to defy and contradict God Himself face to face, doubting His Word, as it is written in the holy book of Job; who carried Our Lord Jesus Christ through the heavens as he later did to the witches in the Middle Ages, and, they say, continues to do to the *asuang* of the Philippines, has now become so bashful that he cannot stand the sight of a piece of cloth whereon are painted two arms, and now fears the knots of a rope. But this does not prove anything except that there is some progress in this matter, and the devil has retrogressed, or at the very least, turned conservative, like all who dwell in the shadows, if we are not to attribute to him the weaknesses of a fifteen-year-old maiden.

As we were saying, Padre Salvi was very assiduous in the performance of his duties—too assiduous, according to the *Alferez*. While he preached—he was fond of preaching—the church doors were closed. In this he was like Nero, who did not allow anyone to leave while he was singing in the theater, but the former did so for the good, and the latter for the ruination of souls. All his subordinates' shortcomings were usually punished with fines. He rarely beat them. He was very much different from Padre Damaso, who settled everything with blows and canes, which he dealt laughing and with the best of good will. No one could bear him ill will for this: he was convinced that only with blows can the *indio* be dealt with; this was said by a friar who knew how to write books, and Padre Damaso believed it, for he never argued against what was printed. Many persons could well be accused of this kind of modesty.

Padre Salvi rarely beat anyone, but, as one old philosopher puts it, what he lacked in quantity he had abundance of in quality. However, no one could hold that against him. Fasting and abstinence impoverished his blood, excited his nerves, and as people said, sent the wind went up to his head. Consequently the backs of the altar boys cannot indicate very well whether a priest fasts or eats well.

The only enemy of this spiritual power with leanings towards the temporal was, as we have said, the *Alferez*. He was the only one, for, as the women tell, the devil takes flight before the friar, because one day, having tried to tempt him, he was caught by the priest, who tied him at the foot of the bed, scourged him with the cord, and released him only after nine days.

Consequently, he who after this could still make himself an enemy of a man like Padre Salvi, acquired a worse reputation than the poor and incautious devil. But the *Alferez* deserved his fate. His wife, an old Filipina who wore much rouge and paint, was called Doña Consolacion; her husband and others called her other names. The *Alferez*

avenged his matrimonial misfortunes by getting as drunk
as a wine cask, by ordering more drills for his soldiers
under the sun, while staying under the shade himself, or
more frequently, by beating his lady, who if she was not a
lamb of God who takes away nobody's sins, instead stored
up for him many penances of purgatory, if he was headed
there, which the pious doubted. He and she, as if playing
a joke, thrashed each other beautifully, and gave the
neighborhood free spectacles, vocal and instrumental, with
four-hand piano pieces, loud, with pedal and all.

Every time these scandals reached Father Salvi's ears,
he smiled and crossed himself, immediately reciting one
Our Father. They called him a watchdog, a hypocrite, a
Carlist, a miser. Padre Salvi would only smile to himself
and pray more. The *Alferez* always told the few Spaniards
who visited him the following anecdote:

"Are you going to the convent to visit that little dead
fly of a priest? Careful! If he offers you chocolate, which I
doubt he will...but if he finally offers, be on guard. If he
calls the servant and tells him: 'Fulanito, make a cup of
chocolate, *eh?*' Then you can stay and not worry; but if he
says 'Fulanito, make a cup of chocolate, *ah?*' then pick up
your hat and exit running."

"What?" asked the other man fearfully. "Does he dole
out poison? Good heavens!"

"Man, no; not to that extent."

"So?"

"Chocolate *eh?* means *espeso*, thick; and chocolate *ah*
means *aguado*, watered down."

We believe, however, that this was just a calumny of
the *Alferez's*, *since* the same anecdote has been attributed
to many priests. Unless of course this is a practice special
to the Order.

To annoy him, the military, inspired by his wife,

forbade anyone to take walks after nine o'clock in the evening. Doña Consolacion claimed to have seen the priest disguised in a piña shirt, with a *nito salakot*, taking walks in the late hours of the night. Padre Salvi avenged himself in a holy manner: when he saw the *Alferez* enter the church, he unobtrusively ordered the *sacristan* to close all the doors, and then he went up into the pulpit and started to preach until saints closed their eyes and the wooden dove over his head, the image of the Holy Spirit, murmured "Please!" The *Alferez*, like all impenitents who cannot be corrected thereby, would leave swearing, and as soon as he could, got hold of a *sacristan* or a servant of the priest, detained him, beat him, and made him scrub the floor of the barracks and that of his own household, which thus came to look decent. When the sacristan paid the fine imposed by the priest for his absence, he revealed the reasons. Padre Salvi heard him in silence, kept the money and at once let loose his goats and sheep to graze in the *Alferez's* garden, while he searched for a new theme for another much longer, more edifying sermon. These things did not, however, prevent their shaking hands and speaking courteously when they met.

When her husband fell asleep from wine or snored during his siesta, and Doña Consolacion could not quarrel with him, she would station herself by the window in her blue flannel blouse, cigar in mouth. She, who could not stand the young, would cast her eyes on the young girls and ridicule them. The latter, in fear of her, filed past in embarrassment, unable to raise their eyes, hastening their pace and holding their breath. Doña Consolacion had a great virtue: she seems never to have looked at herself in a mirror.

These are the chieftains of the town of San Diego.

- 12 -

All Saints' Day

Perhaps the only thing that, without dispute, distinguishes man from the animal, is the cult which conquers those who have ceased to be. And strangely enough, this custom appears to be more deeply rooted in nations which are less civilized.

Historians write that the old inhabitants of the Philippines venerated and deified their ancestors. Today it is the other way around: it is the dead who must commend themselves to the living. They also say that the people of New Guinea keep the bones of their dead in boxes and maintain conversations with them. The greater portion of the peoples of Asia, Africa and America give the dead food offerings of the most exquisite dishes from their kitchens, or of the favorite food of the departed; and they give banquets for those whom they suppose to still exist. The Egyptians built palaces, the Muslims little chapels, etc., but the masters in this matter who know the human heart best are the people of Dahomey. These blacks know that man is vengeful, and so they say that to satisfy the dead there is no better act than to sacrifice all of his enemies over the grave; and because man is curious and would not know how to entertain himself in the other life, they send him each year mail wrapped in the skin of a decapitated slave.

We are different from the others. Regardless of the inscriptions on tombs, almost no one believes that the dead rest and, even less, that they are at peace. The most optimistic imagine that their great grandparents still roast in purgatory, and if they are not damned, will still be able to keep them company for many years. Let whoever would like to contradict us visit the churches and the cemeteries of the country during this day; let him observe, and he will see. But since we are in the town of San Diego let us visit its cemetery.

Towards the west, nestled in the rice fields, is not the town proper, but the barrio of the dead. A narrow pathway, dusty on hot days and flooded on rainy days, leads to it. It has a wooden door, and is fenced partly with stones and partly with bamboo stakes which seem to segregate it from the community of men, but not from the priest's goats and some pigs from the neighborhood which come and go to explore among the tombs, or cheer up the solitude of the place.

In the center of that vast space stands a great wooden cross on top of a stone pedestal. Storms have twisted its INRI sheet of tin, and rains have erased the letters.[1] At the foot of the cross, as in the actual and real Golgotha, lies a confusing heap of skeletons and bones which an indifferent gravedigger threw from the holes he was emptying. There they will probably wait, not for the resurrection of the dead, but for the arrival of the animals which, with their secretions, will warm and wash those cold naked bones. One notices recent excavations in the surroundings. Here the land is sunken, over there is a small mound.

The *tarambulo* and the *pandakaki* grow abundantly: the former to prick the legs with its thorny berries; the latter to add its odor to that of the cemetery, as if this were not enough.[2] The ground is, however, covered with some flowers—flowers which, like the skulls, are known only to their Creator: the sheen of their petals is pale and their scent is the perfume of the sepulchres. Grass and vines cover the corners; they clamber over the walls and niches, dressing and beautifying the naked ugliness; at times they penetrate the cracks caused by tremors and earthquakes, hiding from view the emptiness of the tomb.

When we enter, the men have already driven away the animals save one pig, a most obstinate beast. We see it with its tiny eyes, putting its head through a gap in the enclosure, raising its snout in the air as if to say to a woman in prayer:

"Don't eat everything. Leave me something, eh?"

Two men are digging a grave near the wall that seems in danger of collapsing. One is the official gravedigger; he does the job indifferently. He throws out vertebrae and bones, in the same manner that a gardener disposes of stones and dry twigs. The other is worried. He perspires, smokes and spits now and then.

"Listen!" says the one who is smoking, in Tagalog. "Would it not be better to dig somewhere else? This one is new."

"Some graves are as recent as many others."

"I can't take it anymore! That bone that you have cracked is still bloody...hm! And that hair?"

"How finicky you are," reproaches the other, "as if you were a courthouse clerk. If you have disinterred a corpse as I have, in the darkness of a rainy night, a corpse twenty days old...my lantern went out..." The other man was shaking.

"The nails of the coffin came loose, half of the body came out, it stank, and you had to carry it...it was raining and we were both soaking wet, and..."

"Krrr! And why did you dig it up?"

The gravedigger looked strangely at the other.

"Why? Do I know why? I was ordered to!"

"Who commanded you?" The gravedigger took a half step backward and examined his companion from head to foot.

"Man, you are like a Spaniard; the same question was asked of me by a Spaniard, but in secret. So I will give you the same answer I gave the Spaniard: I was ordered by the head parish priest."

"Ah! And what did you do later with the corpse?" pressed the finicky one.

"To the devil with you!... If I did not know you, and know you to be a man, I would say that truly you are a Spanish civilian; you ask questions like the other one. Well, the chief parish priest ordered me to bury the body in the Chinese cemetery, but since the coffin was heavy and the Chinese cemetery far from here..."

"No! no! I will not dig anymore!" the other one interrupts with horror, letting go of his shovel and jumping out of the grave. "I have broken a skull and I fear that I won't be able to sleep tonight."

The gravedigger bursts into laughter, seeing how the other fled, crossing himself.

The cemetery was filling up with men and women

dressed in mourning clothes. Some had been searching for graves for some time, disagreeing among themselves; they separated and each one knelt where it suited him best. Others, those who had niches for their relatives, lighted candles and prayed devoutly. One could hear the sighs and sobs which they tried to suppress or to exaggerate. Now could be heard the zum-zum of *orapreo*, *orapreiss* and *requiem eternam*, pray for us, pray for us and eternal rest, etc.

A little old man with lively eyes entered, bareheaded. Upon seeing him many laughed, some women knitted their brows. The old man seemed oblivious to all those reactions. He headed for the mound of skulls and knelt, his eyes searching for something among the bones. With care, he separated the skulls one after the other, and because he did not find what he was looking for, knitted his brows, moved his head from side to side, looked around him, and finally got up and addressed the gravedigger.

"Oy!" he said. The other raised his head.

"Do you know where I can find a lovely skull, white like coconut meat, with complete dentures? It is the one I placed at the foot of the cross, underneath those leaves?"

The gravedigger shrugged his shoulders.

"Look!" added the old man, showing the latter a silver coin, "I don't have any anything but this; I will give to you if you find it for me."

The luster of the coin made the gravedigger thoughtful. He looked towards the heap of bones and said, "It is not there? Well, I don't know."

"Do you know? When I am paid by those who owe me, I will give you more," continued the old man. "It was my wife's skull; if you find it for me..."

"Is it not there? Well, I don't know. But if you like I

can get you another one."

"You are like the grave you are digging," exclaimed the old man nervously. "You don't know the value of what you are losing. For whom is that grave?"

"How do I know? For a dead person!" the gravedigger answered with ill humor.

"Like the tomb! Like the tomb!" repeated the old man, laughing wryly. "You don't even know what you throw away, or what you swallow. Dig, dig!" And he turned towards the gate.

In the meantime the digger had finished his task; he had accumulated two mounds of fresh and reddish soil on the edges of the grave. He took *buyo* from his *salakot* and started to chew, glancing blankly at those who passed around him.

- 13 -

A Gathering Storm

Soon after the old man had left a carriage stopped on the pathway. It appeared to have made a long trip: it was covered with dust and the horses were sweating.

Ibarra descended, followed by an old man-servant. He dismissed the carriage with a gesture and headed towards the cemetery, silent and grave.

"My sickness and my preoccupations have not allowed me to return," the old man was saying timidly. "Capitan Tiago said he would have a tomb built, but I planted flowers and had a cross made."

Ibarra did not answer.

"There behind that big cross, Señor!" continued the servant, pointing to a corner when they had reached the gate.

Ibarra was so preoccupied that he did not notice the surprised reaction of some persons who recognized him, stopped in their prayers and followed him with curious eyes.

The young man was treading carefully, avoiding the graves which had sunk into the ground. At another time he would have stepped on them; now he respected them—his father lay in a similar condition. He stopped when he reached the other side of the cross, and looked around him. His companion was confused and confounded. He looked for traces on the ground, but nowhere did he see any sign of the cross.

"Is it here?" he muttered under his breath. "No, it is over there, but the soil has been removed!"

Ibarra regarded him with anguish.

"Yes!" he continued. "I remember: there was a stone nearby; the grave was a little bit short; the gravedigger was sick and an associate had to dig it, but we can ask that one what became of the cross."

He proceeded towards the gravedigger who was regarding them with curiosity, and greeted them, removing his *salakot*.

"Can you tell us which is the grave that had the cross?" asked the servant.

The one questioned looked in the direction of the place and reflected.

"A big cross?"

"Yes, a big one," happily confirmed the servant, looking meaningfully at Ibarra, whose features had brightened.

"A cross with designs on it, tied with rattan?" the gravedigger asked again.

"That's it, that's it! Like this, like this," the servant traced on the earth the shape of a Byzantine cross.

"And over the grave there were flowers planted?"

"*Adelfas, sampagas* and *pensamientos*, that's it!" added the servant, filled with joy. He offered him a cigar.

"Tell us which is the grave and where the cross is."

The gravedigger rubbed his ears and replied yawning: "Well, the cross—I have already burned it."

"Burned it? Why did you burn it?"

"Because the head parish priest so ordered."

"Who is the chief parish priest?" asked Ibarra.

"Who? The one who beats up people, the *Padre Garrote*."[1] Ibarra touched his forehead with the palm of his hand.

"But at least you can tell us where the grave is. You must remember." The gravedigger smiled.

"The dead body is no longer there," he calmly replied.

"What are you saying?"

"Oh," continued the man in a jesting tone, "in its place I interred a woman last week."

"Are you mad?" countered the servant. "It has not been a year yet since we buried him!"

"But that's it! I dug it up some months ago. The head parish priest ordered me to take it to the cemetery of the Chinese. But it was so heavy, and that night it rained..."

The man could not go on; he stepped backwards frightened when he saw Ibarra's reaction. Ibarra advanced toward him, grabbed his arm hard and shook him.

"And you did it?" asked the young man in a tone that cannot be described.

"Don't be angry, Señor," answered the gravedigger, pale and trembling. "I did not bury him among the Chinese. It is better to drown than to be with the Chinese, I said to myself, so I threw the dead body into the water."

Ibarra placed both his fists on the man's arms and looked at him for a long time with an indefinable expression.

"You are nothing but a miserable cad!" he said and left hurriedly, stepping on bones, graves, crosses, like a deranged man.

The gravedigger rubbed his arm, grumbling:

"What troubles the dead leave to us! The head parish priest caned me for not burying the body, sick as I was. Now this one almost breaks my arm for disinterring him. What a people these Spaniards are! Yet still, I am going to lose my job!"

Ibarra walked fast, his gaze far away; the old servant followed him, weeping.

The sun was about to set. Thick nimbus clouds covered the skies toward the east; a dry breeze was shaking the treetops, making the reeds groan.

Ibarra was hatless. Not a tear fell from his eyes; from his breast, not a sigh escaped. He was walking as if he were escaping from someone, perhaps from his father's shadow, or from the approaching storm. He crossed the town, heading towards the outskirts for that ancient house which for many years he had not returned to set foot in. It was surrounded by a wall covered with growing cactus plants, which seemed to beckon to him; the windows were open; the *ilang-ilang* was swaying gaily, waving its branches loaded with flowers[2]; the doves were flying around the cone-shaped roof of their dwelling place in the midst of the garden.

The young man, however, was paying no attention to this cheerful scene which greeted his return to his ancestral home: his eyes were fixed on the figure of a priest who was advancing from the opposite direction. It was the parish priest of San Diego, that pensive Franciscan we saw earlier, the *Alferez's* enemy. The wind folded back the wide brim of his hat, pressed on his rough cotton habit, molding his form and showing off the contours of his thin thighs and somewhat bowlegged calves. In his right hand he carried a cane of *palasan* with an ivory handle.[3] That was the first time Ibarra and the friar saw each other.

When they met, the young man stopped for a moment and stared at him. Padre Salvi avoided his glance and pretended that he was distraught and had not seen the other man.

The hesitation lasted a second. Ibarra rapidly advanced towards the friar and stopped him, letting his hand fall with force on the latter's shoulder and in a voice scarcely intelligible, asked:

"What have you done with my father?"

Padre Salvi paled and trembled upon realizing the emotions that had rushed to the young man's face. He could not answer, like one paralyzed.

"What have you done with my father?" Ibarra asked again in a voice choking with emotion.

The priest, gradually forced to a bending position by the hand that gripped him, made an effort to reply:

"You are mistaken; I have not done anything to your father."

"You did not?" the young man continued, holding the other down forcefully until he fell on his knees.

"No! I assure you! It was my predecessor, it was Padre Damaso!"

"Ah!" exclaimed the young man, releasing him and slapping his own forehead. He left the poor Padre Salvi and proceeded in haste in the direction of his house.

In the meantime the servant helped Padre Salvi to his feet.

- 14 -
Tasio

The strange old man roamed the streets distractedly. He had been a former student of Philosophy, who left his studies to obey his old mother. It was not due to lack of means or capacity to learn. It was, in fact, precisely because his mother was rich, and it was said that he had talent. The good woman feared that her son might become a sage and abandon God, and so she made him choose between becoming a priest or leaving San Jose College. He, being in love, opted for the latter and got married. Orphaned and widowed in less than a year, he sought comfort in books to assuage his loneliness, in cockpits and in doing nothing. But he became so taken up with books and with purchasing them that he completely neglected to attend to his fortune, and gradually became impoverished.

The well-educated called him Don Anastasio or the philosopher Tasio; and the badly brought up, who were in the majority, dubbed him Tasio the mad man for his rare insights and strange ways of dealing with other men.

As we have said, the afternoon threatened a storm; flashes of lightning illumined the leaden sky with pale light; the atmosphere was heavy and the air very humid.

The philosopher seemed to have already forgotten his precious skull: now he was smiling, gazing at the dark clouds.

Near the church he met a man attired in a woolen jacket, carrying in his hand more than an *arroba* of candles and a tasselled cane, the insignia of authority.

"You seem happy," the man said in Tagalog.

"Actually, *Señor Capitan*; I am happy because I nourish a hope."

"Ha? And what is that hope?"

"The storm!"

"The storm! Undoubtedly you are thinking of bathing?" asked the *Gobernadorcillo* in an ironic tone, looking at the old man's modest attire.

"Bathing? Not a bad idea, especially when one encounters garbage," answered Tasio in the same tone, although somewhat deprecatingly, looking his interlocutor in the face. "But I am waiting for better things."

"What then?"

"Some thunderbolts that kill people and burn houses," the philosopher answered seriously.

"Ask then, all at once, for the deluge!"

"We all deserve it, you and me! You, *Señor Gobernadorcillo*, you have there an *arroba* of candles from the Chinese store. For more than ten years, I have been proposing to every new *capitan* the purchase of lightning rods, and they all laugh at me; and they buy firecrackers and rockets and pay for the ringing of the bells. Even more, you yourself, on the day after my proposal, commissioned the Chinese foundry to make a small bell for Santa Barbara,[2] when science has verified that it is dangerous to touch the bells during a storm. Tell me why, in the seventies, when a thunderbolt struck Biñan, it fell exactly on the tower, destroying the clock and the altar? What was the little bell of Santa Barbara doing?"

At that moment a lightning bolt flashed.

"Jesus, Mary and Joseph! Blessed Barbara!" murmured the *gobernadorcillo*, turning pale and crossing himself.

Tasio roared with laughter.

"You are worthy of the name of your patron saint," he said in Spanish, turning his back on him and heading for the church.

The *sacristanes* inside were setting up a bier surrounded with wax candles in wooden candelabra. It consisted of two large tables, one on top of the other, covered with black cloth bordered in white. Here and there one could see painted skulls.

"Is it for the souls or for the candles?" he asked. And seeing two boys—one ten years old, the other approximately seven—he approached them without waiting for the sacristans' reply.

"Are you coming with me, boys?" he asked. "Your mother has prepared for you a supper fit for priests."

"The *sacristan mayor* does not want us to leave until 8 o'clock, Señor," replied the older one. "I expect to collect my salary and give it to our mother."

"Ah! and where are you going?"

"To the tower, Señor, to toll the bells for the souls."

"You are going up to the tower? Then be careful! Do not go near the bells during the storm!"

He left the church, but not without casting a look of

compassion on the boys, who were climbing the ladder to the tower to get to the choir loft.

Tasio rubbed his eyes, looked up again and murmured: "Now I would be sorry if those thunderbolts fell."

Head bowed, he pensively directed his steps to the outskirts of town.

"Please come in before you proceed," a voice said in Spanish from a nearby window.

The philosopher raised his head and saw a man thirty to thirty-five years of age smiling at him.

"What are you reading there?" asked Tasio upon entering the house, pointing to the book the man had in his hand.

"It is a book for the occasion: *The Pains Suffered by the Blessed Souls in Purgatory*," answered the other man, grinning.

"My man, oh man, oh my man!" the old man exclaimed in different tones, as he entered the house. The author must have been smart.

At the top of the stairs he was received very cordially by the owner of the house and his young wife. He was called Don Filipo Lino and she, Doña Teodora Viña. Don Filipo was the *teniente mayor*[3] and the head of a party, almost liberal, if you could call it that, and if it is possible to have parties in the towns.

"Did you see at the cemetery the son of the late Don Rafael who has just arrived from Europe?"

"Yes, I saw him as he was getting out of the carriage."

"They say he had gone to look for his father's grave. The blow must have been terrible." The philosopher shrugged his shoulders.

"Don't you feel concerned about that tragedy?" asked the young married woman.

"Madam already knows that I was one of the six pallbearers who accompanied the body. I was the one who introduced myself to the *Capitan General* when I saw that here the whole world, and even the authorities, were silent before such a major act of desecration. And that despite my preferring always to honor a good man in·his lifetime and not after his death."

"And then?"

"You already know, Madam, that I am not in favor of a hereditary monarchy. Because of the drops of Chinese blood my mother has given me, I think a little like the Chinese: I honor the father in his son, not the son in his father. Each one receives a reward or punishment for his deeds, but not for the acts of others."

"Did you have a mass offered for your late wife as I advised you yesterday?" asked the lady, changing the course of the conversation.

"No," answered the old man, smiling.

"What a pity!" she exclaimed with true compunction. "They say that tomorrow until ten o'clock in the morning the souls of the dead roam freely, awaiting the intercession of the living; that a mass during these days is equivalent to five masses during the other days of the year, or to six, as the priest said this morning. "Ho! ho! Does that mean that we have a day of grace for payment which we must take advantage of?"

"But Doray!" Don Filipo intervened, "you know that Don Anastasio does not believe in purgatory."

"I don't believe in purgatory?" the old man protested, half rising from his seat. "I even know its history!"

"The history of purgatory!" exclaimed the couple in great surprise. "Let's hear it! Tell it to us!"

"You don't know it, yet you order masses for the souls there and you talk about its pains? Very well, since the rain has started and looks as if it will last a long time, we have enough time not to get bored," replied Tasio, pausing for a moment of reflection.

Don Filipo closed the book he had in hand and Doray sat at his side, prepared not to believe anything that Tasio was going to say. The latter started:

"Purgatory existed long before Our Lord Jesus Christ came to the world. It must have been located in the center of the earth, according to Father Astete, or in the vicinity of Cluny, according to the monk spoken of by Father Girard. The place is not important. And now, who were roasting in those fires which had been burning since the beginning of the world? Its very ancient existence is proven by Christian philosophy, which says that God did not create anything new after he took His rest."

"It could have existed *in potentia*, but not in *actu*," interpolated the *teniente mayor*.

"Very well! However, I will tell you that some knew it as having existed in *actu*. One of them was Zarathustra or Zoroaster, who wrote part of the Avesta and founded a religion which had a lot in common with our own. And Zoroaster, according to the sages, existed at least 800 years before Christ. I say at least, because Gaffarel, after an examination of the testimonies of P'ato, Xantus of Lydia, Pliny, Hermipus and Eudoxus, believed it to be 2,500 years before our era. Be that as it may, what is certain is that Zoroaster spoke of the existence of some kind of purgatory and prescribed the means of deliverance from it. The living can redeem the souls of those who died in sin by reciting passages from the Avesta and doing good works, on the condition that he who prays should be a relative up to the fourth generation. The time for this takes place each year and lasts five days.

"Much later, when this belief had been affirmed among the people, the priests of that religion saw in it potential for a great business, and they exploited those "profoundly dark prisons in which remorse reigns," as Zoroaster says. They established then that for the price of one *derem*, a coin of little value it is said, one can save the soul a year of tortures; but since for that religion there were sins costing from 300 to 1,000 years of suffering—like falsehood, bad faith, not keeping one's solemn word, etc., the result was that the ruffians pocketed millions of derems. Here you will see something already similar to our purgatory, but with the difference understood to come from the difference between religions."

A flash of lightning followed by the deafening roar of thunder caused Doray to rise and, crossing herself, say: "Jesus, Mary and Joseph! I leave you two. I am going to burn a palm that has been blessed, and light candles of penitence."

The rain started to fall in torrents. Tasio the Philosopher continued, as he watched the young woman leave:

"Now that she has gone we can talk of this matter more reasonably. Doray, although a bit superstitious, is a good Catholic, and I don't want to pull th faith out of her heart; faith that is simple and sincere is distinguished from fanaticism as flame is from smoke, and music from babble. Imbeciles, like the deaf, confuse them. Between ourselves we can say that the idea of purgatory is good, holy and reasonable. It continues the union between those who have left and those who are left behind, and obliges a commitment to a greater purity of life. The evil lies in its abuse.

"But let us see now how Catholicism inherited this

idea which is not contained in the Bible or in the holy gospels. Neither Moses nor Jesus Christ makes the least mention of it, and the only passage cited from the Book of the Machabees is insufficient, besides the fact that this book had been declared by the Council of Laodicea as apocryphal, and the Catholic Church included it only later. Paganism, too, has nothing similar to it.

"The passage often quoted from Virgil about *Aliae panduntur inanes*, or others being suspended in a vacuum, giving Saint Gregory the Great the occasion to talk of drowning souls, and for Dante to amplify the idea in his *Divine Comedy*, cannot be the origin of this belief. Neither the Brahmans nor the Buddhists, nor the Egyptians, who gave Greece and Rome their Charon and their Averno, have anything like this idea. Neither is it spoken of in the religions of the nations of North Europe. These are the religions of warriors, bards and hunters, but not of the philosophers; notwithstanding the fact that they have kept their beliefs, even rituals, Christianized. These, however, did not accompany their hordes in the sacking of Rome, or in their seating themselves in the capitol. The religion of mists vanished with the noonday sun.

So then, the Christians of the early centuries did not believe in purgatory. They died with the joyful hope of seeing God face to face. The first fathers of the Church who seem to have mentioned it were Saint Clement of Alexandria, Origen and Saint Irenaeus, perhaps influenced by the Zoroastrian religion which was flourishing then and widespread throughout the Orient. We read at every step criticism of Origen's orientalism. Saint Irenaeus proved the existence of purgatory by the fact of Christ's stay for three days in the tomb in the depths of the earth, three days of purgatory, and deduced from this that each soul had to remain in purgatory until the resurrection of the flesh, even though "Today you will be with me in Paradise," would seem to contradict it. Saint Augustine also speaks of purgatory, but if he does not affirm its existence, neither does he believe it impossible, supposing it possible that punishments for our sins can continue in the other life.

"The deuce with Saint Augustine!" Don Filipo exclaimed. "He was not satisfied with what we suffer here, and wants it to continue!"

"Well, that is how it goes; some believed, others did not. Even when Saint Gregory came to admit it in his *de quibusdam levibus culpis esse ante judicium purgatorius ignis cedendus est* (It is to be believed that the fire of purgatory is for the lesser faults), there was nothing definite about it until the year 1439—that is, eight centuries later—when the Council of Florence declared that there should exist a purifying fire for souls that died in the love of God, but have not yet satisfied divine justice. Ultimately the Council of Trent, under Pius IV in 1563 in the 25th session, released the decree on purgatory which begins: *Cum Catholica Ecclesia Spiritu Santo edocta ets., etc.* (with the Catholic Church guided by the Holy Spirit etc.), and which says that the offerings of the living, prayers, alms and other works of piety, are the most efficacious means of releasing the souls, although these the sacrifice of the mass comes before them.

"The Protestants, however, do not believe in it and neither do the Greek fathers, for they do not have a biblical foundation and they say that the time of grace, merit and demerit ends with death, and that *quodcumque ligaberis in terra* (whatsoever you will bind on earth) does not mean until purgatory, etc. But this can be contested by the fact that purgatory, being located in the center of the earth, falls naturally under the dominion of Saint Peter.

"We would not finish our conversation if I were to tell you all that has been said on this matter. Someday, when you wish to discuss the subject further, come to my house and we will open books. We will talk freely and quietly about it. Now I am leaving. I don't know why this evening, Christian piety permits robbery—you, the authorities, allow it, and I fear for my books. If they steal in order to read them I would allow it, but I know that many want them burnt as an act of charity to me. This kind of charity, worthy of the Caliph Omar, is to be feared. Some, on account of these books, already believe I am damned."

"But I suppose that you believe in damnation?" asked Doray, who appeared carrying in a hot pan some dried palm leaves which emitted a delicate smoke and an agreeable perfume.

"I do not know, Madam, what God will do with me," answered old man Tasio, "when I am dying I will surrender myself to Him without fear. Let Him do with me howsoever He wishes. But a thought comes to my mind."

"And what thought is that?"

"If the Catholics are the only ones who can be saved, and of these only five per cent, as many priests say; and since the Catholics form only a twentieth part of the earth's population, if we are to believe what statistics say; after having condemned thousands and thousands of men who lived in the innumerable centuries before the coming of the Savior to this world, and after the son of God has died for us, now only five out of every twelve hundred can be saved? Oh, certainly not. I prefer to say and believe with

Job: 'Why torment a wind-blown leaf, or pursue a withered straw?' No, so much misfortune is impossible; to believe it is to blaspheme, no, no!"

"What do you want? Justice? Divine Purity?"

"Oh, but justice and divine purity saw the future before creation," answered the old man, shuddering and standing up. "Man, the creation, is contingent and not necessary, and this God should not have created him, no, if to make one happy he must condemn hundreds to eternal damnation, and all for inherited sins or for a moment of weakness. No, if this be true, smother your sleeping child; if this belief is not a blasphemy against this God who must be the supreme Good, then the Phoenican Molok, who fed himself with human sacrifices and innocent blood, and in whose entrails burned the infants wrenched from their mothers' bosoms, this sanguinary god, this horrible divinity, would be by his side a weak maiden, a friend, the mother of humanity."

Filled with horror, the madman or philosopher abandoned the house, running into the streets in spite of the rain and the darkness.

A blinding flash of lightning accompanied by a dreadful peal of thunder sowed the air with lethal sparks, and illumined the old man who with his hands raised to heaven, shouted:

"You protest! Of course I know that you are not cruel; of course I know that I must call you only the All Good."

The lightning flashed anew; the storm worsened.

•

- 15 -
The Altar Boys

The peals of thunder reverberated at short intervals, following one after the other, each sound preceding the dreadful zigzag of lightning: it could be said that God was writing His name in fire, and that the eternal vaults of heaven were trembling in fear. The rain poured in torrents and, whipped by the winds, which hissed mournfully, crazily changed direction every so often. The bells tolled a sound full of terror and mournful pleading, and in the brief silence following the robust roar of the unchained elements, they sadly groaned their plaint.

The two boys we saw talking with the philosopher were in the second section of the tower. The younger one, who had big black eyes and a timid appearance was trying to press his body to that of his brother, who had the same features as his, except that the look in the latter's eyes had more depth, and his features were more defined. Both boys were poorly clad in clothes filled with darning and patches. They sat on a piece of wood. Each one had a cord in his hand, the end of which was lost in the third storey, up among the shadows. The rain pushed by the wind reached up to them and tried to blow out a melting candle which burned on a big rock which they used on Good Friday to imitate the sound of thunder, making it roll over the sounds of the choir.

"Pull on your cord, Crispin," said the older boy to his brother.

The latter pulled, hanging on the cord. A weak lament was heard above, which instantly drowned in a clap of thunder multiplied by a thousand echoes.

"Ah! if we were only at home with Mother," sighed the younger, looking at his brother, "there we would not be afraid."

The elder did not answer; he was looking at the melting candle and seemed worried.

"There no one will say that I steal," continued Crispin. "Mother would not allow it. If she found out that they beat me..."

The elder turned his gaze away from the flame, raised his head, biting forcefully on the thick cord, which he pulled violently, causing a loud resonant vibration.

"Are we always going to live like this, brother?" Crispin continued. "I wish I would get sick at home tomorrow; I want to have a long illness so that Mother can take care of me and will not allow me to return to the convent. Thus, they will not call me a thief, nor will they beat me. And you too, brother, you should get sick with me."

"No!" answered the older one. "We will all die— Mother from sorrow, and we from hunger."

Crispin did not reply. "How much are you earning

this month?" he asked his brother after a moment's pause.

"Two pesos. I have been fined three times."

"Pay what they say I have stolen, so they won't call us thieves; pay it, brother."

"Are you mad, Crispin? Mother will have nothing to eat. The *sacristan mayor* says you have stolen two *onzas*, and two *onzas* make thirty-two pesos."

The young one counted with his fingers until he reached thirty-two. "Six hands and two fingers, and each finger a peso," he murmured thoughtfully, "and each peso how many *cuartos?*"[1]

"One hundred sixty."

"One hundred sixty cuartos; one hundred sixty times a cuarto? Mother! And how much is one hundred sixty?"

"Thirty-two hands," answered the elder.

Crispin paused for a moment, looking at his small hands.

"Thirty-two hands!" he repeated, "six hands and two fingers, and each finger thirty-two hands...and each finger a cuarto... Mother! so many cuartos. One wouldn't be able to count them in three days...and one could buy slippers for the feet, and a hat for the head when the sun is hot; and a big umbrella when it rains; and food, and clothing for you and Mother, and..." Crispin grew pensive.

"Now I am sorry I did not steal!"

"Crispin!" his brother scolded him.

"Do not be angry! The priest said he would beat me to death if I cannot produce the money; if I had stolen it, I could make it appear...and if I die, at least you and Mother would have clothes! I should have stolen it!"

The elder remained silent, and pulled at his cord. Then he answered, sighing, "What I fear is that Mother will scold you when she learns about this."

"Do you think so?" asked the little one, surprised. "You will tell her that they have already beaten me up a lot. I will show her my bruises, and my torn pocket. I do not have more than a cuarto, which they gave me at Christmas; the priest took it away yesterday. I have never seen such a beautiful coin! Mother will never believe it, she wouldn't!"

"But if the priest says so..."

Crispin started to cry, murmuring between sobs, "Then you go home alone; I don't want to go home. Tell Mother I am sick. I don't want to go home!"

"Don't cry, Crispin," said the elder, "Mother will not believe it. Don't cry. The old man Tasio said a good supper awaits us..."

Crispin raised his head and looked at his brother.

"A good supper! I have not yet eaten; they won't give me anything to eat until the two onzas appear... But what if Mother should believe it? You tell her that the *sacristan mayor*[2] lies; also the priest who believes him, that all of them lie; that they say we are thieves because our father is a man of vices who..."

A head appeared, emerging at the top of the ladder leading to the main part of the church. This head, like Medusa's, froze the words on the lips of the child. It was an elongated head, lean, with long black hair, a pair of blue glasses hiding one blind eye. It was the *sacristan mayor*, who was wont to appear without a sound, without notice.

The two brothers froze.

"You, Basilio, I impose on you a fine of two reales for not tolling the bell in unison," he said with a cavernous voice as if he had no vocal chords. "And you, Crispin, will stay tonight until what you have stolen appears."

Crispin looked at his brother as if imploring for help.

"We already have permission... Mother is waiting for us at 8 o'clock," murmured Basilio timidly.

"You are not leaving at 8 o'clock either; not until ten."

"But *Señor*, nine o'clock would be too late to walk home, and our home is very far away."

"Are you ordering me?" answered the man in an irritated voice. And getting hold of Crispin's arm he tried to drag him away.

"Sir, it has been a week since we have seen our mother!" pleaded Basilio, holding on to his little brother as if to protect him.

The *sacristan mayor* slapped him, separated the boys and pulled Crispin away. The latter started to cry, and prostrated himself on the floor while begging his brother:

"Don't leave me; they will kill me!"

But the *sacristan mayor*, not minding him, dragged Crispin down the ladder, until they disappeared into the shadows.

Basilio was left speechless; he could not utter a single word. He heard the sound of blows on his brother's body against the ladder steps, the scream, the slaps. Then the heart-rending sounds gradually diminished in the darkness.

The boy was not breathing: he was listening, standing on his feet, eyes wide with fear, fists clenched.

"When will I be able to plow a field?" he muttered between his teeth, and went down in haste. Upon reaching the choir loft he listened with attention; his little brother's soft voice sounded farther away, and his cries "Mother! Brother!" were completely extinguished by a door closing. Trembling, sweating, he paused for a moment. He bit his wrist to suppress a cry which rose from his heart, and allowed his gaze to wander in the semi-darkness of the church. The oil lamp burned faintly; the catafalque was in the center; all doors were shut; the windows had grilles.

Suddenly he climbed the ladder, passed the second level where the candle was still burning and climbed to the third. He untied the cords which held the clappers of the bells, and came down again, pale, his eyes glistening, but not from tears.

The rain was stopping, and the skies were gradually clearing.

Basilio knotted the strings together, tied one end to a balustrade, and without remembering to put out the candle, glided along into the darkness.

Some minutes later, voices and two shots were heard from one of the streets, but nobody was alarmed, and everything again settled down into silence.

- 16 -

Sisa

The night is dark: the neighbors sleep in silence; the families, after remembering their dead, surrender themselves to peaceful and contented slumber. They have recited three rosaries with requiems, the novena for souls, and burnt many wax candles before the sacred images. The rich and the affluent have fulfilled their duties to the benefactors who bequeathed them their fortunes.

The following day they would hear three masses said by each priest; give two pesos for another mass for their intentions, and then buy the papal bull of dispensation for the dead, full of indulgences. In truth, divine justice does not seem to be as demanding as human justice.

But the poor man, the indigent who hardly earns enough to keep himself alive, and has to bribe the petty directors, clerks and soldiers to let him live in peace—he does not sleep with the tranquility described by the courtly poets, who themselves, perhaps, have not suffered the pangs of misery. The poor man is sad and pensive. If he has said few prayers that night, he has prayed much, with tears in his eyes and grief in his heart. He does not have the novenas; neither does he know the ejaculations, nor the verses, nor the *oremus*[1] composed by the friars for those who have no ideas or feelings of their own; neither does he understand them.

He prays in the language of his misery. His soul weeps for himself and for the dead ones whose love had been a blessing to him. His lips may pronounce salutations, but his mind cries out his complaints and accusing laments. Will you be satisfied, you who blest poverty and you tormented shadows, with the simple prayer of the poor, offered before a badly wrought likeness under the light of a *timsim*[2], or would you prefer candlesticks before the images of bloody Christs, of Virgins with small mouths and crystal eyes, and the masses in Latin mechanically recited by a priest? And you, the religion preached for a suffering humanity, you must have forgotten your mission to comfort the oppressed in their misery, and to humble the powerful in their pride, and now have promises only for the rich, for those who can pay you?

The poor widow keeps watch over her children sleeping at her side. She is thinking of the bulls of dispensation she has to purchase for the repose of her parents' souls and that of her deceased spouse. "One peso," she muses, "one peso is one week of love for my children; one week of laughter and happiness; my savings of one month, a dress for my daughter who is turning into a woman."

"But it is necessary that you extinguish those flames," says a voice she has heard preaching. "It is necessary that you make a sacrifice." Yes! It is necessary. The church will not gratuitously save for you the souls of your loved ones; it does not distribute bulls of dispensation gratis. You should buy them. Instead of sleeping the night, you will work. Your daughter: let her in the meantime show her chaste nakedness; fast, for heaven is costly. Definitely it seems that the poor do not enter heaven.

These thoughts swirl in the space around her that separates the *sahig* occupied by the humble pallet, from the *palupu* from where the hammock hangs and rocks the child to sleep.[3] His breathing is easy and rested; every now and then he swallows his saliva and articulates sounds. The hungry stomach dreams of eating, not satisfied with what his older brothers gave him.

The cicadas keep singing monotonously, uniting their eternal and continuous note with the chirp of crickets hidden in the grass, or of the mole which emerges from its hole in search of food, while the gekko, no longer fearful of the water, disturbs the concert with its obnoxious voice, showing its head in the hole of a rotten tree trunk. The dogs howl sadly out there on the street, and the superstitious who listen are convinced that the animals see the spirits and shadows. But neither the dogs nor the insects see the sorrows of people and yet, how many exist!

Away, far from the town, at a distance equivalent to an hour's walk, lives the mother of Basilio and Crispin. Wife to a heartless man, she endeavors to live for her sons while her husband roams, and plays with fighting cocks. His appearances are infrequent and always painful. He had despoiled her of her few pieces of jewelry to feed his vices, and when the suffering Sisa had nothing more to sustain a husband's caprices, he began maltreating her. Weak of character and with more heart than brain, she knew only how to love and to weep.

Her husband was her god; her sons were her angels. He knew to what point he was adored and feared, and behaved like all false gods. Each day he became more cruel, more inhuman, more willful.

When Sisa consulted him, when once he appeared with a visage more somber than ordinary, about her plan to make Basilio a *sacristan*, he continued to stroke the fighting cock; he did not say yes or no. He only asked if they would earn much money. She dared not insist, but the extremity of her situation and the desire to have the boys learn to read and write in the town school obliged her to proceed with her plan. Still her husband said nothing.

That night, around 10:30 or 11:00, when the stars already shone in the heavens which the tempest had left, Sisa was seated on a wooden bench, contemplating some branches half-burning on her stove, which was fashioned from stones more or less angular. In a little kettle settled on a tripod or *tunko* rice was cooking, and over the coals were roasting three dried sardines, which are sold three for two *cuartos*.

With her chin resting on the palm of her hand, she gazed at the yellowish and weak flame of the flickering bamboo, whose fleeting coals quickly turned to ashes. A sad smile lingered on her face. She remembered the witty riddle of the kettle and the fire, which Crispin once made:

> *Naupu si Maitim, sinulut ni Mapula*
> *Nang malao' y kumara-kara.*

> Black sat down, caressed by red
> soon after simmering broke out.

She was still young, and one could see that once she must have been lovely and full of charm. Her eyes which, like her soul, she bequeathed to her sons, were beautiful, with long lashes and a profound look; her nose was proper, her pale lips of graceful design. She was what the Tagalogs would describe as *kayumangging-kaligatan*, that is brown-skinned but of a clean and pure complexion. However, sorrow or perhaps hunger has begun to sap the pale cheeks; the abundant tresses, once her pride and ornament, remain well-groomed: they are, not out of coquetry but by habit, coiled in a simple bun at the nape held fast without pins or combs.

She had been staying home for several days without going out, doing some sewing which had been entrusted to her to finish as soon as possible. In order to earn money she did not attend mass that morning for she would have wasted two hours, at least, going to and returning from the town—poverty forces one to sin! Having finished her work, she took it to the owner, who only promised to pay.

Throughout the whole day she had been thinking of the pleasures of the evening: she knew her sons were coming and thought of giving them a treat. She bought sardines, gathered the best tomatoes from her small garden knowing that these were Crispin's favorite food. She asked her neighbor Tasio, who lived half a kilometer away from her home, for some dried meat of wild boar and a leg of wild duck, food Basilio favored.

Full of hope she boiled the whitest rice which she herself had harvested from a garden plot. It was in truth a supper fit for the priests, for her poor sons.

But by an unfortunate chance her husband arrived and ate the rice, the dried meat, the duck's leg, five sardines and the tomatoes. Sisa said nothing. It was as though she herself had consumed the meal. After satisfying himself he remembered to ask about his sons; then Sisa was able to laugh and, contented, promised herself not to sup that night, for what was left was not enough for three. The father had asked about their sons, and for her this was more than a meal.

Afterwards, he took up his fighting cock and wanted to leave.

"Don't you wish to see them?" she asked tremulously. "The old man Tasio told me they would be a little bit late; Crispin has already learned to read—and perhaps Basilio will bring his salary!"

Her husband paused upon hearing this last piece of information. He hesitated, but his good angel prevailed.

"In that case keep one peso for me," he said, and took his leave.

Sisa wept bitterly, but remembering her sons, dried her tears. She boiled another measure of rice and prepared the three sardines left. Each one would have one-and-a-half pieces.

"They'll bring good appetites," she thought. "The way is long, and hungry stomachs have no hearts."

Tense and attentive to the least movement, she waited expectantly for the sound of footsteps: those of Basilio, strong and clear; those of Crispin, light and uneven, she thought.

The *kalao*[4] in the forest had already sung two or three times since the rain stopped, yet her sons had not yet arrived.

She placed the sardines inside the kettle to keep them warm, and went to the entrance of the hut to look in the direction of the path. In order to distract herself she started to sing in a low voice. She had a lovely voice. Whenever her sons heard her sing a *kundiman*[5] they would burst into tears, not knowing why. But that night her voice shook and the notes came out weak.

She stopped singing and focused her sight on the darkness. Nobody was coming from town, only the raindrops, moved by the wind, falling from the wide leaves of the banana plants.

All of a sudden she saw a black dog appear before her. The animal was dragging something along. Sisa, frightened, picked up a stone and cast it at the dog. The dog started to run, howling plaintively.

Sisa was not superstitious, but she had heard so much about presentiments and black dogs that she was filled with terror. She hurriedly closed the door and sat herself near the light. The night is hospitable to beliefs, and the imagination fills the atmosphere with spectres.

She attempted to pray, to invoke the Virgin, and God, to take care of her sons, above all, her little Crispin. Distracted, she forgot her prayers as she thought only of them, remembering the features of each one, those features which continually smiled at her in her dreams and in her vigils. But suddenly her hair stood on end, her eyes opened wide: illusion or reality, she was seeing Crispin on his feet near the stove, there where he was wont to sit in order to converse with her. Now he was saying nothing; he was looking at her with those big pensive eyes, and smiling.

"Mother! open up! open up!" said Basilio's voice from outside.

Sisa trembled, and the vision disappeared.

- 17 -

Basilio

"Life is but a dream."

B asilio could scarcely enter the house. Staggering, he fell into his mother's arms.

An inexplicable chill seized Sisa when she saw he had come alone. She wanted to talk, but could not emit a sound; she wanted to embrace her son but did not have the strength. To weep was impossible.

But at the sight of the blood that bathed his forehead, she was able to scream in a tone which betrayed a broken heart.

"My sons!"

"Don't be alarmed, Mother!" answered Basilio. "Crispin is in the convent."

"In the convent? He stayed behind in the convent? Is he alive?"

The boy raised his eyes towards his mother.

"Ah!" she exclaimed, passing from a great anguish to a greater happiness. Sisa wept, embraced her son, covering his bloodied forehead with kisses.

"Crispin alive! You left him in the convent... And why are you wounded, my son? Did you fall?"

She examined him carefully.

"The *sacristan mayor*, when he took Crispin away, told me that I could not leave until 10 o'clock. Since it was getting late I escaped. In town the soldiers called, 'Who goes there?' I started to run. They fired and a bullet grazed my forehead. I was afraid they would catch me and make me clean up the headquarters while beating me, as they did to Pablo, who up to now is unwell."

"My God! my God!" murmured his mother, trembling. "You have saved him!"

And she added, while searching for pieces of cloth, vinegar and gauze bandages:

"A finger's width more and they would have killed you; they kill me through my son! The *guardia civil* have no regard for mothers!"

"You must say that I fell from a tree. No one must know that they are after me."

"Why did Crispin stay behind?" Sisa asked after dressing her son's wound.

The latter regarded her for a moment, then embraced her. Little by little, he told her about the *onzas*. He did not, however, mention the tortures to which his younger brother had been subjected.

The tears of mother and son became as one.

"My good Crispin! Accusing my good Crispin! It is because we are poor, and the poor have to suffer everything," murmured Sisa, looking at the slowly diminishing *tinhoy*[1] with tear-filled eyes.

They remained in silence for some time.

"Have you eaten? No? There are rice and dried sardines."

"I don't feel like eating; water, I want only water."

"Yes!" his mother sadly replied. "I know that you do not like dried sardines. I had prepared something else for you, but your father came, my poor son!"

"Father came?" Basilio asked his mother, instinctively examining his mother's face and hands. The question crushed Sisa's heart. She understood only too well what was implied and she hastened to answer:

"He came and asked a lot of questions about you; he wanted to see you both. He was very hungry. He said that if you continued to be good he would return and stay with us."

Basilio interrupted his mother: "Bah!" and he puckered his lips in disgust.

"Son!" she scolded him.

"Forgive me, Mother," he answered in all seriousness: "Aren't we better off, just the three of us——you, Crispin and I? But you are crying. I haven't said anything."

Sisa sighed. "Are you not going to eat? Then let's lie down to sleep for it is getting quite late."

Sisa closed the door and covered the scanty coals with ashes so as not to extinguish them completely, the same way a man covers up the feelings of his soul—covers them with the ashes of life which are called indifference, so that they are not extinguished by the quotidian treatment of our fellowmen.

Basilio murmured his prayers and lay down near his mother, who was praying on her knees.

He was feeling hot and cold; he tried to close his eyes, thinking of his younger brother who that night had been expecting to sleep in his mother's bosom. Now he would be sleeping trembling with terror in his dark corner of the convent. His ears seemed to catch the echo of those screams as he heard them in the tower; but natural weariness began to confuse his thoughts and the spirit of dreams descended on his eyelids.

He saw a room in which two candles were burning. The priest with a reed cane in hand was somberly listening to the *sacristan* who was speaking in a strange language with horrible gestures. Crispin was trembling and turning his tear-filled eyes everywhere as if looking for help or support, or for a place to hide. The priest turns towards the child and, irritated, questions him, and the whip falls with a hissing sound. The boy runs, trying to hide behind the *sacristan*, but the latter catches hold of him, keeps him down and holds him out to the fury of the priest. The miserable boy fights back, kicks, screams and throws himself down on the floor; he rolls over, gets up, flees; he stumbles and falls, parries the blows with his bruised hands, screaming and covering his face. Basilio sees him twist around, hitting the floor head first, sees and hears the hissing of the whip! Desperate, his brother rises; mad with pain he throws himself against his executioners and bites the hand of the friar. The latter yells, lets the reed whip fall. The *sacristan mayor* seizes a cane, strikes the boy on the head and he falls, stunned. The priest, seeing his hand wounded, kicks the boy, who no longer resists, or screams. He rolls on the floor, an inert lifeless mass, leaving a wet trail.

Sisa's voice called Basilio back to reality.

"What ails you? Why do you cry?"

"I dreamt...God!" Basilio exclaimed raising himself up covered with sweat. "It was a dream. Tell me, Mother, that it was a dream, just a dream, nothing more!"

"What did you dream about?"

The boy did not answer. He sat down to dry his tears and his sweat. The hut was still in darkness.

"A dream! a dream," Basilio repeated in a low voice.

"Tell me what you dreamed; I cannot sleep!" said his mother as Basilio lowered himself to lie down.

"Well," said he in a low voice, "I dreamed that we went out to collect ears of corn...in a field with many flowers growing... the women's baskets were full of corn... The men also had baskets filled with corn...and the children too. I don't remember any more, Mother, I don't remember the rest!"

Sisa did not insist; she did not take dreams seriously.

"Mother, I have thought of a plan tonight," said Basilio after a brief silence.

"What kind of plan?" she asked.

Sisa, humble in everything, was humble too with her own children. She believed they were wiser than she was.

"I don't want to be a sacristan anymore."

"What then?"

"Listen, Mother, to what I have thought of. Today the son of the late Don Rafael arrived from Spain. He must be as good as his father was. Well then, tomorrow you get Crispin out, you collect my salary and you tell them I will no longer be a sacristan. As soon as I get well, I will go and see Don Crisostomo and I will plead with him to admit me as tender of his cattle—the cows and the carabaos. I am old enough. Crispin can study at the home of the old man Tasio, who's not given to beating and is good, even if the priest does not believe it. What do we have to fear from the priest, anyway? Can he make us poorer than we already are? Believe it, Mother, the old man is good. I saw him several times in church when there was no one else; he kneels and prays, believe it.

"So, mother, I will no longer be a sacristan. I earn little, and what I earn is turned into fines. All complain of the same things. I will be a cowhand and I will take good care of what is entrusted to me. I will make myself loved by the owner! Perhaps he will allow us to milk a cow so we can drink milk. Crispin likes milk very much. Who knows? He may gift us with a calf, a young female cow, if he sees I am behaving well. We will take good care of it and fatten it like our hen.

"I will gather fruits from the woods and sell them in town together with the vegetables from our garden patch, and thus we will have money. I will set up nooses and traps to catch birds and wild mountain cats; I will fish in the river and when I am older I will hunt. I can also cut wood to sell or to give to the owner of the cows and so we will make him happy. When I can plough, I will ask him to grant me a piece of land on which to plant sugar and corn, and you won't have to sew until midnight. We will have new clothes every *fiesta*; we will eat meat and big fish. In the meantime I shall live free; we will see each other all the days and eat together. And since the old man Tasio says Crispin is very intelligent, we will send him to Manila to study; I will support him by working. True, mother. And he will become a doctor. What do you say?"

"What can I say but yes," replied Sisa, embracing her son.

She noticed that Basilio had not taken his father into account in the future he planned, and she wept in silence.

Basilio went on talking about his projects with the confidence of his age, which sees only what it wishes to see. Sisa said yes to everything which to her seemed good. Sleep once more gradually descended on the boy's tired eyelids, and this time the Ole-Luköie described by Andersen opened its beautiful umbrella, full of happy pictures.

Basilio sees himself already a cowhand, with his little brother. They are gathering guavas, *alpay*[2] and other fruits in the woods. They flit from branch to branch lightly like butterflies; enter the grottos and see the shining walls. They bathe in the springs; the sands are like golden dust and the stones like the jewels in the Virgin's crown. The little fishes sing and laugh at them, the plants bow their branches loaded with coins and fruits. Then he sees a bell hanging from a tree, and a long rope for tolling it; to the rope is tied a cow with a nest of birds between its horns, and Crispin is inside the bell. And thus he dreamt.

But his mother, who was not of his age, and had not run for an hour, was awake.

- 18 -
Souls in Anguish

It must have been seven in the morning when Padre Salvi finished saying his last mass. The three were offered within the space of one hour.

"The Padre is sick," the devotees said; he does not move with his customary elegance and pace.

He divested himself of his vestments without a word, without looking at anyone, without the least comment.

"Watch out," whispered the *sacristanes* among themselves, "the inquiry progresses! Fines will rain down, and all on account of the two brothers!"

He left the sacristy to go to the parochial house, where in the vestibule, which was being utilized as a schoolroom, some seven or eight women were waiting for him, seated on benches. A man was pacing from one end of the room to the other. When they saw him coming, they stood up; a woman advanced to kiss the friar's hand, but the priest made a gesture of impatience, stopping her in her tracks.

"He must have lost one *real*, the miser!" the woman exclaimed with sarcastic laughter, offended by such a reception. Not giving his hand to kiss, to Sister Rufa, and she a monitor of the confraternity! That was unheard of.

"This morning he did not sit in the confessional!" added Sister Sipa, a toothless old hag. "I wanted to go to confession so I could receive communion and gain indulgences."

"Well, I pity you," said a young woman with plain features. "This week I gained three plenary indulgences and I offered them for the soul of my husband." "That was not well done, Sister Juana!" said the offended Rufa. "One plenary indulgence would have been enough to release him from purgatory. You should not waste the holy indulgences. Do as I do."

"I said to myself: the more, the better," replied the simple Sister Juana, smiling. "But tell me, what do you do?"

Sister Rufa did not answer immediately. First she asked for a *buyo*, chewed it, looked at her audience who were listening with attention, spat on one side and said, while chewing tobacco:

"I do not waste a single holy day! Ever since I joined the confraternity, I have gained 457 plenary indulgences, and 760,598 years of indulgences. I record all my gains because I like to keep my accounts clean. I don't want to deceive or be deceived."

Sister Rufa paused, and then continued chewing. The other women were looking at her in admiration, but the man who was pacing stopped and told her a bit disdainfully: "Well I, only this year, I have gained 4 plenary indulgences more than you, Sister Rufa, and 100 years more, and notwithstanding that I have not prayed much."

"More than I? More than 689 plenaries, 994,856 years?" repeated Sister Rufa with some disdain.

"That's it, 8 plenaries more and 115 years more in a few months," replied the man from whose neck dangled scapulars and greasy rosaries.

"It is not strange," said Rufa, surrendering. "You are the *maestro* and the head of the confraternity in the province!"

The man smiled, feeling flattered.

"It is not strange for me to earn more than you. In fact, I can almost say that even in my sleep I gain indulgences."

"And *maestro*, what do you do with them?" asked four or five voices at the same time.

"Pssh!" answered the other with a smirk of utmost disdain: "I scatter them around, here and there!"

"Well, in that case, I cannot praise you, *maestro!*" protested Rufa. "You will go to purgatory for wasting indulgences! You already know that for every word one utters in vain, he suffers 40 days of fire, according to the priest; for each palm length of thread, 60 days; for each drop of water, 20 days. You are going to purgatory!"

"I'll know how to get out of there!" answered Brother Pedro with sublime confidence. "I have taken so many souls out of the fire! I have made so many saints! And besides, in *articulo mortis* I can still gain, if I want to, at least seven plenaries and in dying I will be able to save others!"

And having said this he moved away proudly.

"However, you should do what I do: I don't lose a day and I keep my accounts in order. I don't want to cheat or be cheated!"

"What do you do then?" asked Juana.

"Well, you should imitate what I do. For example: I gain a year of indulgences. I jot it down in my notebook and I say: Blessed Padre, sir St. Dominic, please do me the favor of seeing if there is any one in Purgatory who might need exactly a year—not a day more, not a day less. I toss a coin. If it is heads, no; if it is tails, yes. Well, let us suppose that it is tails, then I write paid; if it turns out tails, then I keep my indulgence. In this way I make groupings of 100 years which I have listed. It is a pity that we cannot do with them as we do with money: give them out with interest. More souls would be saved. Believe me. Do as I do."

"Well, I do better than that!" replied sister Sipa.

"How much better?" asked Rufa in surprise. "That cannot be! What I do cannot be improved upon!"

"Listen for a moment and you will be convinced, sister," answered old Sipa in a disagreeable tone.

"Let us see! let us see! let's listen," said the others.

After a ceremonious cough, the old woman spoke:

"You know very well that praying 'Blessed-be-thy-Purity' and 'My Lord Jesus Christ, most sweet Father,' ten years are gained for each letter."

"Twenty—no, less—five," chorused the voices.

"One more, one less—it does not matter. Now when a man servant or a maid breaks a plate, a glass or cup, etc. I make him or her pick up all the fragments, and for each piece, even the tiniest, he has to recite 'Blessed be thy Purity' and 'My Lord Jesus Christ, most sweet Father,' and the indulgences gained I dedicate to the souls. At home all know this except the cats."

"But these indulgences are gained by the servants and not by you, sister Sipa," objected Rufa.

"And my cups and my plates, who will pay me for

them? The servants are content to pay for them this way and I too; I do not beat them, except for a conk or pinch here and there."

"I am going to follow that"—"I will do the same thing"—"And I!" exclaimed the women.

"But if the plate broke into only two or three pieces, you do not gain much," observed the obstinate Rufa.

"Aba!" answered old Sipa, "I make them pray all the same. I glue the pieces together and we don't lose anything."

Sister Rufa no longer knew what to object to.

"Allow me to ask you about a doubt I have in mind," timidly asked the young Juana. "You ladies, you understand so well these things of heaven, purgatory and hell. I confess my ignorance of these matters."

"Speak out!"

"I find many times in the novenas and in other books this recommendation: Three Our Fathers, three Hail Marys and three Glory be's."

"Well?"

"So I would like to know how to pray these: three Our Fathers one after the other, three Hail Marys one after the other, and three Glory be to the Fathers, or, an Our Father, a Hail Mary and Glory be to the Father three times?

"Well that's it, three times an Our Father..."

"I beg your pardon, sister Sipa!" interrupted Rufa. "They should be prayed in another manner: Don't mix the male with the female. The Our Father is male, the Hail Mary, female and the Glory be's are the children."

"Eh! begging your pardon, sister Rufa. Our Father, Hail Mary and Glory be are like rice, viands and sauce, a dish of the saints..."

"You are mistaken! You see, those of you who pray thus will never obtain what you are asking for!"

"And you, because you pray in this manner, do not obtain a single thing from your novenas!" countered old Sipa.

"Who doesn't?" said Rufa, standing up. "Lately I lost a little pig. I prayed to St. Anthony and I found it. And I sold it at a good price, aba!"

"Yes? That is why your neighbor was saying that you sold her pig!"

"Who? That shameless one! Do you by chance think I am like you?"

The *maestro* had to intervene to make peace; then no one remembered the Our Fathers; only pigs were discussed.

"Come on! come on! There must not be a quarrel for a little pig, sisters! Holy Scriptures give us an example: the heretics and Protestants have no quarrel with our Lord Jesus Christ who drove to the water a herd of swine which belonged to them; and we who are Christians, and members besides of the Confraternity of the Holy Rosary, shall we quarrel over a little pig? What will our rivals of the Confraternity of Tertiaries say of us?"

All were silent, admiring the profound wisdom of the *maestro;* and fearing what the Tertiary Confraternity would say. The former, satisfied with such obedience, changed the tone of the conversation and proceeded:

"Soon the parish priest will have us called. We will have to tell him of our choice of preacher among the three he proposed yesterday: Padre Damaso, or Padre Martin or the assistant priest. I do not know if the Tertiaries have already chosen. It is imperative that we decide."

"The assistant..." murmured Juana timidly.

"Hm! The assistant priest does not know how to preach," said Sipa. "Padre Martin is better."

"Padre Martin!" exclaimed another with disdain. "He

has no voice. Padre Damaso is better."

"Him, that's it," exclaimed Rufa. "Padre Damaso, yes, knows how to preach. He is like a comedian, that's it!"

"But we don't understand him!" Juana demurred.

"Because he is very profound! and as long as he preaches well..."

And while they were at this, Sisa arrived, a basket on her head; greeted them and climbed the stairs.

"That one is going up! Let us go up too!" they said.

Sisa felt her heart beating violently as she climbed the stairs. She did not know what to say to the priest to soften his anger or what reasons to give, to plead for her son. That morning, in the first hues of dawn, she had gone down to her garden patch to harvest her best vegetables, which she placed in a basket between banana leaves and flowers. She went to the river bank to look for *pako*[1] which she knew was the priest's favorite, when made into a salad. She put on her best clothes and with the basket carried on her head, without awaking her son, departed for the town.

She was trying her best to make the least noise while climbing the stairs slowly, listening watchfully, to see if by chance she might hear a well-known voice, fresh and childish.

But she neither heard nor saw anyone. She headed for the kitchen.

There she looked into every corner. The servants and the sacristan received her indifferently. She greeted them; they hardly returned the greeting.

"Where can I leave these vegetables?" she asked, making nothing of the obvious offense.

"There...! anywhere!" said the cook without even looking at her, absorbed in his work: he was plucking the feathers of a chicken.

Sisa laid on the table in an orderly manner on the

table the eggplants, the bitter melon, the *patolas*[2], the ferns and the tender *pako* leaves. And then she placed the flowers on top, half smiled and asked a servant who seemed more tractable than the cook:

"Can I talk to the Padre?"

"He is sick," he answered in a low voice.

"And Crispin? Do you know if he is in the sacristy?"

The servant regarded her with surprise.

"Crispin?" he asked, knitting his brows. "Is he not at your home? Are you saying he is not?"

"Basilio is at home, but Crispin remained here," answered Sisa. "I want to see him."

"Yes," said the servant, "he remained, but afterwards... afterwards he escaped, stealing many things. The priest ordered me early this morning to go to headquarters to inform the *Guardia Civil*. They must have already gone to your house in search of the boys."

Sisa covered her ears; she opened her mouth as if to speak, but no words escaped her lips.

"Indeed! With such sons as you have," added the cook. "It shows you are a faithful spouse: like father like sons. Careful with the younger one. He will be worse than his father." Sisa broke out in bitter sobs, dropping on a bench.

"Don't cry here!" the cook shouted at her. "Don't you know that the Padre is ill? Go and cry in the street!"

The poor woman, almost pushed forward, rushed down the stairs at the same time as the sisters were murmuring and making conjectures about the priest's illness.

The unfortunate mother buried her face in her handkerchief and suppressed her sobs.

Upon reaching the street she looked around her, vacillating. Then, as if she had finally made up her mind, she quickly departed.

- 19 -

The Travails
of a Schoolmaster

The common crowd is stupid; and since it pays for it,
It is proper to speak to it foolishly to please it.

Lope de Vega

The lake, surrounded by its mountains, sleeps peacefully with that hypocrisy of the elements, as if the night before it had not made common cause with the tempest. With the first reflections of light, which awaken the phosphorescent inhabitants of the waters, grayish silhouettes are etched far away, almost at the edge of the horizon. These are the fishing boats retrieving the nets; *cascos* and *paraos* with sails.

Two men, attired in mourning black, are contemplating the waters from a certain height. One of them is Ibarra, and the other is a youth of humble appearance and melancholic features.

"Here it is!" the latter is saying. "It is here that your

father's corpse was thrown. We were brought here by the gravedigger, Lieutenant Guevara and me."

Ibarra effusively grasped the young man's hand.

"You don't have to thank me," averred the latter, "I owed your father many favors, and the only thing I did was to accompany him on his way to the grave. I came here without knowing anyone, without any recommendation, without money, as I am today. My predecessor had left the school to sell tobacco. Your father protected me; secured a house for me and facilitated all that was necessary for the improvement of education. He would come to the school and distribute some coins to poor boys who were diligent in their studies. He provided them with books and paper. But this, like all good things, did not last long!"

Ibarra uncovered his head and seemed to pray for a long time. Then he turned to his companion and said: "You were saying that my father helped poor boys— and now?"

"Now they do what is possible and write when they can."

"And the cause?"

"The cause lies in their torn shirts and in the eyes that are full of shame."

Ibarra kept silent.

"How many pupils do you have now?" he asked with some interest.

"More than two hundred on the list, and in the classroom twenty-five."

"Why is this so?"

The schoolteacher smiled sadly to himself.

"To tell you the reasons is to relate a long and tiresome story," he said.

"Do not attribute my question to a vain curiosity," said Ibarra, looking gravely at the distant horizon. "I have reflected better and I believe that fulfilling the thoughts of my father is worth more than weeping for him, more than avenging him. His tomb is sacred Nature, and his enemies were the people and a priest. I forgive the former because of their ignorance, and I respect the latter because of his character and because I want religion, which educates society, to be respected. I want to be inspired in the spirit of the one who gave me my being. For this I would like to know the obstacles to education here."

"The country will bless your memory, Sir, if you bring to fulfillment your late father's beautiful projects," said the schoolteacher. "Do you want to know the obstacles to education? So then—in the circumstances we are in, without powerful assistance, learning can never be a reality: first, because in the children there is no stimulus or encouragement; and second, because even if there were, they are vanquished by the lack of means and by many preoccupations. They say that in Germany the son of a peasant studies eight years in the town schools. Who in this country would want to dedicate half of that time when the results are negligible? They read, write and commit to memory pieces or parts and sometimes a whole book in Spanish, without understanding a word of their contents. What benefit can the son of peasants obtain from the school?"

"And you, you who see the evil, why have you not thought of correcting it?"

"Ay!" replied the teacher sadly, moving his head, "one poor single teacher alone cannot fight against prejudices, against certain influences. The school would need, first and foremost, to have a place of its own, not as it is now, where I teach beside the parish priest's carriage under the convent house. There, the boys, who like to read aloud, naturally bother the Padre. At times he would come down upset, especially when he has one of those attacks; he shouts at them and insults me at times. You understand that in this way one cannot teach or learn; the child has no respect for the teacher, whom he saw ill-treated, and who did not attempt to insist on his rights. For the schoolmaster to be listened to, for him to have his authority uncontested, he needs prestige, a good name, moral strength, a certain freedom of action.

"Allow me to give you some sorry details. I wanted to introduce reforms—I was laughed at. In order to remedy that evil I was telling you about, I attempted to teach Spanish to the children because besides the government ordering it, I also considered it an advantage for everyone. I used the simplest method, teaching phrases and names without resorting to grand rules, expecting to teach them grammar after they had learned to understand the language. At the end of a few weeks the more alert could understand me, and were composing some phrases."

The schoolmaster paused and seemed to hesitate. Then, as if he had come to a decision, he continued:

"I ought not to be ashamed of the history of my grievances. Anybody in my place would have done the same. As I was saying, I began well; but several days later, Padre Damaso, who was then the parish priest, had me called by the *sacristan mayor*. Because I knew his character and feared to make him wait I went up immediately, greeted him and said 'good morning' in Spanish. In response to my greeting he extended his hand for me to kiss, then withdrew it and without answering my greeting, he broke out in a roar of laughter and made fun of me. I was disconcerted. In front of me was the *sacristan mayor*. At that moment I did not know what to say. I remained looking at him, but he went on laughing. I was getting impatient. I saw myself doing a reckless thing: to be a good Christian and at the same time a worthy being are not incompatible. I was going to ask him, when all of a sudden, passing from laughter to insult, he told me slyly: 'So it is a good morning, ha? Good morning! It is funny! So you already know how to speak Spanish?' And he continued laughing."

Ibarra could not refrain from smiling.

"You are laughing," replied the teacher, also laughing himself. "I confess that at that moment I did not feel like laughing. I was on my feet. I felt the blood rush to my head, and a flash of lightning darkened my brain. I saw the priest far away, very far away. I advanced towards him to answer him, not knowing what I was going to say. The *sacristan mayor* placed himself between us, the priest stood up and told me seriously in Tagalog: 'Don't use borrowed clothing with me. Be content to speak in your own language and don't spoil Spanish—it is not for the likes of you. Do you know the teacher Ciruela?[1] Well, Ciruela was a teacher who did not know how to read, and he put up a school.' I wanted to detain him, but he entered his room and closed the door violently.

"What was I to do, I, who can scarcely manage with what I get as salary? In order to collect it I need the good graces of the parish priest and have to make a trip to the capital of the province. What could I have done against him, the first moral authority—political and civil—in a town, supported by his order, feared by the government, rich, powerful, consulted, listened to, believed in and always catered to by all?

"If he insults me, I must keep silent; if I reply I am thrown out of my job, losing my career forever, and not by this will education be benefited. On the contrary, all would take the side of the priest; I would be execrated and be dubbed vain, proud, arrogant, a bad Christian, badly educated, even anti-Spanish and a subversive. A schoolteacher is not expected to be knowledgeable and zealous. What is required of him are resignation, humiliation, inertia and, God forgive me if I have reneged on my conscience and reason, but I was born in this country; I have to live, I have a mother, and I abandon myself to my fate like a corpse dragged by the waves."

"And on account of this obstacle you feel discouraged forever? And in this manner you have lived since?"

"Oh! to have taken warning from this!" he replied. My misfortunes would have been less! True, since then I have hated my profession; I thought of taking another job like my predecessor, because work, if taken up with disgust and with a vengeance, is a martyrdom, and because the school reminds me each day of my affront, making me spend very bitter hours. But what is to be done? I could not disappoint my mother. I had to tell her that her three years of sacrifice to give me this career make my happiness today. It is necessary to make her believe that the profession is most honorable, the work pleasant, the way is paved with flowers; that the fulfillment of my duties gives me only friends, that the town respects me and fills me with worthy regard. Otherwise, without ceasing to be unhappy, I would only make someone else miserable, which, besides being useless, is a sin. So I stayed in my job and did not want to lose my spirit; I decided to fight."

The schoolmaster paused briefly and continued: "Since that day when I was so grossly insulted, I examined myself and I saw myself actually an ignoramus. I made myself study Spanish day and night, and all that had to do with my profession. The old philosopher lent me some of his books; I read what I could lay my hands on, and I analyzed what I was reading. The new ideas I have acquired here and there changed my perspective. I saw many things under a light different from what I saw before. I saw errors where before I saw only truths, and truths in many things which seemed errors to me.

"For example, the whippings which from time immemorial have been a distinctive feature of schools, and which used to be considered the only efficacious means of making pupils learn—or so we have been accustomed to believe—seemed to me later a deterrent to the improvement of the child, and which rendered him considerably useless. I became convinced that it was impossible to reason, with the paddle or the punishment in view. Fear and terror upset the most serene pupil— besides, a child's imagination is more alive, more impressionable. Moreover, to fix an idea in the child's mind, it is necessary that peace reign, outside and inside, that there be a serenity of spirit, material and moral tranquility and gentle encouragement. I believe that before anything else the child should be inspired with confidence, security and esteem for himself. I understand, besides, that the daily spectacle of whippings destroys compassion in the heart and extinguishes that flame of dignity, the lever of the world, losing with it the feeling of shame which is difficult to restore. I have observed also that when one is whipped, one finds comfort in seeing others suffer, too, and smiles with satisfaction while listening to the other's sobs; and he who is assigned to give the whippings obeys on the first day with repugnance. Later he gets

said the Capitan of the police force.

"And I... and I... if an old man is needed..." another stammered and straightened himself in a display of pomposity.

"Accepted! Accepted!" shouted many voices.

The *Teniente Mayor* paled with emotion. His eyes filled with tears.

"He is weeping out of spite," thought the intransigent, and he shouted:

"Accepted, accepted without argument!"

And satisfied with his vengeance and the defeat of his adversary, the man started to praise the young man's project.

The latter proceeded.

"One-fifth of the funds raised can be used to obtain and distribute some prizes, for example to the best child in school, the best carabao herder, the best laborer, the best fisherman, etc. We could organize regattas or rowing contests on the river and on the lake, horse racing, raise greasy poles for a climbing contest and establish other games in which our peasants could take part. I will concede, for reasons of our own inveterate customs, a display of fireworks: wheels and rockets are very beautiful and amusing, but I don't believe that we will need the detonators proposed by the *Teniente Mayor*. To enliven our fiesta, two bands of musicians would be sufficient. Thus we will avoid quarrels and enmities which make veritable fighting cocks of the poor musicians who come to enliven our own celebration with their own contributions. They retire afterwards badly paid, badly fed, confused and sometimes wounded.

"With the remaining funds we can begin the construction of a small building to serve as a school, as we cannot expect God Himself to come down and build it for us. It is sad, indeed, that while we have a first-class cockpit our children learn little at the priest's stable. This is a light sketch of the project: to perfect it, that is everybody's job."

Happy murmurs were heard in the hall. Almost all gave assent to the young man's proposal; only a few murmured their opposition:

"Innovations! New things! In our youth..."

"Let us accept it for the time being; let us humble him," and they pointed at the *Teniente Mayor*.

When silence was finally restored, everybody was in agreement. The only requisite lacking was the *Gobernadorcillo's* decision.

The latter was agitated and troubled. He passed his hands over his forehead and finally was able to blurt out with downcast eyes:

"I also agree...but, ehem!" The whole tribunal listened in silence.

"But?" asked Capitan Basilio.

"I agree completely," repeated the *Gobernadorcillo:* "I mean I am not in agreement... I say yes, but..."

And he rubbed his eyes with the back of his hand. "But the priest," continued the hapless man—the parish priest wants something else."

"Does the priest pay for the feast or do we ourselves pay for it? Has he donated even a *cuarto?*" exclaimed a strident voice.

Everybody looked in the direction of the one asking these questions: it was Tasio, the philosopher.

The *Teniente Mayor* was immobilized, with eyes fixed on the *Gobernadorcillo*.

"And what does the priest want?" Capitan Basilio asked.

"Well, the parish priest wants six processions, three sermons, three high masses...and if there is money left, the

Tondo *komedya* and songs in between the acts."

"But we don't want that!" said the young ones and some old men.

"The parish priest wants it this way!" repeated the *Gobernadorcillo*. "And I promised him that his wishes would be fulfilled."

"Then why have you summoned us?"

"Precisely to inform you."

"And why didn't you say so in the beginning?"

"I wanted to tell you gentlemen, but Capitan Basilio spoke, and I did not have time...the priest must be obeyed!"

"He has to be obeyed," some of the old men repeated. "We have to obey, otherwise the *Alcalde* will put us all in prison!" added the other old men sadly.

"Well, obey and make the fiesta yourselves," exclaimed the young men standing up. "We are withdrawing our contributions."

"All has already been collected!" said the *Gobernadorcillo*. Don Filipo approached him and said bitterly:

"I sacrificed my pride in favor of a cause; you sacrificed your dignity as a man in favor of a bad cause and you pulled everything down."

Ibarra said to the schoolmaster:

"Do you want something from the capital of the province? Today I am leaving—immediately."

"Do you have business to attend to?"

"We have a business," Ibarra replied mysteriously.

On the way out the old philosopher Tasio said to Don Filipo, who was cursing his fate:

"The fault is ours! You did not protest when you were given a lackey for a leader; and I, woe is me! I had forgotten about it."

- 21 -

A Mother's Story

I wandered uncertain—I flew wandering,
A single moment—without rest...

(Alaejos.)

S isa fled towards her hut with that upheaval in the thoughts that churn within us when, in the midst of a misfortune, we see ourselves abandoned by all, and our hopes desert us. Everything seems hemmed in by the darkness surrounding, and if we see the least glimmer of light in the distance we run towards it, and proceed, oblivious that in the midst of our path an abyss might open.

The mother wanted to save her sons: but how? Mothers do not stop to ask by what means, when it concerns their own flesh and blood.

She rushed headlong, hounded by fears and sinister premonitions. Had they already captured her son Basilio?

Where had Crispin gone?

Approaching her dwelling she recognized the helmets of two soldiers over the fence of her orchard. What went on in that poor mother's heart was indescribable: her mind went blank. She was by no means unaware of the ruthlessness of these men who held no respect for persons—no, not even for the richest in the town. What would happen now to her and her sons accused of theft? The civil guards are not human beings: they are only civil guards, they are deaf to pleas and are accustomed to see tears.

Instinctively Sisa raised her eyes to heaven, and the heavens seemed to smile with unspeakable serenity; white clouds swam in the transparent blue. She stopped to control the trembling of her whole body.

The soldiers were leaving her place and they were alone. They had not caught anyone save the hen that Sisa had been fattening. She breathed in relief and gathered courage.

"How kind-hearted they are, and what good men!" she murmured almost crying with joy.

Had the soldiers burnt her hut but set her sons free, she would have blessed them all the same.

She again looked thankfully towards the sky—her native skies fluted by thin specks of clouds and a flock of herons in flight. Her confidence gradually restored, she continued on her way.

Upon approaching these men who were so feared, Sisa pretended not to be aware of them or of her fowl which was chirping for deliverance; she stared everywhere but at them. She had scarcely passed them by when she wanted to run, but prudence guided her steps.

She had not gone very far when she heard them

calling her in an imperious tone. She trembled, but proceeded on her way as if she had not heard them. They called her again, this time yelling at her with an insulting word. She turned pale and trembled, despite her efforts to remain calm. One of the guards was beckoning her with his hand.

Sisa, like a robot, came nearer, felt her tongue paralyzed with terror and her throat drying.

"Tell us the truth: otherwise we will tie you to that tree and shoot you!" one of them said with a threatening voice.

The woman turned her gaze towards the tree.

"Are you the mother of the thieves, you?" asked the other soldier.

"Mother of the thieves!" Sisa repeated mechanically.

"Where is the money that your sons gave you last night?'

"Ah, the money..."

"Don't you deny it, or it will be worse for you!" added the other one. "We have come to arrest your sons and the elder escaped; where did you hide the younger?"

When she heard this Sisa sighed with relief.

"Sir," she replied, "it has been many days since I have seen my son Crispin. I hoped to see him this morning in the convent, but only there was I told that..."

The soldiers exchanged meaningful glances.

"All right!" exclaimed one of them, "give us the money and we will leave you in peace."

"Sir," pleaded the unfortunate woman, "my sons do not steal even when they are hungry. We are accustomed to suffering hunger. Basilio has not brought me even a *cuarto*. Search all corners in my dwelling. If you can find a single coin, you may do with us as you please. We who are poor, we are not all thieves!"

"Well then," replied the soldier slowly, fixing his eyes on those of Sisa, "you will come with us. Your sons will have to show up and give up the money they have stolen. You follow us!"

"Me?... follow you?" murmured the woman, backing off and looking with fear at the soldiers in uniform.

"And why not?"

"Ah! have pity on me," she pleaded almost on her knees. "I am very poor; I do not have gold or jewelry to offer you. The only possession I have you have already taken, the hen that I intended to sell...take with you everything that you may find in my hut, but leave me here in peace, leave me here to die!"

"Come on! you have to come with us, and if you don't follow us willingly, we will tie you up."

Sisa broke out in bitter weeping. These men were inflexible.

"Let me at least follow you at some distance!" she pleaded when they brutally handled and pushed her forward.

The two soldiers, somewhat moved, conferred between themselves in a low voice.

"All right," said one of them, "since from here up to the entrance to town you might run away, you will walk between us two. Once we are there you may walk about twenty steps ahead, but beware! don't enter any shop; don't stop either. Let us proceed quickly!"

All her supplications were in vain, as were her reasons, and useless her promises. The soldiers said they were conceding too much, which might compromise them.

Seeing herself marching between the two, she felt she could die of shame. It is true no one was in sight, but what about the breeze and the light of the day? True modesty sees glances from all sides. She covered her face with her handkerchief and thus, going on blindly, she wept bitterly in humiliation. She was aware of her misery. She knew she had been abandoned by all including her own husband, but until now she had considered herself honorable and respected; until now she had regarded with compassion those women shockingly attired whom the town called the soldiers' concubines. Now it seemed to her that she had descended one level lower than these in the social scale.

The sound of horses' hooves was heard. These were those that carried fish for the interior towns: men and women forming little caravans mounted on rickety ponies with loaded baskets hanging from the animals' flanks. Some of these, passing by her hut, had asked for drinking water and gifted her with some fish. Now, in passing by her side, it seemed to her that she was being trampled under foot, run over, and that their glances, whether of compassion or of disdain, penetrated the handkerchief on her face, wounding her with sharp arrows.

At last the caravan proceeded on its way, leaving Sisa and the soldiers behind. Sisa sighed with relief. For a moment she removed the handkerchief from her face, to see if they were still far from the town. She saw some remaining telegraph poles before they reached the guardhouse. Never had this distance seemed so long.

Bamboo clumps of luxuriant foliage grew alongside the highway. In other times she would stop in their shade. Here she and her lover would rest; with a tender exchange of words he would relieve her of her basket of fruits and vegetables—ay! that was like a dream. The lover became husband; the husband was made into a *barangay* head and then misfortune started knocking at her door.

As the sun's heat was becoming intense, the soldiers asked her if she wanted to rest.

"No, thank you!" she replied with a shudder.

When they approached the town she was seized with terror; she looked in anguish around her: vast ricefields, a small irrigation canal, thin trees—there was not a precipice or a boulder in sight against which she could smash herself. She regretted having followed the soldiers all this way; she wished she were at the bottom of the deep river flowing past her dwelling—a river with elevated banks littered with sharp rocks was offering her sweet release from all her woes! But the thought of her sons, of Crispin, whose fate she did not yet know, enlightened her in that darkness and she was able to murmur resignedly:

"Later... after all this we will go and live in the depths of the forest!"

She dried her eyes, endeavored to keep calm and, addressing her guards, told them in a low voice:

"We are already in the town!"

Her tone could not be defined. It was a lament, reproach, complaint: it was a prayer, pain and grief condensed into sounds.

The soldiers, moved, responded with a gesture. Sisa advanced rapidly forward and managed to display an air of tranquility.

At that moment the church bells started ringing to announce that the first mass had ended. Sisa quickened her steps so as not to meet, if that was possible, the people coming out. But it was useless. There was no way of avoiding the encounter.

She greeted with a bitter smile two of her acquaintances whose glances were a question mark. From thence, to spare herself from further mortification, she lowered her head and fixed her eyes on the ground. She walked in a stumbling fashion on the stones of the path.

The people paused for a moment upon seeing her; they talked among themselves but followed her with their eyes. All this she saw and felt even if her eyes were constantly fixed on the ground.

She heard the impudent voice of a woman almost yelling behind her: "Where did you arrest her? And the money?"

It was a woman who was not wearing an overskirt or tapis around her; with an underskirt or saya of yellow and green, and a blouse of blue gauze. It was easy to identify her as a mistress of soldiers.

Sisa felt that she was being slapped in the face. That woman had undressed her naked before the crowd. She raised her eyes for a moment to have her fill of irony and contempt. She saw the crowd far, far away from her, but she felt the cold steel of their looks and their whispers. The poor woman walked without feeling the ground.

"Hey! over here!" one of the guards shouted at her. Like a broken-down mechanical doll she swiftly turned on her heels. Without a thought, and seeing nothing, she ran to hide herself.

Seeing a door with a guard standing by, she tried to force her way in, but another voice even more imperious kept her from her purpose. With uncertain steps she headed in the direction of that voice. She felt that she was being pushed in the back. She closed her eyes; took steps. Lacking the strength to move further she let herself fall on the floor, first on her knees, and then she seated herself on the floor. She was convulsed with bitter sobbing—a dry sobbing that was tearless and without words.

This was the barracks. Here there were soldiers, women, pigs and fowl. Some were mending their clothes while a mistress was lying down on a bench, pillowed on a man's thigh, smoking and looking at the ceiling in boredom. Other women helped the men to clean garments, or weapons etc., singing lewd songs in low voices.

"It seems that the chickens have escaped! You have not brought anything but the hen," a woman said to the newcomers. It was not known whether she was alluding to Sisa or to the hen which continued chirping.

"Yes, the hen is always more valuable than the chicks!" she replied to herself when the soldiers failed to answer her.

"Where is the sergeant?" one of the guards asked in a peevish tone. "Have they already reported to the *Alferez?*"

The shrugging of shoulders was the only reply to this query. No one bothered to ask about the fate of the hapless woman.

There Sisa passed two hours in a state of semi-imbecility, huddled in a corner, head hidden between her hands, hair disheveled and in disarray. At noontime the *Alferez* was informed. The first thing that he did was to give no credence to the priest's accusation.

"Bah! this case has to do with that stingy friar!" He ordered that the woman be released and that no one should bother himself further with the case.

"If he wants to retrieve what was lost, let him ask St. Anthony or complain to the Nuncio! Let him go along with that!"

Consequently, Sisa was summarily thrown out from headquarters, almost forced out because she was too stunned to move.

When she found herself in the middle of the street,

she mechanically walked swiftly in the direction of her hut, head uncovered, hair dishevelled and eyes fixed on the distant horizon. The sun was at its zenith, not a cloud to veil its heat and light. The breeze scarcely moved the leaves of trees; the day was almost dry; not a bird dared leave the shelter of its branches.

Sisa finally reached her hut. She entered mute and silent, surveying everything with a look. She went out and started to walk around in all directions. Then she ran to the house of old Tasio and knocked at the door, but the old man was not in. The unhappy woman returned to her hut and started to call, shouting: Basilio! Crispin! stopping every now and then to listen with attention. Her voice echoed, repeating her call. The gentle murmurs of the neighboring river, the rustle of the bamboo leaves were the only sounds in that solitude. She called again, climbed a bank, went down the ravines, descended to the river. Her eyes wandered with a sinister expression. They would brighten up now and then with a strange light; then they would darken like the skies during a stormy night. One can almost say that the light of reason was ebbing close to extinction.

She returned home, climbed into her hut and sat down on the pallet where they had slept the night before. She raised her eyes and saw a torn shred from Basilio's shirt hanging in one corner from a bamboo cane of the partition which was close to the precipice. She stood up, picked up the piece and examined it in the sunlight. The shred was stained with blood. But perhaps Sisa did not see it, for she went down from her hut and continued to examine it beneath the burning light of the noonday sun, raising it aloft. She felt a darkening of light around her. The light seemed to her not enough, so she gazed directly at the sun with wide open eyes.

She continued to wander around, screaming or howling strange sounds. Whoever heard her would take fright. Her voice had a strange quality unlike the sound produced by human vocal chords. If, on a stormy night with the wind blowing furiously as if beating with invisible wings against a host of shadows that haunt you; if you found yourself in a solitary ruin, listening to sad laments, moans and sighs, and if you heard sighs and plaints that you supposed were the impact of the wind lashing against the tall towers or dilapidated walls, but which filled you with terror and made you tremble despite yourself: well, the accents of that mother's plaints were more mournful than those unknown sounds on dark nights when the storm unleashes its fury.

Thus did night find her. Perhaps heaven would allow her some hours of sleep, in which some kindly angel wing would blot out from her features and memory the ravages of suffering. Perhaps such sufferings would be beyond frail human measure, and Mother Providence might intervene with a tender touch of forgetfulness. Be that as it may, the result was that the following day Sisa wandered aimlessly, smiling, singing or talking, communing with all of nature's creation.

- 22 -
Lights and Shadow

Three days had passed since the events that we have narrated. Those three days and nights the town of San Diego devoted to making preparations for the fiesta and commenting on and prattling about it at the same time.

While they were relishing the thought of the coming festivities, some spoke ill of the *Gobernadorcillo*, others of the *Teniente Mayor*, others of the youth; and there was no lack of those who would blame everybody for everything.

They noted the arrival of Maria Clara, accompanied by Tía Isabel. They were delighted by this because they liked her, and even as they admired her beauty, they also wondered at the changes suffered by the character of Padre Salvi. "He is much distracted during the Holy Sacrifice; he does not talk much with us, and looks to our eyes thinner and more taciturn," said his penitents. The cook saw him lose weight by the minute, and complained that little honor was bestowed on his dishes. But what exacerbated the public gossip even more was the fact of having seen in the convent more than two lights during the night while Padre Salvi was on a visit to a particular house, the house of Maria Clara! The pious women crossed themselves, but continued gossiping.

Juan Crisostomo Ibarra had sent a telegram from the provincial capital greeting Tía Isabel and her niece, but not explaining the cause of his absence. Many believed he had been imprisoned for his conduct with Padre Salvi in the afternoon of All Saints Day. But the chatter reached a climax when on the afternoon of the third day they saw him get down from a coach in front of the house of his betrothed and courteously salute the religious who was also going there.

About Sisa or her sons nobody was concerned.

If we go now to the house of Maria Clara, a beautiful nest among orange trees and *ilang-ilang*, we will come upon these two young people leaning on a window sill overlooking the lake. They are shaded by flowers and vines clambering on wires and bamboos, and exhuding a faint perfume.

Their lips are whispering words, softer than the murmur of the leaves and more fragrant than the air permeated with aromas which wander from the garden. It is the hour when the sirens of the lake, taking advantage of the shadows of the rapidly descending dusk, show their happy heads on top of the waves to admire and salute the dying sun with their songs. They say that their eyes and locks are blue, that they are crowned with the white and red flowers of aquatic plants; they say that, now and then, when the white waves reveal their sculptured forms, whiter than the foam itself, and when the night has completely descended, they begin their divine frolic, and let us hear melodies as mysterious as those of harps produced by the wind. They also say...but let us return to our young couple and listen to the tailend of their conversation. Ibarra is saying to Maria Clara:

"Tomorrow before dawnbreak your wish will be complied with. Tonight I will arrange for everything so that nothing will be missing."

"Then I will write my friends, so that they will come. Do something so that the priest does not come along."

"And why not?

"Because he seems to be watching me. His deep and somber eyes disturb me; when they fix on me, I am afraid. When he talks to me, he has a voice... he speaks to me of unusual things, very incomprehensible, very strange... Once he asked me if I had not dreamed of my mother's letters; I believe he is half mad. My friend Sinang, and Andeng, my sister by a wet nurse, say that he is somewhat touched in the head because he does not eat or bathe, and stays in the dark. Do what you can so he does not come along."

"We can do no less than invite him," answered Ibarra thoughtfully. "The customs of the country require it; he is in your house, and besides he has treated me with civility. When the *Alcalde* consulted him about the business that I had spoken to you about, he had nothing but praises for me and did not attempt to put up even the smallest obstacle. But I see that you are distressed. Do not worry, he will not be able to accompany us in the same boat."

They heard light steps; it was the priest, who came nearer, a forced smile on his lips.

"The wind is cold," he said, "when one catches a cold, it does not leave until the warmth comes. Are you not afraid of freezing?" His voice was trembling and his gaze was directed at the faraway horizon. He did not look at the young couple.

"On the contrary the night appears to us pleasant, and the wind delicious," answered Ibarra. "In these months we have our autumn and our spring; some leaves fall but the flowers always bloom." Padre Salvi sighed.

"I find beautiful the marriage of these two seasons where the winter cold does not intrude," continued Ibarra. "February brings forth the buds on the branches of the fruit trees and in March we will have the ripened fruits. When the hot months come we will go to another part of the country."

Padre Salvi smiled. They began to speak of trivial things, of the times, of the town, of the fiesta. Maria Clara looked for a pretext and moved away.

"And since we are talking of fiestas, permit me to invite you to the one we celebrate tomorrow. It is a countryside fiesta given mutually by our friends and ourselves."

"And where will it be held?"

"The young ones want it in the stream which runs in the nearby forest, near the *balete*; that is why we will rise early so that the sun does catch up with us."

The religious reflected, and after a moment replied:

"The invitation is very tempting, and I accept, to prove that I hold no rancor. But I will have to go much later, after I have complied with my duties. Happy are you who are free, totally free."

Minutes afterwards, Ibarra bade farewell, to take care of the preparations for the following day. Night had already descended.

On the street, he was approached by one who greeted

him respectfully.

"Who are you?" Ibarra asked him.

"You do not know my name, sir," answered the stranger. "I have been waiting for you for two days."

"And why?"

"Because nobody has had pity on me. Because they say I am a thief, sir. But I have lost my children, my wife has gone mad, and everybody says I deserve my fate."

Ibarra quickly sized up the man and asked:

"What do you want now?"

"To implore your compassion for my wife and children."

"I cannot be detained," replied Ibarra. "If you wish, come with me; you can tell me what happened while we walk."

The man thanked him and they quickly disappeared into the shadows of the poorly lighted streets.

- 23 -
The Fishing Excursion

The stars were still shining in the blue vaults of heaven; the birds were still perched on the branches when a merry group was already traversing the town streets, headed for the lake, illuminated by the clear light of the peat torches commonly called *huepes*.

Five lively maidens, hands linked, or with arms around each other's waists, were on their way to the lake with rapid strides, followed by some old women and a host of maids carrying supplies and utensils in baskets jauntily perched upon their heads. At the sight of those smiling faces which reflected the gaiety and the aspirations of care-free youth, their dark abundant tresses and the wide folds of their attire tossed by the breeze, we could easily have mistaken them for the deities of the night in flight from the ensuing day, had we not known that they were Maria Clara with her four friends: jovial Sinang, her cousin; the formal and sedate Victoria; the beauteous Iday and pensive Neneng, the timid and unassuming beauty.

They were talking in high spirits, laughing gaily, pinching each other, whispering among themselves and then exploding into bursts of laughter.

"Hush! you will awaken all the people who are still asleep!" admonished Tía Isabel. "We didn't make so much noise when we were young."

"You did not get up from bed as early as we have, and neither were the old men such sleepyheads," replied little Sinang.

They kept silent for a moment and tried to lower their voices, but soon they forgot; they laughed loudly, filling the air with their joyful youthful accents.

"Pretend that you are offended; don't speak to him!" said Sinang to Maria Clara. "Scold him so that he doesn't get spoiled!"

"Don't be too demanding," said Iday.

"Be demanding, don't be a fool! A fiancé should obey while he is still a fiancé; later, as a husband, he will do as he pleases," counselled Sinang.

"What do you understand about these things, little girl?" reprimanded her cousin Victoria.

"Hush! here they come!"

As a matter of fact, a group of young men carrying big bamboo torches was approaching. They were marching in a somewhat somber mood to the sound of a guitar.

"Sounds like a beggar's guitar," said Sinang, laughing.

When the two groups met it was the women who assumed a formal attitude and a serious demeanor, as if they had never learned to laugh. Only the men were talking, greeting and smiling at them, asking them questions and obtaining half replies.

"Are the waters calm? Do you think we will have fine

weather?" the mothers were asking.

"Don't be alarmed, ladies; I know how to swim well," replied a tall thin young man.

"We ought to have heard mass first," sighed Tía Isabel, clasping her hands.

"There is still time, Señora; Albino who was once a seminarian, can say mass in the banca," replied another, pointing to the tall thin youth.

The latter, who appeared rather crafty, upon hearing himself alluded to, assumed a somber demeanor, slyly aping Padre Salvi.

Ibarra, without dropping his sober mien, shared the merriment of his companions.

When they reached the beach, joyful exclamations of wonder involuntarily escaped from the lips of the women. They saw two large boats joined together, picturesquely adorned with wreaths of flowers and leaves, with embossed cloths of various colors; small paper lanterns hung on the improvised covering, alternating between roses and carnations, fruits like pineapple, kasuy, bananas, guavas, lanzones etc.

Ibarra had brought along his carpets, rugs, tapestries and cushions, and formed them into makeshift comfortable seats for the ladies. Even the guide poles and the oars were also decorated. In the best adorned boat there were a harp, guitars, accordions and a carabao horn. In the other boat a clay stove was burning, brewing tea, coffee and *salabat* or ginger brew for breakfast.

"The women over here! over there, the men!" ordered the mothers upon embarking. "Be still. Don't move so much or we might capsize!"

"Make the sign of the cross first," said Tía Isabel, crossing herself.

"And are we being left here alone, just by ourselves?" Sinang asked, making a face. "Just us? *aray!*"

The *aray* was provoked by the mother pinching her daughter.

The boats were slowly rowed farther away from the shore, the light of the lanterns reflecting on the mirror-like surface of the lake. The first hues of dawn tinged with color the eastern horizon.

Silence reigned: the youth, in the segregation ordained by the mothers, seemed dedicated to meditation.

"Be careful!" Albino, the ex-seminarian, cried out to another youth. "Step firmly on the plug which is under your foot!"

"Why?"

"The water may get in: this boat has many holes!"

"Ay! we are sinking!" screamed the frightened women.

"Don't be alarmed, ladies," the seminarian assured them. "This banca is secure; it does not have more than five holes, not very large ones."

"Five holes! Jesus! Do you want us to drown?" exclaimed the terrified women.

"No more than five, ladies, and only this big," assured the seminarian, forming a small circle with his index finger and thumb. "Step firmly on the plugs to keep them in place."

"My God! Holy Mary! The water is coming in!" screamed an old woman who felt she was getting wet.

There was a slight commotion; some were screaming, others thought of jumping into the water.

"Keep the plugs in place, there!" continued Albino pointing to the place where the maidens were.

"Where? Where? Oh Lord! We don't know where! For pity's sake, come over!" begged the terrified women.

It was necessary for the five young men to transfer to the other boat to calm the frightened mothers. What a coincidence! It seemed that there was danger beside each of the five girls, while the five older women together did not have a single hole to worry about. And even more of a coincidence! Ibarra found himself seated beside Maria Clara; Albino, near Victoria and so forth. Tranquility was restored in the circle of the concerned mothers, but not in that of the young people.

Because the waters were completely calm, the fish pens not far away, and it was still very early, it was decided that the oars be laid down, and that all should have breakfast. The lanterns were put out; dawn already illumined all of space.

"Nothing can compare with *salabat*, taken in the morning before hearing mass!" commented Capitana Tica, Sinang's mother. "Have *salabat* and rice cakes, Albino, and you will have more appetite to pray."

"It is what I do," replied the latter. "I intend to go to confession."

"No!" Sinang was saying, "take coffee first—it will give you happy thoughts."

"Yes, right now, because I am feeling somewhat depressed."

"Don't do that!" warned Tía Isabel. "Take tea with *galletas*; they say that tea soothes one's thoughts."

"I will also take tea with cookies!" answered the accommodating seminarian. Fortunately, not one of these drinks is Catholicism.

"But, can you...?" asked Victoria.

"Take chocolate too? Of course. As long as breakfast is not delayed too much..."

The morning was lovely: the waters were beginning

to sparkle, and with the light direct from heaven and that reflected by the waters, there came about a special clarity, brilliant and fresh, which illuminated the objects around almost without a hint of shadows, saturated with the colors we visualize in some seascapes.

Almost everybody was overjoyed; they breathed in the light breeze that was beginning to waken. Even the mothers, however full of warnings and suggestions, were laughing and teasing each other.

"Do you remember?" one said to Capitana Tica, "do you remember when we bathed in the river, when we were still unmarried? We would slide down with the current in our little boats made of banana trunks, with fruits of different varieties between sweet-smelling flowers. Each one carried a small banner with our names on them..."

"And when we returned home," added another, without allowing the first speaker to finish her story, "we found the bamboo bridges destroyed and so we had to wade the streams... the rogues!"

"Yes," agreed Capitana Tica. "But I preferred to wet the borders of my skirt rather than show my feet. I knew that behind the clumps of reeds on the bank there were eyes spying on us."

The younger women who heard these revelations smiled and winked. The rest were engrossed in their own conversations and paid no attention.

Only one man, who served as helmsman, remained silent and indifferent to all that gaiety. He was a man of athletic build, with arresting features because of the haunting sadness of his eyes and the severe outlines of his lips. The unkempt black hair hung carelessly on his strong neck. He wore a shirt of dark coarse cloth, suggesting within its creases powerful muscles that moved his bare sinewy arms to handle like a feather the wide and enormous oar serving as rudder to the two boats.

Maria Clara had more than once surprised him observing her. He would instantly shift his gaze somewhere else—far away towards a mountain or to the bank. The young woman sympathized with his solitude and, taking some biscuits, she offered them to him. The helmsman regarded her with some surprise, but this look lasted for only a second; he took a biscuit and thanked her briefly in a hardly audible voice.

And no one thought of him again. The gay laughter and the witty sallies of the young men did not ease up a single facial muscle. He did not smile at the pert Sinang receiving a pinch for her quick remarks, causing her to knit her brows for a moment and then to bounce back again to her merriment.

After breakfast they continued their excursion towards the fish pens.

There were two of these situated not far from each other. Both belonged to Capitan Tiago. From afar they could see some herons perched atop the bamboo stakes of the fish enclosure, while some white birds called *kalaway*[1] by the Tagalogs, were flying in different directions, filling the air with their strident squawks, their wings grazing the surface of the lakes.

Maria Clara's gaze followed the herons, which took flight in the direction of the nearby mountain as the boats approached.

"Do these birds build nests on the mountain?" she asked the helmsman, more to get him to talk than to be informed.

"Probably, Señora," he replied, "but no one till now has seen their nests."

"These birds do not have nests?"

"I suppose they must have; otherwise they would be very unfortunate."

Maria Clara failed to note the tone of sadness with which the helmsman uttered these words.

"And therefore?"

"They say, Señora," answered the young man, "that the nests of those birds are invisible, and that they have the faculty of making invisible those who have possession of them and, like the soul that can be seen only in the glossy mirror of the eyes, it is only in the mirror of the waters that these nests may be seen."

Maria Clara became pensive.

In the meantime they had arrived at the *baklad*.[2] The old boatman tied the boats to a bamboo stake.

"Wait!" Tía Isabel told the son of the old boatman who was about to come up with his *panalok*, a bamboo rod with a net pocket. "We must have the *sinigang* ready so that the live fish can pass from the water to the broth."

"Good Tía Isabel!" exclaimed the seminarian, "she does not want the fish to be out of the water for more than a moment."

Andeng, Maria Clara's foster sister, had the reputation of being an excellent cook despite her clean and joyous mien. She prepared the rice water for stewing the fish, adding to it tomatoes and *kamias*, helped—or hindered—in this by some vying for her favor. The girls cleaned the squash vine tendrils, the snow peas, and cut the *paayap* into short pieces the length of cigarettes.[3]

Beauteous Iday took up the harp to while away the time and calm the impatience of the guests who wanted to see how the fish would come out of the trap alive and twisting. Iday not only played the harp well; she also had beautiful fingers.

The young people clapped their hands; Maria Clara gave Iday a kiss. The harp was a favorite instrument in that province and was highly appropriate for the occasion.

"Victoria, sing the Marriage Song," the mothers requested.

The men clamored and Victoria, who had a lovely voice, complained that she was hoarse. The Marriage Song is a beautiful Tagalog elegy in which are painted all the miseries and sadness of married life without missing any of its blessings and joys.

They therefore asked Maria Clara to sing.

"All my songs are sad," she protested.

"It doesn't matter," they all said.

It did not require more coaxing for her to accede. She picked up the harp, strummed a prelude and sang in a vibrant voice, harmonious and full of feeling:

> *Sweet are the hours in one's own land*
> *Where all is loved under the sun,*
> *Life is the breeze in her fields sweeping,*
> *Death is welcome, and love more caring!*
>
> *Do you have a country, do you?*
> *Because I weep so,*
> *Do not ask about my country*
> *Not of me!*
>
> *Warm kisses on the lips play,*
> *from a mother's breast awaking,*
> *The arms search, round her neck to cling,*
> *And the eyes smile as they gaze.*
>
> *Do you have a mother, do you?*
> *Because I weep so,*

Do not ask about my mother
Not of me!

Sweet is death for one's own land,
Where all is loved under the sun;
Dead is the breeze for him who has not
A country, a mother and a love![4]

The voice died away, the song stopped, the harp was silent and still they continued to listen. No one applauded. The eyes of the maidens filled with tears. Ibarra seemed bothered and the young pilot gazed impassively at the distance.

All of a sudden a thunderous noise was heard. The women screamed and covered their ears. It was the ex-seminarian Albino who blew with all the power in his lungs on the carabao horn, the *tambuli*. Laughter and liveliness returned; the tear-filled eyes brightened into merriment.

"But, are you trying to split our eardrums, you heretic?" Tía Isabel yelled at him.

"Madam!" the former seminarian solemnly declared, "I have heard of a poor trumpeteer out on the banks of the Rhine, who, by playing the trumpet, married a rich noble damsel."

"That is true! the Trumpeteer of Sackingen!" added Ibarra who could not refrain from taking part in the lively conversation.

"Did you hear that?" continued Albino. "Well, I just want to find out if I would have the same luck!"

And he started to blow the horn again with more gusto than before, bringing it close to the ears of the young women who had been saddened. Naturally, there was a slight commotion. The mothers made him refrain from blowing again, pummelling him with their slippers or pinching him.

"Aray! aray!" he exclaimed feeling his arms. "Such distance between the Philippines and the Rhine river! *oh tempora! oh mores!* Some get concessions, others, contusions!"

Everybody was laughing now, even the sedate Victoria. But Sinang, she of the merry eyes, was whispering to Maria Clara: "You lucky girl! If I only could sing like you!"

Andeng finally announced that the *sinigang* was done and ready for the fish.

The young son of the fisherman climbed over the end or pocket of the fishtrap, to which the narrowing stake fences led. Here might have been inscribed Dante's *Lasciate ogni speranza voi ch' entrate*—Abandon all hope ye who enter here"—if the unfortunate fish had known how to read Italian and understand it. Fish that entered the trap did not emerge except to die. The trap was a space almost circular in shape, approximately one meter in diameter, so contrived that a man could stand on top and scoop the fish out with the small net.

"There I certainly would not be bored fishing with a rod!" said Sinang, highly pleased.

Everyone was attentive. Some already imagined the fish wriggling and struggling in the net, their scales glistening. When the young man dipped the net in, however, no fish jumped out.

"It should be full," said Albino in a low voice. "It has not been visited for more than five days."

The fisherman withdrew the rod...ay! not a single fish adorned the net. The drops of water that fell, reflecting the light of the morning sun, seemed to mock them with their silvery laughter. An *ah* of admiration, of disappointment, of annoyance escaped from everybody's lips.

The young man repeated the same operation with the same results.

"You don't know your business," Albino told him. He climbed up to the enclosure and snatched the net from the young man's hands. "Now you'll see! Andeng, open the kettle!"

But Albino did not know his business either. The net stayed empty. Everybody laughed at him.

"Don't make so much noise, for the fish can hear you and won't allow you to catch them. The net must be torn!" But the net had all its meshes intact.

"Allow me," said Leon, Iday's sweetheart.

He made sure that the stakes were firm, examined the net and, satisfied with what he saw, he asked:

"Are you sure the trap has not been visited since five days ago?"

"Very sure! The last time it was, was for the vigil of All Saints' Day."

"Well then, the lake is either enchanted or I will catch something."

Leon dipped the net into the water, but surprise registered on his face. Silently he gazed at the neighboring mountain and continued exploring the water with the rod, then, without withdrawing it, he murmured in a low voice:

"A crocodile!"

"A crocodile!" they repeated.

The word leaped from mouth to mouth amidst dismay and general stupefaction.

"What are you saying?" they asked him.

"I say there is a crocodile caught," affirmed Leon and, pushing the handle of rod into the water, continued:

"Do you hear that sound? That is not the sand; it is the tough hide, the crocodile's back. Do you see how the fence stakes shake? It struggles but it is all coiled up. Wait...it is big, its body measures almost a yard or more in girth."

"What is to be done now?" was the question.

"Catch it, of course," said a voice.

"Jesus!, and who will catch it?"

No one volunteered to go down into the water. It was very deep.

"We should tie him to our boat and drag him in triumph!" said Sinang. "It ate up the fish that we should be eating!"

Maria Clara murmured, "I have never seen a live crocodile!"

The helmsman stood up; he took a long rope and climbed nimbly to the platform. Leon made way for him.

With the exception of Maria Clara, nobody had noticed him until then. Now they were admiring his splendid physique.

To everyone's great surprise and despite their warning shouts the helmsman jumped into the enclosure.

"Here, take this knife with you," shouted Crisostomo drawing a wide Toledo blade.

But the water had already risen in a fountain of spray and the depths closed on him mysteriously.

"Jesus, Mary and Joseph!" exclaimed the women. "A misfortune will befall us! Jesus, Mary and Joseph!"

"Don't alarm yourselves on his account, ladies," said the old boatman. "If there is anyone in this province who can do it, it is he."

"What is his name?" they asked.

"We call him the helmsman. He is the best that I have

seen—yet he has no love for the work."

The water moved, was agitated. It seemed that a deadly battle was being waged in the deep; the trap shuddered. All were silent, holding their breath. Ibarra tightened his convulsive grip on the handle of the sharp knife.

The struggle seemed to have ended. The young man's head surfaced on the water and was greeted with glad shouts; the women's eyes filled with tears.

The helmsman clambered up, carrying in his hand the end of a rope and, once aboard, pulled on it.

The monster appeared, it had the rope tied around its neck and under its forelegs. It was large, of the size Leon had described; patterned, and on its back grew green moss, which is to the crocodile what gray hair is to man. It was bellowing like a bull, thrashing the bamboo fence with its tail, holding on to the stakes and opening its fierce black jaws, showing its long teeth.

The helmsman was pulling it up to the platform all by himself. No one thought of assisting him. Now out of the water and situated on the platform, he squatted on top of the crocodile and with his strong hands snapped closed its jaws and tried to fasten them together with heavy knots. The reptile made a last effort to release itself: it arched its body, slashed the platform with its powerful tail and escaped, leaping into the lake outside the fence and dragging its captor behind it. The helmsman is a dead man! Everybody screamed in horror.

Quick as a lightning flash another body plunged into the water. They hardly had time to recognize that it was Ibarra. Maria Clara did not faint, because Filipina women do not yet know how to faint.

They saw the waves take on the color of blood. The

young fisherman also plunged into the water, bolo in hand. His father followed suit. They were barely out of sight, however, when the spectators saw Ibarra and the helmsman appear on the surface holding on to the carcass of the reptile. It had its white belly ripped, and the knife stuck in its throat.

It is impossible to describe the rejoicing. A thousand arms were extended to pull them out of the water. The old women went wild with joy—they laughed, they prayed. Andeng forgot that her *sinigang* broth had been boiling three times over; all the liquid had spilled out and put out the fire. The only one who was speechless was Maria Clara.

Ibarra was unhurt; the helmsman had a slight scratch on his arm.

"I owe you my life," he said to Ibarra, who was wrapping himself in woollen shawls and rugs. There was a note of regret in the helmsman's voice.

"You are too daring," Ibarra replied. "Next time do not tempt God."

"Had you not returned..." murmured Maria Clara, still pale and trembling.

"Had I not returned and you had followed me," the young man answered, completing her thought, "then at the bottom of the lake I would have been with my family."

Ibarra had not forgotten that there rested the remains of his father.

The older women no longer wanted to visit the other *baklad*. They wanted to leave, alleging that the day had begun badly and that many misfortunes might still occur.

"All because we did not go to mass!" sighed one of them.

"But señoras, what misfortune has befallen us?" asked

Ibarra. "The crocodile was the only unfortunate one!"

"Which goes to prove," concluded the ex-seminarian, "that in all its miserable life this accursed reptile had never heard mass. I never saw it among the numerous crocodiles which frequented the church."

The boats then headed for the other fishtrap. It was necessary for Andeng to prepare another *sinigang* broth.

Day was advancing; the breeze was fluttering; the waves had awakened and were rippling around the dead crocodile, raising, in the language of the poet P.A. Paterno, "mountains of foam, of flowing brilliance, rich in the colors of the sun."

Again music sounded: Iday played the harp; the men the accordions and guitars more or less in tune, but the best was Albino playing his guitar really out of tune and off the beat in each instant; most of the time forgetting the tune and passing into an entirely different melody.

They visited the other fishtrap without much confidence. Many expected to find the crocodile's mate, but Nature plays tricks, and the net always came up full of fish.

Tía Isabel was in command: "The *ayungin* is good for *sinigang*; leave the *biâ* for the *escabeche*, the *dalag* and the *buan-buan* for *pesâ*; the *dalag* lives long. Put them in the net so that they remain in the water. The lobsters to the frying pan! The *banak* is good for broiling wrapped in banana leaves and stuffed with tomatoes.[5] Leave the rest to serve as decoys: it is not good to empty the trap completely," she added.

They decided to disembark on the shore near that forest of ancient trees belonging to Ibarra. There in the shade and close to the crystal clear stream they would have lunch among the flowers or under improvised shelters.

Music filled the air; the smoke from the earthen stoves rose eddying into gay and tenuous whirlwinds; the water sang inside the kettles, perchance words of comfort for the poor fish, maybe with sarcasm and irony; the body of the crocodile slowly revolved in the water, sometimes exposing its white shattered belly, sometimes its colored moss-covered back—and man, Nature's favorite, had no qualms about committing what the Brahmins and the vegetarians describe as so many fratricides.

- 24 -
In the Woods

E arly, very early in the morning, Padre Salvi had said his mass and cleansed within a few minutes a dozen dirty souls. This was not an habitual practice for him.

It seemed that after reading some letters, which had arrived carefully sealed with wax, the worthy curate lost his appetite, leaving his chocolate to cool completely.

"The Padre is getting sick," said the cook while preparing another cup. "It has been days since he has eaten. Of the six dishes that I place on the table he scarcely touches two."

"It is because he does not sleep well," replied the servant: he has had nightmares since he changed his room. His eyes are more sunken than ever; he is getting thinner and thinner from day to day and his color has become sallow."

As a matter of fact, it evoked compassion to see Padre

Salvi. He neither touched his second cup of chocolate nor tasted the pastries from Cebu: he traversed the spacious living room in a pensive mood, crumpling within his bony palms some letters he read from time to time. Finally he asked for his carriage, fixed himself up and asked to be taken to the forest of the fateful *balete* tree which is the camping ground of excursionists.

Upon reaching the edge of the forest he dismissed his vehicle and entered the woods alone. A gloomy pathway winds torturously through the thicket, leading to a stream formed by various hot springs like many along the slopes of Mount Makiling. Its banks are decked with wild flowers, many of which have not yet been given their Latin names, but which undoubtedly are known to the golden insects of the woods, to the butterflies of every size and hue, blue and yellow, black and white, multi-colored, glittering, showing off the rubies and emeralds of their wings; and to the thousands of beetles of metallic sheen powdered with fine gold. Only the humming of these insects, the chirping of the crickets filling the air day and night, the song of the birds or the brittle snap of a rotten branch falling through the underbrush, break the silence of that mysterious, eerie place.

He wandered for some time among the thick creepers, trying to avoid the thorns which caught at his cotton habit as if to detain him; the roots protruding from the ground every so often tripped one unaccustomed to walking. All of a sudden he stopped in his tracks. Gay laughter and fresh young voices reached his hearing; the voices and laughter came from the direction of the stream, and were coming closer each time.

"I will see if I can locate a nest!" a lovely sweet voice which the priest recognized, was saying. "I wish to see him without his seeing me. I wish to follow him everywhere he goes."

Padre Salvi hid himself behind a thick trunk and prepared to eavesdrop.

"You mean you want to do to him what the priest is doing to you: watch you everywhere you go?" said a gay voice.

"Take care, jealousy makes one thin and gives sunken eyes!"

"No, it is not jealousy—it is curiosity!" replied the silvery voice, while the joyful one repeated: "Yes, jealousy! jealousy!" and then burst into laughter.

"If I were jealous, instead of making myself invisible, I would make him invisible so that no one could see him."

"But you wouldn't be able to see him either, and that's not good! The best we can do is to find the nest and give it to the priest, then he can watch us all he wants without our needing to see him...! How does that appeal to you?"

"I don't believe in this story of herons' nests," answered another voice, "but should I ever feel jealous I would know how to watch and make myself invisible."

"And how? how? Would you be a Sister Eavesdropper?"

Gay laughter ensued upon remembrance of convent schooldays.

Padre Salvi, from where he was hiding, saw Maria Clara, Victoria and Sinang, crossing the stream. The three were wading with their sights focused on the mirror-like surface of the water, searching for the mysterious heron's nest. Their legs were wet up to the knees, the wide folds of their bathing skirts outlining the gracious curves of their thighs. Their hair hung loose and their arms were bare. They wore striped gay-colored blouses. They continued in their quest for the fabled nests, at the same time picking flowers and herbs that grew along the bank.

Pale and motionless, the religious Actaeon[1] watched this chaste Diana: his sunken eyes glistening at the sight of her beautifully molded white arms, the graceful neck ending in a suggestion of bosom. The diminutive rosy feet playing in the water aroused strange sensations and feelings in his impoverished, starved being and made him dream of new visions in his fevered mind.

Those sweet figures disappeared at the bend of the curve behind a clump of reeds and took beyond earshot their cruel allusions. Like one drunk, unsteady and covered with sweat, Padre Salvi left his hiding place, gazing around him with a dazed look. He halted motionless, uncertain, took a few steps as if to follow the girls, but turned and, moving along the bank, tried searching for the other members of the party.

Not far from him he saw in midstream a sort of bathing pavilion fenced by stakes, its roof covered thickly with palm leaves, from whence issued peals of laughter and female voices. It was also decked with palm leaves, flowers and pennants. Beyond he saw a bamboo bridge and farther away from it men bathing in the stream while a host of servants—male and female—were milling around improvised clay stoves; or busy dressing fowl, washing rice, roasting a pig and so forth.

On the opposite bank, in a clearing that had been made, groups of men and women were gathered under the shelter of canvas awnings hung from the branches of aged trees surrounded by stakes recently planted. There were the *Alferez*, the assistant parish priest, the *Gobernadorcillo*, the *Teniente Mayor*, the schoolmaster and many past and present *barangay* captains, even Don Basilio,

Sinang's father and the adversary of the late Don Rafael in
an old lawsuit. Young Ibarra had told him: "We are
discussing issues—to discuss does not necessarily mean
to be enemies." And the famous spokesman of the
conservatives enthusiastically accepted the invitation by
sending three turkeys and placing his servants at the young
man's disposal.

The priest was welcomed with due respect and
deference by all, including the *Alferez*.

"But where did Your Reverence come from?" asked
the *Alferez* upon seeing the priest's face filled with scratches
and his habit covered with leaves and pieces of dry twigs.
"Did Your Reverence suffer a fall?"

"No! I lost my way!" answered the priest, lowering
his eyes to examine his habit.

Bottles of lemonade were uncorked; young green
coconuts were split open for those coming from the bath
to drink their fresh water and to partake of their tender
flesh, whiter than milk. Moreover, the young women were
each given wreaths of *sampaguita* flowers interwoven with
rosebuds and *ilang-ilang* blossoms to perfume their loose
tresses. The guests sat or settled down on hammocks
suspended from the branches of trees; or else entertained
themselves around a great stone slab on which were
assembled some playing cards, chessboards and pieces,
pamphlets, pebbles and cowries for native games.

They showed the priest the crocodile carcass, but he
seemed distraught, and he paid attention only when he
heard that the wound on the reptile's throat was inflicted
by Ibarra. Besides it was not possible for anyone to meet
the celebrated and unknown helmsman: he had
disappeared before the *Alferez*'s arrival.

At last, Maria Clara emerged from the bath

accompanied by her friends, fresh as a rose opening its petals with the first dew, covered with sparks of fire from the early morning sun. Her first smile was for Crisostomo, and the first cloud on her brow for Padre Salvi. The latter noticed this but gave no sign.

It was time for lunch. The priest, the assistant and the *Alferez*, the *Gobernadorcillo* and some more *capitanes* with the *Teniente Mayor* sat themselves at a table over which Ibarra presided. The mothers would not allow any male guest to sit at table with the young ladies.

"This time, Albino, you are not inventing holes as in the boats," said Leon to the ex-seminarian.

"What? what is that?" asked the older women.

"The boats, ladies, were as whole and sound as this plate," elucidated Leon.

"Jesus, you rascal!" exclaimed Tía Isabel smiling.

"Have you already heard, Señor *Alferez*, of the criminal who mistreated Padre Damaso?" Padre Salvi asked the former during the meal.

"Which criminal, Padre *Cura?*" countered the *Alferez* looking at Padre Salvi across the glass of wine he was imbibing.

"Who else can he be but the one who ambushed and manhandled Padre Damaso on the way!"

"Manhandled Padre Damaso?" asked a chorus of voices. The assistant priest seemed to smile.

"Yes, and Padre Damaso is now confined to bed. It is believed that he is the same Elías who threw you down into a mudhole, Señor *Alferez!*"

The *Alferez* blushed with shame or from the wine.

"Well, I thought," continued Padre Salvi, with a certain sarcasm, "that you knew about the incident—you being a commander of the Civil Guards!"

The soldier bit his lips, mouthing a poor excuse.

At this very moment there appeared on the scene a pale thin woman miserably attired. No one saw her come so silently and so unobtrusively, making the least possible noise—at night they would have mistaken her for a phantom!

"Give that poor woman something to eat!" the older women said. "*Oy*, come here!"

But she proceeded on her way and approached the table where the priest sat. The latter turned, recognized her and suddenly dropped the knife from his hand.

"Give this woman food!" ordered Ibarra.

"The night is dark and boys disappear," muttered the beggar.

But at the sight of the *Alferez*, who addressed her, the woman took fright and started to run, disappearing among the trees.

"Who is she?" Ibarra asked.

"An unfortunate woman driven out of her mind by terror and pain," replied Don Filipo. "She has been thus since four days ago!"

"Is she, by chance, a certain Sisa?" queried Ibarra, manifesting interest.

"Your soldiers arrested her and made her a prisoner," continued the *Teniente Mayor* with some bitterness. "They led her across the whole town for I don't know what matters regarding her sons that...no one has been able to explain."

"What?" asked the *Alferez* turning to the priest. "Isn't she the mother of your two bell-ringers?"

The priest nodded.

"Who have disappeared without anybody knowing their whereabouts?" Don Filipo added very severely, fixing his gaze on the *Gobernadorcillo*, who lowered his eyes.

"Look for that woman," Crisostomo commanded his servants. "I have promised to try to ascertain the whereabouts of her sons..."

"You said that they have disappeared?" asked the *Alferez*. "Your altar boys have disappeared, Padre *Cura?*"

The latter gulped down the glass of wine before him and nodded his head in assent.

"*Carambas*, Padre *Cura!*" exclaimed the *Alferez* with ironical laughter, happy with the thought of taking revenge on the priest, "some pesos disappear from Your Reverence's coffers, and my sergeant is awakened very early to make him search for the money; two altar boys of your household disappear and Your Reverence is silent; and you, Señor Capitan...it is true too that you..."

And he did not finish the sentence but broke into laughter, plunging his spoon into the reddish pulp of a wild papaya fruit.

The priest, confused and losing his head, replied:

"But I am responsible for the money..."

"A good enough reply, Your Reverence, from a shepherd of souls!" interrupted the *Alferez*. "A good answer from a holy man!"

Ibarra wanted to intervene, but Padre Salvi, making an effort to control himself, replied with a strained smile:

"And do you know, Señor *Alferez*, what is being said of the disappearance of those boys? No? Then ask your soldiers!"

"What?" exclaimed that official, losing his gaiety.

"It is said that during the night of their disappearance several shots were heard."

"Several shots?" repeated the *Alferez*, looking at those present. The guests moved their heads affirmatively.

Padre Salvi slowly answered with cruel irony:

"Come on! I see that you do not catch criminals nor do you know what is happening in your own household and yet you want to preach and teach others their duty. You must be familiar with the old adage: The fool knows more about his own household..."

"Gentlemen," interrupted Crisostomo, seeing the *Alferez* turning pale. "In relation to this I would like to know what you think of a project that I wish to propose. I intend to entrust that mad woman to the treatment of a good physician and in the meantime, with your advice and your help, to look for her sons."

The return of the servants who were not able to catch up with the mad woman was able to pacify the two enemies, leading the conversation to another matter.

The luncheon ended, and while tea and coffee were being served, old and young divided into various groups. Some took to the chessboards; others played cards, but the young girls, curious about knowing the future, preferred to ask questions of the wheel of fortune.

"Come, Señor Ibarra!" shouted Capitan Basilio, who was somewhat happy. "We have a lawsuit fifteen years old, and there is no judge in the *Audiencia* to render a verdict; shall we see if we can put an end to it at the chessboard?"

"Instantly and with pleasure!" answered the young man. "Just a moment, for the *Alferez* wishes to leave."

When it was known that they would play chess, all the older men gathered around the chessboard. The game was interesting and attracted even the profane. The older women, however, surrounded the priest to discourse with him on spiritual matters, but Padre Salvi deemed neither the occasion nor the place fitting for that kind of conversation. His answers were vague and his eyes sad; and, somewhat annoyed, wandered aimlessly everywhere except at his interlocutors.

The game started with much seriousness.

"It is to be understood, of course, that if the game ends in a draw we will ask for the case to be dismissed."

In the middle of the game, Ibarra received a telegram which made him turn pale and his eyes glisten. He put it intact into his pocket, not without directing his gaze at the group of young people who were laughing, shouting and interrogating Destiny.

"Check the king!" said the young man.

Don Basilio had no alternative but to hide his king behind his queen.

"Check the queen!" rejoined Ibarra, threatening her with a rook which was protected by a pawn.

Capitan Basilio could no longer protect or withdraw his queen because the king was behind her. He asked for time to reflect.

"With great pleasure!" answered Ibarra. "I have something to say right now to some in that group."

And he rose, giving his opponent fifteen minutes. Iday was holding the cardboard disc on which were written the forty-eight questions, while Albino held the answers.

"It is false, it is not true, it is a lie," screamed Sinang almost sobbing.

"What ails you?" asked Maria Clara.

"Just imagine!... I ask when shall I acquire wisdom, I throw the dice, and that—that sleepless priest reads from the book, "When the frogs grow hair! How do you like that?"

And Sinang makes a face at the ex-seminarian, who continues to laugh.

"Who told you to make that query?" asked her cousin Victoria. "Such questions deserve such answers."

"Ask," they told Ibarra, holding out the wheel to him. "We have decided that whoever gets the best answers will receive a gift from the others. All of us have already asked."

"And who got the best answer?"

"Maria Clara! Maria Clara!" repeated Sinang. "We made her ask, whether you like it or not, 'Is his love faithful and constant?' and the book answered..."

But Maria Clara, blushing profusely, covered Sinang's mouth with her hand and would not allow her to say more.

"Then give me the wheel," said Crisostomo, smiling. "I ask: 'Will my present project prosper?'"

"What an ugly question!" exclaimed Sinang.

Ibarra threw the dice and they looked for the corresponding answer according to the number.

"Dreams are but dreams," read Albino. Ibarra drew a piece of paper out of his wallet and opened it with hands shaking.

"This time your little book is lying!" he exclaimed happily. "Read!"

"School project approved, decree in your favor!"

"What does that mean?" they asked him.

"Did you not say that whoever gets the best answer will earn a gift from each one of you?" he asked in a voice trembling with emotion while he carefully divided the telegram in two parts.

"Yes! yes!" they cried.

"Well then, this is my gift," giving half of the paper to Maria Clara. "I will establish a school in the town for boys and girls; this school will be my gift!"

"And that other half? What is that supposed to mean?"

"This I will give to the one who gets the worst answer!"

"Well then it is to me!" cried Sinang.

Ibarra gave her the other half and rapidly moved away.

"And what does this mean?"

But the happy Ibarra had already left to resume his game of chess with Don Basilio.

Padre Salvi, looking distraught, approached the young people's group.

Maria Clara was drying her eyes from a tear or two of joy.

All the laughter and gaiety ceased, and everyone was silent.

The priest was looking at the young people, unable to utter a single word. They expected him to address them, so they kept silent.

"What is this?" he picked up the book and sort of leafed through it.

"The wheel of fortune, a book of games," explained Leon.

"Don't you know that it is a sin to believe in these things?" and he angrily tore up the pages.

Cries of surprise and indignation escaped from all the young folk.

"It is an even greater sin to dispose of what does not belong to you without the owner's will and consent," Albino answered him, rising. "Padre *Cura*, that is called stealing, and God and men forbid it."

Maria Clara joined her hands and with tears in her eyes regarded the remnants of the book which moments ago had made her so happy. Contrary to what they expected of him, Padre Salvi did not answer Albino. He saw the torn pages being blown and scattered by the wind throughout the woods and over the waters; and he moved away, stumbling on his way, far from the young people, with two hands clasped over his head. He stopped for a few seconds to speak to Ibarra who accompanied him to one of the carriages assigned to the guests.

"He does well to leave, that kill-joy of a monk!" muttered Sinang. "He has a face that seems to say: 'Don't laugh for I know all your sins!'

After the gift he had made to his fiancee, Ibarra was so happy that he started to play recklessly without due reflection. He did not stop to examine the positions of his pieces. As a result, although Don Basilio was on the defensive all the time, the game ended in a draw thanks to the mistake that the young man made.

"Case dismissed! Case dismissed!" Don Basilio cried gaily.

"Dismissed!" repeated the young man, "whatever decision the judges may render."

Both effusively shook each other's hand.

While the guests were celebrating this event, which ended a long-standing feud, the sudden arrival of four civil guards and a sergeant all armed with fixed bayonets, disturbed the happiness of the excursionists and caused fear among the women.

"Quiet, everyone!" shouted the sergeant. "A shot for anyone who moves!" Despite this brutal onslaught, Ibarra stood up and approached him.

"What is it you wish?" he asked.

"That a criminal by the name of Elías be delivered to us this very moment," he answered threateningly.

"A criminal? The helmsman? You must be mistaken!" retorted Ibarra.

"No, Señor! This Elías has been recently accused of

manhandling a priest..."

"Ah! and is that the helmsman?"

"The same, according to our information. You admit into your festivities people of ill-repute, Señor Ibarra."

The latter looked at him from head to foot and answered him with supreme contempt:

"I don't have to give you an account of my actions! Everybody is welcome to our celebration, and you yourself would have been given a place at our table like your commander who till lately was with us."

Having spoken thus he turned his back on the sergeant who was biting his moustache. Aware that his case lay on the weak side, he ordered his men to search among the trees for the helmsman, whose identity was described on a piece of paper.

Don Filipo warned the sergeant: "Note well that this description would pertain to nine-tenths of the natives; do not make a false move!"

Finally the soldiers returned, saying that they had seen neither man nor boat, nor a single man who might be a suspect. The sergeant muttered some words and marched out the way he had come—in Guardia Civil fashion.

Gaiety was gradually restored. There was an avalanche of questions and comments.

"So this is the Elías who flung the *Alferez* into a mudhole!" Leon said thoughtfully.

"And how did that happen, how?" asked some curious ones.

"They say that last September, on a rainy day, the *Alferez* met a man loaded with firewood. The street was like a puddle. There was by the bank only a narrow passage sufficient for one person to pass. They say that the *Alferez*, instead of stopping his mount, spurred it on, shouting at the man with the firewood to withdraw or back out in order to give him way. But the man was not disposed to backtrack the distance he had negotiated because of the heavy load on his shoulders; or he did not want to sink into the puddle, so he forged ahead. The *Alferez*, annoyed, wanted to run over him, but the man picked up a piece of firewood, hit the horse on the head with it, and with such force that the animal fell down and deposited his burden, the rider, into the mudhole. They also say that the man continued his way unperturbed by the five successive shots fired from the *Alferez*'s revolver. The commander was blind with fury and with mud. Since the man was a total stranger to the military he supposed that he was the famous Elías, a recent newcomer of five months ago to the province. Nobody knew where he had come from, and he had made himself known to the Guardia Civil by feats of this sort.

"So he is a bandit?" asked Victoria with a shudder.

"I don't think so, because they say he fought the bandits once on the day that they were sacking a house."

"He does not have the look of a criminal," added Sinang.

"No! except that his eyes are very sad. I didn't see him smile throughout the morning," said Maria Clara thoughtfully.

Thus the afternoon wore on, and soon it was time to return to the town.

They left the woods as the last rays of the dying sun disappeared in the horizon. They passed in silence by the mysterious grave of Ibarra's ancestor. Soon the gay conversation resumed its liveliness, full of warmth, underneath those branches so unaccustomed to hearing many voices. The trees seemed sad, the creepers were swaying as if to say: "Farewell to youth! Farewell to a day's dream!" And now by the light of the huge reddish bamboo torches and to the sound of guitar music let us leave them on their way back to town. The group grew smaller, the lights went out, the singing ceased, the guitars muted as they came nearer the dwellings of man. Put on the mask now that you are among your brethren!

- 25 -
Elias and Salomé

If the honorable civil guards, after disturbing the fiesta, had directed themselves to a place that we know before the sun set that same afternoon, they would have without doubt encountered the one whom they were looking for.

It is a small but picturesque hut built along the shores of the lake on an elevation which spares it from the rise of the waters, among luxuriant bamboo groves, betelnut and coconut trees. Little red flowers like *kamantigi* and *maravilla* grow at the foot of the thick rustic wall made out of cut rocks and not appearing that it was really some sort of stairway which led to the lake. The upper part is made out of nipa palm leaves and cut wood held down by strips of bamboo and adorned with leaves blessed on Palm Sunday, as well as with artificial flowers of *tinsim*, which come from China. An *ilang-ilang* tree pushes through the open window an intrusive branch and saturates the air with aroma. On the apex of the roof cocks and hens roost from time to time, while the rest keep the company of ducks, turkeys and pigeons to finish off the last grains of rice and corn scattered on some kind of patio.

On a *batalan* or bamboo porch, taking advantage of the light of day, a young girl of some seventeen years is sewing a shirt of brilliant colors and transparent weave. Her clothes are ragged but clean and decent. Her blouse, like her skirt and *tapis* are covered with patches and stitches. All her adornment, all her jewelry, consist of a plain turtleshell comb to keep her simply dressed hair in place, and a rosary of black beads hanging from her neck over her blouse.

She is graceful because she is young, has beautiful eyes, a small nose, a diminutive mouth; because there is harmony in her features, and a sweet expression animates them; but hers is not a beauty which instantly arrests attention at sight. She is like one of those little flowers in the field without color or fragrance, on which we step unwittingly, and whose beauty manifests itself to us only when we examine them with care—unknown flowers, flowers of elusive perfume.

Now and then she would look towards the lake whose waters are somewhat disturbed, suspend her work and listen carefully, but not discovering anything, return anew to her sewing with a slight sigh.

Her face lights up at the sound of footsteps; she lets go of her sewing, stands up, smooths the creases on her skirts and waits, smiling, by the small stairway of bamboo.

The pigeons fly, the ducks and chickens squawk and cackle as the taciturn-looking helmsman appears, carrying firewood and a bunch of bananas which he deposits silently on the floor, while he turns over to the young girl a mudfish still stirring and wiggling its tail.

She examines the young man with a worried look, then places the fish in a basin filled with water, and returns to pick up her sewing, seating herself beside the helmsman who has remained silent.

"I thought you would come from the lake, Elías," she says, opening the conversation.

"No, I could not, Salomé," answers Elías in a low voice. "The launch came and scoured the lake. On board is one who knows me."

"God, My God," murmurs the young woman, looking anxiously at Elías.

A lengthy pause follows. The helmsman silently contemplates the swaying bamboos moving from one side to another, rustling their lance-shaped leaves.

"Did you enjoy yourself much?" asks Salomé.

"Enjoy! they, they enjoyed themselves," replies the young man.

"Tell me how you passed the day; hearing it from your lips will please me much, as though I had been with all of you."

"Well...they went...they fished...they sang...and they enjoyed themselves," he answers, distracted.

Salomé, not being able to contain herself any longer, questions him with a look and tells him:

"Elías, you are sad!"

"Sad?"

"I know you well!" exclaims the young woman. "Your life is sad...are you afraid they might discover you?"

Something like the shadow of a smile crosses the young man's lips.

"Is there anything you lack?"

"I do not have your friendship, perhaps? Are we not

poor, one like the other?" replíes Elias.

"Then why are you like this?"

"You have told me many times, Salomé, that I do not say much."

Salomé lowers her head and continues sewing, then in a voice which attempts to appear indifferent, asks once more:

"Were there many of you?"

"There were many of them!"

"Many women?"

"Many."

"Who were the...young women...the beautiful ones?"

"I do not know all of them...one was the betrothed of the rich young man who arrived from Europe," answers Elías in an almost imperceptible voice.

"Ah, the daughter of the rich Capitan Tiago! They say she has become very beautiful?"

"Oh, yes! very beautiful and very kind-hearted," the young man answers, drowning a sigh.

Salomé looks at him for a moment and then bows her head.

If Elías had not been looking at the clouds which at sunset often take capricious shapes, he would have surely seen that Salomé was crying and that two teardrops fell from her eyes on what she was sewing. This time it is he who breaks the silence, standing up and saying:

"Farewell, Salomé, the sun is gone, and as you think it is not good that the neighbors can say that the night has caught me here...but you have been crying!" changing his tone and frowning. "Do not deny it with your smile, you have been crying."

"Well, yes!" she answers smiling, as her eyes fill anew with tears. "It is because I, too, am very sad."

"And why are you sad, my good friend?"

"Because soon I will have to leave this home where I was born and where I have grown up," answers Salomé, wiping away her tears.

"And why?"

"Because it is not good that I live alone. I will go and live with my relatives in Mindoro...soon I will be able to pay the debts my mother left me when she died: the town fiesta comes, and my chickens and turkeys are well-fattened. To leave a home where one has been born and raised is much more than to leave half of one's own self...the flowers, the gardens, my doves! A storm comes, a flood, and everything goes down to the lake!"

Elias becomes thoughtful, and then, taking her by the hand and fixing his eyes on her, asks:

"Have you heard anybody speak ill of you? No? Did I ever molest you once? Neither? Therefore you have become tired of my friendship and want to avoid me."

"No, do not speak that way! If only I would get tired of your friendship!" she interrupts. "Jesus, Mary! I live the day and the night thinking of the hour in the afternoon in which you would come. When I did not know you, when my poor mother lived, the morning and the evening were for me the best that God had created: the morning because I would see the sun rising, reflecting itself on the waters of the lake in whose dark depths rests my father; because I would see my fresh flowers, their leaves which had wilted the day before grown green again; my doves and chickens would greet me happily as if offering me good mornings. I loved the morning because after fixing the hut, I would go in my little boat to sell food to the fishermen who would give me fish or who would allow me to take what was left in the folds of their nets. I loved the evening which provided me with the sleep of the day, which would allow me to dream in silence under these bamboo trees to the music of their leaves, making me forget reality—and because the night would bring back my mother, whom the *pangingi*[1] separated from my side during the day.

"But since I met you, the mornings and the evenings have lost their enchantment, and only the afternoon is beautiful to me. I sometimes think that the morning was created to prepare oneself to enjoy the delights of the afternoon, and the evening to dream and relish the memories and awakened feelings. If only it were my choice to forever live the life I bear... God knows I am happy with my lot; I do not desire more than health to work; I don't envy the rich girls their wealth but..."

"But?"

"Nothing, I do not envy them anything while I have your friendship."

"Salomé," the young man says with sharp regret, "you know my cruel past and you know my misfortune is not of my own making. If it were not for that fate which at times makes me think with bitterness about the love of my parents, if it were not because I do not want my children to suffer that which my sister and I suffered and what I still suffer, months ago you would have been my spouse in the eyes of God, and today we should be living deep in the forest and far away from men. But for this same love, for this future family, I have sworn to extinguish in me the misfortune that from father to son we have come to inherit, and it is necessary that this has to be, because neither you nor I would like to hear our children cursing our love from which only miseries can be their legacy. You do well to go to your relatives' home. Forget me, forget a foolish and useless love. Perhaps there you may find someone who is not like me."

"Elías!" exclaims the maiden with reproach.

"You have understood me wrongly; I speak to you as I would speak to my sister if she were alive; in my words, there is not a single complaint against you, nor hidden thoughts. Why should I hurt you with a reproach? Believe me, go to the home of your relatives; forget me. That, with your forgetfulness, I may be less unfortunate. Here, you have nobody but me, and the day that I fall into the hands of those who persecute me, you will be left alone and solitary for the rest of your life, if it is discovered that you were a friend of Elias's. Take advantage of your youth and your beauty to look for a good husband whom you deserve. No, no, you still do not know what it is to live alone, alone in the midst of humanity."

"I was counting on your accompanying me..."

"Ay!" replies Elías, shaking his head, "impossible, and today more than ever. I have not yet found that which I came to look for here. Impossible. This day I have lost my freedom."

And Elias recounts in a few words what transpired that morning.

"I did not ask him to save my life; I am not grateful for what he did, but for the feeling that inspired him, and I should pay that debt. For the rest of it, in Mindoro as anywhere else, the past will always be there and will inevitably be discovered."

"Well then," Salomé says to him, looking at him lovingly, "at the very least, when I have left, live here, live in this home. It will make you remember me and I will not think, in those faraway places, that my little house has been carried away by the hurricane or the waves. When my thoughts go back to these shores, the memory of you and that of my home will present themselves together. Sleep here where I have slept and dreamed...it would be as if I myself were living with you, as if I were at your side."

"Oh!" exclaims Elías, twisting his arms with despair, "woman, you are going to make me forget..." His eyes burn, but only for a moment.

And pulling himself away from the arms of the young woman, he flees, losing himself in the shadows of the trees.

Salomé follows him with her eyes, remaining still and listening to the sound of the footsteps gradually fading away.

- 26 -

In the Philosopher's Home

In the morning of the following day, Juan Crisostomo Ibarra, after making the rounds of his estate, rode to old man Tasio's home.

There was perfect calm in Tasio's garden; the swallows, hovering over the eaves, scarcely made noise. Moss covered its ancient walls where a variety of creeper had fastened itself, framing the windows of the house, which was like a mansion of silence.

Ibarra carefully tied his horse to a post and, walking almost on tiptoe, crossed the clean and scrupulously kept garden, went up the stairs and, since the door was open, entered.

The first thing that greeted his eyes was the sight of the old man huddled over a book on which he seemed to be writing. Hanging on the walls were collections of insects and leaves, among maps and old shelves full of books and manuscripts.

The old man was so absorbed in what he was doing that he did not notice the newcomer's presence, but when the latter was about to withdraw and refrain from disturbing him...

"Why! You have been here all this time?" he asked Ibarra, somewhat surprised.

"Begging your pardon, Señor," the young man replied. "I see that you are very busy."

"As a matter of fact I was writing a few lines, but there is no hurry, and I want to rest. Can I be of service to you in any way?"

"In many!" answered Ibarra, approaching him. "But..." and he cast a glance at the book lying on the table.

"What! Are you occupied in deciphering hieroglyphics?" asked the young man, surprised.

"No!" retorted the old man, offering Ibarra a chair. "I don't know Egyptian, nor even the Coptic language, but I understand something of the system of writing and I write in hieroglyphics."

"You write in hieroglyphics! And why?" the young man asked, doubting what he was seeing and hearing.

"So that they won't be able to read me now." Ibarra was regarding Tasio with attention, debating whether the old man was mad. He examined the book rapidly to see if the old man did not lie, and saw well-drawn animals, circles and semi-circles, flowers, feet, hands, arms and so forth.

"And why then do you write if you don't want to be read?"

"Because I do not write for this generation. I write for other ages. If the present one were able to read me, they would burn my books, the work of a lifetime; on the other hand, the generation that can decipher these characters would be an educated generation; they would understand me and would say: 'Not all slept during the night of our ancestors.' The mystery, or these curious characters, will save my work from the ignorance of men, as the mystery and the strange rites have saved many truths from the destructive priestly class."

"And in what language are you writing?" asked Ibarra after a brief pause.

"In our own, in Tagalog."

"And the hieroglyphic signs, are they useful?"

"But for the difficulty of drawing which requires time and patience, I can almost assure you that they are more useful than the Latin alphabet. Ancient Egyptian had our vowels; our *o* which alone is final and which is unlike the Spanish *o*, but an intermediate vowel between *o* and *u*. Like ours, the Egyptian did not have the true sound of *e*; in their language are found our *ha* and our *kha* which we don't have in the Latin alphabet exactly as we use it in Spanish. For example in this word *mukha*," he illustrated, pointing to the book, "I transcribe the syllable *ha* more adequately with this figure of a fish than with the latin *h*, which in Europe is pronounced in different ways. For a less strong pronunciation of *h*, in the word *hain*, for example, I use this bust of the lion or these three flowers of the lotus according to the quantity of the vowel. Even more, I have the nasal sound which does not exist in the Hispanized Latin alphabet. I repeat: but for the difficulty in drawing which has to be done perfectly, we can almost adopt hieroglyphics; but this same difficulty obliges me to be concise, and not say more than what is correct and necessary. This kind of work, besides, keeps me company, when my guests from China and Japan leave."

"How is that?"

"Don't you hear them? My guests are the swallows. This year one is missing; some bad Chinese or Japanese youngster must have caught it."

"How do you know they come from those countries?"

"Simple: some years ago, before they left I tied to their feet pieces of paper on which was written the name of the Philippines in English, supposing that they could not go very far, and because English is spoken in almost all these regions. For many years there was no answer to my piece of paper until lately, when I wrote it in Chinese. The following November they returned with other pieces of paper attached to their feet. I had them deciphered: one paper was written in Chinese and it was a greeting from the shores of Hoang-ho. Of the other, the Chinese I consulted supposed that it was written in Japanese. But I am entertaining you with these matters, and I still do not know how I can be of useful service to you."

"I came to speak to you of a very important matter," answered the young man. "Yesterday afternoon..."

"Have they caught that hapless man?" interrupted the old man, showing interest.

"Are you referring to Elías? How did you find out?"

"I have seen the Muse of the Civil Guards."

"The Muse of the Civil Guards?"

"The *Alferez*'s wife whom you failed to invite to your celebration yesterday. Yesterday morning it was known all over town what happened to the crocodile. The Muse of the Civil Guard has as much discernment as malice, and she supposed that the helmsman must have been the dreaded Elías who threw her husband into the mudhole and manhandled Padre Damaso. Because she read all the communiques which her husband should have received, hardly had he reached home drunk and mindless, when she sent the sergeant with the soldiers to get even with you, thus upsetting the gaiety of the fiesta. Beware! Eve was a good woman, produced by the hands of God... Doña Consolacion, they say, is evil and it is not known from whose hands she came! Women, in order to be good, need to have been at least a maiden or a mother." Ibarra smiled slightly, and removing some papers from his wallet, said:

"My late father was wont to consult you on some matters, and I remember the times when he congratulated himself for having followed your advice. I have on hand a little project and I want to be assured of its success."

And Ibarra briefly outlined to him the school project which he had offered to his fiancee, disclosing before the stupefied philosopher the plans received from Manila.

"I would like you to advise me which persons in the town I can count on for the best success of my enterprise. You know the inhabitants well: I have just arrived and am almost a stranger in my native land."

Old Tasio was examining, with tears in his eyes, the plans lying before him.

"What you are going to achieve has been my dream, the dream of a poor fool!" he exclaimed, deeply moved. "And now my first advice for you is not to come to me ever to consult me!"

The young man regarded the older man with some surprise.

"Because sensible-minded persons," he continued with bitter irony, will take you for a mad man, too. The people believe them mad, those who do not think like themselves; that is why they have taken me as such. I am grateful because, woe is me! on the day that they would like me to return to sanity; on that day they would deprive me of the little freedom which I purchased at the expense of my reputation of sanity. And who knows if, after all, they are right? I do not think or live according to their laws; my principles, my ideals, are different. The *Gobernadorcillo* enjoys the reputation of being a sane man because, having learned no more than to serve chocolate and to put up with the evil disposition of Padre Damaso, he is rich today; he affects the petty destinies of his fellow citizens and at times even speaks of justice. 'That is a talented man,' the common people think. "See, with nothing he has grown great!'

"But I—I inherited a fortune and esteem; I have been educated, and today I am poor; they have not entrusted me with even the most ridiculous assignment and everybody says: 'That one is a fool; he understands nothing of life!' The priest dubs me a philosopher as a joke, and makes it understood that I am a charlatan who shows off what he has learned in the University classrooms when that is precisely what is of least use to me. Perhaps I am truly a mad man and they the sane ones, who can tell?"

The old man shook his head as if to ward off a thought, and continued:

"The second thing I advise is for you to consult the priest, the *Gobernadorcillo*, all the persons of position. They will give you bad, stupid or useless advice; but to consult does not mean to obey; follow them always when that is possible, and make it apparent that you do."

Ibarra reflected for a moment and afterwards retorted:

"Your advice is good but difficult to follow! Can I not take my idea forward without a shadow hanging over it? Cannot truth find its way through, since truth has no need to borrow clothes from error?"

"No one loves naked truth for its own sake!" replied the old man. That is good in theory, feasible in a world dreamed of by youth. There you have the schoolmaster who has been agitating in a vacuum; a child's heart that loved good and reaped only ridicule and laughter. You tell me you are a stranger in your own country and I believe you. Since the first day of your arrival you started wounding the self-love of a religious who is reputed to be a saint among the people and a sage among his kind! God grant that this step may not have decided your future!

"Don't think that, because the Dominicans and the Augustinians regard with contempt the cotton habit of the Franciscan, the leather belt and the indecent footwear, and a doctor of Santo Tomas University has recorded that Pope Innocent III has qualified the statutes of this order as more suitable for pigs than for men, they will not all join hands to affirm what one procurator specified: 'The most insignificant lay brother can do more than the government with all its soldiers!' *Cave ne cadas!* Beware lest you fall! Gold is very powerful; the golden calf has already overturned God on His altars many times since the time of Moses."

"I am not a pessimist, nor does life in my country seem dangerous to me," answered Ibarra smiling. "I believe that these fears are a bit exaggerated, and I hope to be able to attain all of my purposes without much resistance from that side."

"Yes, if they extend to you a helping hand; no if they withdraw their hand. All your efforts would rebound against the walls of the parochial house; the friar only has to wave his belt or shake his habit; the *Alcalde*, for whatever pretext, will deny you tomorrow his concession of today; no mother will allow her child to attend school and all your fatigue will have a counterproductive effect; they will discourage those who would attempt to execute generous enterprises."

"Despite everything," countered Ibarra, "I cannot believe in that power you have been describing, and even supposing it were true and admitting it, I would still have the backing of the sane population, the government which is inspired by noble purposes and high objectives, and sincerely desires the welfare of the Philippines."

"The government! the government!" murmured the philosopher, raising his eyes towards the ceiling. "No matter how much it desires to raise the people to its own advantage and benefit and those of the Mother Country: no matter how much an official may remember the generous spirit of their Catholic majesties and pledge himself to it, the government itself does not see, or hear or judge beyond what it is allowed to see by the priest, or by the Father Provincial. It has decided that it rests on them alone; that it stands because they support it; that it lives because they allow it to live; and that the day they are gone it will collapse like a broken mannequin which has lost its legs.

"The government is intimidated by threats to raise the people against it, and the people are cowed into submission by the threat of government forces; hence the origin of a simple game similar to that which happens to timid people visiting gloomy sites: they mistake their own shadows for phantoms, and their own echoes for strange voices. So long as the government does not deal directly with the people it will not shed this guardianship. It will live like those young fools who tremble at the voice of their governess, whose acquiescence they beg. The government has no vision of any bright future; it is merely an arm, the head is the convent. Because of this inertia it allows itself to be dragged from one abyss to another. It becomes a shadow, loses its identity; and, weak and impotent, entrusts everything to mercenary hands. You compare our governmental system to that of other countries you have visited..."

"Oh!" Ibarra interrupted, "that is too much to ask. Let us content ourselves with seeing that our people do not complain or suffer like the people of the other countries, and that that is so, thanks to religion and the magnanimity of the rulers."

"The people do not complain because they have no voice; do not move because they are lethargic, and you say that they do not suffer, because you have not seen their hearts bleed. But one day you will see and you will hear, and ah! woe unto them that build their strength on ignorance or in fanaticism; woe unto them who are engage in deception and work in darkness, believing that all are asleep! When the light of day illuminates the monster of the shadows, the terrible reaction will come: so much strength bottled up over centuries; so much venom distilled drop by drop; so much lament suppressed will come out and explode... Who then will square those accounts which the peoples of the world present from time to time and which history preserves for us, etched on bloody pages?"

"Oh, God! Government and religion will not allow that day to take place!" retorted Ibarra, impressed despite himself. "The Philippines is religious and loves Spain; the Philippines will know how much Spain has done for the nation. There are abuses—yes! there are flaws. This cannot be denied, but Spain works to introduce reforms that would correct them; she thinks out plans, she is not selfish."

"I know, and that is the worst part. The reforms that come from above are rendered null in the lower spheres, thanks to everyone's vices, for example, the avid desire to enrich oneself in a short time, and the ignorance of the people who acquiesce to it. The abuses are not corrected by a royal decree, as long as a conscientious authority does not watch over its execution, while freedom of speech is not granted against the excesses of the petty tyrants.

"The plans remain plans, the abuses, abuses and the ministry, satisfied, will sleep in peace. Even worse: if by chance a high personage arrives with great and generous ideas, promptly he begins to hear, while behind his back they take him for a fool: 'Your Excellency does not know the country; Your Excellency has no knowledge of the native character; Your Excellency will spoil them; Your Excellency will do well to trust in So-and-So, etc.' And since His Excellency has no knowledge of the country (which until now is thought to be in America) and moreover has flaws and weaknesses like all men, he allows himself to be convinced. His Excellency will also recall that to acquire this position he had to sweat much and to suffer more; that he will occupy it for only three years; that he is getting old and it becomes necessary for him not to dwell on quixotic notions but on his future: a tiny hotel in Madrid; a little house in the countryside, and a good income with which to live at court in luxury—this is what he should look for in the Philippines.

"Let us not ask for miracles, let us not ask for concern with what is good for the country of him who comes as a stranger to make his own fortune and leave afterwards. What does it matter to him to earn the gratitude or the curses of a people he does not know, in a country where he does not have his roots, where he has no memories to cherish or loves to keep? For glory to be palatable and agreeable it is necessary that it resound in the ears of our loved ones, in the atmosphere of our home or the

Motherland which will hold our ashes. We want glory to crown us in our graves, to warm the cold of death with its rays, to keep us from being reduced to nothingness, and instead to leave something of ourselves. Nothing of this sort can we promise those who come to shape our destinies. And the worst in all of this is that they leave when they start to realize their duties. But we are getting further from our theme."

"No, before resuming it I need to elucidate certain matters," interrupted the young man vigorously. "I can concede that the government has no knowledge of the people, but I believe the people know less of the government. There are useless officials, evil, if you like, but there are also good ones, and these are not able to accomplish anything because they encounter an inert mass, the population that takes little part in matters that concern them. But I have not come to discuss this issue with you. I came to ask for your advice, and you tell me to bow my head to grotesque idols..."

"Yes! and I repeat it: because here one has to bow one's head or lose it."

"Bow the head or lose it?" repeated Ibarra pensively. "It is a difficult dilemma. But...why? Is my love for my country, then, incompatible with my love for Spain? Is it necessary, perhaps, to lower one's self in order to be a good Christian, prostitute one's own conscience to bring about a good purpose? I love my country, the Philippines, because I owe her my life and happiness, and because all men should love their motherland. I love Spain, the land of my forebears, because despite everything, the Philippines owes and will owe her happiness and her future to Spain. I am a Catholic and I keep pure the faith of my fathers. I do not see why I have to bend my head when I can raise it, surrender it to my enemies when I can humiliate them!"

"Because the field in which you wish to sow is in the power of your enemies. Against them you cannot contend for lack of strength... It is necessary to kiss that hand which..."

But Ibarra did not allow Tasio to continue, but exclaimed, carried away:

"Kiss! But you forget that between them they have murdered my father and thrown him out of his grave... but I, who am his son, I do not forget it and if I don't avenge him it is because I am concerned for the prestige of religion."

The old philosopher bowed his head.

"Señor Ibarra," he answered slowly, "if you keep those memories which I cannot advise you to forget, abandon your enterprise and look elsewhere for the good of your countrymen. The enterprise requires another man because, in order to bring it to fruition, it is not only necessary to have money and to will it. In this our country it also requires self-denial, tenacity and faith, because the ground is ready; only it is sown with discord."

Ibarra understood the value of these words, but not that he should be discouraged. The thought of Maria Clara was in his mind; it was necessary to realize his project.

"Does your experience suggest no more than this hard means?" he asked in a low voice.

The old man took the young man's arm and led him to the window. A cooling breeze, precursor of the north wind, was blowing. He saw the garden before him limited by the wide expanse of forest which served as a park.

"Why don't we behave as does that frail stem loaded with buds and blossoms?" observed the philosopher pointing to a lovely rose bush. "The wind blows, shakes it, and the stem bends as if to hide its precious burden. If the stem were to maintain itself erect, it would break, the wind would scatter the flowers and the buds would perish. The wind passes away and the stem straightens itself, proud of its treasure. Who would accuse it of having bent itself in the face of necessity?

"Over there see that gigantic *kupang*[1], its aerial foliage, in which the eagle's nest is sheltered, swaying majestically. I brought it from the forest a fragile plant; with thin bamboos I supported its stalk for months. If I had brought it strong and full of life it would surely not have survived. The wind would have shaken it before it roots could have anchored in the soil, before it could acclimatize itself to its surroundings and find there adequate nourishment to grow further and increase in size and height. Thus would you end up, tree transplanted from Europe to this stony soil; if it does not look for support, it would fail to grow. You are in unfavorable circumstances, alone and elevated: the ground is unreliable, the heavens announce a coming storm and the tops of your family tree—it has been proven—attract lightning. It is not courage, it is reckless temerity, to struggle alone against the existing order. No one would take to task a pilot for seeking a port at the first threat of an impending storm. To bend down when a bullet whistles by your side is not cowardice. What is bad is to defy it, only to fall and not be able to raise one's self."

"And would these sacrifices produce the fruits I hope for?" asked Ibarra. "Will the priest forget his grievance against me and believe in me? Would they openly assist me in behalf of the education that would compete with the convents for the wealth of the country? Can they not pretend friendship, simulate protection, and beneath, in the shadows, fight and undermine, wound it in the heel to make it vacillate sooner than would a frontal attack? Given the antecedents that you suppose one can expect almost anything."

The old man remained silent without attempting to answer. He meditated awhile and replied:

"If that should happen, if the enterprise fails, what will console you is the thought of having done your part. And even thus, something would be gained: lay the first stone, sow; after the storm is unleashed, some grain of wheat will perhaps germinate, survive the catastrophe, save from destruction the species which would later serve as seed for the sons of the dead sower. The example could encourage others who only fear to start."

Ibarra considered these alternatives, saw his situation, and understood that, despite his pessimism, the old man had reason.

"I believe you!" he exclaimed, stretching out his hand. "It was not for nothing that I solicited your advice. Right now I will go and meet the priest who, after all, has done me no wrong, for not all of us are like my father's persecutor. I must, besides, win his interest in favor of that unfortunate madwoman and of her sons. I have faith in God and in people."

He took his leave, and mounting his horse, rode away.

"Attention!" murmured the pessimistic sage, following Ibarra with his eyes. "Let us observe well how destiny will work out in all this, the drama that started in the graveyard."

This time he had truly made a mistake: the drama had started long before.

- 27 -

The Eve of the Fiesta

We have reached the tenth of November, the day before the fiesta.

Breaking away from the daily monotony, the townsfolk are engaged in unusual activity at home, on the streets, in church, at the cockpit and in the fields.

Windows are decked with banners and hangings of various colors; the air is filled with the explosion of fireworks and the blare of music. The whole atmosphere is pervaded and saturated with rejoicing.

The maiden of the house busies herself with arranging on the table various native fruit preserves in glass containers of pleasing colors over a table covered with white embroidered linen. Chickens are chirping in the patio, hens cackle, pigs snort in fright at man's merrymaking. The servants go back and forth, up and down, carrying gilt-edged chinaware and silverware. Here a plate breaks and someone is scolded; over there they laugh at the simple peasant girl. Everywhere orders are given, people whisper, shout, make comments, conjectures; they encourage each other, and all is confusion, noise and uproar—all of this endeavor and fatigue for the benefit of the guest, known or unknown; to entertain any person whom perhaps no one has met before and will not meet again: so that the visitor, stranger, friend, foe, Filipino, Spaniard, poor man, rich one, leaves contented and satisfied. Gratitude is not demanded, nor is it expected of the guests not to harm the hospitable family while or after they are fed! The rich and those who have spent some time in Manila and are more experienced in these things, have brought beer, champagne, liquors, wine and other provisions from Europe, of which they will scarcely take a bite or swallow a drop. Their tables are elegantly prepared.

The centerpiece is often a huge artificial pineapple, a very good imitation, stuck with toothpicks, daintily fashioned by the prisoners of Bilibid during their moments of leisure; sometimes a fan, a bouquet of flowers, a bird, a rose, a palm leaf or some chains, all carved from one piece of wood: the artist is a condemned criminal, his instrument a broken knife and his inspiration the voice of the club wielder. Beside this gigantic pineapple which is called the toothpick holder, stands a pyramidal mound of oranges, *lanzones, atis, chicos* and even *mangoes,* despite the fact that it is November. On large plates, covered with ornamental paper painted in brilliant colors, are laid hams from Europe and China, a huge pie in the shape of an *Agnus Dei* or of a dove, perchance the Holy Spirit, stuffed turkeys and so forth, and among these the appetizers, bottled pickles of fanciful cut carved from the *bonga* flower and other vegetables and fruits artistically carved and pasted with syrup to the sides of the large glass jars.

They clean the crystal globes which have been inherited by fathers and sons; the bronze napkin rings are polished to brilliance; the kerosene lamps are bereft of the red robes which kept them from flies and mosquitoes during the year, rendering them useless. The hanging crystal pendants of prismatic and almond-shaped drops sway harmoniously against each other; they tinkle as they seem to take part in the feasting; they rejoice and break the light into rainbow colors against the whitewashed walls. The children play, enjoy themselves; they pursue the colors, they stumble, break tubes, but all this does not deter them from enjoying themselves: in other times of the year they would be counting in different ways the tears in their round eyes.

Similarly, like the venerable lamps, the hidden handiwork of the young girls also come out: crocheted veils, mantelpieces, artificial flowers. Antique crystal trays appear, bearing on their surfaces miniature lakes with little fishes, crocodiles, mollusks, algae, corals and rocks of glass of dazzling colors. These trays are covered with cigars, cigarettes and diminutive *buyos* twisted by the dainty hands of the maidens of the house.

The floor of the house shines mirror-like; *piña* or *jusi* curtains adorn the doors; lanterns of crystal or of paper pink, blue green or crimson hang from the windows; the house is full of roses and baskets on porcelain pedestals from China. Even the saints are decked with adornments; the images and relics go on holiday; they are brought out and dusted, their glass covers polished and bouquets of flowers attached to their frames.

On the streets are built at regular intervals artistic arches of bamboo worked out in a thousand ways; they are called *sinkaban* and surrounded by *kaluskus*[1], the sight of which makes the children rejoice. Around the church patio we find a huge and expensive awning supported by bamboo poles, to shield the procession. Underneath, the children play—they run, they climb, jump and tear their new shirts, which they were to show off during the feast.

Over at the plaza a stage has been built of bamboo, nipa and wood. Here the comedy troupe from Tondo will stage marvels to compete with the gods in unbelievable miracles; here Marianito, Chananay, Balbino, Ratia, Carvajal, Yeyeng, Liceria and many others will sing and dance.[2] The Filipino is fond of the theater and passionately attends dramatic presentations; he listens silently to the songs, admires the dance and the pantomime; he does not break out into whistles, neither does he applaud. Does he not like the show? Well he chews his *buyo* or leaves, without disturbing the others who are perhaps enjoying the spectacle. Only at times do the lower class hoot—when the actors kiss or embrace the actresses—but they do not go beyond this. Formerly, only dramas were staged; the town poet would compose a piece which necessarily had combat every two minutes, a funny situation and some terrifying mutations. But since the Tondo artists put up a fight every fifteen seconds, presented two funny pieces and others even more fantastic, they killed their provincial colleagues. The *Gobernadorcillo* was an *aficionado* of the theatre and chose, in agreement with the parish priest, the comedy "Prince Villardo or the nails pulled out of the infamous cave," a piece with magic and fireworks.

The bells peal joyfully from time to time, the same bells that ten days ago tolled sadly. The fire wheels and mortars thunder in the air. The Filipino pyrotechnician, who learned his art without the benefit of a well-known teacher, will show off his skill, preparing the bulls, the castles of fire with Bengal lights, paper globes inflated with hot air, brilliant firewheels, detonators, rockets and so on.

Do we hear musical chords from afar? Well, the children are already running in haste towards the outskirts of the town to await the orchestras and bands. There are five hired bands besides the three orchestras. The Pagsanghan band, owned by the notary public, should not be missing, neither that of the town S.P. de T[3], then of great fame because it was directed by maestro Austria, the vagabond *cabo Mariano* who carries—so they say— fame and harmony at the tip of his baton. The musicians praise his funeral march "The Willow," and deplore his lack of a formal musical education with which, and his genius, he could have given glory to his native land.

The bands enter the town playing lively marches, followed by ragged or half-naked children who have put on their brothers' shirts or their fathers' pants. As soon as the music ceases, they already know it by memory; they hum it, they whistle it with uncanny accuracy, and then they give their verdict.

Meanwhile the carromatas are arriving, the calesas or carriages, the relatives, the friends, strangers, the gamblers with their best fighting cocks and sacks of gold, prepared to risk their fortunes on the green-covered card table, or within the circle of the cockpit.

"The *Alferez* gets fifty pesos a night!" volunteers a plump smallish man within hearing of the recent arrivals. "Capitan Tiago will come and bank the *monte*; Capitan Joaquin is bringing eighteen thousand with him. There will be *liampo*; Carlos, the Chinaman, will put it up with a capital of ten thousand. Big players from Tanauan, Lipa and Batangas as well as from Sta. Cruz will come. It will be a big thing! a big thing. But have some chocolate. This year Capitan Tiago will not relieve us of our money as in the past. It has not cost him but three thanksgiving masses; and I have a *mutya* of cacao. And how is the family?"

"In good health, thank you!" answer the visitors. "And Padre Damaso?"

"Padre Damaso will preach in the morning. He will deal cards with us in the evening."

"Better! much better! So there is no danger at all!"

"We are secure, very secure!"

"Carlos the Chinaman will let go even more!"

And the roundish plump man makes signs as if counting coins.

In the town outskirts, the mountainfolk, the *kasama*[4], put on their best attire bringing with them to the houses of their capitalists fattened hens, wild boar, venison, fowl. They load heavy bull carts with firewood, fruits, the rarest orchids they can find in the forests; others bring *bigâ* with large leaves, *tikas-tikas* with fiery colored flowers to deck the doors of the house.[5]

But where the animation is at its height, akin to a tumult, is around a wide expanse of land a few paces from Ibarra's house. The pulleys screech, shouts are heard, as are the metallic sound of stones being crushed, the hammer driving a nail, the ax hewing the beams. A mass of men dig in the ground and open a wide deep well; others place in rows stones from the town quarries, unload carts, pile up sand, and lay hold of capstans and wheels.

"Here! take that over there! Quick!" a little old man with lively, intelligent features shouts, holding like a cane a meterstick edged in copper, around which a plumbing cord is wound. He directs the proceedings—Señor Juan, master builder, mason, carpenter, whitewasher, locksmith, painter, stonecutter and, on occasions, sculptor.

"It is necessary to finish it right now! Tomorrow no work can be done and the day after tomorrow is slated for the ceremony. Quick!"

"Make the opening as large as this cylinder," he says to some stonecutters who are polishing a square slab; our names will be recorded in there!"

And he repeats to every newcomer what he has been saying a thousand times:

"Do you know what we are building? We are putting up a schoolhouse, a model of its kind, like those in Germany, or even better! The plans were made by Señor R, the architect, and myself. I am the one who directs the works. Yes, sir! see this converted into a palace with two wings: one for boys and the other for the girls. Here in the center a large garden with three fountains; over there on the sides a line of trees, small orchards for the children in which to sow and grow plants during recreation hours, spending the time usefully, and not expending it. Look how deep the foundations go! Three meters and seventy-five centimeters! The building will include storerooms, underground areas, dungeons for the lazy ones near, very close to the games and gymnasium, in order for the punished ones to hear how the diligent ones are enjoying themselves. Do you see this large space? This will be the track for running races and jumping in the open air. The girls will have a garden with arrangements of benches, swings, avenues for rope skipping, fountains, and bird cages etc...this will be magnificent!"

And Señor Juan rubs his hands in glee, thinking of the fame he will gain. "Visitors will come to look, and will ask: 'Who is the great architect who built this?' 'Don't you know? It is unbelievable that you have not met Señor Juan!

Doubtless you must have come from afar,' others will reply."

With these thoughts in mind he went from one end to the other, inspecting and checking everything.

"I find too much lumber for a crane," he says to a sallow-faced man who is directing some workers. Three large lengths of lumber to form a tripod and another three to fasten to each other, would be sufficient for me!"

"Aba!" answers the yellowish man, smiling a peculiar smile; "the more of an apparatus we give to the works, the more and better its effect! The whole outfit will have a different aspect, assume more importance and they will say: 'How much labor it has cost them!' You will see the kind of crane I will build! And then I will deck it with banners, garlands of leaves and flowers...You will say afterwards that you were right in admitting me among your workers, and that Señor Ibarra cannot ask for more!"

The man smiles and laughs. Señor Juan smiles and shakes his head.

At some distance two kiosks can be seen joined to each other by a bower of entwined branches covered with banana leaves.

The schoolmaster and thirty children are weaving wreaths; they fasten pennants to the thin bamboo stakes covered with white embossed linen.

"Endeavor to write well and make your letters clear!" he says to those drawing the inscriptions. "The *Alcalde* is coming; many priests will attend, perhaps even the *Capitan General* who is now in the province! If they see that you draw well, they may praise you."

"And they will provide us with blackboards?"

"Who knows? But Señor Ibarra has already ordered one from Manila. Tomorrow some things will arrive which will be distributed among you as prizes.... But leave those flowers in water; we will make the bouquets tomorrow. You must bring more flowers because we need to cover the table with them; flowers are attractive to the eyes."

"My father will bring *baino* flowers[6] and a basket of *sampagas* tomorrow."

"Mine has brought three loads of sand and he has not received payment."

"My uncle has promised to pay for a teacher!" adds Capitan Basilio's nephew.

As a matter of fact, the project had found favor with everyone. The parish priest asked to sponsor and personally bless the laying of the cornerstone—the first— the ceremony to take place on the last day of the fiesta, being one of its major solemnities. The assistant parish priest himself had timidly approached Ibarra, offering him all the masses paid for by devotees until the building was finished. Even more, the rich and thrifty sister Rufa said that in case funds ran short she would traverse the town to beg for alms with one condition only: that her trip and food, etc. be paid for. Ibarra had thanked her and replied:

"We wouldn't get much, for neither am I rich nor is this building a church. Besides I did not promise to build it at the expense of other people."

The youth, the students who came from Manila in order to celebrate the fiesta, admired Ibarra and took him as a role model; but as often happens when we want to imitate celebrities, we only imitate their trifles if not their defects, for we are not capable of more. Many of these admirers noticed how the young man tied his cravat; others, the shape of his shirt collar, and not a few, the number of buttons on his vest and coat.

The gloomy speculations of old Tasio seemed to have

dissipated for good. Ibarra mentioned this to him one day, but the old pessimist retorted:

"Remember what Baltazar says:

When the greeting on your arrival
Is a happy face and a show of gladness,
Be more careful of a hidden enemy."

Baltazar was as good a poet as a thinker.

These and other things took place on the eve of the fiesta, before the sun set.

- 28 -
At Nightfall

In the house of Capitan Tiago grand preparations had also been made. We know the owner—his fondness for ostentatious display and his pride as a Manilan compelled him to outshine and outdo his provincial neighbors in lavish splendor. He had another reason, too, which obliged him to seek to eclipse the others: his daughter Maria Clara. And his future son-in-law, who was the talk of everyone, was there as well.

As a matter of fact, one of the more reputable newspapers of the capital had dedicated an article to Ibarra on its front page with this headline: "Imitate him!" breaking out into counsels for the young man and giving him some praise. He was called *the illustrious young man and rich financier*; two lines below this, *the distinguished philanthropist*; in the next paragraph, *Minerva's disciple who went to the Mother Country to hail the genuine source of the Arts and Sciences*; some lines below, *the Spanish Filipino*, and so forth.

Capitan Tiago was burning with eagerness to emulate him, and was mulling whether, perhaps, he should also put up a convent at his personal expense.

Several days before, there had arrived at the house where Maria Clara and Tía Isabel were staying, a great number of boxes of provisions and drinks from Europe, colossal mirrors, frames and the young woman's piano.

Capitan Tiago came the day before the fiesta. When his daughter kissed his hand, he gave her a beautiful locket of gold covered with diamonds and emeralds and containing a chip of St. Peter's boat, in which the Lord had sat during the disciples' fishing sorties.

The meeting with his future son-in law could not have been more cordial. Naturally the school was discussed. Capitan Tiago wanted to name it the school of Saint Francis.

"Believe me," he said, "Saint Francis is a good patron saint! If you call it School of Primary Instruction you would gain nothing. Who is Primary Instruction anyway?"

Some of Maria Clara's friends arrived and invited her to take a walk with them.

"But return home soon," said Capitan Tiago to his daughter, who had asked his permission: "You know that Padre Damaso, who has just arrived, will dine with us."

And turning to Ibarra, who had become pensive, he added: "You too, why don't you join us? You will be alone in your house."

"With the greatest pleasure. However, I must be home, should guests arrive," mumbled the young man, avoiding Maria Clara's eyes.

"Bring your friends along," Capitan Tiago answered casually. "There is always food in abundance in my house... Besides, I would like you and Padre Damaso to come to an understanding..."

"There will be time enough for that," replied Ibarra, forcing himself to smile. He stood up and left to accompany the girls.

They went down the stairs—Maria Clara between Victoria and Iday, with Tía Isabel following behind.

The people respectfully gave way for them to pass. Maria Clara was stunning in her beauty. Her pallor had subsided, and even if her eyes were pensive, her lips were smiling. She greeted, with the amiability of a happy maiden, old acquaintances of her childhood days, now admirers of her youthful charm. In less than fifteen days she had recovered that open confidence, that childlike chatter which were missing during her stay within the narrow confines of the convent. It could be said of her that the butterfly, after leaving the cocoon, recognizes all the flowers. It is enough for it to fly for a moment and warm itself in the golden rays of the sun to shed the rigidity of its chrysallis. The young woman's whole being was vibrant with new life: she found everything good and beautiful; she manifested her love with that virginal chastity which knows only pure thoughts and is unaware of the reasons for false modesty. She would cover her face with her fan when merrily teased, but her eyes would smile and her whole being would tremble.

The houses were starting to light up, and on the streets, traversed by the band, the chandeliers of bamboo and wood were lit in imitation of those of the church.

From the streets, through the open windows, people could be seen milling around in the houses in an atmosphere of radiance and the perfume of flowers, to the sound of piano, harp or orchestra. Chinese, Spaniards, Filipinos—all dressed in European or native attire, were crossing the streets. They walked in confusion, elbowing and pushing each other: the servants carrying meat and poultry, students clad in white, men and women risking being run over by carriages and calesas which despite their drivers' *"tabi"*[1] found difficulty in clearing the way.

In front of Capitan Basilio's residence some young people greeted our acquaintances and invited them to visit. The happy voice of Sinang running down the stairs put an end to all excuses for not accepting the invitation.

"Come up for a while so that I can go out with you," she told them. "I am bored in the company of so many strangers who talk only of cocks and cards."

They went up the house.

The living room was full of people. Some came forward to greet Ibarra, whose name was known to all. They contemplated Maria Clara, impressed by her beauty. Some old woman murmured while chewing *buyo:* "She looks like the Virgin!"

There they had to partake of chocolate. Capitan Basilio had become the close friend and champion of Ibarra since the day of the excursion. He had learned from the telegram, gift to his daughter Sinang, that Ibarra knew that the lawsuit had been decided in his favor. Not wanting to be outdone in generosity, he tried to cancel the outcome of the game of chess. But Ibarra did not consent to this. Don Basilio then proposed: the money that he would have paid for legal costs would be used to pay the services of another teacher for the town's future school. Consequently, the orator used his ability so that the other oppositors would desist from their strange pretensions, and said to them:

"Believe me, in lawsuits the one who wins is left without his shirt!"

But he was not able to convince anyone, notwithstanding his quoting the Romans.

After partaking of the chocolate our young people had to listen to the piano played by the town organist.

"When I hear him in church," said Sinang, pointing at the man, "I feel like dancing. Now that he is playing the piano I feel like praying. That is why I am going with you."

"Do you want to come with us tonight?" Don Basilio whispered to Ibarra when they were leaving. Padre Damaso will bank a small game."

Ibarra smiled, and answered with a movement of the head which could have signified a yes as much as a no.

"Who is he?" Maria Clara asked Victoria, indicating with a quick glance a young man who was following them.

"That...that is my cousin," she replied, somewhat taken aback.

"That one is no cousin of mine," quickly retorted Sinang. "He is a son of my aunt."

They passed the parish house, which certainly was not among the less lively. Sinang could not contain an exclamation of wonder upon seeing the lamps burning, the lamps of very ancient vintage that Padre Salvi never allowed to be lit so as not to waste gas. Cries and loud laughter were heard. The friars could be seen walking slowly, moving their heads in rhythm and with huge cigars adorning their mouths. The secular priests who were with them tried to do as the religious did. In their European attire they could have been provincial employees or authorities.

Maria Clara was able to distinguish the plump contours of Padre Damaso's figure beside the elegant silhouette of Padre Sibyla's. The taciturn and mysterious Padre Salvi stood motionless in his place.

"He is sad!" remarked Sinang. "He must be thinking

of the expenses occasioned by so many visitors. But you will see, he won't be paying for them; the sacristans will. His visitors always dine on someone else's account."

"Sinang!" reprimanded Victoria.

"I cannot stand him since he destroyed the Wheel of Fortune. I no longer go to confession to him."

One among the houses was without lights and with closed windows: the house of the *Alferez*. Maria Clara marvelled.

"The witch! The Muse of the Civil Guards, according to the old man!" exclaimed the irrepressible Sinang. "What has she to do with our celebrations? She must be raving mad! Wait till cholera attacks us and you will see her invite everyone!"

"But Sinang!" her cousin again reprimanded her.

"I could never stomach her, and even less since she upset our excursion by sending the guards. If I were an Archbishop I would marry her to Padre Salvi...you will see the kind of children they will have! See how she caused the poor helmsman to be apprehended—the man who jumped into the depths to please..."

She was not able to finish her sentence: in one corner of the plaza where a blind man was singing of the romance of the fishes to the accompaniment of a guitar, a rare spectacle was unfolding.

It was a man wretchedly attired, and sheltered by a wide-brimmed *salakot* of palm leaves. His clothing consisted of a ragged frock coat and a pair of large trousers like those worn loose by the Chinese, torn in many places. Wretched sandals shod his feet. All of his face remained in the shadow thanks to his *salakot*, but from such dark shadows glowed every now and then two bright points which would die down instantly. He was tall, and from the way he moved one could tell that he was young. He laid a basket on the ground and moved away, all the while uttering strange incomprehensible sounds. He remained standing, completely isolated, as if he and the multitude were mutually trying to evade each other. Some women would approach and drop into his basket fruits, fish, rice and other foods. When no one came near the basket anymore, other sounds, sadder still but less mournful, would come out of the shadows—perhaps they were expressions of thanksgiving. He would then pick up his basket and move away to repeat the same action somewhere else.

Maria Clara discerned a grave misfortune and asked, full of interest, about the strange being.

"That is the leper!" Iday informed her. "He contracted leprosy four years ago, some say by taking care of his mother; others say from having stayed long in a damp prison. He lives in the field near the Chinese cemetery. He does not communicate with anyone; everyone avoids him for fear of contamination. If you could see his dwelling! It is the house of *giring giring*[2]; the wind, the rain, and the sun come and go like needle through a cloth. They have forbidden him to touch anything that belongs to the people. One day a child fell into a ditch—the ditch was not deep. He was passing by, and helped the child get out of the ditch. The child's father found out and complained to the *Gobernadorcillo*, who ordered the leper flogged with six lashes in the middle of the street, and the whip burned afterwards. That was awful: the leper fleeing from the blows, the whip-master pursuing him and the *Gobernadorcillo* shouting: "Learn! It is better for one to drown than to get sick like you!"

"That is true!" murmured Maria Clara.

And without being aware of her action, she swiftly approached the unfortunate man's basket and dropped in it the locket her father had just given her.

"What have you done?" chorused her friends.

"I have nothing else to give," she said, hiding tears behind a smile.

"And what would he do with your locket?" Victoria asked her. "One day they gave him money, but he pushed it away with a cane. What would he want it for if nobody would accept it from his hands? If he could only eat the locket!"

Maria Clara regarded with envy the women selling food, and shrugged her shoulders.

But the leper approached the basket, picked up the locket which glowed in his hands, kissed it and, uncovering his head, sank to his knees and buried his forehead in the place trodden by Maria Clara.

Maria Clara hid her face behind her fan and brought her handkerchief to her eyes.

In the meantime, a woman had approached the leper, who seemed to be praying. Her hair was dishevelled and unkempt. The light of the lantern revealed the emaciated features of the mad Sisa.

As he felt her contact, the leper cried out and jumped up. But the mad woman held on to his arm to the great horror of the bystanders, and said to him: "Let us pray!...pray! Today is the day of the dead! Those lights are the life of men; let us pray for my sons!"

"Separate them, separate them! The mad woman will get contaminated!" the crowd was shouting, but no one dared to approach them.

"Do you see that light from the tower? That is my son Basilio who comes down by a rope! Do you see that one from the convent? That is my son Crispin, but I am not going to see them because the priest is sick and has many coins of gold and the coins got lost. Let us pray, let us pray for the soul of the priest! I brought him *amargoso* and *zarzalidas;* my garden was full of flowers, and I had sons. I had a garden, I was taking care of flowers and I had two sons!"

Letting go of the leper, she moved away singing: "I had a garden and flowers, I had sons, a garden and flowers."

"What were you able to do for that poor woman?" Maria Clara asked Ibarra.

"Nothing! these last few days she disappeared from the town and she could not be found," replied a confused Ibarra. "Besides, I have been very busy. But don't get upset; the priest promised to help me, but urged me to be tactful and careful. It seems that this has something to do with the Civil Guards. The priest is highly interested in her case."

"Did not the *Alferez* say he would have the boys sought?"

"Yes, but then he was slightly drunk."

No sooner were the words out of his mouth when they saw the mad woman dragged rather than led by a soldier. Sisa resisted.

"Why are you holding her? What has she done?" queried Ibarra.

"What? Didn't you see how she upsets everyone?" answered the custodian of public order.

The leper gathered up his basket in haste and moved away.

Maria Clara wanted to go home. She had lost all her gaiety and her good humor.

"So there also are people who are not happy!" she murmured. When they reached the door of her home her sadness increased when her betrothed refused to come up, and prepared to leave.

"It is necessary," said the young man.

Maria Clara climbed the stairs, thinking how boring the days of the fiesta would be, when strangers would come visiting.

- 29 -

Letters

Everyone speaks of the fair as it goes for him.

Not having anything of importance happening to our characters on the eve of the fiesta or on the next day, we would gladly omit this part, if we had not considered that perhaps some foreign reader might feel curious and want to know how Filipinos celebrate their feasts. To this purpose, what follows is a faithful transcript of some letters: one of them the work of a correspondent for a serious and distinguished journal in Manila, highly respected for its tone of sober authority. It is up to our readers to rectify some light and normal inaccuracies.

The worthy correspondent for this dignified paper wrote thus:

"The Director...

"My distinguished friend:

"I have never in my life witnessed nor ever again hope to witness in the provinces a religious celebration so solemn, so splendid and so touching as the one that is being held in this town by the very reverend and virtuous Franciscan friars.

"The attendance is very large. I had the good fortune of greeting all of the Spanish residents in this province: three reverend Augustinian Padres from the province of Batangas; two reverend Dominican Padres—one of them the Most Reverend Padre Hernando de la Sibyla who came to honor this town with his presence—its worthy inhabitants must never allow themselves to forget this fact. I also saw a great number of prominent men from Cavite and Pampanga, wealthy men from Manila, and many musical bands—among them the elite orchestra from Pagsanjan owned by the clerk of court Don Miguel Guevara; and a crowd of Chinese and *Indios*, who with the curiosity that characterizes the former and the religiosity of the latter, were waiting expectantly for the day of the solemn celebration, to attend the comic-mimic-lyrical-choreographic-dramatic presentations for which a huge and spacious stage was set up in the center of the plaza.

"At 9 o'clock in the evening of November 10, the eve of the fiesta, after the succulent supper tendered in our honor by the *Hermano Mayor* of the celebration, our attention, together with that of the Spaniards and friars congregated in the parish house, was aroused by the music of two brass bands accompanied by a thick and compact multitude led by the town leaders, and by the noise of firecrackers and detonators. They came to the convent house to take us to the seats reserved for us at the show.

"We could not turn down so gracious an invitation, despite my preference for rest in the arms of Morpheus, god of sleep, to relax my aching body from the shaking and jogging of the vehicle assigned to us by the *Gobernadorcillo* of the town of B.[1]

"So we went down to look for our companions, who were dining in the house owned by the pious and opulent Don Santiago de los Santos. The parish priest, the Most Reverend Padre Bernardo Salvi, and the Most Reverend Padre Damaso Verdolagas—who, by a special concession of the Almighty, has by now recovered from the injuries inflicted on him by impious hands—with the Most Reverend Padre Hernando de la Sibyla and the virtuous parish priest of Tanauan and other Spaniards besides, were the guests of this Filipino Croesus. We had the happy privilege of admiring not only the luxurious and elegant taste of the host—uncommon among the natives—but also the exquisite beauty of the precious, lovely and rich heiress, a consummate disciple of St. Cecilia, playing on her elegant piano the best German and Italian compositions with a mastery that reminded me of La Galvez.[2] It is a pity that so perfect a maiden should modestly hide her talents from the society which has only admiration for her. I should not leave in the inkwell the fact that we were served champagne and fine liquors with the generosity and abundance characteristic of this renowned capitalist.

"We viewed the spectacle. You are already acquainted with our performers Ratia, Carvajal and Fernandez. Their witty sallies were understood and enjoyed only by us. They were lost on the uneducated spectators. Chananay and Balbino were good despite the slight hoarseness of their vocal chords. The latter suffered a tiny break in his voice, but he was admirable on the whole. The Tagalog comedy had a particular appeal for the natives, especially for the *Gobernadorcillo*. The latter rubbed his hands with glee, telling us that it was a pity that the princess was not made to fight the giant who kidnapped her. In his opinion that would have been marvelous, and more so if the giant had become invulnerable except in his navel like a certain Ferragus in the Tale of the Twelve Peers of France. The Most Reverend Padre Damaso, with that goodness of heart that distinguishes him, was of the same opinion as the *Gobernadorcillo,* and added that in such a situation the princess could compel the giant to expose his navel and deal him the coup de grâce.

"It is needless to add that during the show nothing was wanting, due to the thoughtful prodigality of this Filipino Rothschild: sherbets, effervescent drinks, choice sweetmeats galore, wines and so forth flowed with profusion among us who were there. What was much noted, and justifiably so, was the absence of the well-known and illustrious young philanthropist Don Juan Crisostomo Ibarra who, as you already know, is scheduled to preside tomorrow over the laying of the cornerstone of the impressive monument he has set out to build. This worthy descendant of the Pelayos and Elcanos (for according to my information his paternal grandparents belong to our heroic and noble provinces of the North—perhaps they were among the companions of Magellan or Legaspi) had not shown himself the whole day due to a slight indisposition. His name runs from mouth to mouth and is pronounced only with praise redounding to the glory of Spain and of the legitimate Spaniards like ourselves who never belie our blood no matter how mixed it may be.

"Today, the 11th of November, we are witnessing a moving sight. This day, it is publicly known, is the feastday of Our Lady of Peace, and is celebrated by the lay brothers of the Confraternity of the Holy Rosary. Tomorrow will be the feast of the patron, San Diego, honored primarily by the Third Order of Laymen following the Franciscan rule. Between these two entities there is a pious competition to serve God, a piety that in the extreme provokes religious quarrels between them, like the recent dispute over the merits of that great preacher of well-known fame, the so many times renowned Most Reverend Padre Damaso, who tomorrow will occupy the pulpit to preach a sermon which will be, according to the general consensus, an event of religious-literary importance.

"Well, as we were saying, we witnessed a highly edifying and touching spectacle: six young religious, three assigned to say mass and the other three as acolytes, sallied forth from the vestry and genuflected before the altar. The celebrant, the Most Reverend Padre Hernando de la Sibyla, intoned the *Surge Domine* in that magnificent voice of his and with such religious unction that all the world acknowledged and deemed him highly deserving of praise. This signalled the start of the procession around the church.

"The *Surge Domine* over, the *Gobernadorcillo*, in formal evening attire, bearing the tall silver cross, and in his wake the four acolytes swinging censers began the procession. Behind them came the bearers of the silver candelabra, the municipal officials and the precious images dressed in satin and gold: representing Santo Domingo, San Diego and the Virgin of Peace with her magnificent blue mantle set with gilded silver plates—a gift of the virtuous ex-*gobernadorcillo* most worthy of imitation, the never sufficiently acknowledged Don Santiago de los Santos. All these images were carried on silver floats. Behind the Mother of God we Spaniards and the other religious followed: the celebrant marching under a pallium carried by the *barangay* heads. The procession line closed with the

Civil Guards in tow.

"I believe it is superfluous to make mention of the multitude of natives forming the two lines of the procession, piously holding lighted candles in their hands. The orchestra played religious marches as the detonators and the wheels of fire kept up their barrage. Admirable are the modesty and fervor that these acts inspire in the hearts of believers; the unbounded and pure faith they profess for the Virgin of Peace; the solemnity and fervent devotion manifest in this celebration are extolled by those of us who had the privilege of having been born under Spain's sacrosanct and immaculate banner.

"The procession ended, the mass was sung by the theater artists with orchestral accompaniment. After the gospel, the Most Reverend Padre Manuel Martin, Augustinian, who had come from the province of Batangas, climbed the pulpit to preach. He had everyone in the audience absorbed and hanging on to his every word, particularly the Spaniards, with his homily delivered in Spanish courageously and boldly, so fluently, so rich and apt, which filled our hearts with fervor and enthusiasm. This is the kind of preaching proper to what we feel for the Virgin and our beloved Spain, especially when it is possible to put into the text the ideas of a prince of the church, his Eminence Cardinal Monescillo, which surely are also those of all Spaniards!

"The mass over, we went up to the convent house together with the town leaders and other personages of prominence. We were served with finesse, attention and prodigality so characteristic of the Most Reverend Padre Salvi, offered cigars and a sumptuous snack which the *Hermano Mayor* had prepared under the convent for all those who needed to assuage the needs of the stomach.

"During the day, nothing was lacking to make the fiesta exuberant, and to keep up the spiritedness characteristic of the Spaniards, which on occasions such as this one, is irrepressible, demonstrated now in songs, or dances, now in other simple and lively pastimes. They have noble and strong hearts that sorrows and misfortunes cannot vanquish; that given three Spaniards together in one place is sufficient to drive away sadness and discomfort. So there was dancing, too, in many homes, but principally in that of the illustrious Filipino millionaire where we had been invited to eat. I must also add that the banquet, succulent and fittingly served, was in a way a second edition of the nuptials of Cana, or those of Camacho in Don Quijote, improved and augmented various times over. While we were enjoying the feast directed by the competent food master of La Campana, the orchestra was playing harmonious melodies.

"The beauteous damsel of the house was wearing a mestiza dress[3] and a cascade of diamonds, and was as always the queen of the feast. We regretted from the bottoms of our hearts that she was suffering from a slight sprain in a pretty ankle which kept her from dancing, for if we are to judge what all her refinements show as a whole, Señorita de los Santos should dance like a sylph.

"The *Alcalde* of the province arrived this afternoon in order to honor with his presence the ceremonies of the following morning. He has deplored the indisposition of the distinguished property owner, Señor Ibarra, who, thank God, is better, according to what has been told us.

"This evening there was a solemn procession, but I will speak about it in my next letter tomorrow, for besides the detonations which have stunned me and turned me somewhat deaf, I am dropping dead with sleep. So, while

I recover strength in the embrace of Morpheus or in a convent bed, I wish you, my distinguished friend, good night—until tomorrow, which will be the great day.

"Your devoted friend who kisses your hand!

"The Correspondent

"San Diego, November 11."

Thus wrote the worthy correspondent. Let us see now what Capitan Martin wrote to his friend Luis Chiquito:

"Dear Choy:

"Come running if you can, as the fiesta is very merry. Just imagine: Capitan Joaquin almost lost all his money when Capitan Tiago tripled his bet, and this in the openings, so that Cabeza Manuel, the owner of the house, returned each time with less joy. Padre Damaso broke a lamp with a fist blow because until now he has not won a single card; the consul lost with his cocks, and to the bank all his winnings from the feast in Biñang and in that of Our Lady of the Pillar in Sta. Cruz.

"We hoped Capitan Tiago would introduce us to his future son-in-law, the rich heir of Don Rafael Ibarra, but he seems to follow in his father's footsteps, for he has not allowed us to see him. A pity! It seems he will never be of benefit to anybody.

"Carlos the Chinaman is making a huge fortune with the *liampo*. I suspect that he carries something hidden, perhaps a magnet. He complains continuously of pains in his head, which is bandaged, and when the *liampo* dice stops, he bends down gradually, almost touching it as if he would like to inspect it. I am rather suspicious because I have heard stories of this sort.

"Goodbye, Choy; my cocks are doing well and my wife is happy and enjoys herself.

"Your friend,

"Martin Aristorenas."

Ibarra had also received a perfumed note brought by Andeng, Maria Clara's foster sister. She gave it to him on the first day of the feast. It said:

"Crisostomo, it is more than a day that you have not been seen. I have heard that you are somewhat sick. I have been praying for you and have lit two candles for you. Papa tells me that your ailment is not too serious. Last night and today they have annoyed me by asking me to play the piano and inviting me to dance. I did not know there were so many bores on earth! Had it not been for Padre Damaso, who tried to entertain me by telling stories and many things besides, I would have locked myself inside my room and gone to sleep. Tell me what ails you, and I will ask Papa to visit you. For the present I send Andeng to you, to brew your tea. She knows how to do it, perhaps better than your servants do.

"Maria Clara

"P.S. If you do not come tomorrow I will not attend the ceremony. So long."

- 30 -
The Morning

The bands played *diana*—a reveille—with the first streaks of dawn, awakening with joyful airs the town's tired inhabitants. Life and high spirits were reborn; the bells again pealed and the fireworks started.

It was the last day of the fiesta, and the feast proper. It was expected that there would be much to see, more than on the previous day. The venerable Tertiaries of the Third Order were more numerous than their brothers of the Confraternity of the Holy Rosary and were smiling smugly, certain of humiliating their rivals. They had purchased a greater quantity of candles; the Chinese wax-makers were reaping a bountiful harvest, and in a spirit of gratitude thought of having themselves baptized, although many of them asserted that it was not faith in Roman Catholicism but the desire to take native wives. But to this the pious women averred:

"Even if this were so, so many Chinese getting married

all at one time cannot be anything but a miracle; and their wives will eventually convert them."

The people donned their best attire, brought out of their boxes all their jewelry. The gamblers and cockfighters wore embroidered shirts with large brilliant studs, heavy chains of gold and white straw hats. Only the old philosopher Tasio went as usual in his striped sinamay shirt buttoned up to the neck, loose footwear and wide-brimmed gray hat.

"You are sadder than ever," the *Teniente Mayor* told him. "Don't you wish us to enjoy ourselves now and then since there is so much for us to weep about?"

"To be happy does not mean to indulge in foolishness!" replied the old man. "It is the same senseless orgy of the past years! And all for what? To throw money away when there is so much need and misery! Of course it is the orgy, the bacchanal to drown the lamentations of everyone!"

"You already know that I share your opinion," Don Filipo replied, half in earnest and half smiling. "I defended it, but what can one do against the *Gobernadorcillo* and the parish priest?"

"Resign!" retorted the philosopher, moving away.

Don Filipo was left perplexed, following the old man with his eyes.

"Resign!" he muttered, heading for the church. "Resign, yes! If this position were an honor and not a burden—yes, I would resign!"

The churchyard was full of people: men and women, children and old people, attired in their best clothes, milling around, going out and coming in through the narrow gates. One smelled burnt powder, flowers, incense, and perfume; bombs, rockets and firecrackers made the women run and scream, the youngsters laugh. A band was playing in front of the convent; others were leading the municipal authorities to crisscross the streets decked with a multitude of waving banners. The mixture of light and motley colors attracted the eyes, and the din of harmonies thundered in the ears. The bells pealed unceasingly; carriages and calesas crossed the streets and the horses were sometimes so frightened that they reared up on their hind legs and pawed the air, making a free spectacle not included in the program but among the most interesting to the spectators.

The *Hermano Mayor* had sent messengers to summon guests from the streets as in the banquet of the gospel story. The invitation was almost a command—to partake of chocolate, coffee, tea, sweetmeats and so forth. Very often the summons assumed the proportions of a controversy.

High mass was about to begin. It was called the Dalmatic Mass, like the one mentioned yesterday by the worthy press correspondent, with the exception that today the celebrant would be Padre Salvi, and among the persons attending would be the *Alcalde* of the province with many other Spaniards and educated people to listen to Padre Damaso, a preacher of great renown all over the province. The *Alferez* himself, smarting at the past sermons of Padre Salvi, was also present to give proof of his good will, and if possible to make up for the bad times dealt him in the past by the parish priest. Such was Padre Damaso's fame as a preacher that the correspondent wrote the newspaper director in advance the following:

"As I announced to you in my humble report yesterday, thus it happened. We had the rare pleasure of listening to the Most Reverend Padre Damaso Verdolagas, erstwhile parish priest of this town, now transferred to a larger one as a reward for good service. The illustrious sacred orator took the Chair of the Holy Spirit, delivering a most profound and eloquent sermon which edified and awed all the faithful who were anxiously waiting to hear the invigorating fountain of eternal life gush forth from his fecund lips. What sublime concepts! What boldness of ideas! What novelty of phraseology! Elegance of style! Gallantry of imagination! Spontaneity of gestures! Grace and wit in speech—such were the qualities of this Spanish Bossuet[1] who has justly won a high reputation not only among the enlightened Spaniards but even among the illiterate natives and the shrewd offspring of the Celestial Empire."

However, this self-confident correspondent was almost compelled to rewrite what he had previously written. Padre Damaso was complaining of a slight cold he had caught the night before: after singing some popular Andalusian songs he had taken three glassfuls of sherbet and stayed outdoors to watch the show. Consequently, he wanted to give up his assignment as God's interpreter to men, but he was not able to locate a replacement who knew the life and miracles of San Diego. The parish priest did, it is true, but he was to officiate; the other religious unanimously agreed that they could not find a better voice than Padre Damaso's and that it would be a great pity to leave undelivered so eloquent a sermon—the one he had already prepared and learnt by heart.

So his old housekeeper prepared lemonade for him, anointed his chest and neck with oil, wrapped him in hot blankets, massaged him and so forth. Padre Damaso took raw eggs beaten in wine, and throughout the morning neither spoke nor broke his fast; he hardly finished a glass of milk, a cup of chocolate and a dozen cookies, and heroically renounced his daily fried chicken and half a

Laguna cheese, because, according to the housekeeper, chicken and cheese had salt and fat and could provoke a cough.

"All in order to gain heaven and to convert us!" said the emotional sisters of the Third Order upon learning of these sufferings.

"The Virgin of Peace is punishing him," muttered the women of the Confraternity of the Holy Rosary, who could not forgive him for having aligned himself with their enemies.

At half past eight in the morning the procession emerged from under the shelter of the canvas canopy. It was similar to the one of yesterday, but there was a novelty: the Confraternity of the Tertiaries of Saint Francis, old men, old women and some young girls on the way to becoming old maids, were clad in long cotton habits. The poor wore coarse cloth, the rich silk or the Franciscan cotton so called because it is most worn by the Reverend Franciscan friars. All those sacred habits were legitimate; they came from the Franciscan Mother House in Manila where they can be acquired through almsgiving, in exchange for money at fixed prices, if we might allow ourselves this market jargon. This fixed price could go up, never down. Similar habits were also being sold in the same convent and in Saint Clare's monastery, which possess besides the special grace of obtaining many indulgences for the dead wrapped in their folds—the most special grace of being costlier the older, the more useless and ragged they were. We are writing about this just in case some pious readers should need such sacred relics, or some smart rag-picker of Europe wishes to bag a fortune by exporting to the Philippines a shipload of mended and filthy rags. They would cost sixteen pesos each or more, depending on their raggedness.

The statue of San Diego de Alcala was on a float decorated with embossed silver plates. The saint, rather thin-looking, had a bust of ivory with a severe majestic expression despite the abundant curls as kinky as the hair of the Negritos. His vestments were of satin and gold.

He was followed by our venerable father Saint Francis, then the Madonna, as it was yesterday, except that the priest who now walked under the pallium was Padre Salvi and not the elegant Padre Sibyla, he of the courtly ways. Even if the former lacked beauty of features, however, he had more than enough unction; his hands were joined together in a mystical pose, his eyes lowered, and he walked slightly bowed. The pallium bearers were the same *barangay* heads, perspiring with satisfaction upon seeing themselves transformed into semi-*sacristanes*, collectors of tributes, redeemers of the poor and lost humanity, and consequently Christs who shed their blood for other people's sins. The vicar, wearing a surplice, was going from one float to another, waving his censer, the fumes of which regaled from time to time the nostrils of the parish priest, who became even more serious and more grave.

Thus lumbered the procession slowly, with pauses, to the sounds of detonators, chants and religious melodies launched into the air from the bands following each float. Meanwhile, with much zeal the Hermano Mayor was distributing candles which most of the retinue took home with them, providing them with light for four days of card-playing. The curious onlookers would kneel devoutly when the Mother of God passed by, fervently praying Credos and Salves.

The *Alcalde*, Capitán Tiago, Maria Clara, Ibarra,

several Spaniards and young ladies, were watching at one of the gaily decorated windows of the house. The procession stopped in front of the dwelling, and Padre Salvi happened to raise his eyes, but did not make the least gesture of greeting or recognition. He only raised his head, assumed a more erect posture, and the celebrant's cape fell on his shoulders more elegantly and with a certain grace.

In the street, beneath the window, there was a young woman of pleasing countenance, dressed luxuriously, carrying an infant in her arms. She must have been its nurse, because the baby was fair and blond and she was dark, her hair darker than jet.

Upon seeing the priest, the baby extended its little hands, gargled with that laughter of infancy which does not provoke pain nor is provoked by it, babbling: "Pa....pa! papa! papa!" in the midst of a brief silence.

The young woman trembled, clamped her hands over the baby's mouth and moved away, running in confusion. The baby started to cry.

The malicious winked at each other and the Spaniards who witnessed the short scene smiled. The usually pale Padre Salvi reddened like a poppy.

And yet the people were wrong. The priest did not even know the woman, who was a stranger to that place.

- 31 -

In the Church

The structure known to man as the dwelling of the Creator of all that exists was full of people from end to end.

They pushed each other, pressed upon each other, trod on each other: the few who were going out and the many who were entering exhaling *Ayes!* From afar an arm would stretch out to dip a finger in holy water, but for the most part the crush would come and separate hand from font; then a growl would be heard, a woman whose feet had been stepped on would curse, but it did not stop the shoving which went on. Some old men who were able to moisten their fingers in the now mud-colored water, where the whole populace and the visitors as well would dip their fingers, were daubing themselves piously with the consecrated water, and with some effort, the nape of the neck, the crown of the head, the forehead, the nose, the chin, the breast, the navel, with the conviction that sanctifying all those parts so they would not feel pain in the neck, nor headaches, nor tuberculosis nor indigestion. The young people who perhaps were not so sickly or did not believe in that sacred prophylaxis, hardly dipped their fingertips but, so that their elders would not have reason to find fault with them, gestured as if signing their foreheads without touching them, thinking: "It may be holy water and whatever you may wish, but its color...!"

One could hardly breathe; the air was warm and reeked of human animal stench, but the preacher was worth all that trouble and discomfort. His sermon was costing the people two hundred fifty pesos! Old Tasio had said:

"Two hundred and fifty pesos for a sermon! Just one man and only once! A third part of what the comedians earn for three consecutive nights! You must be very rich!"

"What does the comedy have to do with it?" ill-humoredly retorted the nervous Prefect of the Third Order. "With the comedy souls go to hell and with the sermon to heaven! If he had requested a thousand pesos we would gladly have paid him that much and been grateful besides."

"After all, you are right!" the philosopher answered. "I am more amused by the sermon than by the comedy."

"Well, for me not the comedy either!" the other shouted furiously.

"I believe you! You know as much of one as of the other!"

And the impious one moved away, ignoring the insults and gloomy forebodings on his future life uttered by the irritated Tertiary Prefect.

While they were waiting for the *Alcalde*, the people sweated and yawned; fans, hats and handkerchiefs agitated the air; the children screamed and cried. The *sacristanes* had quite a hard time driving them out of the temple. This caused the phlegmatic and conscientious director of the Confraternity of the Holy Rosary to cogitate: "Let the children come to Me, said Our Lord Jesus Christ. It is true, but in this case it must be understood to mean children who do not cry!"

An old woman, one of those cotton-clad devotees, Sister Pute, was telling her granddaughter, a six-year-old child who was kneeling beside her: "You wretch! Pay attention, for you will be listening to a sermon like one heard on Good Friday!"

She pinched her to arouse piety in the child, who grimaced, pouted and scowled.

Some men were squatting and dozing near the confessional. An old man, nodding his head, made an old woman, who was mouthing prayers and running her fingers swiftly over her rosary beads, think that the man's way was the most reverent way of submitting to heaven's designs, and gradually start to imitate him.

Ibarra was in a corner; Maria Clara was kneeling near the main altar space, which the priest had courteously ordered the *sacristanes* to clear. Capitan Tiago, attired in formal evening wear, was seated on one of the pews reserved for the authorities, so that the boys who did not recognize him mistook him for another *gobernadorcillo* and dared not approach him.

Finally the *Alcalde Mayor* emerged with his staff from the vestry and occupied one of the magnificent arm chairs on the carpet. The *Alcalde* was in full gala attire, wearing the sash and the Grand Cross of Charles III and four or five more decorations.

The town did not recognize him.

"Aba!" exclaimed a laborer, "a civilian dressed as a comedian!"

"Simpleton!" retorted his neighbor, elbowing him, "He is Prince Villardo whom we saw last night at the theater!"

The *Alcalde* had advanced in category in the eyes of the people, becoming an enchanted prince, conqueror of giants!

The mass started. Those who were seated stood up; those who were asleep were awakened by the tinkling of the bell and the sonorous chanting of the singers. Padre Salvi, notwithstanding the gravity of his mien, seemed very much satisfied. He was being served by the deacon and subdeacon, and no less than two Augustinians.

Each one sang when it was his turn to sing, with a voice more or less nasal and with obscure pronunciation, except for the officiating priest whose voice had a tremor, and was sometimes out of tune, to the great surprise of those who knew him. He moved, however, with precision and elegance, recited the *Dominus vobiscum*, God be with you, with unction, tilting his head to one side and looking towards the ceiling. To see him welcome the incense smoke one would say that Galen had reason to admit that the passage of smoke can reach the brain through the canals of the nostrils passing through the sieves of the nasal cartilage.[1] Padre Salvi drew himself up, threw his head back and walked towards the center of the altar with such pomposity and gravity that Capitan Tiago found him more imposing than the Chinese comedian of the previous night, who had been dressed as an emperor, overpainted, with little banners down his back, a horsehair beard and high-heeled slippers.

"Undoubtedly," he thought, "one single priest of ours has more majesty than all the emperors put together."

At long last came the much awaited time to listen to Padre Damaso. The three priests sat on the armchairs in edifying postures, as the honored correspondent would put it. The *Alcalde* and other officials holding batons and canes imitated the priests; the music ceased.

That interval from sound to silence awakened our old woman, Sister Pute, who was already snoring, thanks to the music. Like Sigesmundo[2], or rather like the cook of the Tale of Dornroschen, the first thing she did was to strike her granddaughter, who also was sleeping, on the back of her head. The child screamed, but she stopped, her attention arrested by the sight of a woman beating her breast with clenched fists with much conviction and enthusiasm.

All tried to make themselves comfortable—those who had no benches to sit on, squatted, the women on the ground on their own legs.

Padre Damaso went through the crowd, preceded by two *sacristanes* and followed by another friar who was carrying a large notebook. He disappeared for a moment while climbing the spiral stairs, but his round head soon surfaced, then the thick neck followed by the bulk of his body. He directed his gaze everywhere around him, feeling confident and secure and coughing slightly. He saw Ibarra; made a particular movement of the eyes indicating that he was not forgetting the young man in his prayers; then a look of satisfaction at Padre Sibyla, and another of contempt at Padre Manuel Martin, yesterday's preacher. After this review he unobtrusively turned to his companion priest, saying to the latter: "Attention, brother!" The priest opened the notebook.

But the sermon deserves a separate chapter. A youth who had learned stenography and who adored the great orators, took stenographic notes of the sermon. Thanks to this we can reproduce here a portion of the sacred oratory of those regions.

- 32 -

The Sermon

Padre Damaso began his sermon, slowly enunciating in a soft voice: "*Et spiritum tuum bonum dedisti, qui doceret eos, et manna tuum non prohibuiste ab ore eorum, et aquam dedisti eis in siti.* And Thou gavest Thy good Spirit to teach them, and Thy manna Thou didst not withhold from their mouths and Thou gavest them water for their thirst.

"Words uttered by the Lord through the mouth of Esdras, Book II, chap. 9, verse 20."

Padre Sibyla regarded the preacher with some surprise; Padre Manuel Martin paled and swallowed hard—this was a better text than his own.

Padre Damaso either noticed the impression he had created, or was still hoarse, but the fact is that he coughed several times and laid both hands on the edge of the pulpit. The Holy Spirit was over his head, newly painted white, clean, with beak and claws of roseate hue.

"Your highly exalted Excellency (the *Alcalde*), most virtuous priests, Christians, brothers in Jesus Christ!"

Here he made a solemn pause, passed his gaze anew around the congregation, whose attention and gathering satisfied him. The first part of the sermon was to be delivered in Spanish; the second part, in Tagalog, for as the Bible says: "*Loquebantur omnes linguas;* they shall speak in all tongues!"

After the greeting and the pause he majestically extended his right hand towards the altar, fixing his eyes on the *Alcalde*, then he gradually crossed his arms without saying a word, but passing from quietude to movement, he threw back his head and pointed to the main door, slashing the air with the edge of his hand with such impetus that the *sacristanes*, mistaking his gesture for a command, closed the doors. The *Alferez* felt alarmed. He was in doubt about whether to leave or to remain, but the preacher had already started to speak in a strong voice, full and resonant. Undoubtedly, his old housekeeper was knowledgeable about medicine.

"The altar is radiant and resplendent; the main portals are spacious and wide; the air is the vehicle of the divine holy word that will flow from my lips. Listen then, all of you, with the ears of the soul and the heart, so that the words of the Lord do not fall on rocky soil, to be devoured by the birds of hell, but that you instead sprout and grow like holy seed in the field of our venerable and seraphic Saint Francis. You! miserable sinners! captives of the heathens of the soul infesting the seas of eternal life, borne on powerful vessels of the flesh and the world; you! you who are bound by the chains of lust and concupiscence, manning the galleys of infernal Satan, regard him who redeems souls from the captivity of the devil—the intrepid

Gideon, the valiant David, Christendom's victorious Roland, the celestial civil guard braver than all the Civil Guards present and future put together"—(the *Alferez* frowns)—"yes, Señor *Alferez*, braver and stronger—who without any weapon but the cross for a cudgel, conquers boldly the eternal bandit of darkness and all of Lucifer's followers and would have totally uprooted them had spirits not been immortal. This marvel of divine creation, this unbelievable portent is the Blessed Diego of Alcala who, making use of a comparison, since comparisons lead to an understanding of the incomprehensible, as another says, I say that this great saint is only a foot soldier, a steward cook in our powerful order, which is commanded from heaven by our beatific father Saint Francis, to which I have the honor of belonging as a corporal or a sergeant by the grace of God!"

The illiterate *Indios* mentioned by the correspondent were not able to catch anything except for the words civil guard, bandits, San Diego and Saint Francis; they observed the scowl that the *Alferez* put on and the preacher's contentious gesture, and concluded that he was scolding the *Alferez* for not going after the bandits. San Diego and Saint Francis would take care of the matter on hand, and very well too, as proven by an existing painting in the Order's Manila convent in which Saint Francis, using only his cincture as weapon, repelled the Chinese invasion during the first years of the Spanish discovery of the Philippines. They rejoiced and thanked God for this help, never doubting that once the bandits were done away with, Saint Francis would also destroy the Civil Guards. Their attention was doubly focused now on Padre Damaso, who continued:

"Your most exalted Excellency: The great issues are

always great beside the small ones; and the small ones are always small even alongside the great. Thus says history, but since history hits the mark accurately once out of a hundred misses, it cannot be relied upon, being the work of man—and men are prone to making mistakes —*errarle es hominem*[1], to err is human, as Cicero says; and as it is said in my own country: "Whoever has a tongue can be wrong,"—consequently there are more profound truths that history does not contain. These truths, your Excellency, have been revealed by the divine Holy Spirit in His supreme wisdom which was never comprehended by human intelligence since Seneca and Aristotle—those wise religious of antiquity—until our present sinful days; and these truths are that small things are not always small but great, not beside the small ones, but beside the great things of heaven and earth, of the clouds and of the air, of the waters and of space, of life and of death!"

"Amen!" replied the Tertiary prefect, crossing himself.

With this rhetoric learned from a great preacher in Manila, Padre Damaso wanted to surprise his audience and, in effect, his holy spirit, who, enthralled with so many truths, needed to be kicked in the foot to remind him of his mission.

"Evident before your eyes!" said the ghost prompter from below.

"Evident before your eyes is the conclusive and irrefutable proof of this eternal philosophic truth. Evident is that sun of virtues—and I say sun, not the moon—because there is no credit for the moon shining at night; in the kingdom of the blind, the one-eyed man is king. In the night any light can shine, or a tiny star. The greater merit is to be able to shine even in the daytime, as the sun does. Thus Brother Diego shines even in the midst of so many great saints! So you have evident to your sight, to your impious incredulity, the Almighty's masterpiece, to confound the great of the earth—yes! my brethren! evident, evident, patent to all!"

A man stood up, pale and trembling, and hid himself inside the confessional booth. He was an alcohol vendor, who had been dozing and dreaming that the authorities were demanding of him his patent to sell, and he had none. It is certain that he did not come out of his hiding place until the sermon was finished.

"Humble and devout saint! Your wooden cross—(the image had one of silver)—your modest habit honors the great Saint Francis whose sons and imitators we are! We propagate your holy race all over the world, in all its corners, in the cities, in the towns, without distinguishing black from white"—(the *Alcalde* holds his breath)—"suffering privations and martyrdoms, your holy race of faith and armed religion"—(ah! sighs the *Alcalde*—"which maintains the world in equilibrium and keeps it from falling into the abyss of perdition!"

The listeners, including Capitan Tiago himself, gradually started yawning. Maria Clara was not paying attention to the sermon. She knew Ibarra was close by and she was thinking of him while, fanning herself, she looked at the bull of one of the evangelists. It had all the characteristics of a small carabao.

"All of us should learn by heart the Holy Scriptures, the life of the saints, so that I do not have to preach to you, sinners! You should learn things so important and necessary like the Our Father, even if many of you have already forgotten it, living as you do, like protestants and heretics, who have no respect for the ministers of God, like the Chinese, but you are going to be condemned, all the worse for you, you wretched ones!"

"Whatsa matta that pale Lamaso!" muttered Carlos the Chinaman, looking with ire at the preacher, who continued improvising, unleashing a series of insults and curses.

"You will die in final impenitence, you race of heretics! God is already punishing you on this earth with jails and imprisonments! Your families, the women should flee from you, the authorities should hang you all to prevent the seed of Satan from multiplying in the Lord's vineyard! Jesus Christ said: 'If there is a part of your body that is evil and induces you to sin, cut if off and throw it into the fire!'"

Father Damaso was nervous; he had forgotten his sermon and his rhetoric.

"Did you hear that?" a young student from Manila asked his companion. "Will you cut it off?"

"Nay! Let him do it first!" the other answered, pointing to the preacher.

Ibarra became uneasy; he looked around him for an inconspicuous corner, but the church was full. Maria Clara heard and saw nothing. She was examining the picture of the blessed souls in purgatory, souls in the form of women's and men's naked bodies with mitres, cardinals' hats or hoods, being roasted in the fire and holding on to the belt of Saint Francis, which did not break in spite of the weight.

The Holy-Spirit-friar-prompter, with that improvisation, lost the thread of the sermon and jumped over three long paragraphs, prompting badly Padre Damaso, who paused breathless from his tirade.

"Who among you, sinners who are listening to me, would lick the wounds of a poor and ragged mendicant?"

Padre Damaso continued. "Who? Let him respond and raise his hand! No one! I knew it already: except that a saint like Diego of Alcala can do it: he licked all the putrefaction, telling a wondering brother: 'This is the way to cure this sick person!' What Christian charity! What unmatched piety! What virtue of virtues! What inimitable example! What a peerless talisman!..."

The above was followed by a series of exclamations— positioning his arms in the form of a cross, he raised and lowered them as if he wanted to fly or scare the birds away.

"Before he died he spoke Latin without knowing Latin. Marvel at this, you sinners! Although you study it and are flogged for it, you will never speak Latin, you will die without speaking it. To speak Latin is a grace of God. That is why the church speaks in Latin! I also speak Latin! And so! Would God deny this comfort to His dear Diego? Allow him to die without being able to speak in Latin? Impossible. If God could not be just he would not be God. Thus he spoke Latin, and to this the writers of that epoch testify." And he ended his peroration with a piece which he had cost him great effort and which he plagiarized from a great writer, Sinibaldo de Mas:[2]

"I salute you then, illustrious Diego! honor of our order! You are a model of virtues, modest with honor; humble but noble; submissive with self esteem; sober with ambition; loyal even to enemies; compassionate and forgiving; zealous and scrupulous; a devout believer; credulous without guile; chaste but with love; discreet with secrets; long-suffering and patient; valiant and fearless; continent by choice; daring and resolute; obedient with submission; retiring and honorable; zealous of your interests yet detached; fortunate and able; punctilious but well-mannered; shrewd and far-sighted; merciful with piety; circumspect and modest; fearless in righting wrongs; poor and resigned yet industrious; generous though destitute; diligent yet relaxed; frugal but liberal; innocent but discerning; reformer and successful; indifferent yet avid to learn; God created you to enjoy the delights of platonic love! Help me to sing of your greatness and your name higher than the stars, and brighter than the sun which revolves around your feet! Help me, all of you! Ask God for sufficient inspiration by praying the Hail Mary!"

All knelt, raising a murmur like the humming of a thousand flies. The *Alcalde* sank with difficulty to his knees, moving his head in disgust; the *Alferez* was pale and contrite.

"To the devil with the priest!" muttered one of the young men from Manila.

"Silence!" answered the other, "his woman might hear us..."

In the meantime Padre Damaso, instead of praying the Hail Mary, was scolding his holy ghost prompter for having skipped three of his best paragraphs. He took two merengues and a glass of Malaga wine, sure of finding in both a higher inspiration than in all the holy spirits, be they of wood in the shape of a dove, or of flesh in the figure of his distracted friar prompter. He was about to start his sermon in Tagalog.

The pious old woman gave her granddaughter another nudge; she woke up in bad humor and asked:

"Is it already time to weep?"

"Not yet, but do not fall asleep, you wretch!" retorted the good grandmother.

We have only a few notes on the second part of the sermon or that in Tagalog. Padre Damaso improvised in this language, not because he knew that better, but because believing Filipinos in the provinces to be ignorant of rhetoric, he was not afraid of committing errors before them. It was a different story with the Spaniards: he had heard of rules on oratory, and among his listeners there might have been one familiar with such rules—perchance the *Alcalde Mayor*—for whom he wrote his sermons, corrected and polished them, then committed them to memory and rehearsed them one or two days before.

It is well known that none of his listeners understood the whole of the sermon: they were so obtuse of understanding and the preacher so profound that, according to Sister Rufa, the audience waited in vain for an occasion to weep. The pious old woman's wretched granddaughter fell asleep again.

However, this second part obtained more results than the first part for certain listeners, at least, as we will see later on.

He started with a *Maná capatir con cristiano*, My brothers in Christ, which was followed by an avalanche of untranslatable phrases. He spoke of the soul, of hell, of the *mahal na santo pintacasi*, venerable patron saint; of the native sinners, and the virtuous Franciscan priests.

"This is all Greek to me, I am leaving," said one of the irreverent Manilans to his companion.

And, seeing all the doors closed, he left through the vestry, shocking the scandalized people and the preacher, who paled and stopped in the middle of a sentence. Some expected a violent insult from him, but Padre Damaso contented himself with following the departing figure with his eyes, and proceeded with his sermon.

He unleashed a tirade of condemnations against the age; against the lack of respect; against the nascent irreligiosity. This subject seemed his forte, for he showed himself inspired, expressing himself forcefully and with clarity. He spoke of the sinners who do not go to confession; who die in prison without benefit of the sacraments; of accursed families, of arrogant and affected *mesticillos* or insignificant half-breeds, of young *sabihondos* or smart alecks, *pilosopillos* or pseudo philosophers, of *abogadillos* or petty lawyers, *estudiantillos* or pretentious students, and so forth. It is a well-known habit of certain persons; when they want to heap ridicule on their enemies they end their description with *illo* because the mind appears unable to give more and they are happy about it.

Ibarra heard all and understood the allusions to himself. Keeping up an apparent calm, he sought with his eyes God and the authorities; but there were nothing more than images, and the *Alcalde* was dozing.

In the meantime the preacher's enthusiasm was growing by leaps and bounds. He referred to the old times when every Filipino on meeting a priest, uncovered himself, bent one knee to the ground and kissed the hand of the religious. "But today," he added, "he removes only his *salakot* or his felt hat, which is tilted one way so as not to disarrange the hair! You are content with saying: Good morning *among*, master; and there are arrogant *estudiantillos* who know little Latin who, because of having studied in Manila or in Europe, believe it their right to shake our hand instead of kissing it. Ah! the day of judgment is coming soon; the world is coming to an end; many saints have prophesied it. It is going to rain fire and brimstone to punish your pride!"

And he exhorted the people not to imitate those savages; to flee from them, abhor them, because they are excommunicated. "Pay attention to what the holy councils proclaim," he said. "When an *Indio* meets a priest on the street, he must bend his head and offer his neck for the *among* to lean on. If the priest and the *Indio* are both on horseback, then the *Indio* should stop, reverently remove his salakot or hat; and finally, when the *Indio* is on horseback and the priest on foot, the *Indio* should get down from his horse and not mount it again until the priest tells him *sulong!* begone! or is already far away. That is what the holy councils say and he who does not obey will be excommunicated."

"And, when one is on the carabao?" a scrupulous laborer asked his neighbor.

"Then go ahead," answered the latter, who was a casuist.

However, despite the cries and the gestures of the preacher, many were dozing or distracting themselves. Those sermons were the same as the rest. Some devotees tried in vain to sigh and weep over the sins of the impious, but they had to desist, not having partners to share in the experience. Sister Pute thought otherwise. A man seated beside her had been dozing in such a position that he fell on her, crumpling her habit. The good old woman took hold of one of her slippers, and began beating him with it to awaken him, crying out:

"Ay! quit, you savage! beast, demon, carabao, dog, wretch!"

There was tumult. The preacher stopped, knitted his brows, taken aback by such a scandal. Indignation choked the word in his throat and he was able only to growl, smashing his fists on the pulpit edge. This produced results. The old woman let go of her slipper, grumbling and crossing herself repeatedly; she devoutly sank on her knees.

"Aaah! aaah!" he finally exclaimed indignantly, crossing his arms and shaking his head: "And for this I preach to you daily, savages! Here in the very house of God you quarrel and utter evil words, shameless wretches! You don't have any respect for anything anymore. This is the work of the lust and the incontinence of the times! I have already said this, aah!"

And on this theme he continued preaching for half an hour. The *Alcalde* was snoring; Maria Clara was swaying: the poor girl could not refrain from dozing, not finding more pictures to examine or images to look at or distract her. Ibarra was no longer affected by the words and the allusions. He was dreaming now of a little house on top of a hill and saw Maria Clara in the garden. Let the men in their wretched towns drag themselves along the bottom of the valley!

Padre Salvi had the little bell rung twice, but that was putting more fuel to the fire. Padre Damaso was obstinate, and prolonged his sermon. Padre Sibyla bit his lips and repeatedly adjusted his eyeglasses of rock crystal mounted in gold; Padre Manuel Martin was the only one who seemed to listen, because he was smiling.

At last the Lord Himself said: "Enough is enough!" The orator finally grew tired and came down from the pulpit.

All knelt to thank God. The *Alcalde* rubbed his eyes, extended an arm as if to relax himself, letting go of a deep Aah! and yawned.

The mass went on. When Balbino and Chananay sang the *Incarnatus est,* all knelt down; the priests bowed their heads. A man whispered in Ibarra's ears: "During the ceremony of the blessing stay near the priest; don't go down into the excavation, don't go near the cornerstone. Your life is at stake!"

Ibarra saw Elías who, having spoken thus, lost himself in the crowd.

- 33 -
The Hoist

The jaundiced man had kept his word: what he built over the yawning pit was not a simple tripod to hoist down the huge mass of granite or the device Ñor Juan had wanted to suspend with a pulley from the top. It was more than a mechanical device—a crane or derrick. It was an ornament besides, a grandiose imposing showpiece!

The complicated and elaborate scaffolding rose eight meters high, with a frame of four thick posts sunk into the ground serving as support and bound to each other with massive crossbeams forming diagonals, joined one to the other by thick nails sunk only halfway, perhaps so that the apparatus, having a provisional character, could be easily dismantled afterwards. Enormous cables hanging from all sides gave the whole structure a look of solidity and grandeur. The top was decorated with banners and floating pennants of motley colors and huge garlands of leaves and flowers artistically entwined.

At the top, in the shadow projected by the huge posts, the banners and the garlands, hung a large three-wheeled pulley, fastened with heavy cords and iron hooks, and on whose shiny edges passed three even thicker cables holding the enormous granite block which had been hollowed out in the center to fit a similar block, already down in the pit, that had also been hollowed out to form a small space in which to keep the recorded history of the day— newspapers, manuscripts, coins, medals and other mementos for future generations. The cables extended downward to another equally huge pulley at the bottom of the pit, from which they were attached to the drum of a winch anchored to the ground with heavy beams. This winch, which could be activated by two cranks, multiplied the strength of a man a hundredfold with the benefit of the play of cogged wheels, although what was gained in power was lost in speed.

"Look," said the sallow-faced man, turning the crank, "Look, Ñor Juan, how I can make this immense mass go up or down with my strength alone. It is so contrived that at will I can calibrate inch by inch the ascent and descent, such that a man from the bottom of the pit can easily fit the stones together while I maneuver it from here."

Ñor Juan could do no less than admire the man, who was smiling strangely. The curious onlookers made comments and praised the man.

"Who taught you this device?" Ñor Juan asked.

"My father, my late father!" he answered with his peculiar smile.

"And who taught your father?"

"Don Saturnino, Don Crisostomo's grandfather."

"I didn't know that Don Saturnino..."

"Oh, he knew so many things! He not only whipped

his workers and exposed them to the heat of the sun; he knew as well how to awaken the sleepy ones and to put to sleep those who were awake! In due time you will see what my father taught me. You will see!"

And the strange sallow-faced man continued to smile his particular smile.

On a table covered by a Persian rug lay the lead cylinder and the objects to be stored in that kind of tomb—a crystal case with thick walls would hold in trust for the future that mummy of an epoch: the memories of a past.

Tasio, cavillating in a reflective mood nearby, was murmuring to himself: "Perhaps some day, when the work which today begins to be born, ages after many vicissitudes, would have fallen into ruin already wreaked by nature and by the destructive hand of man; and over the ruins moss and ivy would grow, and then when time obliterates the ivy and the moss and the ruins, and scatters their ashes to the winds, erasing from the pages of history their memory and that of the builders, already long lost to men's recollection; perhaps, when the races that now inhabit this land shall have been buried or will have disappeared from the face of the earth, perchance some miner's pick will bring forth from the granite the spark, will disinter from the bosom of this rock mysteries and enigmas.

"Perchance the nation's sages inhabiting these regions will examine as today's egyptologists do, the remains of a great civilization concerned only with eternity, unsuspecting of the long, long night that would befall them. Perhaps some wise mentor will say to his five- or six-year-old pupils in a language spoken by all men: 'Gentlemen, having studied and examined carefully the objects found in the subsoil of our land; having deciphered

some symbols and translated some words, we can say
without the least danger of presumption that such objects
belonged to a barbaric age, to the obscure era we often
call mythical. In effect, gentlemen, in order for you to form
an approximate idea of our ancestors' backwardness, it
will be enough that I tell you: those residing here not only
recognized sovereign kings but also in order to resolve
problems of their internal government they had yet to
cross to the other extreme of the world. It is as if we were
speaking of a body that to move would need to consult its
actual head in the other part of the globe, maybe in places
now covered by the waves.

"'This unbelievable imperfection, for all its
incredibility, becomes believable if we take into
consideration the circumstances of those beings, which I
can scarcely qualify as human! These beings of those
primitive times still had a direct contact with their Creator
(or at least believed they did), because they had His
ministers, beings different from the others, denominated
always by the mysterious characters M R P Padre, about
the interpretation of which our sages are not in accord.
According to our mediocre professor of languages, since
he does not speak more than a hundred of the defective
languages of the past, M R P would mean Most Rich
Proprietor, for these ministers were a species of demigods,
extremely virtuous, highly eloquent orators, most
illustrious and enlightened, and despite their great power
and prestige, never committed the least mistake. This
strengthens my supposition that they were of a breed
distinct from the rest.

"'And if this is not enough to support my opinion,
there is another argument, never denied by anyone and
daily confirmed, that such mysterious beings made God

come down to Earth by pronouncing certain words, for God could not speak except through their mouths; God whose flesh they ate, whose blood they drank; and not a few times they also gave to the common man to eat...'"

These and other things besides, this unbelieving philosopher would put into the mouths of the corrupt men of the future. Old Tasio may be mistaken, which is possible; but let us return to our narrative:

In the kiosks we saw occupied yesterday by the schoolmaster and his pupils, a succulent and abundant luncheon was being prepared. On the table reserved for students, however, there was not a single bottle of wine, but instead fruits in abundance. In the bower joining the kiosks were the seats for the musicians, and a table laden with sweets and confections, with jugs of water crowned with flowers and leaves for the thirsty public.

The schoolmaster had set up for the festive games greased poles, hurdles for races, hanging pots and pans.

The multitude, showing off attires of happy colors, milled around, now under the shade of trees and now under the green bowers, to escape the burning heat of the brilliant sun. The boys climbed the branches over the stones for a better view of the ceremonies, and to make up for their lack of height. They looked at the students with envy. Those were clean-looking and attired in new clothes, occupying the places reserved for them. Their parents were enthusiastic, poor simple peasants; they would see their children eat at a white cloth-covered table as would the priest and the *Alcalde*. It was enough just to think of it not to feel hungry, and such an event would be told by fathers to their sons.

The sound of distant music was soon heard. It preceded a motley crowd of people of all ages dressed in gaudy colors. The yellow-faced man showed signs of nervousness. He examined his contraption with a glance. A curious peasant followed the man's eyes, observing the latter's movements. It was Elías, who was also present at the ceremonies. His wide *salakot* and poor clothing disguised his identity. No one noticed or knew him. He had secured for himself the best place, almost close to the winch at the edge of the excavation.

With the musicians playing came the *Alcalde* of the province, the municipal officials, the friars except Padre Damaso, and the Spanish employees. Ibarra was talking to His Excellency, with whom he had become good friends—ever since Ibarra had complimented him for his sashes and decorations—aristocratic pretensions were among His Excellency's weaknesses. Capitan Tiago, the *Alferez* and some rich people also came along with a host of damsels holding silken umbrellas. Padre Salvi was, as usual, taciturn and pensive.

"You may count on my support in any good action that you perform," the *Alcalde* told Ibarra. "I will provide you with whatever you need, or else I will prevail upon others to help you."

Ibarra felt his heart quicken as they approached the excavation site. Instinctively he threw a glance at the extraordinary scaffolding standing high; saw the yellow-complexioned man greeted him with respect and looked at him fixedly for a moment. He was surprised to recognize Elías. The latter was eyeing Ibarra as if to remind him of his warning in the church.

The priest put on his ceremonial vestments and began the rites: the one-eyed *sacristan mayor* held the book, and an altar-boy the hyssop and the holy water container. The rest were standing around with uncovered heads. A deep hush fell on the crowd. Everyone noticed a break in Padre Salvi's voice despite his praying in a very low tone.

In the meantime the mementos—manuscripts, newspapers, medals, coins and other items—were placed in the crystal container, enclosed and hermetically sealed in the cylinder of lead.

"Señor Ibarra, put the case in its proper space; the priest is waiting!" whispered the *Alcalde* to the youth.

"With great pleasure," the latter replied, "but that would be usurping the Señor notary public's honorable duty! The Señor notary public should attest to this act."

The notary public gravely accepted the case; he went down the carpeted steps leading to the bottom of the pit and, with fitting solemnity, placed it in the hollowed-out granite. The priest then took the hyssop and sprinkled the cornerstone with the sacred water.

It was time for the guests to take turns in laying trowelfuls of mortar on the granite surface so that the second granite block still hanging above the pit would adhere to the one lying at the bottom.

Ibarra presented the *Alcalde* with a trowel with a wide silver blade inscribed with the date of the blessing, but His Excellency delivered first a discourse in Spanish:

"Citizens of San Diego," he said gravely, "we are presiding over a ceremony of importance that you already understand without our mentioning it. A school building is being put up. The school is the base of society; the school is the book wherein is written the future of a people! Show us the school and we will show you the kind of people there are!

"Citizens of San Diego! Bless God for giving you virtuous priests and the government of the Mother Country, which tirelessly spreads civilization in these fertile lands, sheltered under her glorious mantle! Bless God for taking pity on you and bringing you these humble priests who enlighten, guide and teach you the divine Word! Bless the government which has made, makes and will make sacrifices for you and your sons!

"And now the blessing of the first cornerstone of this so transcendental an edifice: We, the *Alcalde Mayor* of this province, in the name of His Majesty the King—God preserve him!—King of the Hispanic territories, in the name of the illustrious Spanish government and beneath the protection of its immaculate and always victorious banner, we consecrate this act and we begin the building of this school!

"Citizens of San Diego, long live the King! Long live Spain! Long live the religious! Long live the Catholic religion!"

"Long live! Long live!" chorused many voices. "Long live His Excellency the *Alcalde*!"

He then majestically descended the steps to the sound of music which began to play, and deposited a few layers of mortar on the granite block and with equal majesty ascended anew.

The employees applauded.

Ibarra offered another trowel of silver to the priest, who looked at Ibarra for a moment and went slowly down. Midway down the stairs he raised his eyes for a second to the overhanging second stone fastened securely by the massive cables. He did the same as the *Alcalde*. This time there was more applause. The employees were joined by some friars and Capitan Tiago.

Father Salvi, seeming to look for someone to hand the trowel to, looked with uncertainty at Maria Clara, but changed his mind and handed it to the notary public. The latter gallantly offered it to Maria Clara. She refused with a smile. The friars, employees and the *Alferez* took their turns. Capitan Tiago was not forgotten. Only Ibarra did not. Orders were about to be given to the sallow-faced man to lower the second stone when the priest remembered the young man and said to him jestingly affecting familiarity:

"Señor Ibarra, are you not going to lay your share of the mortar?"

"I would be another Juan Palomo[1], eating what I cooked," Ibarra retorted in the same tenor.

"Go right ahead!" bantered the *Alcalde,* giving Ibarra a gentle push. "Otherwise I will give orders not to have the stone lowered, and we will be here till the day of judgment!"

With that awful threat, Ibarra consented. He changed the small trowel of silver for a bigger one of iron, making some persons smile. He advanced quite calmly. Elías regarded him anxiously with an undefinable expression, seeming to concentrate his whole life on that one glance. The sallow-faced man was looking at the yawning pit before him.

After a rapid look at the granite block hanging over his head and another glance at Elías and the pale individual, Ibarra told Ñor Juan in a somewhat trembling voice: "Give me the mortar and fetch me another trowel from up there."

The young man was left alone. Elías was no longer looking at him; his eyes were fixed on the hands of the sallow-faced man. The latter was bending over the pit, anxiously following the youth's movements. The rasping of the trowel mixing mortar was heard beside the low murmur of the employees congratulating the *Alcalde* for his speech.

All of a sudden sound exploded! The tackle, tied to

the base of the scaffold, plunged downward, followed by the winch which knocked down the contrivance like a battering ram; the beams tottered, the cables snapped, and everything collapsed in a second with a frightful crash. A cloud of dust rose; a scream of horror from a thousand voices filled the air. The crowd ran wild in all directions, a few towards the excavation. Only Maria Clara and Padre Salvi remained frozen in their places, unable to move, pale and speechless.

When the dust had somewhat settled, they saw Ibarra standing on his feet amidst the timber, posts, cables, between the windlass and the granite block which, upon descending so rapidly, jolted and crushed everything. The young man still held the trowel, looking horrified at the corpse of a man lying at his feet, almost buried beneath the timber.

"You have not died? Are you still alive? For God's sake say something," some employees exclaimed, full of concern and terror.

"A miracle! A miracle!" some cried out.

"Come and remove the body of this hapless man!" said Ibarra, awakened as from a dream.

Upon hearing his voice, Maria Clara felt strength leaving her. She fell almost fainting into the arms of her friends.

Great confusion reigned. Everybody was speaking, gesticulating, running here and there, going down the pit, climbing up, all stricken and dismayed.

"Who is the dead man? Is he still alive?" queried the *Alferez*.

They recognized in the corpse the yellowish man who had stood at the side of the winch.

"Let them investigate the master builder!" was the

first thing the *Alcalde* was able to say.

They examined the body; they felt his chest: his heart was no longer beating. The blow had reached his head and blood was oozing from his nose, mouth and ears. They saw around his neck some strange marks: four deep depressions on one side and another on the opposite, a little bit larger. It looked as if a hand of steel had gripped him like a pair of pliers.

The priests warmly congratulated Ibarra, shaking his hand. The Franciscan of humble aspect, who had served as Father Damaso's Holy Spirit prompter, was saying with tears in his eyes:

"God is just! God is good!"

One of the employees said to Ibarra: "You were there just moments before! When I think of this, if I had been the last, Jesus!"

"My hair stands on end!" said an almost balding man.

"It is good that this happened to you and not to me," murmured a trembling old man.

"Don Pascual!" exclaimed some Spaniards.

"Gentlemen! I was saying that because Señor Ibarra has survived: If I had not come out crushed, the thought alone would have killed me!"

But Ibarra had already left to inquire after Maria Clara's condition.

"Let not this incident deter us from continuing our celebrations, Señor Ibarra," said the *Alcalde*. "God be praised! The dead man is neither a priest nor a Spaniard. We must celebrate your safety. What if the stone had crushed you!"

"There were presentiments, presentiments," said the notary public, "I had already been saying that. I saw that Señor Ibarra was going down against his will, this I saw!"

"The dead man was only an *Indio!*"

"On with the feast! Music! The dead will not rise again because we are sad! Capitan, hold the investigation right here—Call the *directorcillo²*... Arrest the master builder!"

"To the gallows with him!"

"To the gallows! Eh! Music now! Music! To the gallows with the master builder!"

"Señor *Alcalde*," replied Ibarra gravely, "if regrets will not raise the dead, the imprisonment of a man whose guilt we are not sure of, will not accomplish it either. I stand guarantor for this person and I ask for him to be released, at least during these days."

"Well! Well! But it must not happen again."

All sorts of comments were bruited about. The idea of a miracle was already an accepted fact. Yet Padre Salvi seemed none too happy over the miracle, which was attributed to a saint of his order and of his parish. There were none wanting who claimed to have seen a figure, attired in a dark habit like that of the Franciscans, go down into the pit when everything was collapsing. Without doubt it was the same Saint Diego! It was also known that Ibarra had heard mass and the yellowish man did not—clear as the light of the sun!

"You see? you didn't want to go to mass," a mother was saying to her son. "If I had not whipped you to make you go, now you would have found yourself before the town hall like that one in the cart." As a matter of fact, the yellowish man, or his corpse, wrapped in a mat was being conducted to the town hall.

Ibarra ran to his home to change his clothes.

"Bad beginning, hmm!" said Old Tasio, leaving.

- 34 -
Free Thinker

I barra had just finished dressing when a servant announced that a peasant was outside looking for him. Thinking it was one of the workers, Ibarra ordered that the visitor be taken to his office, which was at once a study or library and, at times, a chemical laboratory.

To his great surprise he came face to face with the somber and mysterious Elías.

"You once saved my life," said the latter in Tagalog[1], understanding Ibarra's reaction, "and I have paid you my debt halfway. But you don't have to thank me for anything; quite the contrary, I have come to ask you a favor."

"Say it," the young man replied in the same language, wondering at his countryman's grave manner.

Elías looked Ibarra briefly in the eye and replied:

"When the justice of man seeks to unravel this mystery, I beg you not to reveal the warning I gave you in church."

"Do not worry," answered the young man in a

somewhat peeved tone. "I know they are looking for you. However, I am no tale-bearer."

"Oh! it is not for my sake; it is not for me," Elías answered forcefully and with a certain pride. "It is for your sake. I fear no man!"

Our young man's surprise mounted. The tone in which that rustic peasant and former helmsman spoke was new, and seemed quite out of character with his status and circumstances.

"What do you mean?" he asked, peering curiously at the mysterious man.

"I do not speak in enigmas, and I am trying to express myself with clarity. It is necessary for your greater security that your enemies take you to be unwary and confident."

Ibarra drew back. "My enemies? Do I have enemies?"

"We all have, Señor! From the tiniest insect to man, from the poorest to the richest and most powerful! Enmity is the law of life!"

Ibarra silently regarded Elías.

"You are no helmsman, nor are you a peasant," he murmured.

"You have enemies in the higher as well as in the lower spheres," Elías continued, not minding the youth's words. "You contemplate putting up a vast enterprise, and you have a past behind you; your father, your grandfather had enemies, because they had passions, and in life it is not the criminals who arouse the hatred of others, but the men who are honest."

"Do you know who my enemies are?"

Elías did not reply at once. He reflected.

"I know of one, he who died," he answered. "Last night I discovered that he was up to something against you, because of some words he had exchanged with an unknown stranger who was lost in the crowd. 'This one will not be eaten by the fishes like his father; you will see tomorrow,' he said. These words caught my attention: not only on account of their meaning but also because of the one saying them. Some days ago he had presented himself before the master builder with the expressed wish of directing the work of laying the cornerstone. He did not ask for a big salary, and he boasted of his wide knowledge in this matter. I had no sufficient motive for assuming ill will on his part, but something inside me warned me that my assumptions were correct; that is why I chose to warn you at a moment and at a proper occasion in which you could not ply me with questions. As to the rest: you saw how it turned out."

For a long while Elías was silent; neither had Ibarra answered nor said a word. He was pensive.

"I am sorry that man died!" he said finally. "We could have learned more from him!"

"Had he lived he would have escaped the shaky hand of blind human justice. God had judged him; God executed him! Let God be the only judge!"

Crisostomo looked for a moment at the man speaking thus to him, and saw his sinewy arms full of bruises and large contusions.

"Do you also believe in miracles?" he said smiling, "see the miracle of which the people speak."

"If I believed in miracles, I would not believe in God: I would believe in a man deified; I would believe that man created God in his image and likeness," Elías answered solemnly. "But I believe in Him; I have felt more than once His hand upon me. When all was collapsing, threatening destruction to everything in its way, I laid hold of the criminal; I placed myself beside him: he was wounded, I came out safe and unhurt!"

"You? so you...?"

"Yes! I held him down when he wanted to escape after he had done his fatal job. I saw his crime. I tell you: let God be the only judge between men; let Him be the only one who has the right over life; let not any man ever dream of substituting for Him!"

"And yet, however, this time you..."

"No!" Elías interrupted, divining Ibarra's objections: "It is not the same. When a man condemns others to death, or destroys forever that man's future, he does it without risk unto himself and he avails himself of other people's strength to execute his sentence which, after all, might be mistaken or wrong. But I, in exposing the criminal to the same danger which he himself had prepared for others, shared the same risks. I did not kill him; I left that to God's hand to execute him."

"Don't you believe in chance?"

"To believe in chance is tantamount to believing in miracles; both beliefs assume that God does not know the future. What is chance or contingency? An event that absolutely no one has foreseen. What is miracle? A contradiction, an upsetting of natural laws. Contradiction and lack of foresight in the Intelligence which controls the world's machinery signifies two great imperfections."

"Who are you?" Ibarra again asked with some apprehension. "Have you had an education?"

"I have to believe much in God because I have lost my faith in man," answered the helmsman, evading the question.

Ibarra thought he understood the persecuted young man; he denied the existence of human justice; he refused to recognize man's right to judge his peers; he was protesting against force and the superiority of certain classes of society over others.

"But it is necessary that you admit the need for human justice, however imperfect that would be," he replied. "God, notwithstanding his numerous ministers on earth, cannot...that is, does not proclaim very clearly His judgment to solve millions of disputes provoked by our passions. It is necessary, it is contingent, it is just for man to sit in judgment sometimes over his equals!"

"Yes, in order to do good, not evil; to correct and to improve, not to destroy, because if his judgment errs, he has no power to remedy the wrong that he had committed. But," he added, changing his tone, "this discussion is beyond my capacity, and I am detaining you now that they are waiting for you. Do not forget what I have just told you: You have enemies; keep yourself safe for the good of your country."

And he took his leave.

"When shall I see you again?" asked Ibarra.

"Whenever you wish, and whenever I can be useful to you. I am still in your debt!"

- 35 -
The Luncheon

The visitors of importance were eating in one of the decorated pavilions.

The alcalde occupied one end of the table; Ibarra the other. On the young man's right sat Maria Clara, and on his left the notary public. Capitan Tiago, the *alferez*, the *gobernadorcillo*, the friars, the employees and the few remaining young ladies were seated, not according to rank but according to their preferences.

The lunch was lively and merry enough, but midway an employee of the telegraphic office came in carrying a message and looking for Capitan Tiago. Capitan Tiago asked the guests' permission to open the telegram, and it was of course granted.

The worthy Capitan at first knitted his brows, then raised them: he paled, then brightened up; folding the paper quickly he stood up.

"Gentlemen!" he stammered, all excited: "His Excellency, the Capitan General is arriving this afternoon to honor my household!"

And he started off, taking with him both the telegram and his napkin, but without his hat, followed by exclamations and questions.

An announcement of the *tulisanes* coming to town would not have produced such an effect.

"But, listen! When is he coming? Tell us, your Excellency!"

Capitan Tiago, however, was already out of hearing.

"His Excellency is coming and staying at Capitan Tiago's house!" some said disparagingly, without taking into account the presence of his daughter and future son-in-law.

"He could not have made a better choice," said Ibarra.

The friars looked at each other as if to say: "The Capitan General is up to one of his old tricks again; he offends us. He should lodge in the convent." However, since all thought the same way, they kept quiet and nobody expressed his thoughts.

"I was already informed of this matter yesterday, but His Excellency had not yet decided," said the alcalde.

"Do you know, Señor Alcalde, how long the Capitan General is staying here?" asked the *alferez*, somewhat worried.

"Not with certainty; His Excellency loves to give surprises."

"Here come other messages!"

They were for the alcalde, the *alferez* and the *gobernadorcillo*, announcing the same news. The friars duly noted that none was addressed to the parish priest.

"His Excellency will arrive at 4 o'clock in the afternoon, gentlemen!" said the alcalde solemnly; "We can now eat in peace!"

Leonidas at Thermopylae could not have said it better:

"Tonight we sup with Pluto!"

The conversation returned to its normal course.

"I notice that our great preacher is absent," timidly said one of the employees, one of inoffensive aspect who had so far not opened his mouth until the time to eat, and was speaking for the first time all morning.

All who knew the history of Crisostomo's father made a movement and winked, as if to say: "Come on! Down at the first strike!" but others with more benevolence were saying:

"He must be somewhat tired!"

"Somewhat?" exclaimed the *alferez*. "He must be down and out as they say over here—badly off. Beware of platitudes!"

"A superb sermon, gigantic!" said the notary public.

"Magnificent, profound!" added the correspondent.

"In order to be able to say that much one needs to have the lungs he has," observed Padre Manuel Martin. The Augustinian did not concede him more than his lungs.

"And the facility of expression," added Padre Salvi.

"Do you know that Señor Ibarra has the best cook in the province?" said the alcalde, changing the subject.

"That is what they say, but his lovely neighbor refuses to do honor to the meal. She hardly tastes anything," replied one of the employees.

Maria Clara blushed.

"I thank the Señor...you have too much concern for me, but..." she stammered timidly.

"But you are doing it honor even only with your presence," concluded the gallant alcalde; and turning to Padre Salvi:

"Padre Cura," he said in a loud voice, "I notice that all throughout the day you have been silent and deep in thought."

"The Señor Alcalde is an intense observer!" exclaimed Padre Sibyla in a peculiar tone.

"That is a habit with me," stammered the Franciscan. "I would rather listen than talk."

"Your Reverence always wants to win and not to lose," said the *alferez* jestingly.

Padre Salvi did not relish the joke. His eyes glowered for a moment and he replied:

"The señor *alferez* knows too well that during these days it is not I who gains more or loses!"

The *alferez* covered up the blow with hollow laughter, ignoring the allusion to himself.

"But gentlemen! I cannot understand how one can talk of gains or losses," the alcalde intervened. "What would those lovely and discreet señoritas who honor us with their presence think of us? To me young women are like Aeolian harps in the middle of the night: we must listen to them and lend an attentive ear, so that their undescribable harmonies which raise the soul to celestial spheres of the infinite and the ideal..."

"Your Excellency is waxing poetic!" said the notary public merrily, and both drank to that.

"I cannot do less," said the governor, wiping his lips. "The occasion, if it does not always create a thief, makes a poet. In my youth I composed verses which, by the way, were not bad."

"So Your Excellency has been unfaithful to the Muses in order to follow the Law!" said our mythical correspondent with emphasis.

"Psh! What would you have me do? It has always been my dream to run through the gamut of the social scale. Yesterday I picked flowers and sang songs; today I hold the scales of justice. I serve humanity; tomorrow..."

"Tomorrow your Excellency will throw the scales of

justice into the fire to warm you in the winter of life; and you will take up a minister's portfolio," added Padre Sibyla.

"Psh! yes...no...to be a minister is not exactly my ideal dream: any upstart can go that far. A villa in the north in which to spend summer, a hotel in Madrid and some properties in Andalucia for winter...We will live with memories of our dear Philippines...Voltaire could not have said of me that: *Nous n'avons jamais été chez ces peuples que pour nous y enrichir et pour les calomnier*; we have lived among these people only to enrich ourselves and to calumniate them."

The employees believed that his Excellency had made a joke, and they laughed. The friars did likewise. They did not know that Voltaire was the Voltaire they had many times cursed and consigned to hell. However, Padre Sibyla knew, and he became serious, supposing that the alcalde was making an impious or an heretical statement.

The students ate in the other pavilion, presided over by the schoolmaster. For Filipino children, they were making considerable noise, since at table and before elders Filipino children are more bashful than talkative. Whoever made a mistake handling spoon and fork was corrected by his neighbor. Here a discussion ensued, and both sides had their followers: some said the spoon, some the fork or the knife, and inasmuch as they did not consider anybody an authority, what transpired was like the argument of Christ being God, in short a theological discussion.

The parents would wink at each other, elbow each other and the smiles on their faces clearly manifested the happiness they felt.

"Certainly," a peasant woman was saying to an old man who was grinding *buyo* in his *kalikut*.[1] "Even if my

husband would not like it, my Andoy will become a priest.
We are poor, it is true, but we will work and, if necessary,
beg for alms. There will always be someone to provide
financially so that the poor can be ordained. Does not
Brother Mateo, a man who does not lie, say that Pope
Sixtus was a herdsman of carabaos in Batangas? Well, look
at my Andoy. Is not his face like San Vicente's? And the
good woman felt her mouth water seeing her son take a
fork in both hands.

"God help us!" said the old man, chewing his wad of
buyo. "If Andoy becomes Pope, we will all go to Rome,
heh, heh! I can still walk well. And if I die...heh!"

"Don't worry, grandpa! Andoy will never forget that
you taught him to weave baskets of bamboo and *dikines*."[2]

"You are right, Petra: I too believe that your son will
amount to something big...at least a patriarch. I have not
seen anyone else who made good in so short a time! Yes,
of course he will remember me when he becomes Pope or
bishop and entertains himself weaving baskets for his cook.
He will say a mass for me, heh, heh!"

And the good man, with this assurance, filled his
kalikut again with plenty of *buyo*.

"If God listens to my prayers and my hopes are
fulfilled, I will say to Andoy: 'Son, take away all our sins
and send us straight to Heaven. Then we will have no
further need to pray, fast, nor buy indulgences.' He who
has a Pope for a son can commit all the sins he wants!"

"Send him to the house tomorrow, Petra," said the
old man with enthusiasm; "I will teach him to work
with *nito*!"[3]

"Really grandpa! Do you think that popes still use
their hands? Just being a curate, a priest works only in the
mass...when he keeps turning around! The archbishop no

longer makes turns, he says the mass seated; so the Pope will have to say mass in bed, fanning himself! What did you think?"

"He won't lose anything by learning to weave hats and wallets. It is good that he can sell *salakots* and cigar cases so that he does not have to beg alms, as is being done here every year by the parish priest in the Pope's name. I am filled with pity when I see a poor saint, so I give all that I can save."

Another peasant approached, saying: "It is all decided *cumare*: My son must become a doctor!"

"A doctor! Come on, *cumpare*,"[4] answered Petra. "There is nothing like being a priest!"

"A priest? The doctor charges a lot of money, yet his patients take him for a saint, *cumare*!"

"Please! The priest, making just three or four turns and saying *déminos pabiscum*[5] eats God and receives money. Everybody, including the women; they tell him their secrets!"

"And the doctor? What do you think a doctor does? The doctor sees all that you women have; takes the pulses of maidens...I would like to be a doctor for only one week!"

"How about the priest? Doesn't the priest also see what the doctor sees? And even much better! You all know the saying: 'Plump hen and woman fair make a priest's fare!'"

"So what? Do doctors eat dry sardines? and spoil their fingers eating salt?"

"Does the priest soil his hands as do your doctors? That is why he has large plantations; and when priests work they do so to the sound of music and are helped by the sacristans."

"And how about confessions, *cumare*? Is that not working too?"

"What kind of work is that! How I wish I were hearing the confessions of all the world! How we work and sweat to find out what other men and women, our neighbors, do. The priest does nothing but stay seated, and all tell him everything. Sometimes he falls asleep, but he unleashes two or three benedictions and we become again children of God! I would like to be a priest during one afternoon of Holy Week!"

"And what about preaching? Don't tell me that is not work! Did you see this morning how the senior priest sweated?" objected the man who felt he was on the losing side of the dispute.

"Preaching? Is preaching work? Where has your judgment gone? I wish I were preaching for half a day in the pulpit, rebuking and scolding everyone without anyone attempting to reply, and on top of that being paid for it! I wish I were a priest for no more than a week when those who owe me hear mass! You have only to look at Padre Damaso to see how he much he has been fattened by so much scolding and lambasting!"

As a matter of fact, they saw Padre Damaso come in, ambling with a fat man's gait, half-smiling, but in a manner so malignant that, on seeing him, Ibarra lost the thread of his conversation.

Padre Damaso was greeted with some surprise and reserve, although pleasantly, by everyone except Ibarra. The guests were already being served dessert, and champagne bubbled in their cups.

Padre Damaso smiled somewhat nervously when he saw Maria Clara seated to Ibarra's right, but taking his seat beside the alcalde, he asked in the midst of the general silence:

"As you were saying, gentlemen...please continue."

"We were drinking a toast," said the alcalde, "to those

mentioned by Senor Ibarra, who have helped in his philanthropic enterprise, and we were talking about the architect, when Your Reverence..."

"Well, I don't understand anything about architecture," interrupted Padre Damaso, "but I laugh at the architects and the fools who consult them. There you have it—I drew up the plans for the town church, and it is perfectly constructed, as a British jeweller told me—he had been a guest in the convent. To trace the plans of a building it is enough to have just plain common sense!"

"However," countered the alcalde on seeing Ibarra silent, "when it has to do with a certain kind of construction, for example, this school, we need a highly experienced..."

"A know-how who knows nothing!" sneered the priest. "One has to be more backward than the *Indios* themselves who raise their own homes, not to know how to put up four walls and a covering on top, which is the same as building a school!"

Everyone's gaze shifted to Ibarra, but the latter, although he paled, kept up his conversation with Maria Clara.

"But consider, Your Reverence..."

"See," continued the Franciscan, not allowing the alcalde to speak, "how a lay brother, the most ignorant that we have, has constructed a good hospital, beautiful and cheap. He made his laborers work well and he paid no more than eight cuartos (coppers) a day, even to those who had to come from the other towns. He knew how to deal with them, unlike those self-inflated ones and mesticillos who spoil their workers by paying them three or four silver reales."

"Your Reverence says that he paid only eight cuartos?

Impossible!" The alcalde tried to shift the course of the conversation.

"Yes sir, and that is what every worthy Spaniard should imitate. It is already manifest that since the Suez Canal was opened, corruption has reached these parts. Formerly, when we had to turn around the Cape, not one of these wretches—lost souls—could get in nor go abroad to lose their souls!"

"But Padre Damaso...!"

"You are well acquainted with the *Indio*. As soon as he learns something he pretends to have become a doctor. All those still wet behind the ears go abroad to Europe..."

"But please listen, Your Reverence!" interrupted the alcalde, who was becoming bothered by the aggressive nature of those words.

"All will end as they deserve," continued the priest. "One sees the hand of God intervening. One has to be blind not to see it. They already receive in this life—the fathers of such vipers...they die in prison, heh! heh!. What we were saying is that they have no place where..."

But he did not finish the sentence. Ibarra, livid with rage, had been following him with his eyes. Upon hearing the allusion to his father, he leaped to his feet and struck the friar on the head; he fell flat on his back, stunned.

Surprised and shocked, no one attempted to intervene.

"Keep out!" yelled the young man in a terrible voice, extending a hand to pick up a sharp knife, with his foot laid on the neck of the priest, who was recovering from his stupefied state. "He who does not want to die, keep away!"

Ibarra was not himself; his body was trembling; his eyes were rolling threateningly in their sockets. Padre

Damaso made a great effort to raise himself, but Ibarra, getting hold of the friar's neck, shook him until he forced him down on his knees and made him kneel.

"Señor Ibarra, Señor Ibarra!" stammered some of the guests. But no one, not even the *alferez*, dared to come near, seeing the knife flash, and taking into account the young man's strength and state of mind. All felt paralyzed.

"You, there! You who have been keeping silent! Now it is my turn. I have tried to avoid this confrontation; God has brought him to me; let God be the judge!"

The young man was breathing with difficulty, but with an iron grip he continued subduing the Franciscan who was trying in vain to get loose.

"My heart beats calmly, my hand is sure..."

And looking around him: "Is there someone among you, someone who did not love his father, or who hated his memory, someone born of shame and humiliation?...See? Do you hear that silence? Priest of a God of peace, you mouth sanctity and religion. Your heart is full of malice; you could not have known what a father is. You should have thought of your own! See? Among this multitude that you despise there is not one like you! You are being judged!"

The people around, believing he was about to commit murder, stirred.

"Keep out, all of you!" he shouted again in a threatening voice. "What? Do you fear that I might sully my hand with tainted blood? Did I not tell you that my heart beats calmly? Keep away from us. Listen! you priests, judges, you who believe in other men and attribute to yourselves other rights!

"My father was an honorable man. Ask those people who revere his memory. My father was a worthy citizen: he made sacrifices for me and for the good of his country.

His home was open to all; his table at the disposal of the stranger and the exile alike, who appealed to him in their misery! He was a good Christian. He always did what is good, and he never oppressed the weak nor caused anguish to those already in misery.

"To this one he opened the doors of his home, made him sit at his board, and called him friend. How did he respond? This one slandered, persecuted, armed his ignorance against my father, using the sanctity of his priestly office; desecrated his grave, dishonored his memory and hounded him even in his repose in death. And not content with this, he is now persecuting the son!

"I have fled him, I have avoided his presence...You yourselves heard him this morning profane the pulpit, single me out to public fanaticism, and I kept silent. Now he comes here to pick a quarrel with me; I suffered in silence to your own surprise, but he insults anew the most sacred of memories for all sons.

"You who are present here, priests, judges! Did you see your aged father keeping vigil to labor for you, separate himself from you for your own good; die in loneliness in a prison cell, longing to embrace you, looking for someone to comfort him when he was alone and ill, while you were abroad. Then you hear of his memory being dishonored; you find, when you wanted to pray over it, his grave empty. No? You are silent, so you condemn him!"

He raised his arm, but a young woman, swift as lightning, placed herself between him and the priest, and with her delicate hands stopped the avenging arm. It was Maria Clara.

Ibarra looked at her with a glance bordering on madness. Gradually he loosened his clenched hand, letting go of the friar's body and of the knife, and covering his face with his hands, fled through the multitude.

- 36 -

The Comments

Pretty soon, news of the incident between Ibarra and Padre Damaso spread across town. At first nobody would believe it, but having to concede to reality, people broke out in exclamations of surprise. Each one made his comments in accordance with the measure of his moral values.

"Father Damaso is dead!" some were saying. "When they raised him up the priest's face was covered with blood and he was no longer breathing."

"May he rest in peace, but he had it coming," exclaimed a young man. "Look, what he did this morning in the convent is indescribable."

"What did he do? Did he beat his assistant again?"

"What has he done? Come on, tell us!"

"Did you see this morning a Spanish mestizo leave through the vestry during the sermon?"

"Yes! Of course we saw him. Padre Damaso noticed him too."

"Well, the priest had him summoned after the sermon and asked him why he had left. 'I don't understand Tagalog, Padre,' was his reply."

"And why did you mock me by saying that it was all Greek to you?" shouted Padre Damaso at him, giving him a blow. The young man responded, so both indulged in fisticuffs until someone separated them."

"If this had happened to me..." murmured a student between clenched teeth. "I don't approve of the Franciscan's action," replied another. "Religion should not be imposed on anyone as punishment or penance; but I am glad it happened, because I know that young man; he is from San Pedro Makati, and he speaks Tagalog well. Now he wants to pass for a newcomer from Russia, and he thinks that it is an honor for him to ignore the language of his fathers."

"So that is it: Birds of the same feather are beaten together!"

"However, we should guard against such an act as that of Padre Damaso," exclaimed another student. "To keep silent is to give assent to what happened. It can happen to us too. We are back in Nero's time!"

"You are mistaken!" replied another. "Nero was a great artist, and Padre Damaso is the worst preacher!"

Comments from older persons were of a different character.

While they were waiting for the arrival of the *Capitan General* in a little house outside the town, the *Gobernadorcillo* remarked:

"It is not easy to tell who is right and which is wrong. However, if Señor Ibarra had been more prudent..."

"You probably mean—if Padre Damaso had half of Señor Ibarra's prudence?" Don Filipo interrupted. "The evil lies in that they have exchanged their parts: the young man has shown himself as mature, and the old one as immature."

"And you say that no one intervened and separated them except Capitan Tiago's daughter?" Capitan Martin asked.

"No one among the friars, not even the *Alcalde*? Hm! From worse to worst! I myself would not like to be in the young man's shoes. Nobody can forgive him if he had been a coward! This is going from worse to worst!"

"Do you think so?" Capitan Basilio asked.

Don Filipo, exchanging glances with this gentleman, declared: "I hope the people will not abandon Ibarra. We should remember what his family has done and is doing now. And if the people are intimidated and keep silent, his friends..."

"But gentlemen," interrupted the *Gobernadorcillo*, what can we do by ourselves? What can the people do? Happen what may, the friars are always in the right!"

"They are always right because we always give in to them," Don Filipo answered with some impatience, emphasizing the word "always". "Let us start on equal terms for once, and then we can talk."

The *Gobernadorcillo* scratched his head, and looking upwards replied in an aggressive voice:

"Ah! these hot-headed youths! It seems that you still don't know the kind of country we live in; you don't know our own countrymen. The friars are rich and they are united; and we are poor and divided. Yes! Try to defend him and you will see yourselves facing the music alone."

"Yes," Don Filipo answered bitterly, "that is what will happen while we think in this manner, while fear and prudence are synonymous. We give more attention to an eventual evil than to a necessary good. Instantly, fear, and not confidence, occupies us; each one thinks only of himself, not of the others. That is why we are all weak!"

"Well! Think of others first before you think of yourselves, and you'll see how you are left in the lurch. Don't you know the Spanish proverb: 'Charity rightly understood begins with one's self'?"

"You could better say," retorted the exasperated *Teniente Mayor*, "that cowardice rightly understood begins with selfishness and ends with shame! Right now I am submitting my resignation to the *Alcalde*, as of today. I am fed up with being taken as ridiculous without being useful to anyone. Goodbye!"

The women thought otherwise.

"Ah!" sighed a woman with benign features: "The young will be always thus! If his poor mother were alive, what would she say? Oh God! When I think of my son, who is also a hothead, having the same fate...Jesus! I almost envy his deceased mother. I would die of grief!"

"Not me!" answered another woman. "It would not grieve me if such would be the case with my two sons."

"What are you saying, Capitana Maria?" answered the former, joining her hands together.

"I want sons to defend their fathers' memory, Capitana Tinay. What would you say if one day, and you a widow, you should hear someone malign your husband's memory and your son Antonio lowers his head in shame and keeps silent?"

"I would deny him my blessing!" exclaimed a third, Sister Rufa, "but..."

"Deny him the blessing! Never!" interrupted Capitana Tinay, the woman with benevolent features. "A mother should not say that. But I, I do not know what I would do...I do not know! I believe I would die. My God! but I would not want to see him again. But Capitana Maria, what thoughts you are entertaining!"

Sister Rufa added: "With all of these facts we must not forget that it is a grave sin to lay hands on a sacred person."

"The memory of fathers is more sacred!" said Capitana Maria. "No one, not even the Pope himself, and least of all Padre Damaso, can profane such a sacred memory!"

"That is true!" murmured Capitana Tinay, impressed by the two women's wisdom. "Where do you obtain such good reasons?"

"But how about excommunication and damnation?" replied la Rufa. "What are honor and a good name worth in this life if in the other we are damned? All pass away very quickly, but excommunication...insulting a minister of Jesus Christ! That can be forgiven only by the Pope!"

"God, who commands us to honor father and mother, will forgive; He will not excommunicate. And I tell you: if that young man were to come to my house, I would receive him and talk to him. If I had a daughter, I would love to have him for a son-in-law. He who is a good son will be a good husband and a good father. Believe me, Sister Rufa!"

"But I don't think that way. Say what you will, and even if it seems that you are right, I will always believe more in the priest. First and foremost, I save my soul. What do you say, Capitana Tinay?"

"Ah! what would you have me say? Both of you are right; the priest is also right, but God, too, must have His reasons! I don't know; I am only an ignorant woman. What I intend to do is to tell my son not to study anymore! They say that wise men die by hanging! Holy Mary! my son wants to go to Europe!"

"What do you intend to do?"

"Tell him to stay by my side. Why learn more? Tomorrow or the day after tomorrow we will die; the sage as well as the ignorant will likewise die. The question is to live in peace!"

And the good woman sighed and raised her eyes to heaven.

"Well," said Capitana Maria gravely, "if I were rich like you I would allow my sons to travel. They are young, and one day they will grow into manhood. I have little time left to live. Our sons should aspire to become more than their fathers, and in our bosoms we only teach them to be children."

"Oh! what strange thoughts you entertain!" exclaimed a frightened Capitana Tinay, joining her hands together. "It seems as though you had not borne your sons in grief and pain. You delivered your twins without pain and labor?"

"By the same token that I bore them in pain, raised and educated them notwithstanding our poverty, I do not wish that, after the fatigue that it has cost me, my sons become only half of the men they should be."

"It seems to me that you don't love your sons as God commands!" said Sister Rufa somewhat severely.

"Forgive me, but every mother loves her son in her own fashion. Some love their sons for themselves, others for their sons' sakes and still others, because they love themselves. I am one of those who love their sons for their own sakes. My husband taught me that."

"All your thoughts, Capitana Maria," said Rufa as if preaching, "are not very religious. You must join the lay confraternity of the Holy Rosary, of St. Francis, or Saint Rita or Saint Clare!"

"Sister Rufa, when I have become a worthy sister of

people, I will try to become a sister of the saints," she answered, smiling.

In order to conclude this chapter on comments, and in order for the readers to learn in passing what the simple rustics thought of these matters, we take our readers to the plaza where under the tent some people are conversing. One of them is known to us: the man who dreamed of doctors in medicine.

"What bothers me most," he was saying, "is that now the school cannot be finished!"

"What is that? Why?" the group asked with interest.

"My son will no longer become a doctor but a bullcart driver! Nothing! There will be no school!"

"Who says there will be no school?" asked a rough and robust peasant, with wide jaws and narrow brow.

"I do! The white fathers are calling Don Crisostomo a *plibastiero*.[1] There will be no school!"

All were asking questions with their eyes. It was a new word for them.

"And is that name evil?" the rough peasant finally dared to ask the question.

"The worst that a Christian can call another!"

"Worse than *tarantado* and *saragate*?"[2]

"If that were the only meaning! I have been called that many times, but it did not affect my stomach!"

"Come on! It cannot be worse than *indio*, as said by the *Alferez*!"

The father of the prospective bullcart driver put on a long face; the other scratched his head and became thoughtful.

"Then it must be like *betelapora*[3], which the *Alferez*'s old woman says. Worse than spitting on the host."

"Well, worse than spitting on the host on Good

Friday," he answered gravely. "Now you remember the word *ispichoso*.[4] It is enough for a man to be called that for the civil guards of Villa Abrille[5] to apprehend him, send him to exile or to prison. Well, *plebestiero* is much worse. According to the *directorcillo* and the telegram man: *Plibestiro*, said by a Christian, a priest, or a Spaniard to another Christian like ourselves, seems like *santusdeus* with *requimeternam*.[6] Once you have been called *plibustiero*, you may go to confession and pay your debts, because there is no alternative for you but to be hanged. You know if the *directorcillo* and the telegram man are knowledgeable: one talks with wires and the other knows Spanish and does not handle anything but the pen!"

All were terrified.

"Let them compel me to wear shoes and not drink all my life that horse urine they call beer, but let them not call me *pelbistiro*," the peasant swore, clenching his fists. "As for me, if I were as rich as Señor Ibarra, knowing Spanish as he does, and able to eat fast with knife and spoon, I'd laugh at five priests!"

"The first civilian I see stealing hens I will call *palabistiero*, and I will at once go to confession," one of the crowd of peasants murmured in a low voice, and then left.

- 37 -

The First Cloud

There was no less confusion in Capitan Tiago's house than the people imagined. Maria Clara did nothing but weep, and was not listening to the words of comfort of her aunt and those of Andeng, her foster sister. Her father had forbidden her to speak to Ibarra while he had not been absolved by the priests from excommunication.

Capitan Tiago, who was very much occupied with preparing his house for the worthy reception of the *Capitan General*, had been summoned to the convent.

"Don't cry dear," Tía Isabel was saying while polishing the brilliant mirror's surface with chamois cloth. "They will withdraw the excommunication; they will write the Holy Father...we will give a big sum for alms...Padre Damaso only fainted; he is not dead!"

"Don't cry," Andeng comforted her in a low voice. "I will see to it that you can speak to each other. What are confessionals for, if no one is to sin? Everything is forgiven by telling the priest about it!"

Finally, Capitan Tiago returned. They searched his face for answers to many questions, but Capitan Tiago's face showed signs of discouragement. The poor man was perspiring; he drew his hand across his brow and was not able to articulate a word.

"What is it, Santiago?" Tía Isabel asked anxiously.

He answered with a sigh, drying a tear.

"For God's sake, speak! What happened?"

"What I feared most," he finally broke out half-sobbing. "Everything is lost! Padre Damaso wants the engagement broken, otherwise I would be already damned in this life and in the next! Everyone else tells me the same thing, including Padre Sibyla. I should close the door of my home to him...and I owe him more than fifty thousand pesos! I told this to the Fathers, but they refuse to entertain me. 'Which do you prefer to lose,' they said, 'fifty thousand pesos or your life and soul?' Oh! St. Anthony! If I had only known, if I had only known!"

Maria Clara was sobbing.

"Do not cry, my daughter," he added, turning to her: "You are not like your mother, who never wept. She wept only at the beginning of her pregnancy. Padre Damaso told me of his relative from Spain who has lately arrived, and whom he is reserving to be your betrothed."

Maria Clara covered her ears.

"But Santiago, are you mad? How can you talk to her now of another fiancé! Do you think your daughter changes her fiancés as she changes clothes?"

"That is what I have been thinking about," Isabel. "Don Crisostomo is rich. Spaniards marry only for love of money, but what do you want me to do? They have also threatened me with excommunication. They say that it is not only my soul that is running at risk; it is also my body that is in danger. My body, do you hear? My body!"

"But you are causing your daughter pain! Is not the Archbishop your friend? Why don't you write him?"

"The Archbishop is a friar, too. The Archbishop does only what the friars tell him to do. But Maria, don't cry. The *Capitan General* is coming. He would like to see you, and your eyes will be swollen and red. And oh! I who was thinking of spending a happy afternoon. Without this mishap I would be the happiest of men and everybody would envy me. Calm yourself, my daughter. I am more unfortunate than you are, yet I don't weep! You can have a better man, but I...I will lose fifty thousand pesos! Oh! Virgin of Antipolo, if tonight I would, at least, be lucky!"

Detonations, the roll of carriages, the gallop of horses, music playing the Royal March, announced the arrival of His Excellency the Governor-General of the Philippine Islands. Maria Clara ran to hide herself in her room. Poor maiden! Gross hands are playing with your heart—hands insensitive to its delicate fibers!

Meanwhile, the house was filling with people. Footsteps, commanding voices, sounds of sabers and spurs resounded everywhere. The afflicted young woman lay half-kneeling before a picture of the Virgin in an attitude of sorrowful loneliness, which was captured only by Delaroche, as if he had surprised her on her way back from her son's grave. Maria Clara was not thinking of that mother's grief; she was thinking only of her own pain. With head bowed down to her breast, hands supported against the floor, she seemed like the stem of a lily bent by the tempest. A future dreamt of and cherished through the years, whose illusions, born in infancy and nurtured in youth, gave substance and form to her being, was now to be erased from mind and heart with a single word! It was equal to paralyzing the beat of one and depriving the other of its light!

Maria Clara was as good and pious a Christian as she was a loving daughter. Not only the threat of excommunication frightened her. The command and the endangered peace of her father now also required of her the sacrifice of her love. She felt the impact of that filial affection hitherto unsuspected by her. It was at one time a river that glided gently, with fragrant flowers dotting its banks and its bottom of fine sand. Its current scarcely rippled the wind; it could have been said to meander. But all of a sudden its bed narrowed, its flow was impeded by sharp rocks, old tree trunks were laid across to form a dike—then the river roared, it rose, the waves boiled, shaking plumes of foam, it beat against the rocks and lunged to an abyss!

She wanted to pray, but who prays in moments of despair? We pray when we hope; otherwise we approach God with our complaints. "My God!" her heart cried out, "why separate thus a man, why deny him love from others? You do not withhold from him your sun or your breeze, nor do you hide from him the sight of your heaven. Why deny him love—without your heaven, without the breeze and without the sun, one can live, but without love, never!"

Will those cries which men do not hear reach the throne of God? Will the Mother of the unfortunate hear them?

Ay! the poor maiden, who had never known a mother, dared entrust her pains caused by earthly love to that pure heart which has known only the love of a daughter and that of a mother. In her sorrow she comes to that divinized image of a woman, the most beautiful idealization of the most perfect of creatures; to that poetic creation of Christianity which unites within herself the two most beautiful states of a woman: virgin and mother, without their miseries, whom we call Mary!

"Mother! mother!" she sobbed.

Tía Isabel came to rescue her from her grief. Some of her friends had come, by and the *Capitan-General* wished to speak to her.

"Tia, tell them that I am sick!" she pleaded, terrified. "They will make me play the piano and sing!"

"Your father has promised. Would you embarrass your father?"

Maria Clara rose to her feet, looked at her aunt, twisted her lovely arms and stammered:

"Oh! If I only had..."

But she did not finish the sentence, and started to prepare herself.

- 38 -

His Excellency

"I wish to speak to that young man," said His Excellency to his aide, "he arouses all my interest."

"They have already gone to fetch him, my general! But here is another young man from Manila who insists on being introduced to you. We told him that Your Excellency has no time and has not come to grant audiences, but to see the town and the procession. He replied that Your Excellency always has time to do justice."

His Excellency turned to the *Alcalde*, marvelling.

"If I am not mistaken," the latter replied, bowing slightly, "it is the same young man who had an altercation with Padre Damaso on account of his sermon."

"What, again? Does this friar propose to agitate the whole province, or does he believe himself to be the authority here? Tell the young man to come in!"

His Excellency nervously paced the sala back and forth.

In the antechamber various Spaniards, together with the military and civil authorities of the town of San Diego and of the neighboring towns, crowded in groups, conversing or discussing. The friars were also there, all of them except Padre Damaso. They wanted to present their respects to His Excellency.

"His Excellency, the *Capitan General*, requests Your Reverences to wait for a moment," said the aide. "Come in, young man!"

The youth from Manila who had confused Greek with Tagalog entered the room, pale and trembling.

Everybody wondered: His Excellency must have been so irritated as to make the friars wait. Padre Sibyla was saying:

"I have nothing to tell the *Capitan General*. I am wasting my time here."

"I say the same thing," added an Augustinian. "Shall we take our leave?"

"Is it not better for us to find out what he thinks?" Padre Salvi asked. "We could avoid a scandal...and we could remind him...his duties...regarding religion."

"Your Reverences may come in if you wish," said the aide, escorting the young man who did not understand Greek, and who now was leaving, his face all aglow with satisfaction.

Padre Sibyla entered first; behind came Padre Salvi, Padre Manuel Martin and the other religious. They bowed respectfully, except for Padre Sibyla who, even when he bowed his head, kept a certain air of authority. Padre Salvi, on the contrary, almost doubled his body, bending from the waist.

"Which one of Your Reverences is Padre Damaso?" His Excellency demanded abruptly, without asking them to sit down, nor asking about their health, without addressing them in flowery flattering language, the customary practice among personages in the higher spheres.

"Padre Damaso has not come with us, Sir," replied Padre Sibyla, almost in the same curt tone.

"Your Excellency's servant is lying sick in bed," humbly added Padre Salvi. "After enjoying the pleasure of greeting and inquiring about your Excellency's health, as required of all good servants of His Majesty and of all persons of good breeding, we have also come in the name of Your Excellency's humble and respectful servant who had the misfortune..."

"Ah!" interrupted the *Capitan General*, one foot playing with a chair and smiling nervously: "If all the servants of my Excellency were like His Reverence Padre Damaso, I would prefer myself to serve myself my Excellency."

Their reverences, who had already been stopped short bodily, were stayed as well in spirit by this interruption.

"Take seats, Your Reverences," he added after a brief pause, softening his tone a little.

Capitan Tiago was attired in coattails and walking on tiptoe, leading by the hand Maria Clara, who entered hesitantly and timidly. Still she made a ceremonial and graceful greeting.

"Is the young lady your daughter?" asked the *Capitan General*, manifesting surprise.

"And Your Excellency's, my general!" replied Capitan Tiago very earnestly.

The *Alcalde* and the assistants widened their eyes, but His Excellency, without losing his serious mood, extended a hand to the young woman and told her amiably:

"Happy the parents who have a daughter like you, Señorita! I have been told of you with respect and admiration... I wanted to meet you to thank you for the beautiful act you accomplished today. I am acquainted with *all the facts*, and when I write to His Majesty's government I will not forget your generous gesture. In the meantime, allow me, Señorita, in the name of His Majesty the King, whom I represent here and who loves the *peace and tranquility* of his faithful subjects; in my own name, and in that of a father who also has daughters of your age, to give you the most heartfelt thanks and to propose a fitting reward for you."

"Sir...!" answered Maria Clara, her voice trembling.

His Excellency guessed what she wanted to say, and replied:

"It is all right, Señorita for you to be satisfied by your conscience and by the esteem of your fellow citizens. In truth that is the best reward, and we should not demand more. But please do not deprive me of a lovely occasion to make all see that justice knows how to reward as well as punish, and that she is not always *blind*."

All the words written in italics were pronounced in the most significant manner and in a loud voice.

"Señor Don Juan Crisostomo Ibarra awaits Your Excellency's pleasure," announced an aide in a loud voice.

Maria Clara trembled.

"Ah!" the *Capitan General* exclaimed. "Allow me, Señorita, to express to you the desire to see you again before I leave this town. I still have many important things to tell you. His Honor, Señor *Alcalde,* will accompany me during my stroll, which I want to do on foot, after the conference that I will hold with Señor Ibarra alone!"

"Your Excellency will allow us to remind you," said

Padre Salvi with humility, "that Senor Ibarra has been excommunicated."

His Excellency interrupted the friar, saying:

"I am very happy that I do not have to deplore more than the condition of Padre Damaso, for whom I *sincerely desire* a *complete recovery*, because at his age a *voyage to Spain* for reasons of health cannot be very agreeable. That is why it all depends on him...and in the meantime, may God preserve the health of Your Reverences!"

All withdrew.

"Of course, it depends on him—most certainly!" murmured Padre Salvi on leaving.

"Let us see who will make the trip soon," added another Franciscan.

"I am leaving this very moment," said a very disappointed Padre Sibyla.

"And we, to our province!" the Augustinians said.

All of them could not stomach the thought that, due to a Franciscan's fault, His Excellency had received them very coldly.

In the antechamber they met Ibarra, their host of a few hours ago. No greetings were exchanged, only glances which said many things.

The *Alcalde*, however, when the priests had left, greeted him and shook his hand with familiarity, but the arrival of the aide who was fetching the youth left no time for conversation.

At the door they met Maria Clara: the glances of both young people also spoke volumes, although quite different ones from what the friars expressed with their eyes.

Ibarra was attired in deep mourning. He presented himself serenely and saluted profoundly, although he felt the friars' visit did not augur well for his case.

The *Capitan-General* advanced forward to meet him.

"I feel a great satisfaction, Señor Ibarra, in offering you my hand. Allow me to receive you in the deepest of confidence."

As a matter of fact, His Excellency was contemplating and examining the young man with marked satisfaction on his face.

"Sir!...so much kindness!"

"Your surprise offends me. It means that you did not expect a good welcome: from me; that is tantamount to doubting my justice!"

"A friendly welcome, Sir, for so insignificant a subject of His Majesty as myself, is not justice but a favor."

"Well! well!" said His Excellency, seating himself and signalling Ibarra to do the same. "Let us allow ourselves a few moments of relaxation. I am very much satisfied with your conduct and I have already proposed to His Majesty's government a medal for your philanthropic idea of putting up a school. Had you advised me I would have presided with pleasure over the laying of the cornerstone and perhaps spared you from trouble."

"The school project seems so small to me, and I did not think it worth Your Excellency's while to attend the ceremony, distracting your Excellency's attention from your many duties. Besides, my duty is first to address the first authority of my province."

His Excellency moved his head in deep satisfaction and, adopting this time a more intimate tone, continued:

"Regarding the difficulties that you have had with Padre Damaso, do not harbor fear or rancor. Not a hair of your head will be touched, as long as I govern the Islands, and with respect to the excommunication, I will speak to the Archbishop because it is necessary for us to adapt ourselves to the circumstances. Here we cannot laugh at these things in public as we do on the Peninsula or in cultured Europe. Withal in the future, be more prudent. You have pitted yourself against the religious orders which, because of their importance and their riches, need to be respected. But I will protect you because I like good sons; I like for them to honor the memory of their fathers; I too have loved mine and God alive! I don't know what I would have done in your place."

Switching rapidly from the trend of the conversation, he asked:

"I was informed that you have recently arrived from Europe. Have you been in Madrid?"

"Yes Sir, for a few months."

"Did you perchance speak to my family?"

"Your Excellency had just left when I had the honor of being introduced to your family."

"Then, how did you come without bringing any recommendation?"

"Sir!" said Ibarra, bowing. "I did not come directly from Spain, and because I was told what Your Excellency was like, I believed that a letter of recommendation would not only be useless but also offensive: we Filipinos are all recommended to you."

A smile broke out on the lips of the old soldier, who replied slowly as if measuring and weighing his words:

"I am flattered that you think thus, and thus it should be! However, young man, you must know the burdens that lie on our shoulders in the Philippines. Here, we old soldiers have to do it all and be all: King, Minister of State, of War, of Governance, of Supply, of Grace and Justice, and so forth. What is even worse is that for each thing we have to consult the faraway Mother Country, which approves or rejects, according to the circumstances, sometimes blindly, our proposals. And we Spaniards say: 'He who dares much, achieves little.'

"Besides, generally we come knowing very little of the country and we leave it when we have begun to be familiar with it...I have to be frank with you for it would be useless to appear otherwise. Thus, if in Spain, where each governmental branch has its minister, born and developed in the same locality, where there is press and public opinion, where a frank opposition opens the eyes of the government and enlightens it, everything works defectively and imperfectly, it is a miracle that here things are not in upheaval, lacking those advantages, and with a more powerful opposition living and conniving in the shadows.

"We, the ruling government, are not wanting in good will, but we are obliged to make use of outside eyes and arms, which generally we do not know, and which perhaps, instead of serving the country, are serving only their own interests. This is not our fault; it is due to circumstances. The friars are a big help in meeting the problems, but they do not yet suffice...You inspire me with interest and a desire that the imperfection of our actual governmental system would not prejudice you in any way. I cannot be vigilant for everyone; neither can everyone reach me. Can I be of use to you, is there something you wish to ask of me?"

Ibarra reflected.

"Sir," he answered, "my greatest desire is for the happiness of my country, happiness which I would like to come from the Mother Country and from the efforts of my fellow countrymen, united to each other by eternal bonds of common perspective and interests. What I ask only the government can give after many years of continuous endeavor and suitable reforms."

His Excellency looked at Ibarra with a look that Ibarra met quite naturally.

"You are the first real man I have spoken to in this country," he exclaimed, shaking Ibarra's hand.

"Your Excellency saw only the opportunists within the city; you have not visited the miserable hovels of our towns. Your Excellency would have seen real men—if to be a man it is enough to have a generous heart and simple habits."

The *Capitan General* stood up and paced back and forth.

"Señor Ibarra," he exclaimed, stopping all of a sudden—the young man stood up too—"perhaps I will be leaving within a month. You and your way of thinking, and your breeding, are not for this country. Sell all that you possess, pack your suitcase and come with me to Europe—its climate would suit you well."

"The memory of your Excellency's benevolence I will treasure as long as I live!" answered Ibarra, somewhat moved. "But I must live in this country where my parents had lived..."

"Where they have died—you could say more accurately. Believe me! Perhaps I know your country better than you yourself do. Ah! now I remember," he exclaimed, changing his tone, "you are marrying an adorable maiden, and I am detaining you here. Go! Go to her side and, for your greater freedom send me her father," he added, smiling. "Do not forget, however, that I wish you to accompany me on my walk."

Ibarra saluted and took his leave.

His Excellency summoned his aide.

"I am satisfied," he said, patting his aide twice on the shoulder. "Today I have seen for the first time how one can be a good Spaniard and still be a good Filipino and love his country. Today I have finally shown their reverences that not all of us are their puppets. This young man has given me the occasion, and soon I will have settled all my accounts with the friars! A pity that this youth some day or other...but fetch me the *Alcalde*."

This one presented himself immediately.

"*Señor Alcalde*," he told him on his entrance, "in order to avoid the repetition of scenes such as Your Honor witnessed this afternoon—scenes I deplore because they undermine the prestige of the government and of all the Spaniards, I allow myself to recommend to you efficaciously Señor Ibarra, so that you can facilitate for him the means to carry out not only his patriotic objectives, but also to avoid from now on his being molested by persons of any kind under one pretext or the other."

The *Alcalde* understood the reprimand, and bowed to hide his embarrassment. "Let Your Honor transmit this order to the *Alferez* in command of this section; and verify if it is true that this official does things on his own that are not in accordance with the rules. I have heard more than one complaint about this."

Capitan Tiago came next, all erect and well ironed.

"Don Santiago," said His Excellency in an affectionate tone, "only lately I was congratulating you for having such a daughter as Señorita de los Santos; now I am congratulating you for your future son-in-law. The most virtuous of daughters is most assuredly worthy of the best citizen of the Philippines. May we know when the wedding is due?"

"Sir!" Capitan Tiago stammered, mopping the perspiration from his brow.

"Come on! I see that there is nothing definite yet! If there is a lack of sponsors, I would take great pleasure in being one of the sponsors. It is to remove the bad taste left in me by the many weddings I have sponsored," he added, addressing the *Alcalde*.

"Yes, Sir!" replied Capitan Tiago with a smile that inspired compassion.

Ibarra, almost running, went to look for Maria Clara. He had too many things to tell her and to relate. He heard some merry voices from one of the rooms. He knocked lightly at the door.

"Who is calling?" Maria Clara asked.

"It is I!"

The voices stopped and the door remained closed.

"It is I! May I come in?" the young man queried; his heart was beating violently.

Silence prevailed. Seconds later light steps were heard by the door and the merry voice of Sinang murmured through the keyhole:

"Crisostomo, we are going to the theater tonight. Write down what you have to say to Maria Clara."

And the steps moved away as fast as they had come.

"What does this mean?" murmured Ibarra deep in thought, slowly leaving the door.

- 39 -

The Procession

I n the evening, and with all the lanterns in the windows already lighted, the procession went out for the fourth time, accompanied by the pealing of the bells and detonations.

The *Capitan General*, on foot, left Capitan Tiago's house accompanied by two aides, Capitan Tiago, the *Alcalde* of the province, the *Alferez* and Ibarra, preceded by civil guards and authorities who opened the way for them in the streets. They had been invited to the *Gobernadorcillo*'s house to view the procession; a platform had been erected in front of the house, where a *loa*[1] or an ode would be recited in praise of the patron saint.

Ibarra would have gladly renounced the pleasure of listening to this recitation to view the procession from Capitan Tiago's home, where Maria Clara was staying with her friends, but His Excellency wanted to hear the *loa* and there was no way out of it but to console himself with the thought of seeing Maria Clara later in the theater.

The procession began with the silver candlesticks carried by three gloved *sacristanes*. They were followed by the schoolboys accompanied by the schoolmaster, then the boys with paper lanterns of different shapes and colors dangling from bamboo cane sticks more or less long and adorned according to each boy's fancy, for these lights were at the expense of the barrio children. They complied willingly with this duty imposed by the *matanda sa nayon* or the patriarch of the barrio. Each one imagined and made his lantern according to his fantasy, adorned it with more or less pennants and banners depending on the capacity of his pocket. It was lighted with a candle stub if he had a friend or a relative who was a sacristan, or he bought the little red candle the Chinese use on their altars.

The constables—enforcers of the law—walked between the two parallel lines of participants in the procession to keep order and to keep the line unbroken and straight, and to avoid crowding. To do this they made use of their sticks. With some timely blows conveniently and quite forcefully administered, they managed to convey the glory and splendor of the parade for the edification of souls and the luster of religious pageantry!

At the same time that the constables freely applied those sanctified blows, others, to console those bludgeoned, distributed candles and lights of different sizes and shapes also for free.

"Señor *Alcalde*" said Ibarra in a low voice, "are these blows administered as punishment for sins, or just for a whim?"

"You are right, Señor Ibarra," replied the *Capitan General*, who had heard the question. "This spectacle...so barbaric...shocks the sensibilities and all those who come from other countries. It is time that it should be prohibited."

For no apparent reason, the first saint to appear was John the Baptist. Seeing him, it could be said that the reputation of Our Lord's cousin did not sit well with the townsfolk; the truth is that he had the feet and legs of a maiden and a hermit's face, but he went in his old litter of wood, and was partly hidden by a handful of youngsters who did not bother to light their lanterns, and were punching each other under cover.

"Disgraced!" murmured Tasio the philosopher, who was viewing the procession from the street: "It was useless for you to have been a precursor of the good news, or for Jesus to have given way to you: Your great faith, austerity, your dying for the truth, your convictions: all these men forget when what are taken into account are one's own merits! It is worth more to preach badly in the churches than to be an eloquent voice crying out in the desert—this is what the Philippines has taught you. If you had eaten turkey instead of locusts, dressed in silk instead of animal skins, and had affiliated yourself with an order..."

But the old man stopped his rebuke because Saint Francis was coming next.

"Did I not say so?" he continued, smiling sarcastically, "this one goes in his own palanquin, Holy God! What a palanquin this is! How many lights and how many crystal lanterns! I have never seen you surrounded by such great splendor, Giovanni Bernardone![2] And what music! Your sons heard other melodies after your death. But venerable and humble founder, should you resurrect right now you would see none except degenerate Eliases of Cortona. If your sons should recognize you they would confine you, and you would share the fate of Cesario of Speyer!"[3]

Behind the orchestra came a banner representing the

same saint but with seven wings, carried by lay Tertiary
brothers clothed in cotton habits and praying in loud
plaintive voices. Not knowing why, along came Saint Mary
Magdalene, a most lovely image with luxuriant hair, a
kerchief of embroidered piña held in her fingers covered
with rings, and clothed in silk adorned with sheets of gold.
She was surrounded by lights and incense smoke. Her
tears of glass reflected the colors of Bengal lights, lending
the procession a fantastic glow as the holy sinner wept
tears: now green, now red, now blue and so forth. The
houses did not begin to put their lights on until after Saint
Francis had passed by... Saint John did not enjoy these
honors and he passed by swiftly, perhaps ashamed of his
animal skin attire amid so many people covered with gold
and precious stones.

"There goes our saint," exclaimed the *Gobernadorcillo*'s
daughter to her guests. "I lent her my rings, but this in
order to gain heaven!"

The light carriers stopped around the platform to
listen to the *loa;* the saints, too! These or their bearers like
to listen to the verses. Those who were carrying Saint John,
tired of waiting, squatted down on the ground. They
agreed to leave him on the ground.

"The guard might get angry," objected one of them.

"Jesus! why? in the vestry he stays in the corner amid
the cobwebs..."

And Saint John, left on the ground, became one of
the townsfolk.

Starting with the Magdalene came the women, except
that instead of beginning with the girls, as was the case
with men, the old women came first with the maidens
closing the procession, including the Virgin's float, behind
which came the parish priest under the pallium. This

practice was begun in Padre Damaso's time. He was wont
to say: "The Virgin likes young women, not old ones,"
which caused the latter to put on long faces, but it did not
change the Virgin's taste.

San Diego followed the Magdalene although he
seemed not too happy about this, for he continued
remorsefully as he had been in the morning when he was
behind Saint Francis. Six Tertiary sisters were pulling his
float for what promise or sickness we do not know, but
pull they did, and with such energy! San Diego made a
stop before the platform and waited to be saluted.

But there had to be a wait for the Virgin's float
preceded by figures dressed as phantoms, which frightened
the children—hence the cries and the screams of some
fretful babies. Amid that dark mass of habits, hoods, belts
and cowls and the sounds of monotonous and hoarse
praying, however, were seen like white lilies, or fresh
sampagas[4] among old rags, twelve girls dressed in white,
crowned with flowers, hair in ringlets, with eyes as
sparkling as their necklaces—they appeared like little
fairies of light imprisoned by the specters. Two wide blue
ribbons attach them to the Virgin's float—a sight
reminiscent of doves hovering in the wake of springtime.

Now all the images are attentive, close and pressed
to each other to listen to the verses. All eyes are directed
towards a half-opened curtain—at last a sigh of admiration
escapes from the lips of the spectators.

And it is deserved by a youngster with wings, riding
boots, sash, belt, and plumed hat.

"His Honor the *Alcalde Mayor!*" shouted one, but that
prodigy of creation started to recite a poem in the manner
of the *Alcalde*, who was not offended by the comparison.

Why translate here what was said in Latin, Tagalog

and Spanish verses by the *Gobernadorcillo*'s poor victim? Our readers have already savored Padre Damaso's sermon of this morning, and we do not wish to burden them with so many wonders. Besides, the Franciscan may bear us ill will if we provide him with a competitor. This we would not like to do, being ourselves, fortunately, of a peaceful temperament.

Then the procession proceeded on its way, Saint John following his path of sorrow.

When the Virgin's float passed by Capitan Tiago's house it was greeted by a heavenly song saluting the Virgin in the words of Gabriel, the archangel. It was a voice full of melody and tenderness, suppliant, weeping Gounod's *Ave Maria*, accompanying itself at the piano, which prayed with it. The band stopped its music—the praying stopped, and Padre Salvi himself stopped. The voice trembled and drew forth tears. More than a salutation, it was a prayer, a plaint.

Ibarra heard the voice from the window where he was. Terror and melancholy filled his heart. He understood what that soul was suffering and was expressing in song, and feared to ask himself the reason for such pain.

The *Capitan General* found him gloomy and pensive.

"You will accompany me to the table. There we will discuss the case of those boys who disappeared," the *Capitan General* told Ibarra.

"Am I the cause of such pain?" murmured the young man looking at, without seeing, His Excellency, whom he followed automatically.

- 40 -

Doña Consolacion

Why are the windows of the *Alferez's* house closed? Where were the masculine features and the flannel shirt of the Medusa or Muse of the Civil Guards while the procession passed by? Doña Consolacion must have understood how obnoxious were her forehead furrowed with heavy veins, conductors it seemed not of blood, but of vinegar and gall; the oversized cigar, a worthy decoration of her purple lips; and her envious looks—and giving way to a generous impulse, did not want to disturb with her sinister appearance the people's merriment.

Ah! for her, generous impulses belonged to the Golden Age!

The house is sad because the people are happy, as Sinang said; it displayed no lanterns or banners. Had the sentry not been standing watch before the door, one would think the house uninhabited.

A weak light illumined the disorderly sala, making transparent the dirty shell window-panes on which clung cobwebs and dusty grime. The lady of the house, grown lazy by force of habit, dozed in a large armchair. She dressed as she did every day, that is to say, badly and horribly. A scarf tied around her head hardly concealed her thin short scraggly hair; the blue flannel blouse over the one that should have been white, and a faded skirt which clung to her thin flat thighs, crossed one on top of the other. Her mouth expelled clouds of smoke which she spat out towards the space she stared at when she opened her eyes. If Don Francisco de Canamaque[1] had seen her at that moment, he would have taken her for a town chieftain or a *mankukulam*,[2] then described his discovery with comments in gutter language, invented by him for his own particular use.

That morning the lady did not hear mass, not because she was hostile to it. Quite the contrary: she wanted to show herself to the crowd and to listen to the sermon, but her husband would not let her, and the prohibition was accompanied as usual with two or three insults, oaths and threats of being kicked. The *Alferez* understood that his woman dressed herself ridiculously, that she smelled like one they called mistress of the soldiery; that it was not convenient to expose her to the personages of the capital nor to visitors.

But she did not understand it this way. She thought herself a beauty, attractive, that she had the airs of a queen and that she was better than Maria Clara and dressed more luxuriously. Maria Clara wore an overskirt; she went out with just an underskirt. It was necessary for the *Alferez* to tell her: "You either shut up or I kick you all the way to your d— town!"

Doña Consolacion did not want to be kicked back to her town, but she thought of revenge.

The lady's dark features were never suited to inspiring confidence in anyone, not even when she painted herself, but that morning she caused great alarm, particularly when she was seen pacing from one end of the room to another, silent as if meditating on something terrible or malignant. Her eyes glittered like a serpent's, caught and about to be crushed underfoot. They were cold, luminous, piercing, akin to something slimy, filthy and cruel.

The smallest mistake, the most insignificant unexpected sound, provoked her into coarse and foul insults which nobody dared respond to. To justify one's self with an explanation was another crime to her.

In this way she spent her day. Not finding an obstacle to block her way—her husband had been invited to the feast—she saturated herself in her own bile. It was as if her whole being was charged with electricity, threatening to explode into a terrible tempest. Everything around her bent like rice stalks at the first gust of a hurricane. She found nowhere any point of resistance on which to vent her ill humor. Soldiers and servants had to give way before her.

She ordered her windows closed so as not to hear the merriment outside; charged the sentry not to allow anyone to pass. She tied her scarf around her head as if to keep it from bursting asunder. Although it was still daylight, she ordered that the lamps be lit.

Sisa, as we saw, was detained as a disturber of law and order, and taken to headquarters. The *Alferez* was out then, and the hapless woman had to spend the night seated on a bench, staring indifferently around her. The *Alferez* saw her the next day. Fearing the worst for her during those days of turmoil, and not wishing to create a disagreeable scene, he ordered the soldiers to keep her under guard and to treat her with compassion, giving her food. Thus the deranged woman spent two days.

In the evening, perhaps because of the nearness of Capitan Tiago's house, Maria Clara's sad singing may have reached her ears, or because other chords may have aroused her old songs, or whatever might have been the reason, Sisa also began to sing in her sweet and melancholic voice the *kundimans* of her youth. The soldiers listened to her, moved and silent. Those melodies awakened memories of times when they were still uncorrupted.

Doña Consolacion also heard the songs in her boredom and was informed about the person who was singing.

"Let her come up this very moment," she ordered, after some reflection. Something like the ghost of a smile formed on her arid lips.

They brought Sisa, who appeared undisturbed, showing neither surprise nor fear. She did not seem to see any lady before her. This wounded the Muse's vanity; she had wanted to impress Sisa and inspire her with fear and respect.

Doña Consolacion coughed, made a sign to the soldiers to leave; took hold of her husband's whip, and with sinister accents said to the mad woman:

"*Vamos, magcantar icau.* Come, you sing now!"

Sisa naturally did not understand her. The woman's ignorance appeased the lady's anger.

One of her worthy qualities was pretending to ignore Tagalog, or at least not know it, speaking the language very badly, thus giving herself the airs of a genuine *orofea*[3], as she was wont to say. And she did well because she murdered Tagalog; her Castillian fared no better, with reference to grammar and pronunciation. And yet her husband, the chairs, the shoes—each had contributed a share in instructing her. One of the words that gave her more difficulty then hieroglyphics had given Champollion, was the word *Filipinas*.

The story is told that the day following her wedding, while speaking to her husband who was at the time only a corporal, she had said "Pilipinas." The corporal thought it his duty to correct her and told her, knocking her first on the head: "Say Filipinas, woman! don't be a beast. Don't you know that that is the name of your d— country, coming from Felipe?" The lady, who was dreaming of her honeymoon, wanted to obey, and said "Felepinas." She seemed to be catching on. He increased the blows on her head and upbraided her: "But woman, can you not say: Felipe? Don't you forget it; know that the king, Don Felipe...the fifth...Say Felipe, and add to it *nas* which, in Latin, signifies islands of *Indios*, and you have the name of your d—country!"

La Consolacion, who was a laundress then, feeling her bruise or bruises, repeated, starting to lose her patience:

"Fe...lipe, Felipe...nas, Felipenas, is that it, *ba?*"

The Corporal was left seeing visions. Why had it come out Felipenas instead of Felipinas? One of two things: one either says Felipenas, or has to say Filipi.

That day he considered it prudent to keep silent. He left his wife and went to consult the dictionary carefully. Here his admiration reached its climax: he rubbed his eyes: Let us see...slowly...all the printed words say Filipinas, spelled correctly. Neither he nor his wife was right.

"How is it?" he murmured, "Can history tell a lie?

Does this book not say that Alonso Saavedra gave this name to the country in honor of the crown prince Don Felipe? How did this name become corrupted? He must have been an *Indio*, this Alonso Saavedra?"

About his doubts he consulted Sergeant Gomez, who in his youth had wished to be a priest. Without even deigning to look at him, and exhaling a mouthful of smoke, Gomez answered with the greatest pomposity:

"In olden times they said Filipi instead of Felipe. We moderns, since we became Frenchified, cannot tolerate two i's together. That is why cultured folk, in Madrid especially—you have not been to Madrid?—I said cultured folk are starting to say *menistry, eritation, embitation, endignant,* and so forth which is called catching up with the moderns."

The poor corporal had not been to Madrid. That is why he did not know about this juggling of letters. The things one learns in Madrid!

"So now it should be...?"

"Man, in accordance with the old way, because this country is not yet educated, in the old way: Filipinas!" said Gomez contemptuously.

But the corporal, who was a bad philologist, was, on the contrary, a good husband. His wife must learn too, what he himself had learned, and he continued her education.

"Consola, what is the name of your d— country?"

"What else should I call it? As you have taught me, Felifenas!"

"I will throw this chair at you, you b—! Yesterday you were pronouncing it almost correctly, the modern way; but now it has to be pronounced the ancient way: Feli...no! rather Filipinas!"

"Look! I am not for the ancient. What do you think!"

"Never mind! Say Filipinas!"

"I don't feel like doing it! I am not an old rag...barely 30 little years old," retorted la Consolacion, rolling up her sleeves and preparing for combat.

"Say it you b— or I throw the chair at you!"

Consolacion saw the movement, reflected and stammered, breathing heavily: "Feli...Fele...File..."

Pum! crack! the chair finished saying the word.

And the lesson ended in fisticuffs, scratches, blows. The corporal laid hold of her head by the hair, she, the tufts of hair on his chin and on other parts of the body—to bite she could not for her teeth were all loose—the corporal cried out, let go of her, asked for forgiveness; blood flowed, one eye was redder than the other, a shirt torn to shreds, many hidden parts of the body laid bare but Filipinas did not emerge.

Many adventures of this sort took place every time they dealt with the language. The corporal, considering her linguistic progress, painfully calculated: in ten years time his wife would completely lose the use of her tongue. As a matter of fact, that is what happened. When they got married, she still understood Tagalog and tried to make herself understood in Spanish; now at the time of our narrative, she was no longer talking in any language. She had grown much addicted to the language of gestures, of which she chose the most spectacular and crushing— she could have successfully challenged the inventor of Volapuk.[4]

Sisa, then, was lucky not to have understood her. She unknitted her brows a little bit; a smug smile brightened her face. Undoubtedly she no longer understood Tagalog: she was now *orofea*.

"Orderly, tell this woman in Tagalog to sing! She does not understand me, she does not know Spanish!"

The mad woman understood the assistant and sang the Evening Song.

Doña Consolacion at first listened with mocking laughter, but the mirth gradually disappeared from her lips. She became attentive, then serious and somewhat pensive. The voice, the meaning of the words and the song itself, impressed her. That arid and dried-up heart was perhaps thirsty for rain. She understood the song well: "The sadness, the cold and the moisture falling from heaven wrapped in night's mantle," according to the kundiman, seemed to descend on her heart as well; and "the withered faded flower, which showed its beauty off during the day, desirous of applause and full of vanity, in the evening, after sunset, repentant and disappointed, makes an effort to raise its withered petals to heaven, asking for a bit of shade in which to hide itself and die without the mocking of the light which had seen it in its glory, without seeing the vanity of its pride, and a bit of dew to weep over it. The night bird leaves its lonely retreat, the hollow of an ancient trunk, disturbing the forest melancholy..."

"No, don't sing!" exclaimed the *alferez's* wife in perfect Tagalog, standing up all agitated, "don't sing! Those verses hurt me!"

The mad woman kept quiet. The assistant exclaimed: "Aba, she knows Tagalog *pala!*"[5] and stared at the lady in admiration.

The latter understood that she had betrayed herself, and felt ashamed. Since her nature was not that of a woman, her feeling of shame was converted into anger and hate. She pointed the imprudent one towards the door and kicked it closed behind him. She took a few turns in the room, twisting the whip in her calloused hands and, stopping all of a sudden in front of Sisa, told her in Spanish: "Dance!"

Sisa did not move.

"Dance! dance!" she repeated in a threatening voice.

The mad woman regarded her with vague eyes, without expression. The *alferez's* wife raised one arm, then another, and started to shake her. It was useless: Sisa did not understand.

She began to jump and agitate herself, prodding Sisa to imitate her. Music was heard from afar, the band of the procession playing a grave and stately march, but the lady was jumping furiously following a different tempo, a different music, that which resounded inside her. Sisa looked at her, immobile; something like curiosity was painted in her eyes, and a slight smile played on her pale lips. The lady's dance was amusing to her.

This one stopped as if embarrassed, raised the whip— that terrible whip familiar to thieves and soldiers, made in Ulango[6] and perfected by the *Alferez* with twisted wires— and said:

"Now it is your turn to dance...dance!"

And she started to whip lightly the naked feet of the mad woman, whose face contracted with pain, obliging her to defend herself with her hands.

"Ah! now you are beginning," she exclaimed with savage merriment, and moved from *lento* to *allegro vivace*.

The hapless victim broke out in a cry of anguish and raised her foot forcefully.

"You are to dance, you bitch of an *India*," the lady said, and the whip whistled and vibrated.

Sisa slumped on the floor, laying her hands on her thighs and looking at her executioner with terrified eyes.

Two vigorous lashes on her back made her stand up. She no longer moaned; she made howling sounds. Her thin blouse was torn, her skin was broken, and blood flowed.

The sight of blood excites the tiger. Her victim's blood aroused Doña Consolacion's passion.

"Dance! dance! accursed wretch! Cursed be the mother who gave you birth!" she screamed. "Dance! or die by whiplash!"

And she herself, holding Sisa with one hand and whipping her with the other, started jumping and dancing.

The mad woman finally understood, and began moving her arms in harmony with the music. A smile of satisfaction contracted the lips of the teacher, the smile of a female Mephistopheles successful with a promising student: there were hate, contempt, mockery and cruelty in the smile; more, one single laugh could not have said.

Absorbed in the enjoyment of her spectacle, she did not hear the arrival of her husband until the door loudly opened with a kick.

The *Alferez* appeared pale and gloomy, saw what was happening and hurled a terrible look at his wife. She did not move from her place, and continued smiling mockingly.

The *Alferez* laid his hand as gently and tenderly as he could on the shoulder of the strange dancer and made her stop. The mad woman breathed a sigh and gradually sat down on the floor stained with her blood.

Silence prevailed: the *Alferez* was breathing hard. His wife, who was observing him with a questioning look in her eyes, gathered up the whip and asked him slowly and calmly:

"What is the matter? You haven't even said good evening to me!"

The *Alferez*, without replying, summoned the orderly.

"Take this woman with you. Let Marta treat her and give her another blouse. You will give her food, and a good bed to sleep in...beware of treating her badly! Tomorrow you will take her to Sr. Ibarra's house."

Then he carefully closed the door, fastened the bolt and approached his lady.

"You are asking for me to break you!" he said, clenching his fists.

"What is the matter?" she asked, rising and drawing back.

"What is the matter with me?" he shouted in a voice of thunder, spewing out a blasphemy and showing her a piece of paper with jumbled writing on it: "Did you not write this letter to the *Alcalde* saying that I am being paid for allowing gambling, you bitch? I don't know why I do not crush you!"

"Let's see! I dare you!" she said with mocking laughter. "He who can crush me has to be much more of a man than you!"

He heard the insult but saw the whip. He took one of the plates that was on a table and threw it at her head. The woman, accustomed to these battles, ducked swiftly, and the plate smashed against the wall. A cup and a knife met with the same fate.

"Coward!" she screamed at him, "Don't you dare come nearer!"

And she spat at him in order to exasperate him more. Blind with fury and roaring mad, he threw himself at her, but she, with astonishing speed, lashed at his face with the whip and, running and stumbling against all obstacles, locked herself in her room, closing the door violently. Roaring with anger and pain, the *alferez* went in pursuit and was able only to bang against the closed door—causing him to break out in curses.

"May all your descendants be accursed, you filthy pig! Open, you bitch! Open, or I break your head!" he roared, beating the door with his fists and feet.

Doña Consolacion did not answer. Sounds of furniture and a trunk being moved as if to mount a barricade were heard. The whole house vibrated to the sound of blows, his feet kicking against the door and his imprecations and curses.

"Don't come in! Don't you come in!" the woman was saying in her raucous, disagreeable voice. "If you so much as show your face, I'll shoot you!"

He seemed to have quieted himself little by little, and contented himself with pacing from one end of the room to the other like a caged animal.

"Go out into the street and cool your head!" the woman continued mockingly. She appeared to have finished her preparations for defense.

"I swear, once I lay hold of you not even God Himself will be able to recognize you, filthy pig!"

"Yes," she blurted out. "You can say all you want... You did not want me to hear mass; you did not allow me to fulfill my duties towards God!" this with the mocking sarcasm of which she alone was capable.

The *alferez* picked up his helmet, straightened himself a bit, and marched off with loud, giant strides. After a few minutes he returned, not making the least sound. He had removed his boots. The servants, accustomed to these spectacles, were usually bored, but the removal of the boots called their attention. They winked at each other.

The *alferez* seated himself on a chair near the sublime door and had the patience to wait for more than half an hour. "Have you really left, or are you still there, you bastard?" she asked from time to time, changing the epithets, with the language becoming more colorful.

Finally she gradually removed the furniture. He heard the sound and smiled.

"Orderly, has the Señor left?" Doña Consolacion shouted. The orderly, at a sign from the *Alferez*, answered:

"Yes, madam! He has left."

She was heard to laugh merrily, and she unfastened the bolt.

The husband slowly stood up; the door half opened...

A scream, the sound of a falling body, imprecations, moans, curses, blows, hoarse voices...Who can describe what took place in the darkness of that room?

The orderly, going out into the kitchen, made a significant sign to the cook.

The latter said: "You are going to pay for that."

"Me? The whole town, perhaps! She asked me if he had left, not whether he had returned."

The cook shrugged his shoulders and continued plucking the feathers of a chicken.

- 41 -

Right and Might

It was ten o'clock in the evening. The last batches of rockets soared, lazily illuminating the dark skies, where moments before paper balloons had shone like so many heavenly bodies, lifted easily by smoke and heated air. Some, adorned with fireworks, burst, threatening the houses. Thus one could see men with pails of water and long poles with pieces of cloth at their ends station themselves on the roofs. Their black silhouettes stood out in the faint clarity of the air and seemed like phantoms descending from space to witness men's rejoicing.

There were also a number of fireworks burning, in the shape of wheels, castles, bulls or carabaos of fire, and a great volcano which surpassed in beauty and splendor anything that had ever been seen by the inhabitants of San Diego.

Now the people en masse head for the town plaza to see the show for the last time. Here and there are seen

Bengal lights illuminating the merry groups in a fantastic way. The youngsters bearing torches search in the grass for dud bombs and for other items that could still be used, but the music gives the signal for the show to begin and all leave the meadow.

The great stage is splendidly illuminated: thousands of lights placed around the posts, hung from the ceiling or coming from the floor below; a constable supervises the lighting. When he comes forward to fix it, the audience whistles at him and cries out: "Here he is, here!"

The orchestra players in front of the stage tune up their instruments and play a prelude; behind this is the place mentioned in his letter by the correspondent. The important personages of the town, the Spaniards, and the rich visitors are occupying the aligned chairs. The townsfolk, those without titles or accoutrements, occupy the rest of the square, some carrying their own benches on their backs, not so much to sit on, but to add to their heights, to be able to see better. This provokes noisy protest from those without seats, so that those on the benches step down immediately, but soon climb back as if nothing had happened.

Comings and goings, shouts, exclamations, sounds of laughter, a bench leg that gives way, a firecracker, augment the noise. Over there one leg of a bench breaks, and the occupants fall down to the crowd's amusement—people coming from afar to see, and now being seen. Over there, they quarrel and dispute over a place; a little farther away the tinkling of glass and bottles breaking: it is Andeng carrying refreshments and drinks; with both hands she carefully holds the large tray, but she meets with her suitor, who wants to take advantage of the occasion...

The *Teniente Mayor*, Don Filipo, presides over the

activities; the *Gobernadorcillo* is addicted to *monte*.[1] Don Filipo tells old Tasio:

"What can I do? The *Alcalde* will not accept my resignation. He asked me: "Don't you have enough strength to fulfill your duties?"

"And what did you answer him?"

"Señor *Alcalde!*" I replied, "the strength of a *Teniente Mayor*, be it so insignificant, is like that of all authority: it derives from higher spheres. The King himself receives his authority from the people, and the people from God. This is precisely what I lack, your Honor! But the *Alcalde* refused to listen to me. He told me that we would discuss this later, after the celebrations."

"Then God help you!" said the old man, trying to move away.

"Are you not going to watch the show?"

"Thank you! In order to dream and talk nonsense I suffice unto myself," answered the philosopher with a sarcastic grin. "Just now I remember, however: Have you ever thought of our people's character? Though peaceful, it is fond of warlike spectacles, of bloody struggles; though democratic, it adores emperors, kings and princes; though irreligious, it goes bankrupt in order to celebrate the pageantry of a cult. Our women possess a gentle nature, yet they go wild when a princess wields a lance...Do you know to what this is due? Well..."

The arrival of Maria Clara and her friends cut the conversation short. Don Filipo received them and accompanied them to their seats. Behind them came the parish priest with another Franciscan and some Spaniards. With the priest came other neighbors who had the habit of escorting friars. Don Filipo received them and led them to their seats.

"May God also reward them in the other life!" said the old man Tasio, moving away.

The show started with Chananay and Marianito in *"Crispino e la Comare."*[2] Everyone had ears and eyes focused on the stage except one: Padre Salvi. He seemed to have gone to the theater only to watch over Maria Clara, whose sorrow lent her beauty an aura of perfection and fascination. It was understandable that the Franciscan should be enthralled. But Padre Salvi's eyes, deep in their sockets, did not reveal enthrallment. In his gloomy glance there was something desperately sad. With such eyes Cain must have contemplated from afar the delightful Paradise described by his mother.

The act was about to finish when Ibarra arrived. His presence was the subject of whispers and murmurs; the attention of everyone was fixed on him and on the parish priest.

The young man, however, appeared not to notice it. He greeted Maria Clara and her friends with ease, seating himself by her side. The only one who spoke was Sinang.

"Have you seen the volcano?" she asked.

"No, my little friend, I had to accompany the *Capitan General*."

"What a pity! The parish priest came with us and was telling us stories of the damned. How does that seem to you? Scare us to keep us from enjoying ourselves. Fancy doing that!"

The priest rose and approached Don Filipo, with whom he seemed to be having a lively discussion. The priest was speaking forcefully, Don Filipo with moderation and in a low voice.

"I am sorry I cannot accommodate Your Reverence," the latter was saying. "Señor Ibarra is one of the biggest contributors, and he has the right to be here as long as he does not disturb the peace and order."

"But is it not disturbing the order to scandalize the good Christians? It is tantamount to allowing a wolf to join the flock! You will answer for this before God and before the authorities!"

"I am always responsible for the acts that are derived from my own free will, Padre," replied Don Filipo, bowing slightly, "but my little authority does not entitle me to interfere in religious matters. Those who want to avoid contact with Señor Ibarra, let them not speak to him. Señor Ibarra does not compel anyone either to speak to him."

"But that is giving danger a chance; he who loves danger shall perish in it!"

"I do not see any danger here, Padre. The *Señor Alcalde* and the *Capitan General*, my superiors, have been speaking to him the whole afternoon, and I am not going to start giving them a lesson!"

"If you do not throw him out of here, we will leave."

"I would regret that very much, but I cannot throw anyone out of this place."

The priest regretted it, but he had no choice but to leave. He made a sign to his companion, who stood up regretfully, and both of them left. Their sympathizers followed suit, but not without a look of hatred towards Ibarra.

The murmurs and the whispers soon increased. Several persons greeted Ibarra, saying to him:

"We are for you; do not mind those others!"

"Who are they?" he asked, puzzled.

"Those who left to avoid contact with you."

"To avoid contact with me? Contact with me?"

"Yes! They say you have been excommunicated!"

Ibarra, completely surprised, did not know what to say, and looked around him. He saw Maria Clara hiding her face behind her fan.

"But is it possible?" he finally exclaimed. "Are we still living in the Middle Ages? So therefore..."

Approaching the young ladies and changing his tone, he said: "Forgive me—I had forgotten that I have an appointment. I will return to escort you."

"Don't go, stay!" Sinang told him. Yeyeng is going to dance in *La Calandria*[3], she dances divinely.

"I can't, little friend, but I will return."

The murmuring increased.

Meanwhile, Yeyeng came out dressed flashily, with the song "Do you give your permission?" and Carvajal answering, "Please pass, etc..." Two soldiers from the Civil Guard approached Don Filipo and requested him to suspend the show.

"But why?" Don Filipo asked in surprise.

"Because the *Alferez* and his lady have beaten each other up, and now they cannot sleep."

"Tell the *Alferez* that we have the *Alcalde Mayor*'s permission and against this permission nobody in town has the power, not even the *Gobernadorcillo* who is my only superior," emphasizing these words.

"The show has to be stopped," the two soldiers repeated.

Don Filipo turned his back on them. The guards left.

He did not say anything to anyone about the incident so as not to cause disturbance.

After a passage of the comedy which was well applauded, Prince Villardo presented himself, challenging to combat all the Moors who were holding his father hostage; the hero threatened to cut off all their heads with a single stroke and send them to the moon.

Fortunately for the Moors, who were preparing themselves for combat to the music of the *Himno de Riego*[4], a tumult arose. The orchestra players stopped all of a sudden and, throwing down their instruments, jumped from their places. The valiant Villardo, who had not been expecting an attack from those quarters, and mistook them for allies of the Moors, also threw away his sword and shield and started to flee. The Moors, upon seeing such a terrible Christian flee, conveniently follow suit. Cries, moans, laments, imprecations, blasphemies were heard; the people ran and banged against each other, lights went off, glasses were flung into space—"*Tulisanes! Tulisanes!*," some cried out..."Fire! Fire! Robbers!" others cried. Women and children wept; the benches and spectators tumbled on the ground amid the confusion, turmoil and tumult.

What had happened?

Two soldiers were running after the musicians with clubs in their hands to put a stop to the show. The *Teniente Mayor* with his police squad, armed with old sabers, were able to apprehend the soldiers despite their resistance.

"Take them to the town hall!" yelled Don Filipo. "Beware of letting them loose!"

Ibarra had returned and was looking for Maria Clara. The frightened maidens, pale and trembling, clung to him; Tía Isabel was saying the litany in Latin.

The people recovered from their terror after being made aware of what had taken place. Everybody was indignant. Stones were thrown at the police who were leading away the two Civil Guards. Someone proposed to set fire to headquarters and to roast alive Doña Consolacion together with her husband.

"That's all they are good for!" shouted an irate woman

who was rolling up her sleeves and extending her arms. "To disturb the people! They persecute only respectable men! There go your *tulisanes* and your gamblers. Let us burn their headquarters!"

One, feeling his arm, asked for confession; moans and plaints issued from under the upturned benches—they came from an unfortunate musician. The stage was full of artists and townsfolk who were talking all at the same time. There was Chananay dressed as Lenore in *Il Trovatore*, talking in marketplace language with Ratia, costumed as a school teacher; Yeyeng, wrapped in her silken mantle, with Prince Villardo; Balbino and the Moors endeavored to console the musicians, more or less hurt in the scuffle. Some Spaniards were pacing back and forth talking and gesticulating.

But there was already a crowd of people being formed. Don Filipo knew what they were up to, and made haste to contain them.

"Don't interfere with order!" he shouted. "Tomorrow we will demand redress and obtain justice. I will answer for that justice!"

"No," some retorted; "they did the same thing in Calamba and the same promise was made, but the *Alcalde* did nothing! We want justice by our own hands...Now, to headquarters!"

It was useless for the *Teniente Mayor* to dissuade them from their purpose. The crowd was adamant. Don Filipo looked around him, seeking help, and saw Ibarra.

"Senor Ibarra! Please! Stop them while I summon my police force!"

"What can I do?" asked the perplexed young man, but the *Teniente Mayor* had already left.

Ibarra in turn looked around him, searching without

knowing for whom. Fortunately he was able to distinguish Elías, who was observing the commotion with indifference. Ibarra went to him, took hold of his arm and spoke to him in Spanish: "For God's sake, do something if you can; I can do nothing!"

The pilot must have understood him, for he lost himself among the crowd.

Lively discussions were heard, swift exclamations, then gradually the crowd started to dissolve, each one adopting a less hostile attitude.

And about time, too, for the soldiers were coming out armed with rifles and fixed bayonets.

In the meantime what was the parish priest doing?

Padre Salvi had not yet gone to bed. On his feet, with brows pressed against the window shutters, he looked towards the plaza motionless, except for an occasional sigh. Had there been more light, perhaps it could be seen that there were tears in his eyes. In this condition he remained for almost an hour.

The noise of the tumult in the plaza awakened him from his reverie. He saw the people coming and going, their clamor and voices reaching him vaguely. One of the servants, who was breathless, informed him of what was going on.

A thought crossed his mind. The profligates are wont to take advantage amid the turmoil and confusion of a woman's terror and weakness. All flee and are saved; nobody thinks of anyone else but of himself; her screams cannot be heard; the women faint, they fall and hurt themselves; terror and fear overcome chastity and in the middle of the night...and when they are in love! He imagined Crisostomo carrying a fainting Maria Clara in his arms and disappearing in the darkness.

He went down, jumping down the stairs, hatless, without his cane and, like a mad man, ran towards the plaza.

There he saw the Spaniards who were rebuking the soldiers of the Civil Guards; searched among the seats earlier occupied by Maria Clara and her friends and saw them empty.

"Padre *Cura!* Padre *Cura!*" the Spaniards cried out to him; but he did not mind them. He ran in the direction of Capitan Tiago's house. There he breathed a sigh of relief. He saw through the transparent gallery an adorable silhouette full of grace and the lovely contours of Maria Clara and that of her aunt bearing glasses and cups.

"I see!" he murmured, "it seems that she was only indisposed!"

After a while Tía Isabel closed the shell windows, and the graceful shadow could no longer be seen.

The priest left the place without seeing the multitude. He saw before him the lovely vision of a maiden's bust, sleeping and breathing gently, with eyelids shadowed by long lashes forming gracious curves like those of Raphael's virgins. The small mouth smiled. That semblance breathed chastity, purity and innocence. That face was a sweet vision amid the white sheets of her bed, like a cherub's head among the clouds.

His imagination saw other things besides...but who can write what a passionate mind can imagine?

Perhaps the press correspondent, who ended his description of the feast and of all the events in the following manner:

"A thousand thanks; endless thanks to the timely and active intervention of the Most Reverend Padre Bernardo Salvi who, defying all danger, among that infuriated mob, amid that uncontrollable crowd, hatless, without cane, appeased the fury of the multitude, making use only of his persuasive word, of the majesty and authority which are never wanting to the priest of a Religion of Peace. The faithful religious, with exemplary self-renunciation, gave up the delights of sleep which all of good conscience like him enjoy, to keep his small flock from suffering a misfortune. The inhabitants of San Diego will undoubtedly never forget this sublime gesture of their Pastor; and they will know how to be eternally grateful to him all throughout their lives!"

- 42 -

Two Visitors

In his frame of mind Ibarra found it difficult to sleep. So he went to his lonely study to distract himself and drive away the sad thoughts that assailed his mind. Dawn found him working on an experiment—making various chemical mixtures into which he inserted fragments of bamboo and other substances which he then stored in sealed and numbered containers.

A servant entered, announcing the arrival of a peasant.

"Let him come in," he said, without even turning his head.

Elías came in; he remained silent on his feet.

"Ah! it is you," exclaimed Ibarra in Tagalog when he recognized Elías. "Forgive me for keeping you waiting; I was not aware. I was making an important experiment..."

"I do not want to distract your attention," answered the young helmsman. "First, I have come to ask if you want anything to be attended to in Batangas where I am going right now; and second, to give you some bad news..."

Ibarra looked at the helmsman with questioning eyes.

"Capitan Tiago's daughter is ill," said Elías calmly, "but it is not serious."

"I was afraid of that!" exclaimed Ibarra in a weak voice. "Do you know the nature of her illness?"

"A fever. Now if you have nothing further to command me..."

"Thank you, my friend! I wish you Godspeed...but before that, allow me to inquire: if it is indiscreet you do not have to tell me."

Elías bowed.

"How did you manage to quell the mob last night?" asked Ibarra, looking fixedly at Elías.

"Very simple!" he answered with perfect calm. "Those who were leading the move were two brothers whose father had died from beatings by the Civil Guards. One day I was lucky enough to save them from the same fate suffered by their father. Both are now grateful to me. I appealed to them last night and they took care of dissuading the others."

"And those two brothers whose father had been beaten to death...?"

"They will end up like their father," replied Elías in a low voice. "When a particular family is once marked out for a certain misfortune, all its members must perish. When lightning strikes a tree it reduces the whole tree to ashes."

And seeing Ibarra silent, Elías took his leave.

The latter, finding himself alone, lost the composure he had maintained in the helmsman's presence. He was overcome with grief.

"It is I...who makes her suffer," he murmured.

He quickly dressed himself and went downstairs.

A short man in mourning attire, with a big scar on his left cheek, greeted him with humility, barring his way.

"What do you want?" Ibarra asked him.

"Señor, my name is Lucas. I am the brother of the man who died yesterday."

"Ah! I offer you my condolences...and so?"

"Señor, I want to know how much you are going to pay my brother's family."

"Pay?" repeated the young man, unable to control his disgust. "We will talk about this. Come back this afternoon because today I am in a hurry."

"Just say how much are you willing to pay," Lucas insisted.

"I have told you that we will talk about it another day. Today I have no time," said Ibarra, growing impatient.

"You don't have time today, Señor," he said with bitterness, placing himself squarely before Ibarra. "You don't have any time to spare for the dead?"

"Come back this afternoon, my good man. Today I have to visit a sick person."

"Ah! for someone sick, you forget the dead? Do you think that because we are poor...?"

Ibarra looked at him and cut him short.

"Don't put my patience to a test!" he said and proceeded on his way. Lucas left, looking at him with a smile full of hatred.

"One knows that you are the grandson of him who exposed my father to the sun!" he murmured between clenched teeth. "You still have the same blood!"

And changing his tone he added: "But, if you pay well...we are friends!"

- 43 -

The Espadaña Couple

The feasting and the celebrations are over. The townsfolk of San Diego find themselves again, as in previous years, with their coffers poorer. They have worked hard, sweated much, lost sleep without enjoying themselves or gaining new friends—in short, they have paid dearly for the merrymaking and the headaches. But it does not matter: the following year they will do the same thing, the same in the next century, because this till now has been the custom.

In Capitan Tiago's household there is sadness. The windows are closed; the people inside walk on tiptoe, hardly making a noise. It is only in the kitchen that one can attempt to speak in a loud voice. Maria Clara, the life of the house, is lying ill in bed. The state of her health can be discerned in every face, just as a spiritual malaise can be described from an individual's features.

"What do you think, Isabel? Shall I give alms to the

Cross of Tunasan, or to the Cross of Matahong?" asks the sorrowing father in a low voice. "The Cross of Tunasan grows, but that of Matahong sweats. Which of the two, do you think is more miraculous?"

Tía Isabel reflects, shakes her head and murmurs:

"Grow....To grow is more miraculous than to sweat. We all sweat but we all do not grow."

"It is true, yes, Isabel, but note that to sweat...for a piece of wood which is made into a bench leg, to sweat—that is no petty miracle... Let us see, the best solution is to give alms to both crosses. No one would resent it and Maria Clara would soon recover...Are the rooms ready? You already know that a foreign gentleman is coming with the doctors, a kind of relative of Padre Damaso's. It is important that nothing be wanting."

At the other end of the dining room are the cousins Victoria and Sinang, who have come to keep the sick girl company. Andeng is helping them polish the silver tea set.

"Do you know Dr. Espadaña?" Andeng, Maria Clara's foster sister, asks Victoria with some interest.

"No!" replied the one asked. "The only thing I know about him is that he charges high for his services, according to Capitan Tiago."

"He must be very good then!" says Andeng. "The one who attended Doña Maria charged high for boring a hole in her womb, that is why he is a wise man."

"Silly!" exclaimed Sinang. "Not everyone who charges high fees is a wise man. Look at Dr. Guevara: after showing his ignorance by helping in the delivery and cutting off the baby's head, he charged the widower fifty pesos...He only knows how to collect."

"What do you know?" her cousin asked her, digging

an elbow into the latter's ribs.

"As if I didn't know! The husband, who is a logger, after losing his wife, also had to give up his house, because the *Alcalde,* who is a friend of the doctor's, obliged him to pay...how should I know? My father lent the logger money to travel to Sta. Cruz."

A carriage stopped in front of the house, putting a stop to the conversation.

Capitan Tiago, followed by Tía Isabel, went running down the stairs to welcome the newcomers. They were Dr. Tiburcio de Espadaña, his wife the Dra. Doña Victorina de los Reyes de Espadaña and a young Spaniard of pleasant features and agreeable appearance.

Doña Victorina was wearing a silk gown embroidered with flowers and a hat with a huge cluster of tricolored leaves half crushed by red and blue ribbons. The dust of the highway had mixed with the rice powder that covered her cheeks and—just as we saw her in Manila—she was holding the arm of her lame spouse.

"I have the pleasure of introducing to you, our cousin Don Alfonso Linares de Espadaña!" said Doña Victorina, pointing to the young man. "The gentleman is a godson of Padre Damaso's relative, and a personal secretary yet to Cabinet members."

The young man saluted with grace. Capitan Tiago almost kissed his hand.

While they are sending the various suitcases and bags upstairs, while Capitan Tiago takes them to their rooms, allow us to say something about this couple whom we have already met in the early chapters of our narrative.

Doña Victorina is a woman of some forty-five Augusts, equivalent to thirty-two Aprils, according to her mathematical calculations. She had been pretty in her youth, had a good figure—thus she was wont to say herself—but enamored with the contemplation of her own person, she had looked with great contempt upon her many Filipino admirers, her aspirations being aimed at another race. She did not want to give her diminutive white hand to anyone—but not for lack of confidence, for not a few times had she delivered jewels of inestimable value into the hands of foreign adventurers and nationals.

Six months before the epoch of our narrative, she saw the realization of her loveliest dream, the dream of her whole life, for which she had rejected the expectations of youth and even the promises of love of Capitan Tiago, whispered in her ears in some time past, or sung in some serenade. True, it was the late realization of a dream, but Doña Victorina, even if she spoke bad Spanish, was more Spanish than Agustina of Zaragoza[1], and knew the proverb: "Better late than never." She found consolation in repeating it to herself. "There is no complete happiness on earth," was her other intimate refrain, because both never left her lips in the presence of other people.

Doña Victorina, who had weathered her first, second, third and fourth youth, laying her nets to fish in the sea of worldly waters for the object of her sleepless nights, finally had to content herself with what fate had in store for her. Had the poor woman, instead of her thirty-two Aprils, had only thirty-one—the difference being great in her arithmetic—she would have given back to Fate the prize it offered her, in order to wait for another more in conformity with her tastes. But since man proposes and necessity disposes, she who already had much need of a husband, saw herself obliged to be content with a poor man, cast out of his own province of Estremadura who, after wandering around the world for six or seven years, a modern Ulysses, finally found in the island of Luzon hospitality, money and a bedraggled Calypso, half of his orange, and a bitter one at that! The hapless man was called Tiburcio Espadaña, and although he was 35 years old and looked older, he was, however, younger than Doña Victorina who was only 32. The reason for this is easy to understand but dangerous to tell.

He had come to the Philippines as a petty Customs official of the fifth rank. But he had such bad luck that aside from being seasick often and fracturing a leg during the trip, within fifteen days of his arrival he found himself dismissed from his job, notice of which the *Salvadora*[2] opportunely brought him when he found himself without a penny.

He was through with the sea; he did not want to return to Spain without having made a fortune, so he thought of dedicating himself to something else. Spanish pride kept him from doing manual labor. The poor man would have worked willingly in order to live respectably, but Spanish prestige would not consent to it, and this prestige did not save him from his needs.

In the beginning he lived at the expense of some of his fellow Spaniards, but for Tiburcio, basically an honest man, the bread of charity tasted bitter in his mouth. He lost weight instead of gaining it. Not having any science, money or recommendations, his fellow countrymen advised him—to get rid of him—to go to the provinces and pass himself off as a doctor of medicine. The man at first objected on principle. Although he had been an attendant at the San Carlos Hospital, he knew nothing of the science of healing. His job had been to remove the dust from the benches and to light the stoves—and this had been for only a short time. Necessity was urgent, and his friends dissipated his scruples, so he finally listened to them. He went to live in the provinces and started visiting some sick people, charging a doctor's fee just as his conscience dictated. But like that young philosopher spoken of by Samaniego[3], he ended by charging much and putting a high price on his visits. Because of this he was soon considered a great physician, and he would probably have made his fortune had the Board of Medical Examiners in Manila not noticed his exorbitant fees and the competition he offered others of the same profession.

Private persons and professionals interceded in his behalf. "Man," they told the jealous Dr. C., "let him raise his own small capital so that as soon as he is able to gather six or seven thousand pesos he can return to his own country and live there in peace. After all, what is it to you that he fools these poor gullible *Indios?* They should be smarter. He is an unfortunate man. Don't deprive him of his daily bread. Be a good Spaniard."

The doctor was a good Spaniard, and he consented to close his eyes to what was happening. However, the news reached the ears of the townsfolk. They gradually began to lose confidence in Don Tiburcio Espadaña, who thus lost his clientele and was once more obliged almost to beg for his daily bread. At that time he learned from a friend of his, once an intimate of Doña Victorina, of the lady's predicament, of her patriotism and generous heart. Don Tiburcio saw the heavens open for him, and asked to be presented to her.

Doña Victorina and Don Tiburcio met. "*Tarde venientibus ossa,* for the latecomer, bones"—he would have exclaimed, had he known Latin. She was no longer passable; she was passé. Her luxuriant hair had been reduced—according to her maid—to a tiny bun the size of a head of garlic; wrinkles furrowed her face, and her teeth started to loosen; her eyes had also suffered quite considerably; she had to squint frequently to look a certain distance. Her character was all that was left.

At the end of half an hour of conversation these two people came to an agreement and accepted each other. She would have preferred a Spaniard who was less lame, less stuttering, less bald, less toothless, who sprayed less saliva when he talked, and had more mettle and a superior air—as it was her habit to say. This class of Spaniards, however, had never approached her to ask for her hand.

She had heard it said more than once that "no grass grows on a busy street"; she honestly believed that Don Tiburcio met her needs—a man of intelligence who, thanks to his sleepless nights, was prematurely bald. What woman is not prudent at the age of thirty-two?

Don Tiburcio, for his part, felt a vague melancholy thinking of his honeymoon. He smiled with resignation and evoked in his mind the specter of hunger. He had never had ambitions nor pretensions: his wants were simple, his thoughts limited; but his heart, virgin until then, had dreamt of a very different divinity. In his youth, when he tired of working, after a frugal supper, he was wont to lie on a broken-down bed to digest his *gazpacho*, and would go to sleep thinking of a smiling, caressing image. Later, when disappointments and deprivations mounted, the years passed and the poetic image never came, he thought simply of a good woman, industrious and hard-working, who would bring him a small dowry, to console him after the fatigue of work and scold him now and then—yes, he thought of such reprimands as an occasion of happiness.

But when he was obliged to wander from one country

to another in search no longer of a fortune but of a measure of comfort with which to live in peace the rest of his days; until, encouraged by the relationships of his countrymen who had come from overseas, he sailed for the Philippines, reality ceded to dreams of a proud half-breed, to a lovely *India* with big black eyes, wrapped in silk and gauze, loaded with gold and precious stones, offering him her love, coaches and so forth. He arrived in the Philippines and thought his dreams were being fulfilled, for young women in gilded carriages in the Luneta and the Malecon[4] had looked at him with a certain curiosity.

When, however, he was out of a job, the *mestiza* and the *India* disappeared. With great effort he visualized the image of a widow, but an agreeable one. And so when he saw his dream being fulfilled in part, he became sad, but having a modicum of common sense, he told himself: "That was but a dream: in this world no one feeds on dreams!"

Thus he resolved his doubts. She uses rice powder— so what? When they get married he will see to it that she stops it. She has many wrinkles, but his coat has more holes and mending. She is an old woman with pretensions, imposing and masculine—hunger is more masculine, more imposing and more pretentious still, but then for this the sweetness of genius was born, and who knows? Love modifies characters. She speaks very bad Spanish; he himself does not speak it well either, according to the head of the Bureau of Customs when he was notified of his dismissal and besides, what does it matter? That she is an ugly and a ridiculous old female? He is lame, toothless and bald! Don Tiburcio preferred to take care rather than to be cared for as a victim of hunger. To a friend's sneering remark he would retort: "Give me bread and call me a fool!"

Don Tiburcio was what is commonly called a man who could not harm a fly: he was modest and incapable of harboring an evil thought. In olden times he would have been a missionary. His stay in the country had not given him the conviction of high superiority, of high worth and great importance which within a few weeks are acquired by a majority of his countrymen. His heart could never harbor hatred. He had yet to find a single subversive; he only saw wretches to be conveniently exploited if he did not want to be unhappier than they. When they tried to raise a case against him for passing himself off as a physician he did not resent it; neither did he complain; he acknowledged the justice and would only reply: "But it is necessary in order to live!"

She married him or, vice-versa, he married her and they went to Sta. Ana for their honeymoon; but during the night of the wedding, Doña Victorina had a terrible indigestion and Don Tiburcio gave thanks to God, demonstrating solicitude and care. On the second night, however, he conducted himself as an honorable man. The next day, when he looked at himself in the mirror he smiled with some sadness, showing off his toothless gums. He had aged at least ten years more!

Doña Victorina was pleased with her husband, so she had good dentures made for him. He was clothed and equipped by the best tailors of the city; she ordered chandeliers and *calesas*; sent for the best teams of horses from Batangas and Albay, and obliged her husband to keep a pair for the coming races.

While she was transforming her husband she did not forget her own person. She stopped wearing the silken *saya* and the *piña* bodice and adopted European attire. She substituted for the simple coiffure of the Filipinas fake ringlets and curls. With these and her ill-fitting European costume she disturbed and upset the tranquility of an idle neighborhood.

Her husband never went out on foot—she did not allow him to be seen limping. He would take her for a drive in the most solitary places, to her great annoyance. She wanted to show her husband off in the most public places, but she held her peace out of deference for the honeymoon period.

It was when the moon waned that he sought to speak to her of the rice powder, saying that it was not natural but faked. Doña Victorina knitted her brows and looked at his false teeth. He kept quiet, and she understood his weakness.

Soon enough she thought she was pregnant and started announcing it to her friends.

"This following month, I and Dr. de Espadaña, we are leaving for the *Peñinsula*. I do not want my son to be born here and dubbed a revolutionary."

She annexed a *de* to her husband's surname. The *de* did not cost much, but it gave the name a certain status. She signed as Victorina de los Reyes *de* de Espadaña. This *de* had become an obsession with her. Neither the lithographer who made her cards nor her husband could persuade her to change her mind.

"If I do not put more than one *de* it can be believed that you don't have it, simpleton!" she said to her husband.

She was continually referring to her preparations for the trip. She learnt by memory the names of the various stopovers. It was a pleasure to listen to her: "I am going to see the isthmus in the Suez Canal. De Espadaña thinks that it is the most beautiful, and he has been around the world... Probably I will no longer return to this country of savages.... I was not born to live here; Aden or Port Said would suit me better; since childhood I have believed so, etc., etc." In her geography Doña Victorina divided the world between the Philippines and Spain, unlike the youngsters who divide it into Spain and America or China by another name.

The husband knew that some of the things she mentioned were outrageous nonsense, but he kept it to himself to avoid her shouting at him and ridiculing him for his stammering speech. She pretended to have pregnancy whims to complete her illusions of motherhood. She fancied bright colors in her attire, surrounded herself with flowers and ribbons, promenaded in a long loose gown along the Escolta, but oh! what a disenchantment! Three months passed and her dream vanished. Now that there was no longer a reason for her prospective son to be born a revolutionary she desisted from her plans to travel. She went to consult specialists, midwives, old women and so forth, but to no avail. To the great chagrin of Capitan Tiago, she made fun of San Pascual Baylon; she did not wish to have recourse to another saint—male or female. A friend of her husband's told her: "Believe me, Madam, you are the only strong spirit in this boresome country!"

She smiled without understanding what a strong spirit was. That night, when they were about to retire, she asked her husband:

"Dear," he replied the st...the strongest spirit I know is ammonia. My friend must have spoken rhetorically."

Since then she always said when she could:

"I am the only spirit of ammonia in this country speaking in rhetoric. That is what Don N de N, a Spanish peninsular[5] of great authority told me."

Whatever she said had to be followed. She had come

to the point of completely dominating her husband, who for his part, did not put up any resistance. He had become like a kind of lap-dog to her. If she was annoyed she did not allow him to go out; and when she was really angry she pulled out his dentures, leaving him unsightly for one or two more days, depending."

It had occurred to her that her husband should be a doctor of medicine and surgery, and so she told him.

"My dear, do you want me to be arrested?" he asked, terrified.

"Don't be a fool! Leave it to me to fix," she replied. "You are not going to treat anyone, but I want you to be called a doctor and me a doctora!"

And the next day the lithographer received the order to carve on a slab of black marble: DR. DE ESPADAÑA, SPECIALIST IN ALL KINDS OF DISEASES.

All their servants had to call them by their new titles. As a consequence the number of curls increased, so did the coating of rice powder, the ribbons and the laces. She looked with more contempt than ever on her poor and less fortunate countrywomen, whose husbands were of a lower status than hers. Each day she felt more dignified and elevated. Growing in this manner, at the end of the year she would feel she was of divine origin.

These sublime sentiments did not deter her from daily becoming an old and ridiculous hag. Every time Capitan Tiago met her and remembered he had paid court to her in vain, he would immediately send one peso to the church for a mass of thanksgiving. Despite this, Capitan Tiago highly respected Doña Victorina's husband because of his title of specialist in all manner of diseases. He listened attentively to the few phrases that he, stammering, was able to say. Because of this and because this doctor did not visit everyone as did the other doctors, Capitan Tiago chose him to treat his daughter.

Young Linares's was an altogether different story. When Doña Victorina was making her preparations for her trip to Spain, she thought of an administrator from the Peninsula—she had no confidence in Filipinos. Her husband remembered his nephew in Madrid, who was studying law and who was considered the smartest in the family. They wrote to him, paying beforehand for his trip, but when the dream did not materialize, the young man was already sailing to Manila.

These are the three personages who had just arrived.

While they were taking refreshments Padre Salvi arrived. The couple already knew him. Linares was introduced to the priest, and he blushed at their recital of his various titles.

They spoke of Maria Clara, of course. The maiden was resting and asleep. They talked about the trip. Doña Victorina showed off her garrulousness, criticizing the customs of the provincials: their nipa houses; the bamboo bridges, without forgetting to mention to the priest their friendship with the second corporal; with this *alcalde*, with this Judge, with the manager etc.—all personages of importance who professed a high regard for her.

"You should have come two days ago, Doña Victorina," replied Capitan Tiago during a short pause in the conversation. "You would have met His Excellency the *Capitan-General*. He sat over there."

"What? How is that? His Excellency was here? And in your house? I don't believe you!"

"I tell you that he sat right there! You should have come two days earlier..."

"Ah! what a pity that Clarita did not get sick earlier,"

she exclaimed with true regret. And, addressing Linares, she said:

"Did you hear that, cousin? His Excellency was here. Now you see that De Espadaña was right when he told you that you were not going to the house of a miserable *Indio!* Because you must have known, Don Santiago, that our cousin was in Madrid a friend to ministers and dukes, and ate at the house of the Count of the Belfry."

"Of the Duke of the Tower, Victorina," her husband corrected his wife.

"It is all the same, if you tell me so..."

"Will I be able to see Padre Damaso today in his town?" Linares interrupted, addressing himself to Padre Salvi. "I was told that it is near here."

"He happens to be here and will come presently," replied the priest.

"I am overjoyed. I have a letter for him," exclaimed the young man. "Had it not been for this happy chance which brings me here, I would have come on purpose to visit him."

In the meantime the happy chance had awakened.

"De Espadaña?" said Doña Victorina after the snack, "shall we go and see Clarita?" And to Capitan Tiago: "For you only, Don Santiago, only for you! My husband treats only people with status and even, even! My husband is not like some people here...in Madrid he visited only personages of stature!"

They went to the patient's room.

The room was almost in darkness, the windows closed to avoid the draft. The sparse light that illuminated the room came from two lighted candles in front of the

Virgin of Antipolo.

Her head was bound with a piece of cloth soaked in cologne; she was carefully wrapped in white sheets of several folds, hiding her virginal form. The maiden was lying on her *kamagon*[6] bed covered with curtains of *piña* and *jusi*. Her hair, framing the oval of her countenance, enhanced the transparent pallor of her face, brightened only by large black eyes that were full of sadness. By her bedside were her two friends and Andeng with a branch of white lilies.

De Espadaña felt her pulse, examined her tongue, asked some questions and stammered, shaking his head: "She is s...sick but she can be cured."

Doña Victorina looked with arrogance at those present.

"Lichen with milk in the morning, marshmallow syrup, and two pills of hound's tooth compound," ordered De Espadaña.

"Take courage, Clarita," Doña Victorina was saying as she approached the bed; we have come to cure you...I am going to introduce to you our cousin!"

Linares was absorbed, contemplating those eloquent eyes which seemed to be searching for someone. He did not hear Doña Victorina calling him.

"Señor Linares," the priest said, waking him from his ecstasy, "here comes Padre Damaso."

Just then Padre Damaso arrived, pale and somewhat sad; upon leaving his bed his first visit was to Maria Clara. He was no longer the Padre Damaso of other times, so vigorous and determined. Now he walked silent and with some hesitation.

- 44 -
Plans

Ignoring everyone else, he went straight to the sickbed and took her by the hand.

"Maria! Maria, my child! you are not to die," he said with indescribable tenderness, tears filling his eyes.

Maria opened her eyes and looked at him with a certain strangeness.

Not one of those who knew the Franciscan would have suspected him capable of tenderness; beneath the rough and coarse exterior nobody could believe such a heart existed.

Padre Damaso could not go on, and he left the bedside crying like a child. He went to the gallery to give free rein to his grief beneath the green bowers of Maria Clara's balcony.

How he loves his goddaughter, all were thinking.

Padre Salvi, motionless and silent, biting his lips slightly, was contemplating the friar.

When he had calmed down, Doña Victorina introduced to him the young Linares, who approached him respectfully.

Padre Damaso looked at Linares from head to toe in silence. He took the letter the latter handed him and read it, apparently without understanding its contents, because he asked.

"And who are you?"

"Alfonso Linares, the godson of your brother-in-law"...stammered Linares.

The Franciscan straightened himself, examined the newcomer anew, and his face brightened. He stood up.

"So you are the godson of Carlicos!" he exclaimed, embracing Linares. "Come here that I may embrace you...A few days ago I received his letter...so it is you! I did not recognize you. It is obvious, you had not been born yet when I left Spain; I did not recognize you!"

And Padre Damaso enfolded in his robust arms the young man who reddened, it is not known whether out of embarrassment or suffocation. Padre Damaso seemed to have forgotten his grief completely. After those emotional moments and the usual questions about Carlicos and Pepa, Padre Damaso asked:

"Come on! What does Carlicos want me to do for you?"

"I believe that in his letter he says something..." the young man stammered again.

"In the letter? Let us see! It is true, he wants me to secure for you a job and a wife! Hmm, a job...a job is easy to find. Do you know how to read and write?"

"I have graduated as a lawyer from the Central University!"

"*Carambas*! So you are a shyster, but you don't look

like...you look like a damsel, but all the better! As to
procuring you a wife...hm! hmm! a wife...!"

"Padre, I am in no hurry," retorted a confused Linares.

But Padre Damaso was pacing back and forth in the
hall, muttering:

"A wife, a wife!"

His face was no longer sad nor happy. Now he looked
very sober and seemed to be in deep thought. Padre Salvi
from afar was contemplating the scene.

"I never thought this matter would cause me such
grief!" he murmured with a break in his voice, "but
between two evils let us opt for the lesser one."

And raising his voice and approaching Linares,
he said:

"Come here, young man. Let us talk to Santiago."

Linares paled, and allowed himself to be led by the
priest, who was in a pensive mood.

Then it was Padre Salvi's turn to pace the hall, buried
in thought as usual.

A voice greeting him stopped him in his monotonous
walk. He raised his head and found himself confronting
Lucas, who saluted him humbly.

"What do you want?" was the unsaid question in the
priest's eyes.

"Padre, I am the brother of the man who died the day
of the fiesta," answered Lucas in a tearful voice.

Padre Salvi drew back.

"And so what?" the priest muttered in an
imperceptible voice.

Lucas was making efforts to cry, and was drying his
eyes with a handkerchief.

"Padre *Cura*," he wailed. "I have been to the house of
Don Crisostomo to ask for indemnity...first, he received
me with a kick, deciding that he would not pay me

anything because he had been in danger of being killed himself through the fault of my dear hapless brother. Yesterday I returned to speak to him, but he had already left for Manila, leaving as it were for charity five hundred pesos and charging me never to return. Ah! Father..."

The priest at first listened to him, surprised and attentive. Gradually, at the sight of that farce of make-believe, he smiled with such contempt and sarcasm that if Lucas had seen it he would have escaped in haste.

"And now what is it that you want?" he asked, turning his back on Lucas.

"Ah! Padre, tell me for the love of God what I must do. Your Reverence has always given good advice."

"Who told you so? You are not from here..."

"Your Reverence is known all over the province!"

Irritated, Padre Salvi approached the terrified Lucas, pointing to the door: "Go back to your house and thank Don Crisostomo that he did not send you to prison! Out you go!"

Lucas forgot all about his play-acting and murmured: "Well I thought..."

"Out with you!" Padre Salvi shouted angrily.

"I would like to see Padre Damaso..."

"Padre Damaso is busy... Out with you!" imperiously ordered the priest anew.

Lucas went down the stairs muttering: "Here is another one...if he does not pay well... The one who pays more..."

Capitan Tiago, Linares, even Padre Damaso ran towards Padre Salvi when they heard his voice.

"An insolent vagabond who begs for alms and is not willing to work!" said Padre Salvi, picking up his hat and cane to head towards the convent.

- 45 -

An Examination
of Conscience

Long days and sad nights had passed at her bedside:
Maria Clara suffered a relapse moments after she
had gone to confession. During her delirium she
uttered only one name—that of the mother she had never
known. Her friends, her father, and her aunt, however,
watched by her bedside. Masses and alms were sent to all
the miraculous images. Capitan Tiago promised to give a
sceptre of gold to the Virgin of Antipolo. Finally, the fever
abated by degrees and with regularity.

Doctor de Espadaña marveled at the healing
properties of marshmallow syrup and of the lichen and
milk concoction, prescriptions he had never varied. Doña
Victorina was so pleased with her husband that when one
day he stepped on her long gown, she did not apply her
penal code of taking away his dentures, but contented
herself with saying to him:

"If you were not so lame you would have stepped

even on my girdle." And she was not wearing one!

One afternoon, while Sinang and Victoria were visiting Maria Clara, the parish priest, Capitan Tiago and the De Espadaña couple were taking tea in the dining room and conversing.

"Well I regret it very much," the doctor was saying, "Padre Damaso will regret it, too."

"And where did you say he will be transferred to?" asked Linares of the priest.

"To the province of Tayabas," the priest said casually.

"The one who will feel it too is Maria Clara, when she learns about it," said Capitan Tiago. "She loves him like a father."

Padre Salvi gave Capitan Tiago a side glance.

"I believe, Padre," Capitan Tiago continued, "that all this illness comes from the incident that occurred during the fiesta."

"I am of the same opinion. You have done well in not allowing Señor Ibarra to speak to her. Her illness would have been aggravated."

Doña Victorina interrupted: "And had it not been for us, Clarita would now be in heaven singing praises to God!"

"Amen, Jesus!" Capitan Tiago thought it was his duty to say.

"You were lucky that my husband had no patient of importance at that time, otherwise you would have had to call another doctor; and here in this place, all doctors are ignorant. My husband..."

"I believe and follow what I have said," the priest cut her short, "Maria Clara's confession caused a favorable change in her ailment, and saved her life. A clean conscience is worth more than many medicines. Take note that I do not deny the power of science, least of all that of surgery! But a clean conscience... Read the books of piety and you will see how many cures have been worked by a good confession alone!"

"I beg your pardon," Doña Victorina, somewhat peeved, retorted, "about the power of confession...see if you can heal the *Alferez's* wife with a confession!"

"A wound, Madam, is not an ailment which a good confession can heal. In that case, conscience has no influence!" Padre Salvi replied severely. "However, a good confession will keep the believer safe in the future against blows like those of this morning."

Doña Victorina further added: "They are blows well deserved," as if she had not heard what Padre Salvi had been saying. "That woman is so insolent! In the church she does nothing but stare at me. It is obvious: she is a nobody. Last Sunday I was on the point of asking her if she had found something amiss with my face, but who would want to get soiled talking to people who are not important?"

The priest, for his part, as if he had not heard all this chatter, proceeded:

"Believe me, Don Santiago, in order to put the last healing touches to her sickness it is necessary for her to take communion tomorrow. I will bring her the viaticum... I believe she has nothing to confess, yet...if she wants to get reconciled to God this evening..."

"I don't know," Doña Victorina interrupted, taking advantage of a pause in the conversation. "I cannot understand how there can be men capable of marrying such a scarecrow as that woman. From afar it can be seen where they come from. It is obvious that woman is dying of envy, it is obvious! How much does an *alferez* earn?"

"So, Don Santiago, please tell your cousin to prepare the patient for the communion tomorrow. Tonight I will drop by to absolve her of her little faults..."

And when he saw Tía Isabel about to leave, he told her in Tagalog: "Prepare your niece for confession this evening. Tomorrow I will bring her the viaticum which will heal her promptly."

"But Father," Linares timidly ventured, "might she not think she is in danger of death?"

"Don't you worry about that!" the priest replied without deigning to look at Linares. "I know what I am doing. I have already had so many sick patients. Besides it is for her to say if she wishes or not to take holy communion. You will see that she will say yes to everything."

For the time being it was Capitan Tiago who had to say yes to everything.

Tía Isabel entered the sick room.

Maria Clara continued to be in bed, pale, very pale. Her two friends were by her bedside.

"Take a grain more," Sinang was saying in a low voice, giving her a white pill which she removed from a crystal tube. He says that when you hear noises or a humming in your ears, stop taking the medicine."

"Has he written you again?" the sick girl asked in a low voice.

"No, he must be very busy!"

"No message for me?"

"He says only that he will try to get the Archbishop to lift the excommunication so that..."

The conversation was stopped because Tía Isabel was approaching.

"The Father says that you must prepare yourself for

confession, my dear," said Tía Isabel. "Leave her so she can make her examination of conscience."

"But it has been only a week since she confessed!" protested Sinang. "I am not sick and I do not sin so often."

"Aba! you don't know what the priest says: the just man sins seven times a day. Come on, do you want me to bring you books?—the Anchor, the Bouquet or the Straight Way to Heaven?"

Maria Clara did not answer.

"Come on, you must not tire yourself," added the good aunt to comfort her. "I myself will read to you the examination of conscience, and you will do nothing else but recollect the sins you have committed."

"Write to him not to think of me anymore," murmured Maria Clara into the ears of Sinang when the latter took her leave.

"What did you say?"

But the aunt entered and Sinang had to leave without understanding what her friend had told her.

Tía Isabel placed a chair close to the light, put her spectacles on the end of her nose and, opening a little book, said:

"Pay close attention, dear. I will begin with the Commandments of the Law of God. I will go slowly so that you can meditate. If you do not hear me well, you will let me know so that I can repeat it. You already know that when it is for your good I never tire."

She started to read in a monotonous and nasal voice the considerations pertaining to sinful cases. At the end of each paragraph she made a long pause to give the young woman time to recollect her sins and repent.

Maria Clara was gazing blankly into space. When they had done with the first commandment to love God above all things, Tía Isabel observed her through her spectacles and was satisfied with her pensive and sad attitude. She coughed piously, and after a long pause, they began the second commandment. The good woman read with unction and after taking up the corresponding considerations, looked again at her niece who was turning her head to one side.

"Bah," Tía Isabel told herself, "in this consideration about taking His holy name in vain, the poor little thing cannot have anything to do. Let us go to the third commandment."

And the third commandment was taken piecemeal, commented upon and after reading the cases in which one sins against it, Tía Isabel looked at the bedside, but now raised her glasses and rubbed her eyes. She had seen her niece cover her face with her handkerchief as if to dry her tears. "Hm! ehem!" she said. The poor girl had fallen asleep during the sermon. Replacing her glasses on the tip of her nose, she mused.

"Let us see if by not sanctifying the feasts father and mother have not been honored."

And she read the fourth commandment with even more pauses and more nasally, thinking of lending more solemnity to the act as many friars did. Tía Isabel had never heard a Quaker preach, otherwise she would herself tremble, too.

In the meantime the young lady raised the handkerchief to her eyes many times, and her breathing became more perceptible.

"What a good soul she is!" the old woman thought to herself. "She is so obedient and meek with all. I have committed more sins and I could never truly cry!"

The fifth commandment was taken up with more

lengthy pauses and a perfect twang if that were possible, with so much enthusiasm that she could not hear her niece's deep sobbing. She made only a single pause, after the considerations about homicide committed with weapons, when she perceived the sinner's moans. Then her tone reached the sublime, she read what was left of the commandment with accents that she endeavored to sound threatening; and, seeing her niece continue to sob, "Weep! my dear, weep!" she told Maria Clara approaching the bed. "The more you weep the sooner will God forgive you. Feel contrition not attrition, in your sobbing. Weep! dear, weep! You don't know how I enjoy seeing you weep. Beat your chest, but not too strongly, because you are still sick."

However, as if sorrow needs mystery and solitude in order to grow, Maria Clara, when she found herself taken by surprise, gradually stopped sighing, dried her eyes without saying a word or replying to her aunt.

Tía Isabel continued with her reading, but since the sobs of her audience had stopped, she lost her enthusiasm. The rest of the Commandments made her sleepy and she yawned to the detriment of the monotonous twanging voice, so she stopped.

"If I had not seen it I would not have believed it," thought the old woman. This girl sins like an old trooper against the first five commandments, and from the sixth to the tenth not even a venial sin, quite the reverse from the rest of us. How the world goes now!"

And she lighted a large candle to the Virgin of Antipolo and two smaller candles to the Lady of the Rosary and the Lady of the Pillar, taking care to separate and set apart in a corner an ivory crucifix, as if giving it to understand that the lighted candles were not intended for the crucifix. The Virgin of Delaroche had no share either, because she was an unknown foreigner, and Tía Isabel so far had not heard of any miracle performed by her.

We do not know what actually happened during that night's confession; we respect those secrets. The confession was long and the aunt, who from afar stood watch over her niece, could see that the priest, instead of lending an ear to the patient's words, had his face turned towards her. It seemed as though he were trying to read her thoughts in the girl's lovely eyes, or to guess at them.

Pale and with drawn lips, Padre Salvi came out of the room. Seeing his dark brow bathed in sweat, it seemed as if he were the one who had been confessing and had not deserved absolution.

"Jesus, Mary and Joseph!" said the old woman, signing herself as if to drive away some evil thought, "who can understand these young women nowadays?"

- 46 -
The Fugitives

Under cover of the feeble light which the moon diffuses across the thick foliage of the trees, a man makes his way slowly and cautiously through the forest. From time to time, as if to orient himself, he whistles a particular tune to which another of the same kind responds from afar. The man listens attentively and continues on his way, following in the direction of the faraway sound.

Finally, across the thousand hazards that a virgin forest offers in the night, he comes to a small clearing bathed by the light of a first quarter moon. Tall rocks crowned by trees rise, forming a kind of ruined ampitheatre; newly felled trees, burned trunks fill the center, mingling with huge boulders which nature has partly covered with its mantle of green moss.

The stranger had hardly arrived when another figure, swiftly emerging from behind a big rock, advances, revolver in hand.

"Who are you?" he asks in Tagalog in an imperious voice, cocking his gun.

"Is old man Pablo among you?" the first man asks calmly, ignoring the question and without any semblance of fear.

"Are you referring to the Captain? Yes, he is."

"Tell him then that Elías is looking for him," said the man who was none other than Elías, the mysterious helmsman.

"Are you Elías?" countered the other with a certain respect, and approached him, but without lowering his gun which was still pointed at Elías. "In that case, come!"

Elías followed him.

They penetrated into a sort of cave sunk into the depths of the earth. The guide, who was familiar with the trail, alerted the helmsman when to descend, bend or crawl on his belly. They were not much delayed, however, and arrived at a kind of hall which was meagerly lighted by pith torches, and occupied by twelve to fifteen armed individuals, with grimy faces and sinister attires—some seated, others lying down hardly speaking to each other. Their elbows rested on a stone slab which served them as table, and in deep thought they contemplated the torches which gave little light and much smoke amid all that gloom. One could see an old man with sad features, his head wrapped with a bloody bandage. If we had not known that it was a hideout of bandits, we could say, seeing despair portrayed on the old man's face, that this was the Tower of Hunger on the eve of Dante's Ugolino devouring his sons.

Upon the arrival of Elías and his guide, the men half-raised themselves, but at a sign from the latter they relaxed and contented themselves with examining the helmsman, who was completely devoid of weapons.

The old man slowly turned his head and found himself confronted with the somber figure of Elías, who was contemplating him openly, full of sadness and interest.

"Is it you?" queried the old man, whose eyes, upon recognizing Elías, brightened up a little bit.

"I never thought I would find you in this condition," murmured Elías, shaking his head.

The old man lowered his head in silence and made a sign to the men. These stood up and left the place, but not without stealing glances to gauge Elias's height and muscles.

"Yes!" the old man answered Elías once they were by themselves. "Six months ago I gave you shelter in my house. It was I then who had compassion on you. Now fate has changed; it is you who have compassion for me. But sit down. Tell me why you have come here."

"It has been fifteen days since I learned of your misfortune," replied the young man slowly and in a low voice, his glance directed towards the light. "I immediately started on my way here and I have been searching for you from one mountain to another. I have traversed almost two provinces."

"I had to escape so as not to shed innocent blood. My enemies dared not confront me. I confronted only some miserable wretches who have done me no wrong."

After a brief pause, while Elías tried to read the thoughts in the somber face of the old man, he replied:

"I have come to make you a proposition. I have been searching in vain for any remnant of the family which did mine a great wrong. I decided to leave the province where I was living to go north and dwell among the independent tribes of infidels. Are you willing to leave behind the life you have begun, and live with me? I will be a son to you since you have lost those you had. I have no family. You will be my father!"

The old man moved his head in a negative mood and said:

"At my age, when one embraces a desperate resolve, it is because there is no other. A man who, like me, has spent his youth and mature years working out his own future and that of his sons; a man who has been submissive to the will of his superiors, who conscientiously fulfilled his commitments, suffered all in order to live in the peace and tranquility that was possible; when this man's blood has cooled with time, and he renounces all his past and all his future to the very edge of the grave, it is because in his mature judgment peace does not exist, nor does the supreme good.

"Why live miserably on foreign soil? I had two sons, a daughter, a home. Today I am like a tree despoiled of its branches. I wander as a fugitive, hunted like a beast in the forest, and all for what? Because a man dishonored my daughter, because her brothers demanded an accounting of the infamy, and because that man is highly placed over the rest of mankind with the title of minister of God. Despite everything else, I, the father, disgraced in my old age, have forgiven the injury, indulgent with the passions of youth and the weaknesses of the flesh, and in the face of an irreparable evil, what could I do except hold my peace and save what was left to me? But the guilty one, fearing sooner or later a forthcoming vengeance, sought the undoing of my sons.

"Do you know what he did? No? Do you know that a theft was simulated in the convent and my son figured as one of the culprits? The other one could not be included because he was absent. Do you know of the tortures to which he was subjected? You must know, because they are the same tortures suffered by all the people. I... I saw my son hanged by the hair. I heard his cries; I heard him call me, and I, a coward and accustomed to peace, I did not have the courage either to kill or to be killed. Do you know that they were unable to prove my son's crime? They saw that all was a frame-up.

"As punishment the priest was transferred to another town; my son died as a result of the tortures. The other son who was left was not a coward like his father. The hangman feared the possibility of revenge from the brother, and under the pretext that my son had no residence certificate, which he had forgotten for the moment, he was apprehended by the Civil Guards, ill-treated, harassed and provoked by his injuries to commit suicide.

"And I, I have survived after such a disgrace, but if I did not have a father's courage to defend my sons, I have a heart still beating for vengeance, and I will have my revenge. The malcontents are starting to unite under my command; my enemies have enlarged my field of action. The day I find myself strong enough to face my enemies I will go down to the plains and extinguish the fires of my vengeance and my own existence! And that day will come, or there is no God!"[1]

And the old man, highly agitated, stood up and with eyes that glowed and a cavernous voice, added, tearing his long hair:

"Curses! May I be accursed for detaining the avenging hand of my sons: I murdered them. I should have left the guilty one to die; I should have believed less in the justice of God and in that of men, and today I would still have my sons, perhaps as fugitives, but I would have had them and they would not have died from torture. I was not born to be a father, so I was deprived of them. A curse be upon me for not learning with my years to know the environment in which I lived! But I will know how to avenge myself in fire and blood and in my own death!"

The unfortunate father, in a paroxysm of grief, had pulled off the bandage, laying open the wound on his forehead, which spurted blood.

"I respect your sorrow and I understand your revenge," said Elías. "I, too, am like you. However, I prefer to forget my mishaps lest I shed innocent blood."

"You can forget because you are young and because you have lost no son, nor your last hope! But I assure you I will do no harm to the innocent party. Do you see this wound? Because I could not kill an unfortunate police guard who was only doing his duty, I allowed myself to be wounded."

"But consider," said Elías after a brief silence. "Consider the fearful holocaust of fire and blood in which you would involve our hapless towns. If you achieve revenge by your own hands, your enemies would take terrible reprisals, not against you, not against those who are armed, but against the people who are usually accused as culprits according to custom, and then consider the injustice that would result!"

"Let the people learn to defend themselves; let each one defend himself!"

"You know that it is impossible! Sir, I knew you in other times when you were happy; then you were giving me wise counsel. Will you allow me...?"

The old man crossed his arms and seemed attentive.

"Sir," continued Elías, weighing well his words: "I had the good fortune to lend service to a rich young man of good will, noble, one who loves the good of his country.

They say this young man has friends in Madrid, I don't know, but I can assure you that he is a friend of the *Capitan General*'s. What do you say if we make him the bearer of the people's complaints, if we awaken his interest for the cause of the oppressed?"

The old man shook his head.

"You say that he is rich? The rich do not think of anything but to augment their riches: they are blinded by pride and the pomp of circumstance. Since they are usually well-off, especially when they have powerful friends, not one of them would bother himself in behalf of those who are unfortunate. I know, for I was rich once."

"But the man I am talking about is not like the others. He is a son who has been insulted in the memory of his father; he is a young man who plans to have a family, and for this reason he thinks of the future, of a good future for his sons."

"Then he is a man who is going to be happy. Ours is not a cause for happy men."

"But it is the cause of all men of good will!"

"So be it," responded the old man, seating himself. "Let us suppose that he would consent to transmit our complaints to the *Capitan General*; let us suppose that he finds in the *Corte*[2] representatives who will sponsor our cause. Do you believe that we will obtain justice?"

"Let us try first, before adopting a bloody alternative," answered Elías. It may surprise you that I, another unfortunate, young and in the prime of life, should propose to you, who are old and weak, to have recourse to peaceful means. But I have seen so much misery caused by ourselves as well as by the tyrants; the defenseless are the ones who pay."

"And if we fail in this?"

"Something will always be achieved, believe me; not all of those who govern are unjust. And if we fail to achieve something, or if they are deaf to our voices, if man has become callous to the sad plight of his fellowmen, then you will have me at your command!"

Full of enthusiasm, the old man embraced Elías.

"I accept your proposition, Elías. I know you keep your word. You will come to me and I will help you avenge your ancestors; you will help me avenge my sons, my sons who were like you!"

"In the meantime, Sir, you will refrain from employing all violent measures."

"You will expose the people's complaints; you know them already. When will I know the answer?"

"Within four days send a man to me at the beach of San Diego, and I will tell him what I get from the person in whom I hope...If he accepts, justice will be done to us. Otherwise I would be the first to fall in our struggle."

"Elías will not die; he will be the leader when Capitan Pablo falls after having satisfied his vengeance," said the old man.

And he himself accompanied Elías out of the cave.

- 47 -

The Cockpit

To sanctify Sunday afternoon one generally goes to the cockpit in the Philippines, as to the bullfights in Spain. Cockfighting, a passion introduced into the country and exploited for almost a century, is one of the people's vices, more transcendental than opium among the Chinese.

The poor go there to risk all they have, desirous to gain money without labor. The rich go there to entertain themselves, using the money left from their parties and thanksgiving masses. The fortune they gamble is their own, the cock is trained, with more care perhaps than is the son, his father's successor in the cockpit, and we see no reason to object to it.

Since the government allows it even to the extent of almost recommending that the spectacle be held only in the public plazas during fiestas (so that all can enjoy it and be inspired?) after high mass until dark in the evening (eight hours), we ourselves intend to watch this game to look for some of our acquaintances.

The cockpit of San Diego is no different from those which are found in other towns, except in some details. It is made up of three divisions: the first—or the entrance— is a large rectangle some twenty meters long by fourteen meters wide. It has a door on one of its sides which is generally kept by a woman in charge of collecting the *sa pintû* or the right of entry. From this contribution which each one gives, the government gets a share, some hundreds of thousands of pesos yearly. They say that with this amount which vice pays for its freedom, magnificent schools rise, bridges and highways are built; awards are instituted in order to foster agriculture and commerce...blessed be the vice which produces such bountiful results!

In this first enclosure can be found the vendors of *buyo*, cigars, sweetmeats and food, etc. Here can be found youngsters who accompany their elders—parents or uncles—who initiate them into the secrets of living. This enclosure leads to a larger space, a kind of foyer where the public congregates before the *soltadas*.[1] There the greater number of fighting cocks are tied to the ground by strings fastened to a bone nail or a wooden peg. There can be found the gamblers, the *aficionados* and the skillful binder of the gaff; there they propose bets, consider them, borrow money; there men malign, swear, laugh loud. That one caresses his favorite cock, stroking its shining plumage; this one examines and counts the scales on the cock's legs; relates the achievements of heroic winners. There one sees many with crestfallen visages carrying by the legs a despoiled carcass. The animal which was a favorite for months, fondled, watched over day and night and on which were pinned alluring hopes, now is just a carcass and will be sold for a peseta, to be cooked in ginger and consumed that very night. *Sic transit gloria mundi!* The loser returns to his home awaited by his anxious wife and ragged children, without his little capital and without his cock. Of all that golden dream, of all that solicituous care during the months, from break of day till sunset, of all that fatigue and labor, what is left is just a peseta and ashes, the residue of so much smoke.

In this foyer the less enlightened discuss; the most light-headed examine conscientiously the subject at hand, weigh, contemplate, spread the wings, feel the muscles of those animals. Some are well-dressed, surrounded and followed by the fans of their cocks; others, dirty and unkempt, with the stamp of vice on their squalid features, anxiously follow the movements of the rich, and attend to the bets, for pockets can be emptied, but passion cannot be satisfied. There is not one single face that is not animated: there is no indolent Filipino, nor one apathetic, nor silent; all is movement, frenzy, eagerness. It can be said that they have a thirst further enlivened by the waters of the sewer.

From this place one enters the arena which they call the *rueda*. The space, fenced in by bamboo stakes, is usually more elevated than the two previous compartments. In its upper part, almost reaching the roof, are stands for the spectators, or for the gamblers—which amounts to the same thing. During the fights these stands are occupied by men and boys who shout, cheer, sweat, quarrel and blaspheme. Fortunately almost no woman gets up there. In the ring can be found the prominent men, the rich ones, the famous gamblers, the concessionaire, the referee. The cocks fight on a perfectly levelled ground. Here, destiny distributes to families laughter or tears, feasts or famine.

At the hour when we enter we see the *Gobernadorcillo*, Capitan Pablo, Capitan Basilio and Lucas—the man with the scar on his face, who felt keenly the death of his brother.

Capitan Basilio approaches one of the townsfolk and asks:

"Do you know which cock Capitan Tiago brought?"

"I don't know, sir. This morning two arrived, one of which is the *lásak*, or red and white, that defeated the Consul's *talisain* or green."

"Do you think my *búlik*, my black and white, can fight him?"

"Of course. I will bet my house and my shirt on it."

At that moment Capitan Tiago arrives. He is attired as the big gamblers are, in a shirt of Canton cloth, woolen pants, and straw hat. Behind him follow two servants carrying the *lásak* and a white cock of colossal dimensions.

"Sinang told me that Maria is getting better every day," says Capitan Basilio.

"Did you lose last night?"

"A little. I know you won...let us see if I can get it back."

"Do you want to play the *lásak?*" Capitan Basilio asks, looking at the bird, and asking the servant to give it to him.

"It depends, if there is a bet."

"How much will you bet?"

"Less than two, I don't play."

"Have you seen my *búlik?*" Capitan Basilio asks, and calls a man who brings a small bird.

Capitan Tiago examines it, and after weighing it and analyzing the scales on its legs, he returns the bird to the handler. He asks:

"How much will you put up?"

"What will you bet?"

"Two and five hundred."

"Three?"

"Three it is."

"For the next one!"

The chorus of gamblers and the curious spread the news that two famous cocks would engage in combat. Both have histories and the reputation of winning. Everybody wants to see, to examine the two celebrities; opinions are expressed; prophecies are uttered.

In the meantime, the voices grow in volume; so does the confusion. The ring is invaded, the stands taken by storm. The handlers bring out the two birds—one red and white, the other white—already gaffed but with blades still in their sheaths. Cries are heard for the white; a few shout for the red.

The white is heavily favored and the red handicapped.

The Civil Guards mingle with the crowd. They are not wearing the full and complete uniform of their corps, but they are not in civilian clothes either. They wear denim trousers with red stripes, shirts stained blue by their jackets, garrison caps. This is their disguise in harmony with their behavior: they bet and stand watch; they disturb and talk of maintaining peace.

While there is shouting, hands are extended, jingling coins to make them sound; while the pockets are emptied of their last coin, or where there is none, pledges are made, promising to sell the carabao, the next harvest etc., two young men, apparently brothers, follow the gamblers with envious eyes; they approach and whisper timid words to which nobody listens. They become more and more gloomy and regard each other with disgust and disappointment. Lucas observes them slyly with a malignant smile; he jingles some silver pesos, passes by the two brothers, and looks towards the ring, shouting:

"I pay fifty, fifty against twenty for the white!" The two brothers exchange looks.

"I have been telling you," murmured the older one, "not to bet all the money. If you had only obeyed we would have money now to bet on the red!"

The younger one approaches Lucas, timidly touching his arm.

"Is it you?" exclaims Lucas, turning around and feigning surprise. "Is your brother accepting my proposition, or have you come to place your bet?"

"How do you want us to bet when we have lost all our money?"

"So you accept?"

"He does not want to! If you can lend us something, since you say you know us..."

Lucas scratched his head, pulled at his shirt and replied:

"Of course I know you both; you are Tarsilo and Bruno, young and strong. I know your brave father died as a result of the one hundred daily lashes which those soldiers gave him; I know that you are not thinking of avenging him..."

"Don't meddle in our affairs," interrupted Tarsilo, the older of the two. "That brings bad luck. If we did not have a sister we would have been hanged a long time ago!"

"Hanged? Only cowards are hanged, those who have no money nor protection. Anyway, the mountain is close by."

"A hundred against twenty, I go for the white," yelled a passerby.

"Lend us four pesos...three...two...pleaded the younger

brother. "We will return it doubled; the fight is about
to begin."

Lucas again scratched his head.

"Tst! This money is not mine. Don Crisostomo gave it
to me for those who want to serve him. But I see that you
are not like your father. That one—yes, he was indeed
valiant. He who is not has no right to enjoy himself."

And he walked away, but not too far.

"Let us accept. What difference does it make?
Hanged or shot, it doesn't matter. The poor aren't good
for anything else."

"You are right, but think of our sister."

In the meantime the ring has been cleared. The contest
is about to begin. The voices begin to die down, and only
the two handlers and the skilled gaff binder remain in the
center. At a signal from the referee the binder unsheathes
the steel and the fine blades gleam, threatening, sparkling.

The two brothers approach the circle morose and
silent, leaning their foreheads against the bamboo fence.
A man comes close to them and whispers in their ears:

"*Pare!*[2] a hundred against ten. I go for the white!"

Tarsilo looks at him stupefied. Bruno digs his elbow
into the side of his brother, who replies with a grunt.

The handlers hold the birds skillfully, taking care
not to be slashed. A deep silence reigns. One would think
that those present, except the handlers, were horrible
waxen puppets. One cock is brought close to the other, its
head held tightly so that it can be pecked and provoked,
and vice-versa: in all duels there have to be equal terms,
the same between Parisian gamecocks as with Filipino
gamecocks. Then they are made to look at each other
eyeball to eyeball so that the poor animals might recognize
who had plucked out its feather and whom to fight with.

Their neck plumage starts to bristle and ruffle; they look at each other with hatred in their small round eyes. Thus the moment has arrived: they are lowered to the ground at a certain distance from each other and left by themselves.

They advance gradually; their steps on the hard level ground can be heard. No one is talking now; no one breathes. They raise and lower their heads as if to measure each other with their eyes. The two cocks murmur sounds, perhaps of threat or scorn. They have espied the shining blade scintillating with cold and blue light; the danger stimulates them and they approach each other with determination. But at a step apart they stop, and with fixed eyes lower their heads; the plumage around the neck bristles anew.

At that moment the tiny brain is bathed in blood, anger flashes like lightning, and with natural valor they impetuously lunge against each other, beak against beak, breast against breast, steel against steel and wing against wing. The blows have been evaded in masterful fashion; only a few feathers have fallen. They measure each other again. All of a sudden the white leaps high into the air and slashes with its deadly razor, but the red had bent its legs, lowered its head and the white had slashed only empty air. But as it touches the ground, avoiding getting wounded from behind, it rapidly turns and faces the red. The red attacks with fury, but the white defends itself coolly. It is not the public's favorite for nothing. Everyone, tremulously and anxiously, follows the ups and downs of the fight, with bated breath and one or other involuntary cry. The ground is being covered by red and white feathers dyed in blood, but the duel is not about the drawing of first blood; the Filipinos, following here the laws mandated by government, want a fight to the death, or till the first one flees. Blood already bathes the ground; the blows are sparser, but victory remains uncertain.

Finally in one supreme effort the white hurls itself against the red to give the final blow, nails its gaff on the wing of the red bird, where it is caught in the bones, but the white has been wounded in the breast and the two birds, drained of blood, expended, gasping, one joined to the other, lie still until the white falls, its beak spurting blood; it gives a shuddering kick and agonizes. The red, still pinned on the wing, stands by its side, its legs gradually buckling, and slowly closes its eyes.

The referee, in accordance with government regulations, declares the red the winner. A savage uproar from the public greets the official verdict, a clamor that is heard all over the town, prolonged, sustained and lasting for some time. He who hears it from afar knows then that he who has won is the handicapped, otherwise there would have been less rejoicing. Thus it is with nations. The small nation which wins a victory over a large one tells and sings of it for centuries and centuries after.

"You see?" Bruno said, displeased with his brother, "if only you had believed me today we would have a hundred pesos. It is your fault that we haven't a single *cuarto*."

Tarsilo did not answer, but looked around him with half-closed eyes, as if looking for someone.

"He is over there talking to Pedro," added Bruno. "He gives Pedro money, oh so much money!"

As a matter of fact Lucas was counting some silver coins on the palm of Sisa's husband. They exchange some words in secret and separate from each other with apparent satisfaction.

"Pedro must have entered into an agreement. That

one, he is really determined," sighs Bruno.

Tarsilo remains somber and pensive. He dries the sweat on his forehead with his sleeve.

"Brother," says Bruno. "I am going to make a decision, if you won't. The law prevails: Capitan Tiago's *lásak* should win and we must not lose any opportunity. I want to bet in the next fight. What difference does it make? Thus we will avenge our father."

"Wait!" says Tarsilo, and he looks at his brother fixedly—both are pale—I go with you; you are right, we will avenge our father!"

However, he stops and dries his perspiration again.

Bruno, impatient, asks: "What is keeping you?"

"Do you know what fight follows? Is it worth...?"

"Well, no! Didn't you hear? Capitan Basilio's *búlik* against the *lásak* of Capitan Tiago. According to the law on games, the *lásak* should win."

"Ah, on the *lásak* I would also bet...but first let us make sure."

Bruno makes a gesture of impatience, but he follows his brother. He examines the bird carefully, analyzes, meditates, thinks it over, asks some questions: the wretch doubts. Bruno is nervous and looks at him irritated.

"But don't you see that broad scale near its spurs? Don't you see those claws—what more do you want? Look at the legs! Pull out the wings. And that split scale over the broad one—and that double scale?"

Tarsilo does not hear him. He continues to examine the bird, the sound of gold and silver tinkling in his ears.

"Let us have a look now at the *búlik*," he says in a half-smothered voice.

Bruno taps the ground with his foot, grinds his teeth, but obeys his brother.

They approach another group. There the fighting cock is being fitted with a gaff. They choose the blades, the binder prepares red silken cords, he waxes and rubs it several times.

Tarsilo looks at the bird with brooding and inscrutable eyes. He seems not to see the fighting cock, but something else in the future. He draws his hand across his brow and asks his brother in a husky voice:

"Are you ready?"

"Me? A long time ago—without the need to see!"

"It is because...our poor sister!"

"Aba! Didn't they tell you that the leader is Don Crisostomo? Haven't you seen him take a walk with the *Capitan General*? What danger do we run?"

"And if we die?"

"What difference would that make? Our father was beaten to death."

"You are right!" Both brothers look for Lucas among the groups. As soon as they see him, Tarsilo stops. He exclaims:

"No! Now let's get out of here. We are headed for ruin!"

"You go if you like; I accept the proposal of Lucas."

"Bruno!"

Unfortunately a man approaches them and says:

"Are you betting? I go for the *búlik!*"

The two brothers do not answer.

"I give you odds."

"How much?" Bruno asks the man who starts counting his four-peso coins. Bruno watches breathlessly.

"I have two hundred; fifty against forty!"

"No!" answers Bruno firmly...make it..."

"All right, fifty against thirty!"

"Double it if you want to!"

"Good! The *búlik* is my patron's cock and I have just won. A hundred against sixty."

"The deal is done! Wait, I am going to get the money."

"But I will hold the money," says the man, not having much confidence in Bruno's looks.

"It is all the same to me!" says Bruno, who trusts his fists. And turning to his brother, he says to him:

"If you stay, I am going."

Tarsilo reflects: he loves his brother and his gambling. He cannot leave him alone. He murmurs: "So be it!"

They approach Lucas, who sees them coming, and smiles.

"*Mamâ!*"[3] says Társilo.

"What is it?"

"How much are you giving?" ask the two.

"I have already told you: if you take charge of recruiting those who will attack headquarters, I will give you each thirty pesos and ten for each recruit. If everything comes out satisfactorily, each one will get a hundred and both of you twice as much. Don Crisostomo is rich."

"Accepted!" Bruno exclaims. "And now let's have a look at the money."

"I knew that both of you are brave men like your late father! Come, let them not hear you, those who killed him," says Lucas pointing to the civil guards.

Taking them to a corner, he tells them while he counts the money:

"Tomorrow Don Crisostomo will arrive and bring the weapons with him. The day after tomorrow, by evening, close to eight o'clock, go to the cemetery and I will give you further instructions. You have time to recruit your companions."

They take their leave. The two brothers seem to have exchanged roles. Társilo is calm, Bruno pale.

- 48 -

Two Ladies

While Captain Tiago pitted his *lásak* in the cockpit, Doña Victorina was taking a paséo around town, with the intent to see how the indolent *Indios* took care of their households and their cultivated lands. She had dressed herself as elegantly as she could, putting on top of her silk gown all her ribbons and flowers, to impress the provincials and make them see the gap between them and her sacred person. Leaning on the arm of her lame husband she strutted like a peacock on the streets of the town, amid the wondering and stupefied inhabitants. Cousin Linares stayed at home.

"What ugly houses these *Indios* have!" she was saying, making a wry face. I cannot understand how they can live there; it takes an *Indio* to do that. And they are so proud and ill-mannered! They find themselves among us and they do not even take off their hats! Hit their hats as the priests and the lieutenant of the Civil Guards do; teach them urbanity."

"And if they hit me?" Dr. de Espadaña asked.

"That is why you are a man!"

"B...but I am lame!"

Doña Victorina was in an ill humor; the streets were not paved and the train of her gown grew dusty. Besides, she found herself among many young women who, passing by her side, lowered their eyes and did not admire her elegant costume as they should have. Sinang's coachman, who was driving her and her cousin in a luxurious open carriage, had the nerve to shout to Doña Victorina to "move aside" in such an imposing voice that she had to give way and could only protest: "Look at that brute of a coachman! I am going to tell his master to better educate his servants!"

"Let us return to the house," she commanded her husband.

The latter, fearing a forthcoming storm, pivoted on his crutch and obeyed her mandate.

They encountered the *Alférez*, greeted each other, and this augmented Doña Victorina's discontent. The officer not only did not compliment her on her dress, but also examined her almost with mockery.

"You should not give your hand to a plain *Alférez*," she told her husband after putting some distance between them, "he hardly touched his helmet and you removed your hat. You do not know how to put him in his place!"

"He is the commander h...here!"

"And so what? Are we *Indios*, too?"

"You are right," he replied, not wishing to provoke a quarrel.

They passed in front of the officer's house. Doña Consolacion was at the window, as usual, dressed in flannel and smoking a cigar. Since the house was low, they crossed glances and Doña Victorina had a full glimpse of her: the Muse of the Civil Guard examined her calmly from head to foot and then, pursing her lower lip, spat, turning her face the other way. This stretched the patience of Doña Victorina, and leaving her husband without support, she placed herself squarely before the *Alférez's* wife, trembling with rage and unable to speak. Doña Consolacion gradually turned her head, again calmly appraised her and spat, this time with great contempt.

"What is the matter with you, Doña?" she asked.

"Can you tell me, *Señora*, why you look at me thus? Are you envious?" Doña Victorina was finally able to blurt out.

"Me? Envious? Of you?" the Medusa sneered, "yes, I envy you those curls!"

"Come, woman!" the doctor told his wife. "Don't m... mind her!"

"Leave me to teach this shameless wretch a lesson!" answered the wife, giving a push to her husband, who almost kissed the ground. Turning to Doña Consolacion:

"Watch whom you are dealing with," she said. "Do not think I am a *provinciana*, or a mistress of the soldiers! In my house in Manila *alférezes* do not enter; they wait at the door!"

"Hello! My very excellent *Señora Puput!*[1] *Alférezes* may not enter, only invalids like that one! ha! ha! ha, ha!"

If not for her make-up, one would have seen Doña Victorina blush. She wanted to charge at her enemy, but the sentry stopped her. Meanwhile, the street was filling with curious onlookers.

"Listen! I degrade myself talking to you. Persons of my prominence...Do you wish to wash my clothes? I will pay you well. Do you think that I do not know that you were a laundrywoman?"

Doña Consolacion drew herself up, furious. This matter about the laundry hit her hard.

"Do you think that we do not know who you are and the kind of people you brought along with you? Come on, my husband has already told me! Madam, I at least have not belonged to anyone but one, but how about you? One must indeed be dying of hunger to take on the discards, the rags of all the world!"

The shot hit Doña Victorina on the head. She rolled up her sleeves, closed her fists and, clenching her teeth, started:

"Come down you filthy old sow! I am going to macerate that dirty mouth of yours. Harlot of a full battalion, a whore by birth!"

The Medusa vanished rapidly from the window. Suddenly she was seen coming down in haste, flicking her husband's whip.

Don Tiburcio, pleading, intervened, but they would have come to blows if the *Alférez* had not arrived on time.

"But ladies! Don Tiburcio!"

"Educate well your wife, Sir, buy her better clothes and if you don't have the money, steal it from the people. What are you soldiers good for!" shouted Doña Victorina.

"I am here, madam! Why doesn't your excellency mash my mouth? You are nothing more than tongue and spit, Doña Excellency!"

"Madam," said the furious *Alferez*, "give thanks that I do not forget you are a woman, otherwise I would have kicked you to pieces with all your curls and your ribbons!"

"Se...Señor *Alferez!*"

"Go on, Sir Quack! You do not wear trousers, Juan Lanas!"[2]

"There was an avalanche of words and gestures, of

shouting, insults and injuries. All dirty linen hidden in closets were brought out into the open, and because four talked at the same time and said so many things that degraded certain classes, truths were revealed—we give up on writing what was said. The curious who understood not what they were saying enjoyed the fun no less, and were expectant that matters would end up in an exchange of blows. Unfortunately, the parish priest came and brought peace.

"Gentlemen! Ladies! what a shame! Señor *Alferez!*"

"You are meddling here, you hypocrite, you Carlist!"

"Don Tiburcio, take your wife away with you. Madam, control your tongue!"

"Tell that to those oppressors of the poor!"

"Little by little the dictionary of epithets was exhausted, the recounting of the shameless doings of the two couples, threatening and insulting each other, gradually died out. Padre Salvi went from one to the other, enlivening the scene. If our friend, the correspondent, had been present...!

"This very day we are going to Manila and present ourselves before the *Capitan General!*" an infuriated Doña Victorina was saying to her husband. "You are not a man! A pity the trousers that you waste!"

"B...but woman, how about the guards? I am lame!"

"You should challenge him to a duel with pistol or saber or else...or else..."

And Doña Victorina looked at his dentures.

"Dear, I have never held..."

Doña Victorina did not allow him to finish. With one superb movement she plucked out his dentures, threw them into the middle of the street and stamped on them. He, half sobbing, and she emitting sparks, reached home.

Linares was at that moment talking with Maria Clara, Sinang and Victoria, and having no idea whatsoever of the discord, was not a little distressed when he saw his cousins. Maria Clara, who was seated on an armchair among pillows and blankets, was more than a little surprised at her doctor's new physiognomy.

"Cousin," said Doña Victorina, you challenge now the *Alférez* or else..."

"And why should I do that?" asked Linares, surprised.

"You challenge him right now, otherwise I will tell all here who you are."

"But Doña Victorina!..."

The three friends looked at each other.

"How does this look to you? The *Alférez* has insulted us and he told us you are what you are! That old hag of a wife came down with a whip in her hands...This one..." pointing at her husband, "...and this one allowed himself to be insulted...and he a man!"

"Aba!" said Sinang. "They had a fight and we did not see it!"

"The *Alférez* broke the doctor's teeth!" added Victoria.

"This very day we are leaving for Manila. You will stay here and challenge him; if not I will tell Don Santiago that what you have been telling them is a lie. I will tell him..."

"But Doña Victorina, Doña Victorina!" interrupted pale Linares, drawing near to her, "calm yourself, don't remind me..." and he whispered to her, "Don't be indiscreet, just at this time."

While this was going on, Capitan Tiago arrived from the cockpit, sad and sighing; he had lost his *lásak*.

Doña Victorina did not allow him much time to sigh; in a few words and many insults she recounted what took place, taking care, it is understood, to put herself in favorable light.

"Linares will challenge him to a duel, do you hear me? If not, don't allow him to marry your daughter, don't let it happen. If he has no courage, he does not deserve Clarita!"

"So you are marrying that gentleman?" asked Sinang, her merry eyes filling with tears. "I knew that you were discreet, but not fickle."

Maria Clara paled like wax, half-raised herself and, with terrified eyes, looked at her father, at Doña Victorina and at Linares, who blushed. Don Santiago lowered his eyes and the Doña added:

"Clarita, beware of marrying a man who does not wear trousers—remember this—you expose yourself to insults even from dogs!"

But the young woman did not reply. She told her friends, "Take me back to my room. I cannot walk alone."

They helped her to stand up, their well-rounded arms encircling her waist and, leaning her head on the shoulders of the beautiful Victoria, the maiden returned to her room.

That same night the De Espadaña couple collected their things, presented Capitan Tiago with a bill amounting to some thousands, and the following day very early departed for Manila in Capitan Tiago's carriage. To the timid Linares was relegated the role of avenger.

- 49 -

The Enigma

The dark swallows will return... (Becquer)[1]

Ibarra arrived the following day, as Lucas had previously announced. His first visit was to Capitan Tiago's family, with the purpose of seeing Maria Clara and to let her know that His most illustrious Excellency had already reconciled him to the church. He brought with him a letter of recommendation for the parish priest, written by hand by the Archbishop himself. Tía Isabel was overjoyed. She had a great liking for the young man and did not look favorably on the prospect of her niece's marrying Linares. Capitan Tiago was not at home.

"Come in, come in!" the aunt said in her poor Spanish. "Maria," she said, "Don Crisostomo is back again in God's grace. The Archbishop has de-excommunicated him."

But the young man was unable to advance. The smile froze on his lips and he forgot what he was about to say.

Linares was standing by the balcony at Maria Clara's side, weaving bouquets with the flowers and leaves of the vine. The floor was littered with roses and *sampagas*. Maria Clara was reclining in her chair, wan and pale and in a pensive mood; her eyes were sad. She was playing with her ivory fan which was not as white as her slender fingers.

Linares paled when he saw Ibarra, and Maria Clara's cheeks turned crimson. She tried to stand up but, lacking the necessary strength, she lowered her eyes and dropped her fan.

An embarrassing silence ensued for a few seconds. At last, Ibarra came forward and murmured with a break in his voice:

"I have just arrived and I have come in haste to see you...I find that you are in a better condition than I expected."

Maria Clara seemed to have become speechless. She did not say a single word and remained with her eyes lowered.

Ibarra looked at Linares from head to foot, a look which the timid young man sustained with a certain hauteur.

"Very well, I see that my arrival was not expected," he said slowly. "Maria, forgive me that I have not had myself announced. Some other day I can give you an explanation of my conduct... We will still see each other...surely..."

These last words were accompanied with a look in the direction of Linares. The maiden raised to him her beautiful eyes, full of purity and melancholy, so suppliant and eloquent that Ibarra stopped in confusion.

"Can I come tomorrow?"

"You know very well that to me you are always

welcome," she answered in a hardly audible voice.

Ibarra took his leave outwardly calm, but with a tempest in his mind and a chill in his heart. What he had just seen and felt was incomprehensible. Was it doubt, rejection or betrayal?

"Oh! Just a woman after all!" he murmured.

Without noticing it he arrived at the site of the school construction. The work was far advanced. There was Ñor Juan, with his meter stick and his plumb; he was going back and forth among the numerous workers. He ran to meet Ibarra when he saw him coming.

"Don Crisostomo," he said. "At last you have come. All of us have been waiting for you. Look at the walls, they are one meter and ten centimeters high. Within two days they will reach a man's height. I have been using only *molave, dungon, ipil langil.* I have asked for *tindalo, malatapay,* pine and *narra* for the woodwork upstairs.[2] Do you want to inspect the basement?"

The workers respectfully greeted the youth and redoubled their activity in his presence. He, on his part, tried to show as much as he could that he was well pleased—as much as he could, as permitted by his frame of mind.

"This is the drainage that I took the liberty of adding," Ñor Juan was saying. "The underground ditches lead to a kind of storage about thirty paces from here. It will serve as fertilizer for the garden. These were not included in the plans. Does it displease you?"

"On the contrary, I approve of it and congratulate you for your idea. You are a real architect. From whom did you learn?"

"I taught myself, Señor," the old man modestly replied.

"Ah! before I forget: so that the scrupulous among

you may know, in case some fear to talk with me, I am no longer excommunicated. The Archbishop has invited me to lunch."

"*Aba*, Señor, we pay no attention to these excommunications! We all are already excommunicated. Padre Damaso is, and yet he is as fat as ever."

"How is that?"

"I believe a year ago he caned his assistant, and his assistant is as much of a priest as he is. Who cares about these excommunications, Señor?"

Ibarra saw Elías among the workers. This one saluted him like the rest, but with a look that gave him to understand that he had to talk to him.

"Ñor Juan," said Ibarra, "would you like to bring me the list of the workers?"

Ñor Juan disappeared, and Ibarra approached Elías, who was lifting by himself a huge stone block, and placing it on a cart.

"Señor, can you spare me a few hours of conversation? Take a walk this afternoon by the shore of the lake and embark on my boat. I have to speak to you of grave matters," said Elías who left after seeing Ibarra move his head in assent.

Ñor Juan brought him the list. He read in vain; the name of Elías was not on it.

Ibarra left to see the schoolmaster.

- 50 -

The Voice
of the Persecuted

Before the sun set, Ibarra stepped into Elias's boat, which was on the lake shore. The young man seemed upset.

"Forgive me, Señor," said Elías with a certain sadness upon seeing him. "Forgive me for having presumed to invite you to an appointment. I wanted to talk to you in complete freedom and here we will have no witnesses. Within an hour we will be able to return."

"You are mistaken, friend Elías," said Ibarra, making an effort to smile. "You have to take me to that town with a bell tower that we can see from here. I am bound by fate to go there."

"Fate?"

"Yes! Just imagine! On my way here I met the *Alferez* who was trying to keep me company. I was thinking of you and, knowing that he would recognize you, I had to get rid of him: I had to tell him I was going to that town with a bell tower that can be seen from here, where I will have to stay the whole day, since the man wants to look for me tomorrow afternoon."

"I thank you for your caution, but you should simply have told him that I would accompany you," Elías said casually.

"But what about you?"

"He would not have recognized me, for the only time he ever saw me he did not know how to make out my forebears."

"Today I am out of luck," sighed Ibarra, thinking of Maria Clara. "What is it that you want to tell me?" he asked after a few seconds.

Elías looked around him. They were already far from the shore. The sun had set and, since in these latitudes twilight hardly lasts, the shadows began to lengthen, making brighter the disk of the moon in its fullness.

"Señor," replied Elías gravely, "I am the bearer of the aspirations of many unfortunates."

"Can I do something for them?"

"Much, Sir, more than anybody else."

Elías recounted briefly the conversation he had had with the chieftain of the bandits, omitting mention of the latter's doubts and threats. Ibarra listened attentively, and when Elías finished his narrative there reigned a long silence, which Ibarra was the first to break.

"So what do they wish...?"

"Radical reforms in the armed forces, in the clergy, in the administration of justice—meaning that they are asking for a paternal outlook on the part of the government."

"Reforms? In what sense?"

"For example: More respect for human dignity, more guarantees for the individual's safety, less power to the armed forces, less privileges for this body which easily abuses its power."

"Elías," countered the young man. "I do not know who you are, but I perceive that you are not a common man—you think and act differently from the others. You will understand me if I say that although the state of things is defective, it would still be, even if changed. I could make my friends in Madrid talk by paying them; I could talk to the *Capitan General*, but neither would they achieve anything, nor would he have enough power to introduce so many innovations, nor would I ever take a step in this direction, because I understand very well that although it is true that these entities leave much to be desired, they are at present necessary—they are what we call a necessary evil."

Elías, much surprised, raised his head and looked at Ibarra aghast.

"Do you, Sir, also believe in the necessary evil?" he asked in a slightly trembling voice. "Do you believe that in order to do good it is necessary to do evil?"

"No! I believe in it as a violent remedy which we resort to when we want to heal a sickness. Now, the country is an organism which suffers a chronic malaise and to heal it the government has to resort to harsh and violent means if you like, but useful and necessary ones."

"He is a bad doctor, Sir, he who seeks only to correct the symptoms and muffle them without attempting to inquire into the origin of the evil, or knowing it, is fearful of attacking it. The Civil Guard has only this end in view: the repression of crime by terror and force, an end which is not fulfilled or achieved except by chance. Furthermore, Sir, it has to be taken into account that society only has the right to be severe with the failings of individuals after it has illustrated and administered the necessary means for his moral perfection. In our country, since there is no society, because the country and the government do not constitute a unity, the latter should be indulgent, not only because indulgence is needed, but also because the individual, uncared for and abandoned, has less responsibility for the reason that he has not been enlightened. Besides, following your comparison, the treatment applied to the evils of the country is so destructive as to affect even a sound organism, whose vitality weakens and conditions it for evil. Would it not be more reasonable to strengthen the sick body and lessen somewhat the violence of the treatment?"

"To weaken the Civil Guard would be tantamount to exposing to danger the security of the towns."

"The security of the towns!" Elías exclaimed bitterly. "Very soon it will be fifteen years that these towns have had their Civil Guard, and see: we still have bandits; we still hear of towns being sacked; you are still held up in the highways; the robberies continue, and their perpetrators are not investigated; crime prevails and the true criminal roams freely, but not so the peaceful inhabitant of the town.

"Ask every honest citizen if he regards this institution as a blessing, a protection of the government and not an imposition, a despotism whose abuses wound more than do the criminals' violence. These, it is true, are often serious but are rare. Against it one has the faculty to defend oneself, but against the vexations of the legal power, to protest is not allowed, and even if these are not too grievous, they are, however, continuous and sanctioned.

"What is the impact of this institution on the life of our towns? It paralyzes communication, because all fear ill treatment for senseless causes. Attention is paid to formalities but not to the core of the matter, the first symptom of incapacity. Because one has forgotten his residence tax, he is handcuffed and ill-treated; it matters not whether he is a decent person and one highly considered. The officers consider it a primary duty to have themselves saluted by reason of rank or by force, even in the dead of night. Their inferiors ape them in maltreating and despoiling the peasants, and do not lack pretexts. The sanctity of the home does not exist. Lately in Calamba, they raided, passing through the window, the house of a peaceful citizen to whom the officer owed money and favors. There is no security for the individual. When they need to clean headquarters or house, they go out and apprehend any one who does not resist, and make him work the whole day. Do you want more? During the fiestas the prohibited games have continued, but the merriment allowed by law is brutally disturbed. Did you not perceive the people's reaction to them? What did the people achieve in erasing their anger and waiting for the justice of men? Ah! Sir, if this is what you call preserving the peace..."

"I agree that there are evils," replied Ibarra, "but let us accept these evils for the sake of the benefits that go with them. This institution may be imperfect, but, believe me, it prevents, by the terror it inspires, the growth of the number of criminals."

"Or say rather that on account of terror their number increases," rectified Elías. "Before the creation of this body almost all the evil-doers except a few, were criminals because of hunger. They pillaged and robbed in order to live. However, once the need was over and the highways were free once more, the poor but valiant local police with their obsolete weapons were enough to make them flee, this force so often calumniated by those who have written about our country, those whose rights were to die, whose duty was to fight, and whose recompense was ridicule. Today there are bandits and they are so for life. A mistake, a crime inhumanly punished, the resistance against the abuses of this power, the fear of cruel reprisals throw them out of society forever and condemn them to kill or be killed. The terrorism of the Civil Guard closes against them the doors of repentance, and since a *tulisan* or a bandit fights and defends himself in the mountains better than does a soldier whom he derides, the result is that we are not capable of extinguishing the evil we have created.

"Remember what the prudence of the *Capitan-General* de la Torre[1] achieved: the amnesty he granted to these hapless wretches has proven that in those mountains still beat the hearts of human beings who only yearn for pardon. Terrorism is useful when the people are enslaved, when the mountains have no caves, when power places behind each tree a sentry and when the slave's body has only guts and hunger. But when the desperate one who fights for life feels the strength of his arm, his heart beats and his whole being is filled with bile. Will terrorism be able to put out the fire on which it pours more fuel?"

"You confuse me, Elías, by talking this way. I could believe you are right if I did not have my own convictions. But take note of this—do not be offended for I exclude you and take you for an exception—consider who these are who press for reforms! Almost all of them are criminals or on the verge of criminalism!"

"Criminals or future criminals—but why are they such? Because their peace has been broken, their happiness wrenched from them; they have been wounded in their most cherished affections. When they asked justice for protection they became convinced that they can expect it only from themselves. But you are mistaken, Sir, if you think criminals only ask for it. Go from town to town, from house to house, listen to the silent sighs of families; you will be convinced that the evils the Civil Guard correct are the same, if not less, than the evils they continually cause. Are we to infer from this that all the citizens are criminals? Then what is the use of defending the others? Why not destroy all of them?"

"There is an error in your reasoning which escapes me at this moment, some error in theory which can be refuted by experience, for in Spain, in the Mother Country, this body serves and has been serving effectively."

"I do not doubt it. Perhaps over there it is better organized, the personnel more select, perhaps because Spain needs it, but not the Philippines. Our customs, our character, which are always being invoked when they wish to deny us a right, are altogether forgotten when they want to impose something on us. And tell me, Sir, why this institution has not been adopted by other nations which, being neighbors to Spain, should resemble her more than does the Philippines? Is it because of this that they have less robberies in their trains, less mutiny, less murders, less assassinations and less stabbings in their great capitals?"

Ibarra lowered his head as if reflecting, then raising it, he replied:

"This question, my friend, deserves more serious study. If my investigations show that these complaints are legitimate and well-founded, I will write to my friends in Madrid, since we do not have representatives. In the meantime believe that the government, to make itself respected, needs an entity with unlimited power, and the authority to impose it."

"That is so, Sir, if the government were at war with

the people; but for the good of the government we should not make the people believe that they are at odds with the government. Besides, if this were so, if we prefer strength to prestige, we should consider well those to whom we give this unlimited power, this authority. So much power in the hands of men, and ignorant men at that, full of passions, without moral education, without proven integrity, is a weapon in the hands of a mad man amid a defenseless multitude. I will concede and I want to believe that the government needs this arm; well, let it choose this arm well, let it choose the most worthy, and since it prefers this authority let the people give it, or at least make believe that it knows how to give this authority."

Elías spoke with passion, with enthusiasm, his eyes glowing, his voice resonant, vibrant. There was a solemn pause. The boat, unmoved by paddle, seemed to float motionless over the waters; the moon shone majestically in the dark blue sky; some lights were gleaming on the distant shore.

"And what else are they asking?" Ibarra queried.

"The reformation of the clergy," answered Elías in a sad, discouraged voice. "The unfortunate ones ask for greater protection against..."

"Against the Religious Orders?"

"Against their oppressors, Sir!"

"Have the Filipinos forgotten what they owe to these religious orders? Have they forgotten how much they are beholden to those who rescued them from error to give them the gift of faith, to those who had shielded them against the tyrannies of civil power? This is the evil result of not teaching the history of our country."

Elías, aghast, could hardly believe what he heard.

"Sir," he replied gravely, "you are accusing the people

of ingratitude. Permit me—I, one of the people who suffer—to defend them. Favors done, so that they may have the right to be acknowledged, must not be self-serving. Let us skip the missionary duty of Christian charity, so often handled as a pretext: let us omit history. Let us not ask what Spain has done to the Jewish people who had given all of Europe One Book, One Faith and One God; what she did to the Arabs who gave her culture, and themselves tolerated her own religion and awakened her national pride and self-consciousness, dormant and almost wiped out during the Roman and Visigothic dominations.

"You say that she has given us the true faith and rescued us from error? Do you call faith, those external practices, religion, the trade of scapulars and leather belts; truth, those miracles and tales which we hear daily? Is that the law of Jesus Christ? For this it was not necessary for God to have Himself crucified nor for us to be eternally beholden. Superstition already existed long before this. What was needed was only to perfect it and to raise the price of the goods. You will say that no matter how imperfect is our religion today, it is preferable to what we previously had. I agree, and I am convinced of its truth, but it is too expensive, since in exchange we have given our own nationality, our independence; for it we have given her priests our best towns, our fields and still give up our own savings in the buying of religious objects. An article made by foreign industry has been introduced to us, we paid well and we are at peace. If you speak of the protection it gave against the Spanish land grantees, I could answer you that precisely because of these Religious Orders we fell into the power of the *encomenderos*.[2]

"But no! I admit that true faith and a genuine love for

humanity guided the first missionaries who arrived at our shores. I acknowledge our debt of gratitude to those noble hearts. I know that Spain then abounded with heroes of all categories: in the religious as well as the political, in the civilian and in the military. But because their ancestors were men of righteousness, shall we consent to the abuses of their degenerate descendants? Because they did us a great good, would we be guilty if we prevented them from doing us evil? The country does not seek the abolition of the clergy. It is asking only for reforms as required by the present circumstances and according to its pressing needs."

"I love our country as much as you can love her, Elías; I understand something of what you wish for her. I have listened with attention to what you had been saying, but withal, my friend, I believe we are viewing things with the eyes of passion. I see less need for reform here than in any other place."

"Is it possible, Sir?" exclaimed Elías, throwing up his hands despondently, "you do not see the need for reforms here? You whose family misfortunes..."

"Ah! I forget myself and I forget my own mishaps when the security of the Philippines and that of Spain are involved," Ibarra quickly replied. "To keep the Philippines it is necessary that the friars continue as they do, and in the union with Spain lies the welfare of the country."

Ibarra had already finished speaking, but Elías was still listening. His face was sad and his eyes had lost their brightness.

"The missionaries conquered the country, it is true," he replied. "Do you think that the Philippines will be preserved by the friars?"

"Yes! only by them. Those who have written about her also believe this."

"Oh!" Elías exclaimed, throwing down the paddle in the boat, much discouraged. "I did not think you had such a poor idea of the government and of the country. Why don't you despise one and the other? What would you say of a family which lives in peace only because of the intervention of a stranger? A country that obeys because it is deceived, a government which commands because it resorts to deception, a government which does not know how to inspire love and respect for its own sake! Begging your pardon, Sir, I believe that your government is stupid and suicidal when it rejoices in that belief! I thank you for your kindness in listening to me. Now, where do you want me to take you?"

"No! replied Ibarra. "Let us thresh this out. It is necessary to know which of us is right in a matter of such consequence."

"Forgive me, Sir," said Elías shaking his head. "I am not eloquent enough to convince you, even if it is true that I have had some education. I am an *Indio*, my existence is doubtful to you, and my words are always suspect. Those who have expressed a contrary opinion are Spaniards and as such, even if they speak of trivialities and stupidities, their accent, their titles and their race consecrate them, give them such authority that I desist forever from arguing against them.

"Besides, when I see you, who love your country, you whose father rests beneath these tranquil waters, you who have been provoked, insulted and persecuted, maintaining such opinions in spite of everything, in spite of your education, I start to doubt my own convictions, and to admit the possibility that the people may be mistaken. I have to tell those unfortunate ones that they who placed their confidence in men, must henceforth place it in God and in their own strength. Again I thank you. Tell me where I am to take you."

"Elías, your bitter words have pierced my heart. They also cause me to doubt. What would you have me do? I have not been brought up among the people whose needs, perhaps, I am not aware of. I spent my childhood in a Jesuit school, I grew up in Europe, I have been developed by books and I have read only what men have been able to bring to light. What remains behind in the shadows, what writers failed to write about, I ignore. For all that, I love, as you do, our country, not only because it is the duty of each man to love the country to which he owes his being and which, perhaps, should be his last refuge, not only because my father had taught me thus, because my mother was a native and because all my most lovely memories dwell in her; I love her besides because I owe her and will owe her my happiness!"

"And I because I owe her my misfortune!" murmured Elías.

"Yes, my friend, I know that you suffer. You are unfortunate and this makes you see the future as dark; it influences your way of thinking. Because of this, I listen to your complaints with certain mental reservations. If I could only appreciate the motives, part of that past..."

"My misfortunes recognize a different origin. If I knew that it could be useful, I would relate them to you; other than that I do not make a mystery out of my past. It is sufficiently known to many."

"Perhaps getting acquainted with the past will correct my judgment. I do not put my trust in theories; I am guided by facts."

"If that is so," Elias answered after a thoughtful pause, "I will tell you briefly my history."

- 51 -

The Family of Elias

"Sixty years ago my grandfather lived in Manila. He served as bookkeeper in a Spanish merchant's establishment. My grandfather was then very young; he was married and had a son. One night, it is not known how, the warehouse caught fire. The fire spread through the establishment and to other houses. The losses were heavy, someone had to be blamed and the merchant accused my grandfather. In vain he protested his innocence, but since he was poor and could not pay for able lawyers, he was condemned to be scourged in public and taken through the streets of Manila. Not long ago this was in use, this infamous punishment the people call "caballo y vaca," a thousand times worse than death itself. My grandfather, abandoned by all except his young wife, was tied to a horse, followed by a cruel multitude, and flogged on every street corner, before other men, his brothers, and in the neighborhood of the numerous temples of a God of peace.

"When the unfortunate man, forever branded, had satisfied the vengeance of men with his blood, his tortures and his cries, they had to untie him from the horse because he had lost consciousness. It would have been better for him if he had died then. They gave him his freedom in one of those gestures of refined cruelty. His wife, pregnant at that time, begged in vain from door to door for work or alms, in order to take care of her sick husband and her poor son, but who would trust the wife of a despicable arsonist? His wife was obliged to resort to prostitution."

Ibarra got up from his seat.

"Oh, don't be upset! Prostitution was no longer a disgrace for her, nor an insult to her husband. Honor and shame no longer existed. Her husband was healed of his wounds and, with his wife and son, hid in the mountains of this province. Here the wife gave birth to a misshapen and diseased foetus, which had the good fortune to die. Thus they lived for a few months, wretched, isolated, hated and avoided by all. My grandfather could no longer bear his misery and, less courageous than his wife, hanged himself in his despair upon seeing his wife sick and deprived of all care and help. The corpse rotted before the very sight of the son, who could hardly take care of his sick mother. The stench led to its discovery by the authorities. My grandmother was accused of and condemned for not informing them. Her husband's death was attributed to her, and it was believed that she, the wife of a wretch who turned later into a prostitute, was capable of anything. If she swore, she was called a perjurer; if she wept they called her a liar, and a blasphemer when she called upon God. However, they had some consideration for her left, and waited for her to deliver another baby, with which she was pregnant, before giving her the lash. You know that the friars spread the belief that the only way to deal with the natives is to flog them; read what Padre Gaspar de S. Agustin says.[1]

"Thus condemned, a woman will curse the day her child is born: which, besides prolonging the torment, is tantamount to a violation of her maternal feelings. Unfortunately the woman delivered safely, and also unfortunately the child was born healthy and strong. Two months later she served her sentence to the great satisfaction of the men who thought they were fulfilling a duty. No longer safe in those mountains she fled to a nearby province with her two sons. Here they lived like beasts: hating and hated.

"The older of the two brothers, who remembered in the midst of such misery his happy childhood, became a bandit as soon as he was strong enough to stand on his own. Very soon the bloody name of Bàlat spread from province to province, terror of the towns, because he carried out his vengeance by fire and blood. The younger, who had received Nature's gift of a good heart, resigned himself to his fate and to infamy by the side of his mother. They lived on what the forest gave, donned the rags thrown to them by wayfarers. She had lost her name and she was known only by titles: the delinquent, the whore, the one who had been flogged; he was known only as the son of his mother. Because of the gentleness of his nature no one could believe him to be the son of the arsonist, and because anything about the morality of the *Indios* can be doubted. In the end the infamous Bálat one day succumbed to the power of Justice, which demanded of him a strict accounting of his crimes, and yet had not done anything to teach him what was good.

"One morning the younger brother, looking for his mother who had gone to the forest to gather mushrooms and had not yet returned, found her stretched on the ground by the wayside beneath a cotton tree, face turned towards the sky, eyes wide open and fixed, fingers clenched into the soil which was stained with blood. The young man raised his eyes to look in the direction of the woman's gaze. He saw a basket hanging from a branch. Within the basket he saw the bloody head of his brother."

"My God!" exclaimed Ibarra.

"That is what my father could have said," continued Elías coolly. "The men had dismembered the highwayman and buried the trunk, but the other parts were scattered and hung in different towns. If you ever go from Calamba to Sto. Tomas, you will still see a wretched *lomboy* tree where, rotting, a leg of my uncle hung. Nature has cursed it: the tree neither grows further nor bears fruit. They did the same with other parts of his body, but the head, as the best part of the individual, one that can be recognized easily, they put in a basket and hung in front of his mother's hut!"

Ibarra lowered his head.

Elías continued: "The younger brother fled like an accursed creature from town to town, across mountains and valleys. When he thought that no one would recognize him, he found work in the household of a rich man in Tayabas. His industry and gentle disposition won him the esteem of those who knew nothing of his past. By dint of hard work and thrift he was able to save a small capital and, since misery had passed and he was young, he dreamt of happiness. His good looks, his youth and his somewhat comfortable state won for him the love of a young woman of the town. He was afraid to ask for her hand in marriage, for fear that his past would be known. But love conquers all and both yielded to themselves. To save the maiden's honor the young man risked everything. He asked for her hand; papers were required and the past came to light.

"The young woman's father was rich, and was able to have the man accused in court. He did not try to defend himself; he admitted everything and was sent to prison. The young woman delivered twins: a boy and a girl, who were brought up in secret, made to believe in a deceased father, which was not a difficult thing to do, for the children at a very early age saw their mother die. Besides, we didn't think much of tracing genealogies since our grandfather was rich and our childhood was a happy one. My sister and I were brought up together, we loved each other as twins, who had not known any other love.

"I was sent very young to the school of the Jesuits, and in order not to be totally separated, my sister went to the La Concordia convent school for girls.[2] At the end of our brief education, because we only wanted to be farmers, we returned to the town to take possession of the inheritance from our grandfather. We lived happily for some time, the future smiled on us, we had many servants, our fields harvested bountifully and my sister was on the eve of getting married to a young man she adored and who reciprocated her devotion.

"Because of financial matters, and because of my arrogant character at that time, I was alienated from the good graces of a distant relative who one day threw in my face my somber past, and my infamous paternity. I believed it to be a calumny and I demanded satisfaction. The tomb in which so much rottenness lay was reopened and the truth came out to confound me. To my misfortune we had, for many years, an old servant who put up with all my whims without ever leaving us; contenting himself to weep and sigh amid the jeerings of the other servants. I don't know how my relative found out. This old man was summoned to court and was made to talk and to tell the truth. The old servant was our own father, who stayed close to his beloved children, and whom I had maltreated many times!

"Our happiness vanished, I renounced our inheritance, my sister lost her betrothed and, with my father, we abandoned the town for any other place. The thought that he had contributed to our misfortune shortened the days of the old man, from whose lips I learned all about the painful past. My sister and I were left alone.

"She wept much, but in the midst of so much sorrow which became our lot, she could not forget her love. Without complaining and without saying a word she saw her old love wed another. I saw her gradually wither away without being able to comfort her. One day she disappeared. In vain I searched for her everywhere, in vain I asked about her, until six months later, I learned that after a flood, there had been found on the Calamba lakeshore, among the ricefields, the corpse of a young woman who had drowned or been murdered. A knife was buried in her breast. The town authorities had the facts published in the neighboring towns. Nobody came forward to claim the body; no young woman had disappeared. By the signs given me afterwards, by the dress, the jewels, the beauty of her face, and her luxuriant tresses, I was able to recognize in them my poor sister.

"Since then I have wandered from province to province; my fame and my history are on many lips. Deeds are attributed to me, at times I am calumniated, but I do not pay much heed to the opinions of men and I go on my way. I have here given you a brief sketch of my history and the history of one of the judgments of men."

Elías kept silent and continued paddling.

"I am beginning to believe that you have enough reason," Crisostomo murmured in a low voice, "when you say that justice should procure what is good to reward virtue and to educate criminals. Only...this is impossible, utopian. Where can one obtain so much money to pay so many new employees?"

"What then are priests for, they who proclaim their mission of peace and charity? Is it more meritorious to moisten with water the head of a child, give him salt to eat, than to awaken in the darkened conscience of a criminal that spark given by God to each man to look for what is good? Is it more humane to accompany a criminal to the gallows, than to accompany him along the difficult path which leads from vice to virtue? Are not spies also being paid, hangmen, civil guards? This matter of being dirty also costs money."

"My friend, neither you nor I—much as we would be willing—we would not be able to achieve it."

"By ourselves alone, it is true, we are nothing. But embrace the cause of the people, make common cause with the people, do not ignore their voices, give an example to others, launch the idea of what is called the motherland!"

"What the people want is impossible; it is necessary to wait."

"Wait! To wait is to suffer!"

"If I ask for reforms, they will laugh at me."

"And what if the people support you?"

"Never! I will never be the one to lead the multitude to obtain by force what the government believes to be untimely, no! And if I ever come to see that multitude rise up in arms, I will place myself by the side of the government and I will fight them, because in that mob I would not see my country. I desire its good, that is why I am putting up a school: I will seek for that good by means of instruction, by progressive advancement. Without light there is no way."

"Without struggle, too, there is no freedom," answered Elías.

"But I do not wish that kind of freedom!"

"Without freedom there is no light," replied the helmsman quickly. "You say that you know very little of your country; I believe you. You do not see the forthcoming struggle, you do not see the cloud in the horizon; the struggle begins in the sphere of ideas to come down to the arena which will be dyed in blood. I hear God's voice. Woe unto those who want to resist Him. History has not been written for them!"

Elías looked transfigured. He was on his feet with head uncovered. His manly features, illuminated by the moonlight, bore something of the extraordinary. He shook his abundant mane and continued:

"Do you not see how everything awakens? The sleep lasted for centuries, but one day lightning struck, and the lightning, in destroying, brought forth life. Since then new aspirations work the spirits and these aspirations, today separate, will one day unite, guided by God. God has not failed the other peoples, neither will he fail ours; his cause is the cause of freedom."

A solemn silence followed these words. Meanwhile, the boat, impelled only by the waves, neared the shore.

Elías was the first to break the quiet.

"What message shall I take to those who sent me?" he asked, changing the tone of the conversation.

"I have already told you: I deplore their condition but let them wait, for evils are not corrected by other evils and in our misfortune all of us share in the guilt."

Elías did not reply; he lowered his head, continued paddling and, reaching the shore, took leave of Ibarra saying:

"I thank you, Sir, for the patience you have accorded me. For your sake I ask you henceforth to forget me and not to recognize me in whatever situation you may encounter me."

Having said this, he turned to his boat and paddled it in the direction of a thick bush on the shore. During the long transit he remained silent; he seemed to see no other thing than the thousands of brilliant gems that his paddle churned up and returned to the lake, where they vanished mysteriously into the blue depths.

At last he reached the shore. A man came out of the thicket, and approached him. He asked:

"What shall I say to the Captain?"

"Tell him that if Elías does not die first, he will keep his word," he sadly replied.

"So when will you rejoin us?"

"When your captain believes that the hour of danger has come."

"Very well, goodbye!"

"If I do not die before that," Elías murmured as the other departed.

- 52 -
Changes

T he shy Linares was serious and uneasy. He had just received a letter from Doña Victorina, which read thus:

"Estim cazin: In tree deys I want to noe from U if alredy de alferez kild U or U kild him I no want to pas a dey mor wizout satz animal get hiz punizmen if pasez diz time U neber chalend I tel Don Santiago dat U neber segretary, nor waz gibing jokz to Canobas nor goz palzy to the general Don Arseño Martines I tel Clarita all iz jokin an I no gib U no cuarto mor anlez him U chalend I promiz ol U wish zo U ar alredy chalend him U I warn der ar no x-queuzes nor motib.

> Ur cazin who lav U wid hart,
> Victorina de los Reyes de De Espadaña.
> Sampaloc, Mondey, 7 at night."

The matter was a serious one. Linares knew the character of Doña Victorina and what she was capable of. To speak to her of reason was just like talking of honesty and good manners to a Customs officer of the treasury who is determined to discover contraband where there is none. To plead was useless; to deceive, worse. There was no other recourse but to challenge the *alferez*.

"But how?" he was saying, pacing alone. "What if he receives me in an ugly mood? If I meet his wife? Who would want to be my second? The parish priest? Capitan Tiago? Cursed be the day when I listened to her counsel, that nuisance! Whose idea was it anyway to give myself airs, to put up a bluff and make up those tall tales? What will that young lady say of me? Now I am really sorry to have been secretary to all the Cabinet ministers!"

The good Linares was in this sad soliloquy when Padre Salvi arrived. The Franciscan was, in truth, thinner and paler than usual, but his eyes glittered with a singular light and on his lips there was a strange smile.

"Señor Linares, all alone?" he greeted the young Spaniard, heading for the living room from whose half-opened door escaped some notes of the piano.

Linares wanted to smile.

"And Don Santiago?" added the priest.

Capitan Tiago presented himself that very moment, and kissed the hand of the priest and relieved him of his hat and cane, while smiling the smile of the blessed.

"Come! come!" said the priest, entering the living room followed by Linares and Capitan Tiago. "I have good news to share with you. I have received letters from Manila which confirm the one brought by Señor Ibarra...so after all, Don Santiago, the impediment is removed."

Maria Clara, who was seated at the piano between her two friends, half rose from her seat, but she lost her strength and seated herself again. Linares paled and looked at Capitan Tiago, who lowered his eyes.

"That young man seems very charming to me," continued the priest. "In the beginning I misjudged him...he is somewhat quick-tempered, but afterwards he knows well enough to make amends, so that one cannot hold a grudge against him. If it were not for Padre Damaso..." And he threw a quick glance at Maria Clara who was listening without moving her eyes from the music sheet, despite the hidden pinches of Sinang, who thus expressed her delight; had she been alone she would have danced!

"Padre Damaso...?" Linares asked.

"Yes, Padre Damaso has said," continued the priest without taking his eyes from Maria Clara, "since, as....baptismal sponsor he could not allow...but finally I believe that if Señor Ibarra begs him for forgiveness, which I doubt not, everything will be settled."

Maria Clara rose from her seat, made excuses and retired to her room accompanied by Victoria.

"And if Padre Damaso does not forgive him?" Capitan Tiago asked in a low voice.

"Then...Maria Clara will see...Padre Damaso is her father...spiritual; but I believe they will come to an understanding."

In that very moment steps sounded. Ibarra appeared, followed by Tía Isabel. His presence produced varied reactions. He greeted affably Capitan Tiago, who did not know whether to smile or to weep; Linares, with a deep nod. Padre Salvi stood up and extended his hand so affectionately that Ibarra could not suppress a look of surprise.

"Do not be surprised," said Padre Salvi, "just now we were praising you."

Ibarra thanked him and approached Sinang.

"Where have you been the whole day?" asked this

one with her youthful chatter. "We were asking and saying, where did this soul redeemed from Purgatory go? And each one of us said something else."

"May I know what you have been saying?"

"No that is a secret, but I will tell you when we are alone. Now tell us where you have been, to see which among us was able to guess."

"No, that is also a secret, but I will reveal it to you when we are just by ourselves, with the permission of these gentlemen."

"I should say so, I should say so. It is the last straw," said Padre Salvi.

Sinang took Crisostomo to another end of the living room; she was very thrilled with the idea of keeping a secret.

"Tell me, my little friend," Ibarra asked: "Is Maria angry with me?"

"I do not know, but she says it is better for you to forget her, and she starts to cry. Capitan Tiago wants her to marry that gentleman over there, so does Padre Damaso, but she does not say either yes or no. This morning when we were asking about you and I said: Has he gone to make love to someone, she answered me, 'I hope he has,' and broke into tears."

Ibarra was serious.

"Tell Maria I want to speak to her alone."

"Alone?" Sinang asked, knitting her brows and looking at Ibarra.

"Entirely alone, no, but I do not want that one to be present."

"It is difficult, but do not worry, I will tell her."

"And when shall I know the answer?"

"Tomorrow. Come to the house early. Maria does not

ever want to be alone. We keep her company. Victoria sleeps by her side one evening, and I, the next. Tomorrow is my turn. But listen: what of that secret you were going to tell me? You are leaving without telling me that which is important."

"It is true! I have been to Los Baños town.[1] I am going to do business with coconuts. I am thinking of putting up a factory. Your father will be my partner."

"Is that all? What a secret!" Sinang exclaimed in a loud voice with the tone of an embezzled usurer. "I thought..."

"Careful! I do not allow you to spread the news."

"As if I would," Sinang replied wrinkling her nose. "If it had been something more important, I would tell it to my friends, but buying coconuts! coconuts! Who is interested in coconuts?"

And she hastened to look for her friends.

A few moments later Ibarra took his leave, seeing that the conversation was about to languish. Capitan Tiago had a sweet and sour look on his face; Linares was quiet and observant; the priest, pretending to be in a merry mood, was talking of strange things. Not one of the young women had come out again.

- 53 -

The Card of the Dead and the Shadows

The cloudy sky hides the moon. A cold wind, harbinger of the coming December, sweeps away some dry leaves and the dust on the narrow pathway that leads to the cemetery.

Three shadows are talking to each other in a low voice under the gateway.

"Have you spoken to Elías?" asks a voice.

"No, you already know he is odd and cautious, but he must be on our side. Don Crisostomo has saved his life."

"For that same reason I joined," said the first voice. "Don Crisostomo had my wife treated by a doctor in Manila. I am taking charge of the parish house to settle my accounts with the priest."

"And we, the barracks, to show the Civil Guards that our father had sons."

"How many will you be?"

"Five...five is enough. Don Crisostomo's man says we will be twenty."

"And if all does not go well?"

"Quiet!" said one and all fell silent.

In the semi-darkness one could see a shadow loom stealthily alongside the fence; from time to time it stopped, as if it turned its head and looked back.

And for good reason. About 20 paces behind it came another shadow, more bulky, and which appeared more shadowy than the first; very lightly it treaded the ground, vanished swiftly as if swallowed by the earth every time the first shadow stopped and turned its head.

"I am being followed," said the first shadow. "Could it be a Civil Guard? Did the *sacristan mayor* lie to me?"

"They said that this is the meeting place;" murmured the second shadow, "there must be something fishy about this affair when the brothers hide it from me."

The first shadow finally reached the entrance to the graveyard. The first three moved forward.

"Is that you?" they were asked.

"Is it you?"

"Let us separate, because they have followed me. Tomorrow you will have the weapons and it will be at night. The call is: 'Long live Don Crisostomo.' Now, go!"

The three figures disappeared behind the wall. The recent arrival hid himself behind the gate and waited in silence.

"Let us see who is shadowing me," he muttered.

The second shadow arrived with much caution and stopped as if to look around him.

"I am too late!" he said in a muted voice. "Perhaps they will come back."

And because it was beginning to drizzle and threatening to pour thick and fast for a long time, he thought to take shelter under the gateway.

Naturally he encountered the other.

"Ah! who are you?" asked the recent arrival in a virile voice.

"And who are you?" replied the other coolly. A momentary pause. Both were trying to recognize each other by the timber of the voice and to distinguish the features.

"And what are you waiting for here?" asked the one with the virile voice.

"For the hour to strike eight for me to have the card of the dead. I want to win a large amount tonight," replied the other smoothly. "How about you?"

"For...the same thing."

"Aba! I am glad. Then I will not be without company. I brought a deck of cards with me; on the first stroke of eight I will deal them by chance; on the second, boldly; those that move are the cards of the dead and they have to be disputed with swords. Do you have your own deck?"

"No!"

"Therefore?"

"Very simple. As you deal for them, I expect they will deal for me."

"And if the dead do not deal?"

"That cannot be helped. The game has not yet been made obligatory among the dead..."

There was a moment's pause.

"Are you armed? How are you going to fight with the dead?"

"With my fists," answered the larger of the two.

"Oh! damn it! Now I remember: the dead will not pick when there is more than one alive, and we are two."

"Is that so? Well, I do not want to go."

"Neither do I...I lack money," answered the smaller one, "but we can do one thing. Let us play between us two, and he who loses leaves."

"So be it..." answered the other testily.

"Then let us go in...Do you have matches?"

"They entered and searched for an appropriate place in that semi-darkness. They found a niche and sat down. The shorter one drew from his *salakot* a pack of cards and the other lighted a match.

By the flame they stared at each other, but judging by the expression on their faces, they did not know each other. Of course we recognize in the taller one with the virile voice, Elías; and in the smaller, Lucas with the scar on his cheek.

"Cut," he said, without taking his eyes off Elías.

He moved away some bones which he found in the niche, and drew an ace and a horse. Elías was lighting matches one after the other.

"On the horse," he said. To identify the card he placed a vertebra on top.

"Call," said Lucas, and after four or five cards drew an ace.

"You have lost," he said, and added: "Now leave me alone to attend to my business."

Without saying a word, Elías left, losing himself in the shadows.

Some moments later the clock in the church struck eight, and the belfry tolled the hour for the Holy Souls. Lucas did not invite anyone to gamble with him; he did not even conjure up the dead as required by superstition, but uncovered himself and muttered some prayers, crossing and signing himself with the same fervor as did the Prefect of the Confraternity of the Holy Rosary at the same moment.

All night it continued raining. By nine o'clock the streets were dark and abandoned. The oil lamps which every household must hang up hardly illuminated a space of one meter radius. They seemed to have been lit just to enable one to see the shadows.

Two Civil Guards patrolled the street near the church from one end to the other.

"It is getting cold," said one in Tagalog with a Visayan accent. "We have not caught a single *sacristan*; there is no one to fix the *Alferez's* chicken coop...With the death of the other one, they have gotten scared; this bores me."

"Me, too," replied the other. "Now no one steals, nor robs, nor riots, but thank God: they say that Elías is in town. The *Alferez* says that he who captures him will be free from scourging for three months."

"Ah! do you know his description by heart?" asked the Visayan.

"Of course: height, tall according to the *Alferez*; regular, according to Padre Damaso; complexion, brown; eyes, black; nose, regular; mouth, regular; beard, none; hair, dark..."

"And other distinguishing marks?"

"Black shirt, black trousers, woodcutter..."

"He will not escape. I seem to see him already."

"I will not confuse him with another even if they look alike."

And both soldiers continued their patrol.

By the light of the lantern we see again two shadows, one behind the other, walking cautiously. An emphatic: "Who goes there?" stops both, and the first shadow answers in a shaking voice: "Long live Spain!"

The soldiers drag him out and take him under the light of the lantern to identify him. It was Lucas, but the soldiers were not sure, and looked at each other in consultation.

"The *Alferez* did not say that he has a scar," said the

Visayan in a low voice. "Where are you going?"

"To have a mass offered tomorrow."

"Did you not see Elías?"

"I do not know him, Sir!" Lucas replied.

"I am not asking you whether you know him, stupid! We do not know him either. I am asking you if you have seen him."

"No, Sir!"

"Listen well: I will give you his description: Height, sometimes tall, at times regular; hair and eyes, dark; everything else about him is regular," said the Visayan. "Do you know him now?"

"No, Sir," replied Lucas in a daze.

"Then, go, you fool!" And they gave him a push.

"Do you know why Elías seems tall to the *Alferez*, and to the priest regular?" asked the Tagalog thoughtfully of the Visayan.

"No!"

"Because the *Alferez* was flat on his back on the mud when he saw him; and the priest was on his feet."

"It is true," the Visayan exclaimed. "You are smart...How come you are a Civil Guard?"

"I have not always been one—I have been a smuggler," replied the Tagalog boastfully.

But another shadow drew their attention. They gave him the "Who goes there?" and brought him under the light. This time it was Elías who presented himself.

"Where are you going?"

"Sir, I am pursuing a man who beat and threatened my brother. He has a scar on his face and his name is Elías!"

"Hah!" exclaimed both and looked at each other terrified. And forthwith they dashed in the direction of church where minutes before Lucas had disappeared.

- 54 -

A Good Day Is Foretold by the Morning[1]

Soon enough the news spread throughout the whole town that many lights had been seen in the cemetery the night before.

The head of the Tertiary Order spoke of lighted candles and described their shapes and sizes; he could not say quite exactly how many there were, but had counted more than twenty. Sister Sipa of the Confraternity of the Holy Rosary could not stand it that one from a rival confraternity should brag that she alone had seen this miracle of God. Sister Sipa, even if she did not live close by, heard laments and wails, to the extent that she believed she recognized in the voices certain persons known to her in another time...but, for Christian charity, she was not only forgiving them, but also praying for them and withholding their names, for which all declared her an instant saint. Sister Rufa does not have in truth such a fine sense of hearing, but she cannot suffer Sister Sipa to claim what she may have heard and she had not. That is why she had a dream and there had appeared many souls, not only of dead people but also of live ones. The souls in anguish asked for a share in the indulgences which she had accumulated and recorded. She could mention their names to the interested families, and would only ask for small alms to relieve the Pope of his needs.

A youngster, a shepherd, who attempted to assert not having seen anything more than a light and two men with *salakots*, scarcely escaped from blows and insults. In vain he swore; there were his carabaos which came with him and they could testify.

"Do you think you know better than the prefect and the Sisters of the Confraternity, you free mason, you heretic?" they told him, looking at him with suspicious eyes.

The parish priest climbed to the pulpit and again began to preach about Purgatory, and the pesos came out of hiding to pay for a mass.

But let us leave the souls in anguish behind, and listen to the conversation between Don Filipo and the old Tasio, sick in his lonely house. It has been days since the philosopher or madman has left his bed, having been laid prostrate by a rapidly progressing ailment.

"In truth, I do not know whether or not to congratulate you on the acceptance of your resignation. Before, when the *Gobernadorcillo* ignored brazenly the wishes of the majority, it was proper for you to resign; but now when you are at odds with the Civil Guard, your resignation is inconvenient. In times of war one should remain in his post."

"Yes, but not when the commanding officer prostitutes himself," replied Don Filipo. "You already know that the following morning the *Gobernadorcillo* set free the soldiers

I was able to apprehend, and refused to move one step farther. Without the consent of my superior I cannot do anything."

"You, alone—nothing, but with the others you could do much. You should have taken advantage of this situation to give an example to other towns. The rights of the people are above the *Gobernadorcillo's* ridiculous authority; it was the beginning of a good lesson but you lost it."

"And what could I have done against the representative of powerful vested interests? Take Señor Ibarra, for example. He yielded to the beliefs of the crowd. Do you think that he believes in excommunication?"

"You and he are not in the same situation. Señor Ibarra intends to plant ideas and to do so, he has to yield and adjust himself to what is at his disposal. Your mission was to agitate, and to agitate requires strength and drive. Moreover the struggle must not be mounted against the *Gobernadorcillo*; the word should be against him who abuses his power; against him who disturbs public peace and order; against him who fails in his duties; and you would not have been alone, for the country today is no longer the same as it was twenty years ago."

"Do you think so?" asked Don Filipo.

"And you do not feel it?" answered the ancient, propping himself up on his bed. "Ah! it is because you have not known the past; you have not studied the impact of the European immigration; of the advent of new books and the journey of the youth to Europe. Study and compare: it is true that the Royal and Pontifical University of Sto. Tomas still exists with her most enlightened cloister, and some intellects still indulge in the exercise of formulating distinctions and conclusions to the subtleties of scholasticism.[2] However, where will you find nowadays the metaphysical youth of our own times, with prehistoric learning, who, with brains tortured, died philosophizing in some provincial nook without beginning to understand the attributes of being, without resolving the matter of essence and existence, pretentious concepts which have made us forget what is essential, our own existence and proper self?

"Look at the child of today: full of enthusiasm at the sight of broader horizons, he studies History, Mathematics, Geography, Physics, Literature, Physical Sciences; Languages—all subjects which we in our time listened to with horror as if they were heresies; the greatest free-thinker of my time declared these subjects inferior to the Categories of Aristotle and the laws of syllogism. Man has finally understood that he is man. He has renounced the analysis of his God, to penetrate the impalpable, in what he has not seen, to set up laws about the phantoms created by his mind; man understands that his heritage is the vast world whose dominion is within his reach. Tired of a useless and presumptuous endeavor, he bows his head and examines all that surrounds him. Do you see today how our poets are born? The muses of nature open her treasures for us little by little, and they begin to smile as if to encourage us to advance further. Scientific experiments have given us their first fruits; what we lack now is the time to perfect them. Our new lawyers are being cast in the new mold of the philosophy of law— some are beginning to shine in the midst of the darkness that surrounds our courts and are drawing attention to change in the march of time. Listen to our youth talk, go to the centers of learning, and other names resound in the walls of the cloisters where before we heard only of

Saint Tomas, Suarez, Amat, Sanchez and others, idols of my era.

"In vain do the friars clamor from the pulpit against the moral degeneration, as the fish vendors clamor against the avarice of their buyers, without taking into account that their merchandise is spoiled and worthless. In vain do the convents extend their roots and branches to stem the new tide of ideas in the towns; the old gods are gone; the roots of the tree can starve the plants that thrive on her, but cannot pluck the life of other things which, like the bird, soar to the skies!"

The philosopher was talking with animation, his eyes flashing.

"However, the new seed is small; if everybody chews on it, the progress, which we bought too dearly, can be suffocated," objected Don Filipo, incredulous.

"Choked? By whom? By man, that puny little dwarf? Choke Progress, the potent offspring of Time and Action? When was Progress ever choked? Dogma, the gallows and the bonfires, in trying to stifle it, pushed it. "*E pur si muove*; nevertheless it moves," said Galileo when the Dominicans obliged him to declare the earth did not move; the same phrase can be applied to human progress. Some wills may suffer violence, some individuals may be sacrificed, but it does not matter: Progress will follow its course and from the blood of those who fall now, vigorous shoots will sprout.

"Consider the Press itself, no matter how reactionary it wishes to be, it also takes, without desiring to, a step forward. The Dominicans themselves do not escape this law and they imitate the Jesuits, their irreconcilable enemies. They give feasts in their cloisters, put up small theaters, compose poems, because they are not lacking in intelligence despite their belief that they are still in the 15th Century. They understand that the Jesuits have reason and will still play a part in the future of the young people they have educated."

"According to you, the Jesuits go with progress?" Don Filipo asked admiringly. "Then why are they fought in Europe?"

"I will answer you like an old scholastic," replied the philosopher, lying down again on his bed, and assuming his usual sardonic attitude. "There are three ways of going along with progress: forward, sideways and backward. The first ones guide it; the second, allow themselves to be led; the last are dragged, and to these belong the Jesuits. They would like to take the lead, but seeing it strong and with other tendencies, they capitulate. They prefer to go along instead of being trampled or left along the way among the shadows.

"Now we in the Philippines are at least three centuries behind the cart; we are barely beginning to emerge from the Middle Ages; that is why the Jesuits, who are reactionary in Europe, seen from here, represent progress. The Filipinos owe to the Jesuits their new-born indoctrination in the natural sciences, soul of the 19th century, just as to the Dominicans their scholasticism, now dead in spite of Leo XIII. There is no Pope who can resurrect what common sense has executed... But where have we gone?" he asked, changing his tone.

"Ah! we were talking about the actual condition in the Philippines... Yes, we are now entering an era of conflict—I mean that you, our generation, belong to the night; we are going. The struggle is between the past, which grapples and grasps, with curses the tottering feudal stronghold, and the future, whose song of triumph can be heard from afar amid the splendors of a fresh new dawn bringing the good tidings from other lands...Who will succumb and be buried in the crumbling ruins of the past?"

The old man fell silent, and seeing that Don Filipo was looking at him thoughtfully, smiled and continued:

"I can almost guess what is in your mind."

"Really?"

"You are thinking that I could well be wrong," he said, smiling sadly. "Today I am feverish. I am not infallible. As Terence says: *"Homo sum et nihil humani a me alienum puto;* I am a man, and I do not judge what is not human as alien to me.'* But sometimes to dream is allowed, why not dream of pleasant things in the last hours of existence? And what next, I have lived only on dreams! You are right: I dream! Our young men think of nothing but loves and pleasures. They spend more time and effort in seducing and dishonoring a young woman than thinking of the good of their country. In taking care of the household and God's family, our women neglect their own. Our men are active only for vice and heroic only in shame. Childhood awakens in darkness and routine; youth lives its best years without an ideal. And the mature, sterile, only serve to corrupt youth with their example...I am glad to die...*claudite jam rivos, pueri;* lower the curtain, children."[3]

"Do you need some medicine?" Don Filipo asked, to change the trend of the conversation which had cast a shadow on the sick man's face.

"Those who are dying need no medicine; those who remain need it. Tell Don Crisostomo to visit me tomorrow. I have important things to tell him; within a few days I go. The Philippines is in darkness!"

After a few minutes more of conversation, Don Filipo left the sick man's house in a grave and thoughtful mood.

- 55 -

Discovery

*There is nothing concealed that
will not be disclosed, or hidden
that will not be made known.*

(Luke 12:2-NIV)

The church bells herald the evening prayer. Upon hearing this religious pealing all stop, leave their occupations and uncover their heads: the laborer who comes from the field suspends his song, stops the rhythmic gait of the carabao which he mounts, and prays; the women make the sign of the cross in the middle of the street and move their lips with affectation so that no one will doubt their devotion; the man stops stroking his cock and prays the Angelus for luck to favor him; in the homes people pray in loud voices. All sounds that are not of the Ave Maria are dissipated, muted.

The parish priest, however, hat on, crosses the street

and scandalizes many old women; and more scandalous still, the priest is headed towards the *Alferez's* house. The devotees believe it is time to suspend the movement of their lips to kiss the hand of the priest, but Padre Salvi does not even notice them. Today, he does not find pleasure in placing his bony hand on a Christian nose, from there to slide surreptitiously (as observed by Doña Consolacion) onto the bosom of a gracious maiden who bows to ask for blessing. Something important must preoccupy him to make him thus forget his own interests and that of the church.

He virtually hurtles up the stairs and knocks impatiently at the door of the *Alferez*, who appears frowning, followed by his other half, who smiles like one damned.

"Ah, Padre *Cura!* I was about to see you about your goat..."

"I have come on a very important matter..."

"I can no longer allow it to keep on breaking down my fence...If I see it again I will shoot it."

"That is if you survive until tomorrow," said the priest breathlessly, making his way to the living room.

"What? Do you think that an infant of seven months can kill me? I will crush him with a kick!"

Padre Salvi drew back, looking instinctively at the *Alferez's* feet.

"Of whom are you speaking?" he asked, trembling.

"Who else but that stupid dolt who has challenged me to a pistol duel at a hundred paces?"

"Ah!" breathed the priest, and added, "I came to speak to you of a very urgent matter."

"Don't bother me with your matters. It probably will be the same as that of the two boys."

Had the light not been of oil and the lamp not so dirty, the *Alferez* would have noticed the priest's pallor.

"Today, it seriously concerns the lives of many," answered the priest in a stifled voice.

"Seriously?" the *Alferez* repeated, turning pale. "Is that young man such a good shot?"

"I am not talking about him."

"Of whom then?"

The friar looked, pointed at the door, which the *Alferez* closed in his own fashion with a kick. The *Alferez* found his hands superfluous and would not have lost anything had he been left handless. An imprecation and a roar came from behind the door.

"Brute! You have broken my head!" screamed his wife.

"Now let us have it out," he said coolly to the priest.

The priest looked at him for some time, then asked with the nasal monotonous voice of a preacher:

"Have you seen how I came, running?"

"By God, yes! I thought you had diarrhea."

"Well then," said the priest, ignoring the grossness of the *Alferez*, "when thus I fail in my duty it is for grievous reasons."

"And what else?" asked the soldier, tapping the floor with his foot.

"Calm yourself!"

"Then why come in such a hurry?"

The priest came closer and mysteriously asked:

"Don't you know anything new?"

The *Alferez* shrugged his shoulders.

"You admit that you know absolutely nothing?"

"You want to speak to me of Elías, who last night was sheltered by your *sacristan mayor*?"

"No! I am not telling you of those tales," replied the

priest with ill humor. "I speak of a great danger!"

"Well, damn, out with it, so?"

"Come now!" said the friar slowly and with some contempt. "You will come to realize the importance which we religious have: the least lay brother is worth a regiment, and so a parish priest."

And lowering his voice with an air of great mystery:

"I have discovered a great conspiracy."

The *Alferez* started, and regarded the priest with astonishment.

"A terrible and well-planned conspiracy which will strike this very night!"

"This very night?" exclaimed the *Alferez*, springing up to the friar and running for his pistol and saber hanging on the wall.

"Whom do I arrest, whom do I arrest?" he yelled.

"Calm yourself! There is still time, thanks to the haste with which I came; until eight o'clock..."

"I will shoot them all!"

"Listen, this afternoon a woman, whose name I must not reveal (it is a secret of confession), approached me and revealed all to me. At eight o'clock they will seize the barracks by surprise; sack the parish house, take the launch and murder all of us Spaniards."

The *Alferez* was stupefied.

"The woman has not told me more than this," added the priest.

"She did not say more? Then I will arrest her!"

"I cannot consent to that. The confessional is the throne of the God of all mercies!"

"No God nor mercies are of any worth to me! I will arrest her!"

"You are losing your head! What you should do is to

prepare yourself; arm your soldiers quietly and set them in position for an ambush; send me four guards for the convent and advise those on the launch."

"The launch is not here. I will ask for help from the other garrisons!"

"No! it will be noticed, and they will not go ahead with what they are planning. What is important is that we catch them alive and we make them sing, I say that you will make them sing; I, as a priest, should not get mixed up in these matters. Be alert! This is a chance for you to win for yourself crosses and stars; I only ask that it be on record that it was I who warned you."

"It will be placed on record, Padre; and perchance it may win for you a bishop's mitre!" answered the *Alferez* beaming, casting a glance at the sleeves of his uniform.

"So then you are to send me four disguised guards, eh? Be discreet! Tonight at eight, stars and crosses will rain!"

While this was taking place, a man ran up the pathway to the house of Crisostomo and climbed the stairs hurriedly.

"Is the master in?" Elías asked the servant.

"He is in his study, working."

Ibarra, to distract his impatience while waiting for the hour to give Maria Clara his explanations, had gone to work in his laboratory.

"Ah, is it you, Elías?" he exclaimed. "I have been thinking of you. Yesterday I forgot to ask you the name of that Spaniard in whose house your grandfather lived."

"Sir, this has nothing to do with me..."

"See," continued Ibarra, not noticing Elias's agitation, and holding a piece of bamboo over the flame: I have made a great discovery—this bamboo does not burn..."

"Sir, it has nothing to do now with this bamboo. It has to do with you...you must get your papers together and escape this very minute!"

Ibarra regarded Elías with surprise; seeing the latter's serious countenance, he dropped the object he held in his hands.

"Burn everything that can compromise you and within an hour find yourself a safer place."

"And why?" Ibarra finally asked.

"Place in safety all that is of value to you..."

"Why?"

"Burn all papers written by you or to you—even the most harmless that can be interpreted wrongly."

"But...why?"

"Why? Because I have just discovered a conspiracy that is being attributed to you in order to destroy you."

"A conspiracy? And who is plotting it?"

"It has not been possible for me to find out its author. A moment ago I just spoke with one of the wretches paid to participate, whom I was not able to dissuade."

"And this one, did he not tell you who it is that is paying him?"

"Yes, he required me to keep it secret. He said it was you!"

"My God!" exclaimed Ibarra, terrified.

"Sir, do not hesitate. Let us not lose time. The conspiracy may break out, perhaps this very night!"

Ibarra, his eyes almost out of their sockets and hands pressed to his temples, seemed not to have heard him.

"The blow cannot be stopped," continued Elías. "I have come too late. I don't know the leaders...save yourself, Sir! Preserve yourself for your country!"

"Where can I escape to? This evening I am expected!"

Ibarra exclaimed, thinking of Maria Clara.

"To any town, to Manila, to the house of some authority, but another place, so that no one can say you are directing the movement."

"And what if I myself denounce the conspiracy?"

"You, denounce?" exclaimed Elías, regarding Ibarra and drawing back. "You would be considered a traitor and a coward in the eyes of the conspirators and pusillanimous in the eyes of others; it could be said that you baited them to gain credit for yourself; it could be said..."

"But what am I to do?"

"I have already told you: destroy all papers relative to your person, take flight and await the course of events."

"And Maria Clara?" the young man exclaimed. "No! I would rather die!"

Elías wrung his hands and said:

"Well, at least ward off the blow; prepare yourself for when they accuse you!"

Ibarra looked around him in a daze.

"Then help me! Over there in that folder I have my family's letters. Pick out the letters written by my father which may perhaps implicate me. Check the signatures."

And the young man, stunned and bewildered, opened and closed drawers, gathered up papers, read through letters rapidly, tore some up and kept others, selected books and leafed through them and so forth. Elías was doing the same, less upset, but with the same zeal. But he stopped; his eyes widened; he was turning back and forth a paper he was holding, and he asked with a voice that shook:

"Did your family know Don Pedro Eibarramendia?"

"Of course!" answered Ibarra, opening a drawer and lifting up a sheaf of documents. "He was my great-grandfather."

"Your great grandfather? Don Pedro Eibarramendia?" Elías asked again, his face livid and features altered.

"Yes," replied Ibarra, distraught. "We shortened the family name, which was too long."

"Was he a Basque?" asked Elías, approaching him.

"Yes, a Basque...but what is the matter with you?" he asked Elías, surprised.

Elías closed his fists and pressed them against his brows, looking at Crisostomo, who drew back at the sight of the man's facial expression.

"Do you know who Don Pedro Eibarramendia was?" he asked between clenched teeth. "Don Pedro Eibarramendia was the wretch who calumniated my grandfather and caused all our misfortunes...I was looking for that family name. God is delivering you to me...me an accounting for our miseries!"

Crisostomo gazed at Elías terrified, but Elías shook him by the arm and told him in a voice full of bitterness and hatred:

"Look at me well: see if I have suffered, and you are alive, you love, you have a fortune, a home, you enjoy people's consideration, you live...you live!..." Completely outside himself, Elías ran towards Ibarra's small collection of weapons ... but as he laid hold of two daggers, he let them drop and looked bewildered at Ibarra, who stood motionless.

"What was I going to do?" he murmured and fled from the house.

- 56 -

The Catastrophe

Capitan Tiago, Linares and Tía Isabel are having supper in the dining room. From the living room is heard the clatter of dishes and silverware. Maria Clara says she has no appetite, and sits at the piano accompanied by the merry Sinang who whispers mysterious phrases into her ear. Padre Salvi paces restlessly from one end of the living room to the other.

It is not that the convalescent is not feeling hungry, no; it is that she expects someone's arrival, and takes advantage of the time when her Argus[1] cannot be present: the dinner hour for Linares.

"You will see how that spectre stays until eight," murmurs Sinang, pointing to the priest. "He should be coming at eight. That one there is in love like Linares."

Maria Clara looks at her friend in shock. The latter, without noticing her, proceeds with her irreverent chatter:

"Ah! Now I know why he does not leave despite my

hints: he does not want to waste light in the convent. Do you know? Since you fell ill, the two lamps that he used to burn have been allowed to die... But look at him! How he ogles, and with what gall!"

At that very moment the house clock strikes eight. The priest trembles and seats himself in a corner.

"He is coming," says Sinang, pinching Maria Clara. "Do you hear?"

The church bells ring eight, and all stand up to pray. Padre Salvi, in a weak voice that shakes, leads the prayer, but each one has his own thoughts, and no one pays attention to him.

Hardly had the prayer finished when Ibarra arrived. The young man wore mourning, not only in his attire, but also in countenance, so much so that Maria Clara, upon seeing him, stood up and moved forward to greet him and ask what the matter was with him.

At that moment a volley of shots is heard. Ibarra stops in his tracks; his eyes dart around; he is speechless. The priest hides himself behind a column. Fresh shots, more explosions are heard from the convent side, followed by shouts and running feet. Capitan Tiago, Isabel and Linares enter the living room in haste, shouting: *"Tulisan, tulisan!"*[2] Andeng follows them, brandishing a roasting spit and running protectively towards her foster sister.

Tía Isabel falls on her knees, weeping and praying the *Kyrie eléison;* Capitan Tiago, pale and trembling, carries a chicken liver on a fork, which he offers sobbing to the Virgin of Antipolo. Linares has his mouth full and is armed with a spoon; Sinang and Maria Clara embrace each other. The only one who remains motionless, as if petrified, is Crisostomo, whose pallor is indescribable.

The shouts and the blows continue; windows are

slammed shut all around; whistles are heard and, every now and then, a shot.

"*Criste eléison!* Santiago! the prophecy is being fulfilled...close the windows!" Tía Isabel sobs.

"Fifty big bombs with two thanksgiving masses!" answers Capitan Tiago; "*ora pro nobis!*"

Gradually, a terrible silence ensues. The voice of the *Alferez* is heard. He shouts, running:

"Padre *Cura!* Padre Salvi! Come here!"

"*Miserere!* the *Alferez* asks for confession!" Tía Isabel cries out.

"Is the *Alferez* wounded?" Linares finally asks. "Ah!"

And now he notices that he has not yet swallowed what he has in his mouth.

"Padre *Cura!* Come out now! There is nothing more to fear!" the *Alferez* continues shouting.

Padre Salvi, pale and shaken, finally decides to come out of his hiding place, and goes down the stairs.

"The *tulisanes* have killed the *Alferez!* Maria, Sinang, to your room! Lock the door! *Kyrie eléison!*"

Ibarra also heads for the stairs in spite of Tía Isabel, who warns:

"Do not go out, you have not gone to confession, do not go out." The good old woman had been a good friend of his mother.

But Ibarra leaves the house. It seems to him that everything has whirled around him and that there is no ground to stand on. His ears are ringing, his legs heavy and moving unsteadily; waves of blood, light and darkness play in his retina.

Despite the light of the moon shining brightly in the heavens the young man stumbles along his way across stones and pieces of wood on the deserted street.

Near the barracks he sees soldiers with fixed bayonets talking animatedly; thus he passes unnoticed.

In the town hall, blows, cries and curses are heard. The voice of the *Alferez* overpowers and drowns out everything.

"To the stockade, handcuff them! Shoot whoever moves. Sergeant, you will stand guard. Today, nobody has leave, not even God Himself! Captain, do not go to sleep!"

Ibarra hastens his pace towards his house. His servants await him, gravely disquieted.

"Saddle the best horse and go to sleep," he tells them.

He enters his study and hastily packs a satchel. He opens a safe, takes all the money there and places it in a sack. He gathers all his jewelry, takes a portrait of Maria Clara from the wall, arms himself with a dagger and two pistols and goes towards a cupboard where some tools are kept.

At that moment three strong sharp raps are heard on the door.

"Who goes there?" asks Ibarra in a melancholy voice.

"Open in the name of the King; open at once or we will break down the door!" answers an imperious voice in Spanish.

Ibarra looks towards the window, his eyes glinting. He cocks his revolver, but changing his mind, sets down his weapons and himself opens the door as the servants also appear.

Three soldiers immediately seize him.

"Give yourself up in the name of the King!" says the Sergeant.

"On what grounds?"

"Over there where we are going they will let you

know. We are not allowed to tell you."

The young man reflects for a moment, and perhaps not wanting the soldiers to discover his preparations for flight, takes up a hat and says:

"I am at your disposition. I suppose it will be only for a few hours."

"If you give us your word that you will not attempt to escape we will not handcuff you: this is a concession from the *Alferez*, but if you try to escape..."

Ibarra goes with them, leaving his servants in consternation.

In the meantime, what has happened to Elías?

Upon leaving Crisostomo's house, he ran like one deranged, without any sense of direction. He crossed fields, reached the forest in the grip of a deep violent agitation. He was running away from the town; he was fleeing from all human contact; he was fleeing from the light; the moon upset him; and he plunged deep into the mysterious shadows of the woods. There, now stopping in his tracks, now wandering through unknown trails, leaning against the aged tree trunks, entangling himself in the underbrush, he looked towards the town which lay at his feet, bathed in the light of the moon which extended into the plains, stretching from the shores of the lake.

The birds, awakened from their sleep, took flight; giant bats, owls, eagles fluttered from branch to branch with strident cries and stared at him with their round eyes. Elías neither heard nor saw them. He believed himself haunted by the angry ghosts of his forebears; he saw hanging from every branch the sinister basket with the bloody head of Bálat, just as his father had told him; he thought he stumbled at the foot of every tree on the corpse of the old woman; he seemed to see hanging among the shades the rotting skeleton of his infamous grandfather...and the skeleton and the old woman and the head were shouting at him: "Coward! Coward!"

Elías left the mountain, fled and descended to the lake, to the shore, where he ran agitated; but there, far away in the middle of the waters, where the moonlight seemed to lift a mist, he thought he saw a shadow rising and swaying, the shadow of his sister with her blood-stained breast, her hair loose and streaming in the wind.

Elías fell on his knees on the sand: "You too!" he murmured, stretching his arms out.

But with eyes staring at the mist, he slowly rose to his feet and stepped forward into the water as if following someone. He walked down the slow incline which formed the bank; soon he was far from shore, the waters rising up to his waist and he went on and on as if fascinated by a seducing spirit. The waters reached his breast...but the discharge of firearms resounded, the vision vanished and the youth returned to reality.

Thanks to the tranquility of the night and to the greater density of the air, the sounds of firing reached him clearly and distinctly. He stopped, collected his wits and noted that he was in the water. The lake was calm and he could make out the lights in the fishermen's huts. He returned to the shore and headed towards the town, for what, he himself did not know.

The town seemed uninhabited; the houses were all shut up. The animals themselves, the dogs which are wont to bark during the night, had hidden in fright. The silvery light of the moon added to the sadness and the solitude.

Fearing to meet the civil guards, he penetrated into the orchards and gardens. In one of these he thought he perceived two human figures; but he continued on his way and, leaping over walls and fences until he laboriously reached the other end of the town, directed himself towards the house of Crisostomo. At the gate were the servants, commenting and lamenting the arrest of their master.

Informed of what had happened, Elías walked away, then round to the back of the house, leaped over the wall, climbed to the window and entered Ibarra's study, where the candle Ibarra had left still burned.

Elías saw the papers and the book, found the weapons and the sacks containing the money and jewelry. He reconstructed in his imagination what had taken place there and, seeing so many compromising papers, thought of gathering them together, throwing them out of the window and burying them.

He glanced at the garden, and by the light of the moon he saw two civil guards come in with a civilian; their helmet and bayonets gleamed.

He came to a decision: he piled up clothes and papers in the center of the room, emptied on top a kerosene lamp and set them on fire. He buckled on the weapons in haste, saw the portrait of Maria Clara, hesitated...put it in one of the sacks and, taking them with him, jumped out through the window.

He was just on time; the civil guards were forcing entry into the room.

"We are going up to seize your master's papers," said the *directorcillo*.

"Do you have permission? Otherwise you may not go upstairs," said an old man.

The soldiers removed him with blows of gun butts and climbed the stairs...but a thick dense smoke filled the whole house and gigantic tongues of fire lunged from the living room, licking at the doors and windows.

"Fire! fire!" shouts everyone.

Everyone makes haste to save what he can, but the fire reaches the laboratory-study and the inflammable materials explode. The civil guards withdraw. Their way is barred by the fire which roars and sweeps everything in its path. In vain is water drawn from the well; everyone is shouting, asking for help, but they are isolated. The fire reaches the other rooms and lifts up to the sky thick spirals of smoke. Now the house is engulfed by the flames; the heated wind feeds them.

Some peasants come from afar; they arrive to witness the huge bonfire, the end of that ancient edifice that the elements had so long respected.

- 57 -

Fact and Fancy

With God's help, dawn finally came to the terrified town.

The street on which the barracks and the courthouse are situated remained deserted and solitary; the houses showed no signs of life. Despite this, the wooden shutter of a window opened loudly and a child's head appeared, turning in all directions, stretching its neck to look around...*plas!* the sound announced the brusque contact of tanned leather with fresh human hide. The boy's mouth made a grimace, his eyes closed, he disappeared and the shutter closed again.

The example was given; that opening and shutting had been heard, without doubt, because another window slowly opened and the head of an old wrinkled toothless woman cautiously appeared. It was the very same Sister Pute who had created such an uproar while Padre Damaso was preaching. Children and old women are the representatives of curiosity on the earth; the former by their eagerness to learn; the latter by their zeal to remember.

Undoubtedly, nobody would dare give her a spanking, and thus she remained, looked afar and knit her brows; gargled, spat noisily and then crossed herself. The house in front also opened timidly and a little window gave way to Sister Rufa, she who neither deceived nor wanted to be deceived. Both looked at each other for a moment, smiled, made signs and crossed themselves again.

"Jesus!" exclaimed Sister Rufa. "It was like a mass of thanksgiving with all the fireworks!"

"I have not witnessed a similar night since Bálat sacked the town," replied Sister Pute.

"So many shots! They say it was old man Pablo's gang!"

"Were they *tulisanes?* That cannot be! They say they were the police force against the civil guards. That is why Don Filipo is in prison."

"*Sanctus Deus!* Holy God! They say there are at least fourteen dead!"

Other windows were opening, and different faces emerged, exchanging greetings and making comments.

In the light of the day which promised to be splendid, soldiers were seen coming and going, confusedly, like grey silhouettes.

"There goes another dead man," said one from a window.

"One? I see two!"

"And I...but anyway, do you know what it was all about?" asked a man with sly features.

"The municipal policemen, of course!"

"No sir, it was an uprising at headquarters!"

"What uprising? The priest against the *Alferez?*"

"Well, nothing like that," said the one who had asked

the question. "They are the Chinese who have risen up."
And he closed his window again.

"The Chinese?" repeated everyone with great
astonishment.

"That is why you do not see anyone!"

"They must have all been killed."

"I thought they were going to do something bad.
Yesterday..."

"Oh, I already foresaw that. Last night..."

"What a pity!" exclaimed Sister Rufa. "To all die when
Christmas is approaching, when they come with their
gifts...They should have waited for the New Year...!"

The street was gradually becoming livelier. First it
was the dogs, the chickens, pigs, and doves that attempted
to circulate; these animals were followed by some ragged
youngsters, arm in arm, who sidled up timidly towards
the barracks; then some old women with handkerchiefs
on their heads tied under their chins, big rosaries in hand,
making believe they were praying so that the soldiers
would allow them entry. When they saw that they could
walk about without being shot at, the men started to come
out, affecting indifference. In the beginning, their steps
were limited to the fronts of their own houses, where they
stroked their fighting cocks; then they lengthened their
strides, stopping every now and then, and thus they
reached the front of the town hall.

Within a quarter of an hour different stories went
around. Ibarra, with his servants, had wanted to abduct
Maria Clara, and Capitan Tiago had defended her, helped
by the civil guards.

The number of the dead was now not fourteen but
thirty. Capitan Tiago had been wounded and was leaving
that very hour with his family for Manila.

The arrival of two municipal policemen carrying in a litter a human form and followed by a soldier produced a great sensation. It was known that they came from the convent; by the form of the feet dangling from the stretcher, one conjectured who it was. A little farther it was reported who it was; farther away, the dead multiplied and the mystery of the Holy Trinity was verified. Then it was the renewal of the miracle of the loaves and fishes, and the dead reached thirty-eight.

At seven thirty, when other civil guards arrived from the neighboring towns, the story that circulated was clearer and more detailed.

"I have just come from the courthouse, where I have seen Don Filipo and Don Crisostomo prisoners," a man was saying to Sister Pute. "I have spoken to one of the municipal policemen who was on duty. Well, Bruno, the son of the man who was beaten to death, told the whole story last night. As you know, Capitan Tiago was getting his daughter married to the young Spaniard. Don Crisostomo, offended, wanted to avenge himself and tried to murder all the Spaniards, even the priest. Last night they raided the headquarters and the convent; and happily, by God's mercy, the priest was in Capitan Tiago's house. They say that many escaped. The civil guards burnt down the house of Don Crisostomo, and if they had not apprehended him earlier, they would also have burned him."

"They burned his house?"

"All the servants have been arrested. Look—the smoke can still be seen from here," said the narrator, approaching the window. "Those who come from there tell of sad happenings."

All looked towards the indicated site: a light column

of smoke was still rising slowly to the sky. All made more or less pious comments, more or less reproachful.

"Poor young man!" exclaimed an old man, the husband of Sister Pute.

"Yes!" she answered him, "but remember that yesterday he did not have a mass offered for the soul of his father, who undoubtedly needed it very badly, more than the others did."

"But woman, don't you have any compassion...?"

"Compassion for the excommunicated? It is a sin to have it for the enemies of God, say the priests. Do you remember? On holy ground he was walking as if in a farm yard?"

"But the farm yard and the cemetery and the poultry yard are alike," replied the old man, "except that in one nobody enters except the animals of one species!"

"Come on!" sister Pute shouted at him, "you are still defending one whom God is clearly punishing. Watch out that you are not arrested yourself. Prop up a falling house and it will fall on you."

The husband was silenced by that argument. The old woman continued: "After mauling Padre Damaso, he had nothing left to do but kill Padre Salvi."

"But you cannot deny that he was good as a youngster."

"Yes, he was good," replied the old woman, "but he went to Spain; all who go to Spain come back heretics, the priests have said."

"Oho!" countered the husband, who saw that he could get back his own. "And the priest, and all the priests, and the Archbishop and the Pope and the Virgin, are they not from Spain? Aba! they are all heretics too? Aba!"

Happily for Sister Pute the arrival of a maid running all excited and pale cut the discussion.

"Somebody is hanging in the neighbor's kitchen garden," she said breathlessly.

"A man hanging!" all exclaimed, stupefied.

The women crossed themselves; no one could move from his seat.

"Yes, sir," continued the maid, trembling. "I went to pick some peas...I looked into the neighbor's kitchen-garden to see if there were any...I saw a man swinging in the air. I thought it was Teo, the servant who always gives me...I approached to... to get peas and I saw it was not he, but another, a dead man. I ran, ran and..."

"Let us go and look," said the old man, rising, "take us to the place."

"Don't go!" cried Sister Pute, holding him by the shirt. "A misfortune will befall you! Did he hang himself? All the worse for him!"

"Let me see him, woman. Go to the town hall, Juan, to make a report. He might not be dead yet."

And he proceeded towards the kitchen-garden, followed by the maid, who was hiding behind his back. The women and Sister Pute herself came behind them, filled with fear and curiosity.

"There he is, Sir," said the maid, stopping and pointing with a finger.

The committee stopped at a respectable distance, leaving the old man to advance alone.

A human body, hanging from the branch of a *santol* tree, was swaying gently, pushed by the breeze. The old man regarded it for some time. He saw the rigid feet, the arms, the soiled clothes, the bent head.

"We must not touch him until the police arrive," he said in a loud voice. "He is already stiff. He has been long dead."

The women gradually approached.

"It is the neighbor who lived in that hut, he who arrived two weeks ago. Do you see the scar on his face?"

"Ave Maria!" exclaimed some of the women.

"Shall we pray for his soul?" asked a young woman after looking at and examining the corpse.

"You silly heretic!" Sister Pute scolded her. "Do you know what Padre Damaso said? To pray for the damned is to tempt God. He who kills himself is condemned irretrievably; that is why he is not buried in consecrated ground."

And she added: "It had already seemed to me that that man was going to end badly. I could never find out on what he lived."

"I saw him speaking twice to the *sacristan mayor*," observed a young woman.

"You can be sure it was not to go confession or to have a mass said!"

The neighbors came along, and soon quite a number surrounded the body which was still swinging. In half an hour a constable, the *directorcillo* and two policemen arrived. They lowered the body and placed it on a litter.

"People are in a hurry to die," said the *directorcillo*, laughing while he removed a pen from behind an ear.

He asked misleading questions, took the statement of the maidservant whom he tried to trap, now looking at her with stern eyes, now threatening her, then attributing to her words she had never said, so much so that believing she was going to prison, she began to cry and ended with a declaration that she was not looking for peas but that...and was taking Teo to be a witness.

In the meantime, a peasant with a wide *salakot* and a large patch on his neck, was examining the body and the rope.

The face was not as livid as the rest of the body. Above the marks of the rope could be seen two scratches and two small bruises. The bruises caused by the rope were white and bloodless. The strange peasant meticulously examined the shirt and the trousers, noted they were full of dust and newly torn in some parts; but what called his attention the most were the seeds of *amor seco* that clung even to the collar of the shirt.

"What do you see?" asked the *directorcillo*.

"I was trying to see, sir, if I could recognize him," stammered the peasant, half uncovering himself—that is, lowering his salakot even more.

"But haven't you heard that he is a certain Lucas? Are you asleep?"

Everyone burst into laughter. The peasant, abashed, mumbled some words, bent his head and walked away slowly.

"Hah, where are you going?" the old man shouted at him. "That is not the way out; that is the way to the dead man's hut!"

"The fellow is still asleep!" sneered the *directorcillo*. "We have to empty a bucket of water over his head."

The crowd laughed again.

The peasant left the place where he had played such a sorry part and headed for the church. At the vestry he asked for the *sacristan mayor*.

"He is still asleep," they answered him rudely. "Don't you know that last night they sacked the parish house?"

"I will wait till he wakes up."

The church attendants regarded him with the ill humor characteristic of people accustomed to ill treatment.

In one corner, which remained in shadows, the one-eyed man was sleeping on a long chair. His eyeglasses were up on his forehead among the long unkempt hair; his breast, rickety and squalid, was bare and heaved with regularity.

The peasant sat himself nearby, ready to wait patiently, but he dropped a coin and started to search for it under the chair of the *sacristan mayor* with the help of a candle. The peasant noted that there also were *amor seco* seeds on the trousers and shirt sleeves of the sleeper, who finally woke up, rubbed his one sound eye and rebuked the peasant in a bad temper.

"I wanted to have a mass said, Sir!" the latter retorted in an apologetic tone.

"All the masses have already been said," said the one-eyed man, softening his tone a little. For tomorrow, if you like...Is it for the souls in Purgatory?"

"No, Sir," replied the peasant, giving him a peso; and looking at him fixedly in his one eye, added:

"It is for a person who is soon to die."

And he left the vestry.

"I could have caught him red-handed last night!" he said, sighing as he removed the patch and straightened himself to recover the face and the height of Elías.

- 58 -

Woe to the Vanquished!

My joy in a well.[1]

Guardias civiles pace in front of the town hall with a sinister air, threatening with their rifle butts the brash youngsters who stand up on tiptoe or on each other's backs to see something through the bars.

The town hall no longer presents the festive aspect of the day when the fiesta program was discussed. Now it is somber and none too reassuring. The soldiers and the municipal police who occupy it hardly speak or, if at all, do so in hushed voices and a few words. On the table, the *directorcillo*, two clerks and some soldiers are scribbling on papers; the *Alferez* is pacing back and forth, looking fiercely at the door from time to time. Themistocles himself, before the Olympic Games after the Battle of Salamis, could not have appeared prouder. Doña Consolacion is yawning in a corner of the room, showing her blackened gums and jagged teeth. Her cold and sinister eyes are fixed on the prison cell door, which is covered with indecent scrawls. She was able to persuade her husband, whom victory had rendered complacent, to allow her to be present during the interrogation and perhaps the consequent tortures. The hyena smells the stink of rotting flesh; it licks its chops and appears bored with the delay in the proceedings.

The *Gobernadorcillo* is contrite; his chair, that great armchair placed beneath the picture of His Majesty, is vacant and seems destined for another person.

At about nine o'clock the parish priest arrived, pale and frowning.

"Well you didn't keep us waiting, did you?" the *Alferez* told him.

"I'd rather not be present," replied Padre Salvi in a low voice, ignoring that sarcastic tone. "I am very nervous."

"Since no one else could come so as not to leave his post, I deemed that Your Reverence's presence...You know that they are to be taken away this afternoon."

"Young Ibarra and the *Teniente Mayor*...?"

The *Alferez* pointed towards the cell.

"Eight are there," he said. "Bruno died at midnight, but his statement is on record."

The priest greeted Doña Consolacion, who responded with a yawn and with an aah! and occupied the armchair under the picture of His Majesty.

"We can begin," he said.

"Bring out the two who are in the stocks!" commanded the *Alferez* in a voice that he endeavored to make as terrifying as he could. Turning to the priest and changing his tone, he added:

"They were put in the stocks, skipping two holes!"

For those who are not familiar with these instruments of torture, let us tell them that the stocks are one of the most deceptively innocent-looking. The holes in which the legs of the detained are placed, are about a hand's breadth apart; skipping two holes, the prisoner would find himself in a somewhat strained position with a singular discomfort at his ankles and his legs almost a yard apart. It does not kill instantly, as one can well imagine.

The warden, followed by four soldiers, withdrew the bolt and opened the door. A nauseating stench and a thick humid air escaped from the dense gloom in which some cries and sobs were heard. A soldier lighted a match, but the flame died in that rotten spoiled air, and they had to wait for the air to be renewed.

By the vague light of a candle they could make out some human forms: men clasping their knees and hiding their heads between them, lying face down, standing and facing the walls, etc. One could hear a bang and squeak accompanied by curses. The stocks were opened.

Doña Consolacion was inclined slightly forward, stretching the muscles of her neck, eyes protruding, staring at the half-opened door.

Between two soldiers appeared a somber figure, Tarsilo, the brother of Bruno. He had handcuffs on his wrists; his clothes were torn, revealing a well-muscled body. His eyes were fastened insolently on the wife of the *Alferez*.

"He is the one who fought with the most bravery, and ordered his companions to flee," said the *Alferez* to Padre Salvi.

Behind came another of wretched appearance, lamenting and weeping like a child. He was limping and his trousers were bloodied.

"Mercy, sir, mercy! I will never go into the patio again!" he was crying.

"He is a scoundrel," observed the *Alferez*, talking to the priest. "He wanted to flee, but had been wounded in the thigh. These two are the only ones we have alive."

"What is your name?" the *Alferez* asked Tarsilo.

"Tarsilo Alasigan."

"What did Don Crisostomo promise you if you attacked the barracks?"

"Don Crisostomo never communicated with us."

"Don't you deny it! That is why you were able to surprise us."

"You are mistaken. You beat our father to death. We are avenging him and nothing more. Search for your two companions."

The *Alferez* regarded the sergeant with surprise.

"They are there on a cliff. There we threw them yesterday; there they will rot. Now kill me; you will not learn anything more!"

Silence and general surprise.

"You are going to tell us who your other accomplices are!" threatened the *Alferez*, brandishing a whip.

A smile of contempt surfaced on the lips of the prisoner.

The *Alferez* conferred a few moments, in a low voice, with the priest and, turning to the soldiers: "Take him to where the corpses are!" he commanded.

In a corner of the courtyard, in an old cart, five corpses were piled up, half covered by a piece of torn matting, soaked in filth. A soldier paced back and forth spitting frequently.

"Do you know them?" asked the *Alferez*, lifting the matting.

Tarsilo did not answer. He saw the corpse of the husband of the mad woman with two others, that of his brother, riddled with bayonet wounds and that of Lucas still with the rope around the neck. His look became more somber and a sigh escaped from his breast.

"Do you know them?" he was asked again.

Tarsilo kept silent.

A whistle cut the air and the whip struck him on the shoulders. He shuddered; his muscles contracted. The lashes were repeated, but Tarsilo remained impassive.

"Beat him till he falls apart or until he talks," shouted the *Alferez*, exasperated.

"Come on, talk!" the *directorcillo* urged him. "They are going to kill you anyway!"

They took him back to the courthouse hall where the other prisoner was calling on the saints, teeth chattering and knees bending.

"Do you know that man?" Padre Salvi asked.

"This is the first time I have seen him," Tarsilo answered, looking at the other with compassion.

The *Alferez* gave him a fist blow and a kick.

"Tie him to the bench."

Without taking off his handcuffs, which were stained with blood, he was tied to a wooden bench. The hapless one looked around him as if searching for something, and saw Doña Consolacion; he laughed contemptuously. Those present were surprised; onlookers followed his gaze and saw the woman, who was biting her lips slightly.

"I have never seen a woman so ugly!" Tarsilo exclaimed amid general silence. "I would prefer to lie on a bench, tied as I am, than beside her, like the *Alferez*."

The Muse blanched.

"You are going to beat me to death, Señor *Alferez*," he continued. "Tonight I will be avenged when your wife embraces you!"

"Gag him!" screamed the *Alferez*, furious and trembling with rage.

It seemed that Tarsilo had only wanted the gag, because when he had it, his eyes beamed a ray of satisfaction.

At a signal from the *Alferez*, a guard, armed with a whip, began his gruesome task. All of Tarsilo's body contracted; a half muzzled prolonged groan was heard despite the piece of cloth which gagged his mouth. He lowered his head; his clothing was soaked in blood.

Padre Salvi, pale and with a strained look, rose painfully to his feet, made a sign with his hand and left the hall, staggering. In the street he saw a young woman leaning her back against the wall, rigid, motionless, listening attentively, staring into space, twitching hands extended against the aging wall. The sun fully bathed her. She seemed to be counting without breathing, voicelessly, the biting blows and that heartbreaking groan. She was Tarsilo's sister.

In the meantime, the scene was continuing in the courthouse hall; the unfortunate victim, exhausted by pain, grew silent and waited for his torturers to tire. Finally the soldier let his arm fall, panting. The *Alferez*, blanching with fury and wonder, made a sign to the soldier to untie him.

Then Doña Consolacion stood up and whispered a few words into her husband's ears. He moved his head in a sign of understanding.

"To the well with him!" he ordered.

The Filipinos know what this means. In Tagalog they translate it into *timbain*.[2] We do not know who invented this procedure, but we believe it must be very old. "The truth coming out of a well" may be a sarcastic interpretation.

In the middle of the courtyard rises the picturesque mouth of a well made roughly of unpolished stones. A rustic apparatus of bamboo forming a lever, serves to draw from the well slimy, dirty and foul-smelling water. Broken pottery, garbage and other liquids are tossed in there. The well is like the prison: whatever society discards or gives up as useless is amassed there; an object that falls inside it, no matter how good it was, is lost forever. However, it has never been closed up. Sometimes prisoners are condemned to penetrate and deepen it, not because something useful is expected to come out of that punishment, but because of the difficulties that the work involves. A prisoner who once went down into the well caught a fever, of which he eventually died.

Tarsilo contemplated all the soldiers' preparations with a fixed gaze. He was very pale and his lips trembled or murmured a prayer. The pride of his despair seemed to have vanished, or at least been weakened. Several times he bent his haughty neck and lowered his eyes to the ground, resigned to suffering.

They took him close to the mouth of the well, followed by Doña Consolacion who was smiling. The hapless young man cast a glance of envy at the heap of dead bodies, and a sigh escaped his breast.

"Speak now!" the *directorcillo* urged him again. "They will hang you all the same. At least you would die without having to suffer too much!"

"You will leave here only to die on the gallows," a policeman told him.

They removed his gag and hung him by his feet. His head would be lowered first and kept some time under water, as is done to a bucket, except that the man is given more time.

The *Alferez* went off to look for a timepiece and to count the minutes.

In the meantime, Tarsilo hung, his long hair streaming in the air, his eyes half closed.

"If you are Christians, if you have hearts," he pleaded in a low voice, "lower me quickly, or do it so that my head hits the wall and it kills me. God will reward you for this good deed...maybe some day you will find yourself in my place!"

The *Alferez* returned and presided over the descent, timepiece in hand.

"Slowly, slowly!" screamed Doña Consolacion, following the hapless one with her eyes. "Be careful!"

The lever was descending slowly. Tarsilo's head grazed against the protruding stones and the filthy plants which grew among the fissures. Then the lever stopped moving. The *Alferez* counted the seconds.

"Up!" he commanded roughly after half a minute.

The silvery and harmonious sounds of the drops of water falling on water, announced the prisoner's return to daylight. This time, since the counterbalancing weight was greater, he shot up more quickly. Pebbles and shingles were pulled out of the walls and fell noisily.

His forehead and hair covered with loathsome ooze, his face full of wounds and abrasions, his body wet and dripping, he appeared before the eyes of the silent crowd. The wind made him shiver with cold.

"Do you want to confess?" they asked him.

"Take care of my sister," murmured the unfortunate one, looking entreatingly at a policeman.

The bamboo lever creaked again, and the doomed man disappeared anew. Doña Consolacion observed that the water remained tranquil. The *Alferez* counted off a minute.

When Tarsilo returned upward, his features were contorted and bluish. He looked towards the spectators with bloodshot eyes open.

"Are you going to talk?" the *Alferez* asked again, sounding discouraged.

Tarsilo shook his head and they lowered him again. His eyelids were starting to close, the pupils of his eyes continued gazing at the sky where white clouds were floating. He bent his neck to keep on seeing the light of day, but he was soon submerged in water and a sordid curtain fell and shut out for him the spectacle of the world.

A minute passed. The Muse in observation saw great bubbles of air rise to the surface.

"He is thirsty," she said, snickering.

Then the water was again undisturbed.

This time it lasted a minute and a half before the *Alferez* gave a sign. Tarsilo's features were no longer contorted. The half-opened eyelids revealed the white eyeballs; from his mouth oozed vile water with streaks of blood. The wind was blowing cold but his body no longer shivered.

All looked at each other in silence, pale and in consternation. The *Alferez* made a sign for them to detach him; he moved away, thoughtful. Doña Consolacion touched the lighted end of her cigarette several times to the bare legs, but the body did not react or quiver, and it doused the fire.

A policeman muttered: "He strangled himself. See how his tongue turned as if he had wanted to swallow it!"

The other prisoner had witnessed the scene, perspiring and shaking. He looked looking around him like a deranged person.

The *Alferez* assigned the *directorcillo* to question him.

"Sir, sir!" he whimpered, "I will say anything you like."

"Well, let us see. What is your name?"

"Andong, Sir!"

"Bernardo...Leonardo...Ricardo...Eduardo...Gerardo... or what?"

"Andong, Sir!" repeated the imbecile.

"Put him down as Bernardo or whichever," decided the *Alferez*.

"Surname?"

The man regarded him with terror.

"What name do you want added to the name Andong?"

"Ah, Sir! Andong Half-Wit, Sir!"

The laughter could not be contained; the *Alferez* himself stopped in his tracks.

"Your occupation?"

"Pruner of coconut trees and servant to my mother-in-law."

"Who ordered you to attack headquarters?"

"No one, Sir!"

"What do you mean, no one? Don't lie or they will lower you down the well. Who ordered you? Tell the truth!"

"The truth, Sir!"

"Who?"

"Who, Sir!"

"I am asking you. Who ordered you to stage a revolution?"

"Which revolution, Sir?"

"That for which you were in the barracks yard last night."

"Ah, Sir!" exclaimed Andong, blushing.

"Who then was to blame for that?"

"My mother-in-law, Sir!"

Laughter and surprise followed these words. The *Alferez* stopped and looked severely at the wretch who, believing that his words had produced a good effect, continued, encouraged.

"Yes, Sir, my mother-in-law does not give me anything to eat other than what is rotten and no good, so last night when I came, my stomach ached. I saw the courtyard close by and I said to myself: 'It is night and nobody will see me.' I entered...and when I was getting up many shots resounded. I was tying my underwear!"

A whiplash cut off the words. The *Alferez* ordered: "To prison with him. This afternoon, to the provincial capital!"

- 59 -
The Culprit

Very soon the news that the detainees were to be taken away spread around town; at first it was heard with dread, then came tears and lamentations.

The families of the detainees ran about, confused. They went from the convent to the barracks, from the barracks to the courthouse, and not encountering solace anywhere, filled the air with cries and weeping. The parish priest had shut himself up as being sick. The *Alferez* had added to his guards, who received the supplicant women with rifle butts. The *Gobernadorcillo*, who was useless, seemed more stupid and useless than ever. In front of the prison those who still had strength, ran from one end to another. Those who did not, sat on the ground calling out the names of their loved ones.

The sun burnt hot, but none of the hapless women thought of leaving. Doray, Don Filipo's merry and happy wife, wandered about disconcerted, carrying her baby in her arms; both were weeping.

"Go home!" they told her. "Your son will catch a fever."

"Why live if he does not have a father to bring him up?" answered the desolate woman.

"Your husband is innocent. Perhaps he will come back."

"Yes, after we are all dead!"

Capitana Tinay wept, and called for her son Antonio. The courageous Capitana Maria looked through the small barred window behind which were her twins, her only sons.

The mother-in-law of the coconut tree pruner was there. She was not weeping. She walked, gesticulated with sleeves rolled up, haranguing the passers-by.

"Have you seen anything like it? To apprehend my Andong, to take a shot at him, to place him in the stocks and take him to the provincial capital only for...because he has new underwear? This calls for revenge. The civil guards are abusive! I swear that if I ever come across one of them in a secluded spot in my garden—as has happened many times—I will mutilate him, mutilate him, otherwise...they can mutilate me!"

But there were few persons to be found who would agree with this Islamic mother-in-law.

"For all this, Don Crisostomo is to blame," sighed one woman.

The schoolmaster also wandered about, lost in the crowd. Ñor Juan no longer rubbed his hands; he no longer carried his plumbing line nor his meter stick. The man was dressed in black because he had heard the bad news and, true to his way of looking at the future as something

that had already happened, he was already in mourning
for the death of Ibarra.

At two o'clock in the afternoon an open cart pulled
by two bullocks, stopped before the courthouse.

The cart was surrounded by the crowd, which wanted
to unhitch and destroy it.

"Don't do such a thing," Capitana Maria was saying.
"Do you want them to go on foot?"

This stopped the families of the prisoners. Twenty
soldiers came out and surrounded the vehicle. The
prisoners came out.

The first was Don Filipo, tied up. He greeted his
wife, smiling. Doray broke out in bitter sobs and it took
two soldiers to stop her from embracing her husband.
Antonio, Capitana Tinay's son, appeared, crying like a
child, which increased his family's cries. The half-wit
Andong broke down when he saw his mother-in-law, the
cause of his misadventure. Albino, the ex-seminarian, was
also handcuffed; so were Capitana Maria's twins. These
three young men were serious and grave. The last one to
come out was Ibarra, uncuffed, but led between two
soldiers. The young man was pale; he searched for a
friendly face.

"It is his fault," screamed many voices. "That one is to
blame and he is set loose!"

"My son-in-law has done nothing and yet he is
handcuffed!"

Ibarra turned to his guards:

"Tie me up but tie me well, elbow to elbow," he said.

"We have no orders."

"Tie me up!"

The soldiers obeyed.

The *Alferez* appeared on horseback, armed to the

teeth. Ten or fifteen more soldiers were behind him.

Each prisoner had his own family pleading there for him, weeping for him and calling him endearing names. Ibarra was the only one who had nobody there for him. Ñor Juan himself and the schoolmaster had disappeared.

"What have my husband and my son done to you?" Doray, weeping, asked him. "Look at my poor son! You have deprived him of his father!"

The families' sorrow turned to anger against the young man, who had been accused of provoking the mutiny. The *Alferez* gave the signal to depart.

"You are a coward!" Andong's mother-in-law shouted at him. "While others were fighting for you, you were in hiding, you coward!"

"Damn you!" shouted an old man. "Damn the gold amassed by your family to disturb our peace! Damn you, damn you!"

"May they send you to the gallows, heretic," shouted a relative of Albino's; and, unable to contain himself, he picked up a stone and threw it.

The example was soon followed, and over the hapless youth fell a rain of dust and stones.

Ibarra suffered impassively, without anger, without complaint, the just vengeance of so many torn hearts; Ibarra bore the onslaught. This was the leave-taking, the farewell, given him by his town where he had all his loves. He lowered his head; perhaps he was thinking of a man flogged in the streets of Manila; or of an old woman who fell dead at the sight of the head of her son; perhaps the history of Elías was passing before his eyes.

The *Alferez* thought it necessary to distance the crowd, but the stone throwing and the insults did not cease. Only one mother was not avenging her sorrows on him:

Capitana Maria. Motionless, lips taut, eyes filled with silent tears, she saw her two sons being taken away. Contemplating her immobility and her wordless grief, Niobe no longer remained a fable.

The contingent moved away.

Of the persons who emerged from rarely opened windows, those who showed more compassion for the young man were the indifferent or the curious. All his friends had hidden themselves; yes, even Capitan Basilio who forbade his daughter Sinang to cry.

Ibarra saw the smoking ruins of his home, the home of his fathers where he had been born, where lived the sweetest memories of his childhood and adolescence; tears so long repressed welled in his eyes. He bowed his head and wept, without the comfort of being able to hide his grief, handcuffed as he was, his sorrow not evoking anyone's compassion. Now he no longer had a country, or home, or love, or friends, or a future!

From a height, a man was contemplating the gloomy caravan. He was old, pale, emaciated, wrapped in a woollen blanket, leaning, spent, on a cane. It was Tasio, the old philosopher, who upon hearing news of the events, wanted to leave his bed and be present, but had not been permitted by his strength. The old man followed the cart with his gaze until it vanished in the distance. He remained thoughtful for some time, with head bent; then he rose, and laboriously took the way home, resting at every step.

The following day some herdsmen found him dead on the threshold of his solitary abode.

- 60 -

Patriotism and Self-Interest

T he telegraph transmitted the events secretly to Manila, and thirty-six hours later the newspapers wrote about it, albeit obtusely and not without a few warnings, augmented to, corrected and mutilated by the state attorney. In the meantime, the private accounts emanating from the convents were the ones first circulated by word of mouth, in secret, and with great dismay for those who came to know. The incident, in a thousand distorted versions, was believed with more or less readiness, depending on the favored or contrary feelings and the way of thinking of each one.

Although the public peace appeared undisturbed, what was least apparent revolved in the peace of the home, like that of a pond: while the surface appears smooth and untroubled, in the bottom the mute fishes swarm, dart about and pursue each other. Crosses, medals, epaulettes, jobs, prestige, power, influence, dignities and so forth, started to flutter like butterflies in a golden atmosphere for a part of the population. For the other part, a dark cloud rose on the horizon and, projecting from its grey depths like black silhouettes prison bars, chains, even the sinister shadow of the gallows. They imagined hearing in the air the interrogations, the sentences, the screams drawn by the tortures. The Marianas[1] and Bagumbayan appeared enveloped in a tattered and blood-stained veil: fishermen and fish in troubled waters. Destiny showed up the events to the imagination of the Manilans like certain Chinese fans: one face painted in black; the other gilded with gold, brilliant colors, birds and flowers.

In the convents reigned the greatest turmoil. Carriages were hitched, Fathers Provincial visited each other, held secret conferences. They presented themselves in the palaces to offer their support to the government which was overrun by the gravest of perils. There was again talk of comets, allusions, pinpricks, and so forth.

"A Te Deum, a Te Deum," a friar in a convent was saying. "This time let no one be absent from the choir. It is no little goodness of God's to be able to show now, precisely in these critical times, how valuable we are!"

"With this little lesson our little General Bad-Omen[2] must be biting his lips," replied another.

"What would have happened to him without the religious orders?"

"And to better celebrate the fiesta let the Brother Cook and the Procurer be advised...let us rejoice for three days!"

"Amen! Amen! Long live Salvi! Long live!"

In another convent they were speaking in a different manner.

"You see, that one was a student of the Jesuits. The dissidents come from the Ateneo," said a friar.

"And the anti-clerics!"

"As I have already said: the Jesuits are ruining the country; they are corrupting the youth. Nevertheless they are tolerated because they trace a few smudges on paper when there is an earthquake..."

"And only God knows how they do it!"

"Yes! Just try to contradict them! When everything trembles and moves, who has the time to write scrawls? Nothing, it is Father Secchi[3]..."

And they smiled at each other with sovereign disdain.

"But how about the storms and the typhoons?" another friar asked, with scornful irony. "Is their prediction not divine?"

"Any fisherman can predict them!"

"When he who governs is a fool...Tell me how your head is and I will tell you how your legs are. But look how the brotherhood favor one another: the newspapers are almost, almost asking for a mitre for Padre Salvi."

"And he will get it; he will fawn for it!"

"Do you believe so?"

"Why not? These days, for any reason whatsoever, they give it. I know of one who for less got mitred: he wrote a silly little book showing that the *Indios* are not capable of anything beyond manual labor...you know, the usual trivialities!"

"That is true. So many injustices damage the Church!" exclaimed another friar. "If mitres had eyes and could see on what heads..."

"If mitres were objects of Nature," added another with a nasal twang, "*Natura abhorret vacuum*, Nature abhors a vacuum."

"That is how they are held in place, the vacuum sucks them in," replied another.

These and other things besides were being said in the convents, and we give our readers other comments with political color, metaphysical or biting. Let us lead our readers to a particular household. Let us go to Capitan Tinong's house, the hospitable man whom we saw insistently inviting Ibarra to honor him with a visit.

In the rich and spacious sala of his house in Tondo, Capitan Tinong is seated on a wide armchair, stroking his forehead and neck in a disconsolate gesture while his wife Capitana Tinchang is crying and lecturing in front of their two daughters who are mutely listening in a corner, aghast and shaken.

"Ay, Virgin of Antipolo!" cried the woman. "Ay, Virgin of the Rosary and of the Girdle![4] ay! ay! Our Lady of Novaliches!"

"*Nanay...*" replied the younger of the two daughters.

"What did I tell you!" continued the wife in a reproachful tone. "I warned you, ay! Virgin of Carmel![5] ay!"

"But you told me nothing!" Capitan Tinong tearfully attempted to reply. "On the contrary you told me I was doing well to frequent the house and conserve the friendship of Capitan Tiago because...because he is rich...and you told me..."

"What? What did I tell you? I did not say such a thing. I never told you anything! Oh! if only you had listened to me!"

"Now you are blaming me!" he retorted bitterly, slapping the arm of the chair. "Didn't you tell me that I had done well to invite him to dine with us, because since he is rich...weren't you saying that we should not have friends other than rich people? Aba!"

"It is true that I told you that because...because then

there was no other alternative. You did nothing but praise him. Don Ibarra here, Don Ibarra there, Don Ibarra everywhere! abaa! But I did not advise you to see him, nor talk to him during that reunion; you cannot deny that!"

"Did I by any chance know he would be there?"

"Well, you should have known better!"

"How? I didn't even know him!"

"Well, you should have known him!"

"But Tinchang! That was the first time I saw him, and heard about him!"

"Well, you should have seen him before, heard about him before. That is why you are a man; you wear trousers and read *El Diario de Manila!*"[6] she replied undeterred, giving her husband a terrible look. Capitan Tinong was at a loss to reply.

Capitana Tinchang, not content to win this victory, sought to overwhelm him and drew near with clenched fists.

"Is it for this that I have been working years and years, economizing, so that you with your stupidity you can throw away the fruits of my labor?" she rebuked him. "Now they will come to take you away into exile; they will despoil us of our goods, as was done to the wife of...Oh! If I were a man, if I were a man!"

And seeing her husband bow his head, she started to weep anew, but always repeating:

"Ay! If I were a man! ay!"

"And If you were a man," the peeved husband finally asked, "what would you do?"

"What? well...well...well this very day I would present myself to the *Capitan General*, to offer myself to fight against the mutineers, this very moment!"

"But haven't you read what *El Diario* said? Read what

it says: 'The infamous and treacherous rebellion has been suppressed with energy, vigor and strength; and soon the enemies of the Motherland and their accomplices will all feel the weight and severity of the laws...see? There is no longer an uprising."

"It does not matter! You should offer your services as those of 72 did, and saved themselves.'"[7]

"Yes, so did Padre Burg..."

But he was not able to finish his sentence; his wife, running, covered his mouth.

"Go on! Say that name and tomorrow they will hang you in Bagumbayan! Don't you know that it is enough to pronounce it to be sentenced without even filing a case? Go ahead and say it!"

Even if Capitan Tinong had wanted to talk back, he could not very well have done so. His wife had both her hands over his mouth, pressing back his head against the back of the armchair, so that the poor man would have choked to death but for the arrival and intervention of a newcomer.

He was the couple's cousin, Don Primitivo, who knew Amat's book by heart, a man of some forty years, faultlessly groomed, full-bellied and somewhat chubby.

"*Quid video?* What do I see?" he exclaimed upon entering, "and why? *Quare?*"

"Ay, cousin," said the woman, advancing tearfully towards him. "I had you called; I don't know what will become of us...What do you advise us? Tell us, you who studied Latin and know how to argue..."

"But before all else, *quid quaeritis? Nihil est in intellectu quod prius non fuerit in sensu; nihil volitum quin praecognitum;* what do you want? There is nothing in the mind which is not first perceived by the senses, and what is unknown cannot be desired."

And he sat himself down deliberately. As if the Latin phrases had a tranquilizing virtue, the couple stopped weeping and approached him, awaiting counsel from his lips, as once did the Greeks of old before the saving word of the oracle that would rescue them from their Persian invaders.

"Why do you weep? *Ubinam gentium sumus?* Among what people are we?"

"You know of the news of the uprising...?"

"*Alzamentum Ibarrae ab alferesio Guardiae civilis destructum? Et nunc?* The uprising of Ibarra suppressed by the *alferez* of the *Guardia Civil?* So what? Does Don Crisostomo owe you money?"

"No, but you know, Tinong had invited him to lunch; had greeted him on the Bridge of Spain...in broad daylight! They will say that Ibarra is his friend."

"A friend!" exclaimed the surprised Latinist, standing up: "*Amice, amicus Plato sed magis amica veritas,* Friend, Plato is my friend but truth is even more my friend. Tell me with whom you go and I will tell you who you are. *Malum est negotium et est timendum rerum istarum horrendissimum resultatum. Hmm!* The business is bad and I fear a horrible end!"

Capitan Tinong turned dreadfully pale listening to so many words in *um*, the sound presaged ill for him. His wife wrung her hands, pleading, and said:

"Cousin, do not talk to us in Latin now. You know we are not philosophers like you. Talk to us in Tagalog or in Spanish, but give us your counsel."

"It is a pity that you do not understand Latin, cousin; the truths in Latin are Tagalog falsities. For example: *contra principia negantem fustibus est argilendum,* with those who deny principles you argue with fists. In Latin this is a truth like Noah's ark. I tried to put it into practice once in

Tagalog and it was I who was beaten. That is why it is a pity that you don't know Latin. In Latin you could fix everything."

"Well, we also know many *oremus, parce nobis* and *Agnus Dei Catolis,* but right now we won't understand each other. Give Tinong a reason why he should not be hanged!"

"You were wrong, very wrong, cousin, to make friends with that young man," replied the Latinist. "The just pay for the sinners; I would advise you to make your last will and testament...*Vae illis! Ubi est fumus ibi est ignis! Similis simili gaudet; atqui Ibarra ahorcatur, ergo ahorcaberis.* Woe to them! Where there is smoke there is fire! Everyone seeks his partner; thus if they hang Ibarra, ergo, you will be hanged."

And he shook his head, disgusted.

"Saturnino! What is the matter with you?" screamed Capitana Tinchang, filled with terror. "Oh my God! He is dead! Doctor! Call a doctor! Tinong! my Tinong!"

Their two daughters came running and the three broke into lamentations.

"Cousin, he has only fainted, just fainted. I would have been happier if...if...but unfortunately, he has only fainted. *Non timeo mortem in catre sed super espaldonem Bagumbayanis,* better to die in bed than on the scaffold in Bagumbayan. Bring some water!"

"Don't die!" sobbed the wife. "Don't die, they will come to arrest you! Ay! if you die and the soldiers come, ay! ay!"

The cousin splashed water on his face and the hapless man revived.

"Come, stop crying! *Inveni remedium;* I have found the remedy. Take him to bed! Come! courage! I am with you with all the wisdom of the ancients...Have a doctor called; and right now, cousin, you are to go to the *Capitan General* and you bring him a gift, a gold chain, a ring—*Dadivae quebrantant peñas*; gifts will move the hardest rocks—tell him it is a Christmas gift. Close the windows, the doors and to whoever asks for my cousin, say that he is seriously ill. In the meantime, I shall be burning all his papers, letters and books so that they can find nothing, as Don Crisostomo did. *Scripti testes sunt! Quod medicamenta non sanant, ferrum sanat quod ferrum non sanat, ignis sanat*; what is written testifies, what medicines do not cure, iron does; what iron does not cure, fire does."

"Yes, cousin, here: burn it all," said Capitana Tinchang. "Here are the keys, here are Capitan Tiago's letters, burn them. Be sure that not a single newspaper from Europe is left; they are very dangerous. Here are *The Times*, which I was keeping to wrap up soap and clothing. Here are the books."

"Cousin, go to the *Capitan General*," said Don Primitivo. "Leave me alone. *In extremis extrema*, in desperate times, desperate measures. Give me the powers of a Roman leader and you will see how I will save the coun...I mean my cousin."

And he started to give orders and more orders, to pull out and ransack drawers and shelves, to tear up papers, books, letters and so forth. Soon a bonfire was burning in the kitchen; with an axe he hacked apart old guns, flung into the drainage rusty revolvers; the maidservant who wanted to hang on to the barrel of one to use as a bellows received a reprimand:

"*Conservare etiam sperasti perfida?* You would like to conserve it too, perfidious one? To the fire!"

And he continued his *auto da fe*.

He saw an old volume in parchment and read the title: "'Revolutions of Celestial Bodies' by Copernicus pfui! *ite, maledicti, in ignem kalanis!* Go accursed into the stove fire!" he exclaimed, throwing it to the flames. "Revolutions and Copernicus! Crime upon crime! If I had not come on time...'Freedom in the Philippines!' What is this? Tra lala! What books! Into the fire!"

And innocent books written by simple authors were burnt. Not even the Capitan Juan, a guileless little work, was spared. Cousin Primitivo was right: the just suffer for the sinners.

Four or five hours later, in a social gathering of some pretensions in Intramuros, the events of the day were commented upon. Many old women and spinsters, wives or daughters of employees were there, dressed in long loose house gowns, fanning themselves and yawning. Among the men, as well as the women, their features betrayed their learning and origins. There was an elderly gentleman, small and one-armed, who was being treated with much consideration and who displayed, with respect to the rest, a disdainful silence.

"To tell the truth, where before I could not bear friars and officers of the civil guard, ill-bred that they are," a corpulent lady was saying, "now that I see their usefulness and their services, I could almost marry any one of them with pleasure. I am a patriot."

"I say the same," agreed a thin lady. "It is a pity that we no longer have the former Governor. That one would leave the country as clean as a paten."

"And would finish off this breed of little subversives!"

"Don't they say that there remain many islands to be populated? Why don't they deport the many puffed-up natives there? If I were the *Capitan General*..."

"Ladies," said the armless one, "the *Capitan General* knows his duty. According to what I have heard he is much annoyed because he had heaped many favors on this Ibarra."

"Heaped favors," echoed the thin lady fanning herself vigorously. "See how ungrateful these *Indios* are! How can they be treated like human beings? Jesus!"

"And do you know what I have heard?" asked a military man.

"What? Come on! What do they say?"

"Reliable persons," said the officer in the midst of a profound silence, "assert that all that noise about building a schoolhouse was just a tale."

"Jesus! You see?" exclaimed the women, already believing in the tale.

"The school was a pretext. What he wanted to build was a fortress where he could defend himself when we went to attack him..."

"Jesus! Such infamy! Only an *Indio* is capable of such cowardly thoughts," cried the fat lady. "If I were the *Capitan General* they would see...they would see..."

"I say the same," exclaimed the thin lady, addressing the one-armed man. "I would arrest all the pettifogging lawyers, minor priests, traders, and without formal charges deport or send them into exile. We must pull the evil out by its roots!"

"Well, it is being said that that petty subversive is the son of Spaniards," remarked the armless man without looking at anyone in particular.

"Ah! of course," exclaimed the fat lady, undeterred. "They always have to be the half-breeds! No *Indio* understands about revolution! Breed crows... breed crows...!"

"Do you know what I have heard being bruited about?" asked a half-breed, cutting into the conversation. "Capitan Tinong's wife...do you remember him in whose house we danced and supped during the fiesta in Tondo..."

"The one who has two daughters, and so?"

"Well, his wife has just given a present this afternoon, to the *Capitan General*, a ring worth a thousand pesos!"

The one-armed man turned.

"Really, and for what reason?" he asked, his eyes shining.

"The woman said it was a Christmas present..."

"Christmas is a month away."

"They are probably afraid the downpour will catch them...?" remarked the fat lady.

"And so they take cover beforehand," added the thin one.

"An unsolicited apology is an admission of guilt."

"I was thinking of the same thing myself; you have put your finger on the sore spot."

"It will be necessary to look into this," thoughtfully observed the one-armed man: "I fear there is something fishy here."

"Something fishy, I was going to say the same thing," repeated the thin lady.

"And I," said another, interrupting, "Capitan Tinong's wife is very miserly...up to now she has not sent us a gift, even though we have stayed in her house. So, when one so tight-fisted and avaricious lets go of a small gift of a thousand pesos..."

"But is that true?" asked the armless man.

"Certainly, very true! It was told to my cousin by her fiancee, His Excellency's own aide. And I am inclined to believe it is the same ring that her eldest daughter was wearing on the day of the fiesta. She is always loaded with diamonds!"

"A walking shop display!"

"Just a manner of proclaiming, like any other way. Instead of buying a mannequin or paying for a shop."

The one-armed man left the gathering under a pretext.

And two hours later, when everybody was asleep, various Tondo residents received an invitation delivered by soldiers...the authorities could not allow that certain persons of rank and wealth to sleep in houses which were so badly guarded and poorly ventilated; in Fort Santiago and other government buildings, sleep would be more tranquil and refreshing. Among these favored persons was included the hapless Capitan Tinong.

- 61 -
Wedding Plans for Maria Clara

Capitan Tiago was very happy. In all this terrible time nobody had bothered with him: he had not been arrested, he had not been subjected to confinement, interrogations, electrical machines, continuous foot baths in underground cells and other roguish vexations familiar to certain personages who call themselves civilized. His friends, meaning those who used to be his friends—because the man had already reneged on his former Filipino friends from the instant they became suspects to the government—had also returned to their homes after a few days' vacation in the State buildings. The *Capitan General* himself had ordered them thrown out, judging them not worthy to remain inside government property, to the great annoyance of the armless man who wanted to celebrate the coming Christmas in their lavish and rich company.

Capitan Tinong returned to his home sick, pale and

bloated. The excursion had not turned out well for him. He was so changed that he did not say a word or greet his family who wept, laughed, chattered and went wild with joy. The poor man kept to his home so as not to run the risk of greeting a subversive. His cousin Primitivo, with all his wisdom of the ancients, could not draw him out of his silence.

"*Crede, prime*, believe me, cousin," he was saying, "if I had not come on time to burn your papers, they would have tightened the noose around your neck; but if only I had burned down the whole house, they would not have touched a hair of your head. But, *quod eventum, eventum; Gratias agamus Domine Deo quia non in Marianis Insulis es, camotes seminando*: what is done is done; let us give thanks to God that you are not in the Marianas Islands planting camotes."

Happenings similar to that of Capitan Tinong were not ignored by Capitan Tiago. The man was filled with gratitude, without knowing for sure to whom he should be grateful for such signal favors. Tía Isabel attributed the miracle to the Virgin of Antipolo, to the Virgin of the Rosary or at least to the Virgin of Carmel, or at the very least, Tía Isabel was willing to concede, to Our Lady of the Girdle. According to her, the miracle could not go beyond that. Capitan Tiago did not deny the miracle, but he added:

"I believe, Isabel, that the miracle could not have been done alone by the Virgin of Antipolo. My friends must have helped my future son-in-law, Señor Linares, who, as you already know, is on joking terms with Señor Antonio Canovas himself[1], the very same one whose picture was in the *Ilustracion*, the one who did not consider the public fit to see more than half his face.

And the good man could not help but suppress a smile of smug satisfaction every time he heard important news relative to the events. And no wonder! It was secretly whispered that Ibarra would be sent to the gallows, although there was lack of enough proof to condemn him. Lately there had emerged one who supported the accusation: that experts had declared that, in effect, the design of the schoolhouse could well be that of a bulwark, a fortification, although somewhat defective, as nothing better can be expected from the ignorant *Indio*. These rumors reassured him and made him smile.

In the same manner that Capitan Tiago and his cousin Isabel diverged in opinion, the friends of the family were also divided into two factions: one believing in miracles; and the other in political intervention, although the latter was insignificant. On the miracle side there were also subdivisions: The *sacristan mayor* of Binondo, the candle peddler, and the head of a Confraternity saw the hand of God moved by the Virgin of the Rosary; the Chinese wax-maker, Capitan Tiago's supplier of candles when he went to Antipolo, said, fanning himself and swinging a leg:

"No bee stoopid; Milgen Antipolo es wan; shi can mor dan eblybody; No bee stoopid!"

Capitan Tiago held in high esteem this Chinese who passed himself off as a prophet, medicine-man and so forth. Examining the palm of the hand of his late wife, in her sixth month of pregnancy, he prognosticated:

"If no izzy bebe man, an no izzy ded, wilbe good woman."

And Maria Clara came into the world to fulfill the infidel's prophecy.

Capitan Tiago, a prudent and cautious man, could not decide as easily as did the Trojan Paris. He could not give, just like that, the credit to one of the Virgins, for fear of offending the other, which might bring grave consequences. "Prudence!" he told himself. "Let us not spoil it now!"

He was immersed in these doubts when the believers of political intervention arrived: Doña Victorina, Don Tiburcio and Linares.

Doña Victorina spoke for the three men and for herself; mentioned the visits of Linares to the *Capitan General* and insinuated repeatedly the convenience of having a relative of influence.

"No," she concluded, "*az we 'ave zet, he who unner biggah tree tek zhelteh, iz get biggah blowz.*"

"J...j..ust the other way round, woman," the doctor corrected.

For some time now Doña Victorina had pretended to speak with an Andalucian accent by suppressing the *d*, saying *z* for *s*, and this idea no one could get out of her head; first they would have had to pull out her false ringlets.

"*Yez!*" she added, talking of Ibarra. "*Iz wan haz it well ezerb; I zey zo wen firz time 'em I zee: iz wan iz filibazteh. Wat it 'e General zey to yu, primo? Wat yu tel 'im? Wat'z newz on Ibarra?*"

And, seeing that it took time for the cousin to reply, she went on, addressing Capitan Tiago.

"*Belieb me: if ey connem 'im to eath az iz to be ezpect, 'twill be becoz of my cazin.*"

"Madam! madam!" Linares protested.

But she gave him no time to answer.

"*O, wat a 'iplomat yu av becam! We no yu ar an abizer to 'e General ho no manaze wizout yu....Oh! Clarita, iz a plezure to zee yu!*"

Maria Clara appeared still pale, although recovered

from her illness. Her long tresses were gathered with a light blue silk ribbon. She greeted them shyly, smiled with sadness and approached Doña Victorina for the customary kiss.

After the usual exchanges, the pseudo-Andalucian continued:

"*We caim to vizit yu; yu av been zpared tankz to yur connezionz!*" looking significantly at Linares.

"God protected my father," the young woman answered in a low voice.

"*Yez, Clarita, but 'e time ov miracolz az gone naw: we ze Zpaniardz zey: no truzt 'e Virgin, truzt yur legz!*"

"J-j-just the other way round!"

Capitan Tiago, who till then had not found time to talk, attempted to ask giving much attention to the answer.

"So Doña Victorina, you believe that the Virgin..."

"*We caim precizely to spek to yu about 'e Virgin,*" she answered mysteriously, indicating Maria Clara: "*We av to tok of biznez.*"

The young woman understood that she should withdraw. She found an excuse and left, supporting herself on the furniture.

What in this conference was said and discussed is so base and so wretched that we prefer not to refer to it. Suffice it to say that when they took their leave every one was in high spirits, and that afterwards Capitan Tiago told Tía Isabel:

"Advise the hostel that tomorrow we are giving a party! Be off, prepare Maria because we will marry her off quite soon."

Tía Isabel looked at him, horrified.

"You will see: when Señor Linares becomes our son-in-law, we will go up and down all the State houses. They will envy us; they will all die of envy."

And thus it was that at about eight o'clock in the evening of the following day, Capitan Tiago's house was again filled up, except that this time Capitan Tiago invited only the Spaniards and the Chinese; the fair sex being represented by Spanish peninsular ladies and Filipinas.

The greater number of our acquaintances were there: Padre Sibyla, Padre Salvi among various Franciscans and Dominicans; the old teniente of the Civil Guard, Señor Guevara, more somber than before; the *Alferez* who was recounting his battle for the thousandth time, looking at everyone over his shoulders, believing himself a Don Juan of Austria. Now he is a Teniente with the grade of *Commandante*; De Espadaña, who regards him with respect and fear, avoids his eyes; and Doña Victorina is disappointed. Linares had not arrived yet, since as an important personage, he should arrive later than the others. There are those who naively believe that with an hour of delay in everything they become more important.

Among the group of women it was Maria Clara who was the object of the murmurs; the young woman had greeted and received them ceremoniously, without losing her air of sadness.

"Bah! somewhat arrogant!" a young woman was saying.

"Pretty enough," replied another, but he could have chosen another with a less stupid face."

"Money, dear! Attractive males are for sale!"

Somewhere else, it was said:

"Getting married when her first fiancé is about to be hanged."

"That is what I call prudence: having a substitute at hand."

"Well, when I become a widow..."

These conversations were perhaps heard by the maiden, who was seated on a chair, arranging flowers on a tray, because her hand was seen to tremble; she grew paler and bit her lips several times.

In the gathering of men, the conversation was carried on in a loud voice, and naturally it had to do with the latest happenings. Everyone was speaking, even Don Tiburcio, except for Padre Sibyla, who kept his disdainful silence.

"I have heard it said that Your Reverence is leaving town, Padre Salvi?" asked the new Teniente whom his new star had made more amiable.

"I have nothing more to do there; I am to be established permanently in Manila...how about you?"

"I am also leaving town," he said, stretching himself. "The government needs me so that with a roving column I can disinfect the provinces of dissidents."

Padre Sibyla looked the speaker up and down quickly, and turned his back completely.

"Is anything definite known about what is to be done with the chieftain of the little uprising?" an employee inquired.

"You are speaking of Crisostomo Ibarra?" asked another. "The most probable and the most fitting and proper is that he be hanged like those of '72."

"He is being exiled!" said the old Teniente dryly.

"Exiled! Nothing more than exile! But it will be a perpetual exile!" a number of voices exclaimed at the same time.

Teniente Guevara proceeded in a loud stern tones: "If that young man had been more prudent; if he had confided less to certain persons with whom he communicated; if our state fiscals were not so subtle in interpreting documents, that young man, most assuredly, would have been acquitted."

This statement from the old Teniente and the tone of his voice produced great surprise in his audience, which was at a loss what to say. Padre Salvi looked somewhere else, perhaps to avoid the somber look which the old man directed at him. Maria Clara dropped the flowers and remained immobile. Padre Sibyla, who knew how to keep quiet, seemed to be the only one who knew how to ask.

"Are you referring to letters, Señor Teniente?"

"I am only repeating what I was told by the defense counsel who took up Ibarra's case with zeal and interest. Outside of a few ambiguous lines which this young man wrote to a woman before leaving for Europe, lines in which the state prosecutor saw a plan and a threat against the government and which he acknowledged as his, there was nothing of which they could accuse him."

"And the statement of the bandit before he died?"

"The defense counsel nullified it, for, according to the outlaw himself, he and his companions had never communicated with the young man, except through a certain Lucas, who was his enemy, according to what has been proven, and who has committed suicide, perhaps in remorse. It was proven that the documents found on the corpse were forgeries: because the script was similar to that of Señor Ibarra of seven years ago, but not to his present handwriting, which made it appear that the model for the forgeries was that accusing letter. Even more, defense claimed that if Señor Ibarra had not admitted his authorship of this letter, much could have been done for him; but the sight of the letter made him pale; he lost courage and ratified what he had written in it."

"You were saying," a Franciscan queried, "that the letter was addressed to a girl: how did it reach the hand of the prosecutor?"

The Teniente did not answer. He looked for a moment at Padre Salvi and moved away, twisting his pointed gray beard nervously while the rest were making comments.

"One can see the hand of God there!" said one; "even the women hate him."

"He had his house burnt down, thinking that that would save him, but he did not take into account the lady guest, that is, the mistress, the woman!" added another laughing. "It comes from God. Here's to Santiago! And to Spain!"

In the meantime the old officer stopped his pacing and approached Maria Clara who was listening to the conversation frozen in her seat; at her feet could be seen the flowers.

"You are a discreet young woman," the lieutenant told her in a low voice, "you have done well in surrendering the letter...thus you are all assured of an untroubled future."

She saw with vacant eyes, biting her lips, the officer move away. Fortunately Tía Isabel was passing by. Maria Clara had enough strength to take hold of her dress.

"Aunt!" she murmured.

"What ails you?" she asked horrified when she saw the young woman's expression.

"Take me to my room!" she pleaded, clutching the old woman's arm to raise herself.

"Are you ill, my dear? It seems that there is not a single bone in your body. What is it?"

"Just a faintness...the people in the living room...so much light...I need to rest. Tell my father I will go to bed."

"You are cold! Do you want tea?"

Maria Clara shook her head, locked the door of her room and, without any strength left, let her body fall to the floor at the foot of the Virgin's image sobbing:

"Mother, mother, mother mine!"

The light of the moon entered through the window and the door leading to the balcony.

The orchestra continued playing merry waltzes. The sounds of laughter and the hum of conversation filtered to the balcony. Her father knocked at the door several times, as did Tía Isabel, Doña Victorina, and even Linares himself, but Maria Clara did not budge; a lament escaped her breast.

The hours passed. The pleasures of the table came to an end. Sounds of dancing were heard. The taper in the room burned out and was extinguished, but the young woman still remained on the floor motionless, illumined by the moonbeams, at the foot of the image of the Mother of Jesus.

The house gradually fell silent. Lights were put out, Tía Isabel called anew through the door.

"Well, now she has fallen asleep," said Tía Isabel in a loud voice. "As she is young and has no cares she sleeps like one dead."

When all were silent, she rose slowly and looked around her. She saw the balcony, the little trellises bathed in the melancholy light of the moon.

"An untroubled future! Sleeps like the dead!" she murmured in a low voice, and went out to the balcony.

The city slept. Only the clatter of a carriage could be heard every now and then crossing the wooden bridge over the river whose solitary waters calmly reflected the light of the moon.

The maiden lifted her eyes to a sky with the purity of sapphire. She slowly removed her rings, earrings, hairpins and comb and placed them on the balustrade of the balcony and looked down into the river.

A boat, loaded with *zacate*, stopped at the foot of the landing which each house had on the river bank. One of the two who steered it went up the stone steps and climbed the wall; and seconds later his steps could be heard climbing up the stairway to the porch.

Maria Clara saw him stop when he saw her, but only for a moment, because the man advanced gradually and stopped three steps away from the young woman. Maria Clara drew back.

"Crisostomo!" she whispered, full of terror.

"Yes, it is I, Crisostomo," the young man gravely replied. "An enemy, a man who had reason to hate me, Elías, rescued me from prison where my friends had thrown me!"

These words were followed by a sad silence. Maria Clara lowered her head and let both her hands fall.

Ibarra continued:

"By my dead mother's coffin I swore to make you happy no matter what happened to me. You could break your own pledge, she was not your mother; but I who am her son, I hold her memory sacred, and despite a thousand perils I have come here to fulfill my pledge, and chance permits me to speak to you in person. Maria, we will not see each other again. You are still young, but someday your conscience may accuse you...I have come to tell you, before taking my leave, that I forgive you. Now be happy, and farewell!"

Ibarra tried to leave, but the maiden stopped him.

"Crisostomo!" she said, "God has sent you to save me

from despair...Hear! then judge me!"

Ibarra gently tried to disengage himself.

"I have not come for an accounting...I have come to give you peace of mind."

"I do not want that peace of mind with which you gift me; that peace I will have to give myself. You despise me, and your scorn will make life bitter till death!"

Ibarra saw the despair and the grief of the poor girl, and asked her what she wanted.

"I want you to believe that I have always loved you."

Crisostomo smiled bitterly.

"Ah! you doubt me, you doubt your childhood friend who has never hidden a single thought from you," exclaimed the young woman with pain. "I understand you! When you learn the story of my life, the sad story which they revealed to me during my illness, you will take pity on me and you will not have that smile for my agony. Why did you not let me die at the hands of my ignorant doctor? You and I would have been happier!"

Maria Clara paused a moment and continued:

"But you wanted it this way. You have doubted me. May my mother forgive me! One night when I was ill and in pain, a man revealed to me the name of my real father and forbade me your love...unless my real father forgives you the injury you have done him."

Ibarra drew back and looked at the maiden, horrified.

"Yes," she continued. "The man told me that our union cannot be allowed by him because his conscience forbade it and he felt he would be obliged to divulge it in public at the risk of causing a great scandal, because my father is..."

And she whispered into Ibarra's ears a name in such a low voice that he alone heard.

"What was I going to do? Should I sacrifice my love

for the memory of my mother, for my false father's honor and the good name of the real one? Could I have done that without you yourself despising me?"

"But proof, do you have proof? You need proof!" exclaimed Crisostomo furiously.

The young woman removed from her bosom two papers.

"Two letters from my mother, two letters written in the midst of her remorse when she was carrying me in her womb. Take and read them and you will know how she cursed me and desired my death...my death that my own father tried in vain to bring about with drugs. My father forgot, and left these letters in the house where he lived. The man found and kept them, and only turned them over to me in exchange for your letter...to assure him, according to his pledge, that I would not marry you without the consent of my father. Since I have carried them with me in place of your letter, I have felt a chill on my heart. I gave you up, I sacrificed my love...What would one not do for a dead mother and two live fathers? How could I suspect what they would do to your letter?"

Ibarra was dismayed. Maria Clara went on:

"What was there left for me? Could I tell you then who was my real father? Could I tell you to ask his forgiveness, he who had done so much to make your own father suffer? Could I perhaps tell my father to forgive you; could I tell him I was his daughter, he who had so much desired my death? My only refuge was to suffer, to keep the secret to myself and to die suffering... Now, my friend, now that you know the sad story of your poor Maria, would you still have for her that disdainful smile?"

"Maria! You are a saint!"

"I am happy because you believe me..."

"However," added Ibarra, changing his tone, "I have heard that you are getting married..."

"Yes!" sobbed the young woman; "my father requires of me this sacrifice...! He loved me and brought me up and that was not his duty. I am paying this debt of gratitude, assuring him peace through this new relationship, but..."

"But what?"

"I will not forget the oath of fidelity I swore to you."

"What do you intend to do?" asked Ibarra, trying to read her eyes.

"The future is dark and our destiny is among shadows! I do not know what I have to do, but I know for sure that I love only once. Without that love I will never belong to anyone! And you—what is to become of you?"

"I am nothing but a fugitive...on the run. Soon they will discover my escape, Maria..."

Maria Clara took the young man's head in her hands and kissed his lips repeatedly, embraced him and afterwards brusquely pushed him away from her.

"Go! go quickly!" she told him. "Go, farewell!"

Ibarra looked at her with glowing eyes, but at her gesture the young man left staggering, vacillating.

He leapt again over the wall and got into the boat. Maria Clara, leaning over the balustrade, watched him leave.

Elías uncovered his head and gave her a deep, profound bow.

Pursuit in the Lake

"Listen, Señor, to this plan that I have in mind," said Elías thoughtfully as they headed for San Gabriel. "You will hide for now in the house of a friend of mine in Mandaluyong. I will bring you all your money which I saved from the fire and kept at the foot of the balete tree where your grandfather's mysterious grave is. Then you will leave the country..."

"Go abroad?" interrupted Ibarra.

"To live in peace the remainder of your days. You have friends in Spain, you are rich, you can get a pardon. Anyway, a foreign country is for us a better one than our own."

Crisostomo did not reply. He reflected in silence.

At that moment they were entering the Pasig river and the boat began to move upstream. A horseman was galloping in haste along the Bridge of Spain and a sharp and prolonged whistle was heard.

"Elías," replied Ibarra, "you owe all your misfortunes to my family. You have saved my life twice. I owe you not only gratitude but also the restitution of your fortune. You advise me to live abroad. Well, come with me and we will live together like brothers. Here you too are unfortunate."

Elías shook his head sadly and answered:

"That is impossible! It is true that I cannot love or be happy in my own country, but I can suffer and die in it and, perhaps, for it, which is something. Let the misfortunes of my country be my own misfortunes, and since we are not at all united in one noble ideal, since our hearts do not beat in unison under one name, at least our common woe may unite me with my countrymen; at least I can weep with them over our sorrows, and let the same misfortunes oppress all our hearts."

"Then why do you advise me to leave?"

"Because elsewhere you can be happy, but not I; because you are not made for suffering, and because you would come to hate your country if some day you would find yourself unfortunate on its account; and to abhor one's motherland is the greatest misfortune."

"You are being unjust to me!" exclaimed Ibarra in bitter reproach. "Have you forgotten that I had scarcely arrived when I sought what is good for her?"

"Do not take offense, Señor; I am not reproaching you in any way. I wish all could imitate you. But I am not asking of you what is impossible; and do not be offended if I tell you that your heart misleads you. You loved your country because your father had taught you thus. You loved her because in her you had love, wealth, youth. You loved her because here everything had smiled on you; your country has not done you any injustice; you loved her as we love all that makes us happy. But in the day that you find yourself poor, hungry, hunted, betrayed and sold by your own countrymen, on that day you will disown yourself, your country and all mankind."

"Your words wound me," said Ibarra with resentment.

Elías lowered his head, reflected and answered:

"I want to disillusion you, Señor, and save you from a tragic future. Remember when I spoke to you in this very boat, under the light of this same moon, more or less about a month ago? You were happy then. The pleas of the unfortunate did not touch you. You disdained their complaints because they were the complaints of criminals. You listened more to their enemies and, notwithstanding my arguments and pleas, you placed yourself on the side of their oppressors; and it then depended on you whether I should become a criminal myself or allow myself to be killed to honor a sacred pledge. God has not allowed it, because the old leader of the outlaws died...A month has passed and now you think differently!"

"You are right, Elías, but man is a creature of circumstances. I was then blinded, disgusted—what did I know! Now misfortune has suddenly removed the bandage from my eyes. The loneliness, the misery of my imprisonment have taught me otherwise. Now I see the horrible cancer that gnaws at this society, which grips its flesh and which demands violent eradication. These have opened my eyes, they have made me see the wound and compelled me to become a criminal! And since that is how they want it, I will become a subversive, but a true dissident.

"I shall call on all the oppressed, all those who within their breasts feel the beating of a heart, all those who sent you to me...no! I will not be a criminal, never is he a criminal who fights for his country. Quite the contrary!

We, during three centuries, have stretched out our hands to them; we have asked them for love, we wanted to call them brothers, and how have they answered us? With insults, and sarcasm, denying us even our own humanity. There is no God, no hope, no humanity; there is only the right of might!"

Ibarra was in a frenzy; his whole body trembled.

They were passing in front of the Governor General's palace, and noted unusual activity and excitement among the guards.

"Have they discovered the escape?" murmured Elías. "Lie down Señor, so I can cover you with the *zacate*; we are passing by the powder magazine and the sentry might find it odd that there are two of us in this boat."

The boat was one of those slender and narrow canoes that glide over the surface of the water rather than move through it.

As Elías had foreseen, the sentry stopped him and asked him where he had come from.

"From Manila, delivering horse fodder to the judges and the priests," he answered, imitating the accent of those of Pandakan.[1]

A sergeant came out to see what was going on.

"Be gone!" this one told him. "I warn you not to take anyone aboard; a prisoner has just escaped. If you catch him and bring him to me I will give you a good reward."

"Very good, Sir! What does he look like?"

"He goes frocked and speaks Spanish. So beware!"

The boat moved away. Elías turned his head and looked at the silhouette of the sentry standing on the river bank.

"We will be losing a few minutes," he whispered. We must enter the Beata river to make it appear that I am

from Peñafrancia. You will see the river of which Francisco
Baltazar sang."

The town slept in the moonlight. Crisostomo raised
himself to admire the sepulchral peace of nature. The river
was narrow and its banks were evenly formed, planted
with *zacate*.

Elias unloaded his cargo ashore, took a long bamboo
pole and picked up from under the grass some empty
bayones or sacks made of palm leaves. They moved on.

"You are the master of your own will, Señor, and
your own future," he said to Crisostomo, who remained
silent. "But if you will permit an observation, I would tell
you: Consider well what you intend to do. You will start a
war, because you have money and brains and will soon
encounter helping hands; fatally, there are many
malcontents. Besides, in this struggle which you are going
to wage, those who will suffer more are the defenseless
and the innocent. The same sentiments which a month
ago led me to press for reforms now make me ask you
to reflect.

"The country, Señor, does not think of separating itself
from the Motherland. It asks for nothing more than a little
liberty, justice and love. The discontented, the criminals,
the desperate, will support you, but the people will abstain.
You are mistaken, because you see darkness everywhere,
in believing that the country is desperate. The people suffer,
yes; but they still hope; they believe and will rebel only
when they have lost patience—that is, when those who
govern decide to have it so, which is something still far
away. I myself will not follow you; never will I resort to
these extreme measures while I see hope within men."

"Then I shall go on without you!" replied Crisostomo
resolutely.

"Is that your firm decision?"

"My firm and only decision! As my father's memory is my witness! I will not tolerate having my peace and happiness snatched away from me with impunity. I, who only desired the common good; I, who have respected and suffered for the love of a hypocritical religion; for love of a country. How did they repay me? By burying me in a foul prison and degrading my future wife. No! not to avenge myself would be a crime, it would spur them to further injustice! No! Let there be an end to cowardice, weakness, to sighing and sobbing, while there still are life and blood; when insult and challenge are joined by derision! I shall call on the ignorant people; I will make them see their misery; they should not think of brothers: there are only wolves which devour each other, and I shall tell them that against this oppression rises and protests the eternal right of man to secure his liberty!"

"The innocent people will suffer!"

"Much better still! Can you take me to the mountains?"

"Until you are in safety," Elías retorted.

They went out again into the Pasig river. They spoke once in a while of inconsequential things.

"Santa Ana!" murmured Ibarra. "Would you know this house?"

They were passing by the Jesuits' country house.

"There I spent many happy and cheerful days," sighed Elías. "In my time we went there once a month...I was like the others then: I had wealth, family, dreamt and glimpses of a future. In those days I would visit my sister in the neighboring college. She would gift me with a labor of her hands...she was accompanied by a friend, a lovely young woman. All that has passed like a dream!"

They remained silent until they reached Malapad-na-bato.[2] Those who in the evening have gone down the Pasig river on one of those enchanted nights the Philippines offers, when the moon spills melancholy poetry from a limpid blue sky; when shadows hide the misery of man and the silence extinguishes the mean accents of his voice; when Nature alone speaks, they will understand what went through the minds of these two young men.

In Malapad-na-bato, the frontier guard was sleepy, and seeing that the boat was empty and offered no booty to loot according to the traditional custom of his corps and the usage of the post, he easily allowed them to pass.

The civil guard at the Pasig did not suspect anything either, and they were not molested.

Dawn was beginning when they reached the lake, smooth and tranquil like a gigantic mirror. The moon waned and the eastern horizon was dyed in rosy hues. At a certain distance they made out a grey mass that was moving slowly.

"The patrol boat comes," whispered Elías. "Lie down and I will cover you with these sacks."

The silhouette of the tender was becoming clearer and more perceptible.

"It is positioning itself between us and the shore," remarked Elías uneasily.

He changed the course of the canoe gradually, paddling towards Binangonan. To his great dismay he saw the launch also change direction, while a voice shouted at him.

Elías stopped and thought. The shore was still far away, and very soon they would be within range of the guns of the patrol boat. He thought of returning to the Pasig. His boat was faster. Fate however, was against him. Another banca came from the Pasig; and the helmets and bayonets of the civil guards could be seen gleaming.

"We are caught," he whispered, turning ashen.

He looked at his robust arms and taking the only alternative left to him, he began to paddle with all his strength towards Talim island.[3] In the meantime, the sun was coming out.

The boat glided swiftly. In the patrol boat, which was also turning, Elías saw some men on their feet making signs to him.

"Do you know how to handle a *banca?*" he asked Ibarra.

"Yes, why?"

"Because we are lost unless I jump out and lead them away. They will go after me, but I am a good swimmer and a diver...I will keep them away from you and then you try to save yourself."

"No, stay and we will sell our lives dearly!"

"Useless. We are unarmed. With their guns they will shoot us like sitting ducks!"

At that moment a hiss was heard in the water like the sound of hot lead, immediately followed by a detonation.

"You see?" said Elías, laying the paddle in the boat. We will see each other on Christmas Eve by your grandfather's grave. Save yourself!"

"What about you?"

"God has delivered me from greater perils!"

Elías removed his shirt. A bullet tore it from his hands and two shots were heard. Undisturbed, he clasped the hand of Ibarra, who was still lying in the bottom of the boat; he stood up and dove into the water, pushing the small craft away with his foot.

Various shouts were heard, and soon at some distance

the young man's head broke the water as if to take breath, and went down instantly.

"There, there he is!" several voices shouted and the bullets whistled anew.

The patrol boat and the other banca started in pursuit, a slight trail marking their passage, getting farther away from Ibarra's banca, which was bobbing as if abandoned. Every time the swimmer raised his head to breathe, the civil guards and boatmen shot at him.

The chase was taking a long time. Ibarra's little banca was already far away. The swimmer was approaching the shore at a distance of some fifty arms' length. The rowers were getting tired, and so was Elías, because his head was coming up more frequently, and each time in a different direction as if to confuse the pursuers. The telltale wake no longer betrayed his passage under water. They saw him for the last time some ten arms' lengths away near the shore; they fired...after minutes and more minutes had elapsed, nothing more appeared on the tranquil lonely surface of the water.

Half an hour later a rower claimed to have discovered in the water near the shore traces of blood, but his companions shook their heads as if to say yes as well as no.

- 63 -

Padre Damaso
Explains

I n vain are piled on a table the expensive wedding
gifts. Neither the diamonds in their blue velvet cases,
nor the *piña* embroideries, nor the bolts of silk, attract
the eyes of Maria Clara. The young woman sees, without
seeing or reading, the journal which gives an account of
the death of Ibarra, drowned in the lake.

All of a sudden she felt two hands laid over her eyes
and holding her fast and a merry voice—that of Padre
Damaso—saying:

"Who am I? Who am I?"

Maria Clara jumped from her seat and looked at him
with dismay.

"Silly little girl! You were scared, eh? You were not
expecting me, eh? Well I have come from the provinces to
attend your wedding."

And, approaching her with a smile of satisfaction, he
extended his hands for her to kiss. Maria Clara came close,

trembling, and kissed the friar's hand with respect.

"What ails you, Maria?" the Franciscan asked her, losing his merry smile and becoming uneasy. "Your hands are cold, you are pale...Are you ill, my little child?"

And Padre Damaso drew the girl to him with a tenderness that no one could believe him capable of; took hold of the maiden's two hands and questioned her with a look.

"You no longer have confidence in your godfather?" he asked her reproachfully. "Come on! sit here and tell me your little disappointments as you used to do as a child, when you asked for candles to make dolls of wax. You know that I have always cherished you...I never scolded you..."

Padre Damaso's voice was no longer brusque. It had an affectionate tone. Maria Clara began to weep.

"You are weeping, my dear! Why? Did you quarrel with Linares?"

Maria Clara covered her ears. "Not a word about him...not now!" cried the young maiden.

Padre Damaso looked at her, dumbfounded. "You do not want to trust me with your secrets? Have I not always endeavored to satisfy every one of your whims?"

The young woman raised her tear-filled eyes to the priest, looked at him for a while and started again to weep bitterly.

"Do not cry this way, my daughter! Your tears are hurting me. Tell me your pains; you will see how much your godfather loves you!"

Maria Clara gradually drew closer to the priest, sank on her knees at his feet and raising her face bathed in tears, said to him in a scarcely audible voice: "Do you love me still?"

"Child!"

"Then...protect my father and break off my marriage."

And Maria Clara narrated to him her last meeting with Ibarra, omitting the secret of her birth.

Padre Damaso could scarcely believe what he heard.

"While he was alive," she continued, "I was thinking of keeping on: I was hoping, I was trusting! I wanted to live to be able to hear about him...but now that they have killed him, now there is no longer a reason for me to live and suffer."

This she said slowly, in a low voice, calmly, without tears.

"But, silly! Is not Linares a thousand times better than...?"

"While he was alive I could get married...I thought of flight afterwards...my father does not want anything but the connections! Now that he is dead nobody else shall claim me as his wife...When he was alive I could degrade myself, there was left the comfort of knowing he lived and perhaps would think of me. Now that he is dead...the convent for me or the grave!"

The maiden's tone had such firmness that Padre Damaso lost his gaiety and became thoughtful.

"Did you love him so much?" he stammered.

Maria Clara did not reply. Padre Damaso bent his head over his chest and remained silent.

"My daughter!" he said finally in a breaking voice, "forgive me for making you unhappy without knowing it. I was thinking of your future; I wanted your happiness. How can I allow you to marry a native of the country, to see you an unhappy wife and an unfortunate mother? I could not move your mind away from your love and I opposed it with all my strength; I abused my position for you, only for you. If you had been his wife you would weep over your husband's condition exposed to all vexations without any means of defense. As a mother you would weep over the fate of your children; if you educated them you prepared them for an unhappy future. They would make themselves enemies of religion and you would see them swing from the gallows or exiled somewhere else. If you left them ignorant you would see them degraded and tyrannized! I could not consent to that! That is why I sought for you a husband who could make you a happy mother of children; who would command and not obey; who could punish and not suffer...I knew your childhood friend was good. I loved him as much as I loved his father, but I hated them when I saw that they were going to cause your unhappiness, because I love you, I idolize you, I love you as a father loves his child. I have no other love but yours. I have seen you grow up; not an hour passes by without my thinking of you; I dream of you; you are my only happiness..."

And Padre Damaso began to weep like a child.

"Then, if you still love me, do not make me eternally unhappy. He no longer lives. I want to be a nun!"

The old man pressed a hand to his forehead.

"To be a nun! To be a nun!" he repeated. "You do not know, my daughter, the life, the mystery that are hidden behind the cloister walls. You do not know! I prefer a thousand times to see you unhappy in the world than in the cloister...Here your grievances can be aired; there you have only the walls...You are beautiful, very beautiful and you were not born for Him, to be the bride of Christ! Believe me, my daughter, time effaces everything. Later you will forget, you will love, and you will love your husband...Linares."

"The cloister or...death!" repeated Maria Clara.

"The cloister, the cloister or death!" he exclaimed. "Maria, I am old; I will no longer have time for you and your peace of mind...Choose another alternative, look for another love, another young man, no matter who he may be, but not the cloister."

"The cloister or death!"

"My God! my God!" cried the priest, covering his head with his hands. "You are punishing me: so be it, but keep watch over my daughter!"

And, turning to the young woman:

"You want to be a nun? So be it. I do not want you to die."

Maria Clara took hold of both his hands, held them, and kissed them as she knelt.

"Godfather! my Godfather!" she repeated.

Padre Damaso came out sad, head bent and sighing.

"God! God! you exist, since you punish! But take vengeance on me and spare the innocent. Save my daughter!"

- 64 -

Christmas Eve

High up on the slope of the mountain, along a stream, a hut built on twisted tree stumps lies hidden among the trees. Over its roof of cogon grass creep squash vines loaded with gourds and flowers; the rustic dwelling is decorated with deer antlers, the skulls of wild boars, some with long tusks. There live a Tagalog family dedicated to the hunt and the cutting of wood.

Beneath the shade of a tree, the grandfather was making brooms with the stems of palm leaves, while a young woman arranged eggs, lemons and vegetables in a basket. Two children, a boy and a girl, were playing beside another child, wan, listless, with great deep-set eyes, who was seated on a fallen tree trunk. We recognize in his thin features Sisa's son, Basilio, the brother of Crispin.

"When your feet are healed," the girl was saying to him, we will play pico-pico and hide-and-seek. I will play *It*."

"You will climb with us to the summit of the mountain," added the boy, "you will drink venison blood with lime juice and you will get fat. Then I will teach you to jump from one rock to another over the torrent."

Basilio smiled sadly, looking at the wounds on his feet, and then turned his eyes to the sun which was shining brightly.

"Sell these brooms," said the grandfather to the young woman, and buy something for your brothers because today it is Christmas."

"Firecrackers! I want firecrackers!" cried the boy.

"And I, a head for my doll," shouted the little girl, clutching at her sister's skirt.

"And you? What would you like?" the grandfather asked Basilio.

The latter raised himself up with difficulty and approached the old man.

"Señor," he said, "have I then been ill for over a month?"

"Two moons have passed since we found you unconscious and covered with wounds. We thought you would die..."

"May God reward you! We are very poor!" replied Basilio, "but since today is Christmas, I would like to go to town to see my mother and my little brother. They must be looking for me."

"But son, you are not well and your town is far away. You will not reach it by midnight!"

"It does not matter, Señor! My mother and my little brother must be feeling very sad. All these years we have spent this feast together...Last year we ate one whole fish between us three...Mother must have be weeping, looking for me."

"You will not reach the town alive, boy! Tonight we have chicken and dried boar's meat. My sons will be looking for you when they return home from the fields..."

"You have many sons: my mother has only the two of us. Perhaps she thinks I am already dead! Tonight I want to make her happy, give her a present—a son!"

The old man felt his eyes moisten. He placed a hand over the boy's head and said to him, moved:

"You are like a grown-up. Go then, look for your mother, give her her present...from God, as you say. If I had known the name of your town, I would have gone there when your were sick. Go on, my son, may God and the Lord Jesus be with you! Lucia, my granddaughter, will accompany you to the nearest town."

"What! Are you going?" The little boy asked. "Down below there are soldiers, there are many thieves. Don't you want to see my firecrackers? Pum, purumpum!"

"Don't you want to play blind chicken with hide- and-seek?" the little girl asked. "Did you ever hide yourself? Really, nothing is more fun than to be pursued and to hide oneself!"

Basilio smiled, picked up his cane and said, with tears in his eyes:

"I will return soon. I will bring my little brother; you will meet him and play with him. He is about your size."

"Does he limp too when he walks?" the little girl asked. "Then we will make him play home in the pico-pico game."

"Don't forget us," the old man was saying. "Take boar's meat with you and give it to your mother."

The children accompanied him up to the bamboo bridge which spanned the turbulent stream.

Lucia made him lean on her arm, and they were lost to the sight of the children.

Basilio was walking lightly despite his bandaged leg.

The north wind is blowing and the inhabitants of San Diego shiver with cold.

It is Christmas Eve; but the town is sad. Not a single paper lantern hangs from the windows, not a single sound in the houses announces the merriment as in other years.

On the ground floor of Capitan Basilio's house he and Don Filipo are engaged in conversation beside barred windows. (The latter's misfortunes had made them friends.) At another window Sinang, her cousin Victoria and the lovely Iday are looking out into the street.

The waning moon appears on the horizon, gilding the clouds, trees and houses, and projecting long and fantastic shadows.

"Yours is no small luck to get yourself acquitted in these times!" remarked Capitan Basilio to Don Filipo. "Yes, they have burned your books, but others have lost more!"

A woman approached the bars and looked inside. Her eyes were bright, her features emaciated, her hair loose and matted. The moon gave her a peculiar aspect.

"Sisa!" exclaimed Don Filipo, surprised, turning to Don Basilio while the mad woman moved away. "Wasn't she under treatment in the home of a physician?" he asked. "Is she cured?"

Capitan Basilio smiled bitterly.

"The doctor feared that he would be accused of being Don Crisostomo's friend and dismissed her. Now she roams, madder than ever; she sings, is harmless and lives in the forest."

"What else has happened to the town since we left it? I know we have a new parish priest and a new *Alferez*..."

"Terrible times; humanity has retrogressed," murmured Capitan Basilio, remembering the past. Let's see now: the day after you left they found the *sacristan mayor* dead, hanging from the ceiling of his house. Padre

Salvi felt his death keenly, and took possession of all the dead man's papers. Ah! Tasio the philosopher also died, and was interred in the cemetery of the Chinese."

"Poor Don Anastasio," sighed Don Filipo. "And his books?"

"They were burned by the pious busybodies, who believed that thus they were pleasing God. I was not able to save any of the books, not even the works of Cicero...the *Gobernadorcillo* did nothing to prevent it."

Both kept silence. At that moment the sad and melancholic singing of the mad woman was heard.

"Do you know when Maria Clara is getting married?" Iday asked Sinang.

"I do not know," she answered. "I received a letter from her, but I have not opened it, fearing to know the worst. Poor Crisostomo!"

"They say that had it not been for Linares, Capitan Tiago would hang. What could Maria Clara do?" observed Victoria.

A youngster passed by, limping. He was heading in the direction of the plaza where Sisa's singing came from. It is Basilio. The boy had gone to his house, found it deserted and in ruins. After many inquiries, the only thing he learned was that his mother had gone mad and was roaming the town; of Crispin not a single word.

Basilio swallowed his tears, suppressed his grief and, without any rest, went to search for his mother. He arrived in town, asked for her and the singing reached his ears. The hapless boy tried to control the trembling of his legs and wanted to run and throw himself into his mother's arms.

The mad woman left the plaza and reached the house of the new *Alferez*. Now, as before, a sentinel guards the door and a woman's head appears at the window.

However, it is not the Medusa; it is a young woman. *Alferez* and unfortunate are not synonymous.

Sisa started to sing in front of the house, gazing at the moon which was swaying majestically in the blue sky amid the golden clouds. Basilio saw her but dared not approach, waiting perhaps for her to leave the place. He walked to and fro, but avoided coming nearer to the barracks.

The young woman at the window listened attentively to the song of the mad woman and ordered the sentinel to bring the woman upstairs.

Upon seeing the soldier approach, and hearing his voice, Sisa was filled with terror, started to run, and only God knows how a mad person can run. Basilio followed behind her and, fearing to lose her, also ran, forgetting the pain in his legs.

"See how that boy is pursuing the mad woman!" indignantly exclaimed a maidservant who was on the street.

Seeing that he continued running after her, she picked up a stone and threw it at him, saying:

"Here, take that! It's a pity that the dog is tied up."

Basilio felt a blow on the head, but continued running, ignoring it. The dogs were barking at him, the geese honked, some windows opened to give way to the curious; others closed, fearing another night of tumult.

They reached the outskirts of the town. Sisa began to slow down. A great distance was between her and her pursuer.

"Mother!" he cried when he caught sight of her.

The mad woman, upon hearing his voice, started on her flight anew.

"Mother, it is I!" the boy screamed in despair.

The mad woman did not hear; the boy followed

behind her, panting. They had passed the rice fields and were now close to the woods.

Basilio saw his mother enter, and he followed. The shrubs and bushes, the thorny canes, the protruding roots of the trees hampered the movements of both. The boy followed his mother's silhouette, lighted now and then by the moon's rays penetrating through the clearings and the branches. This was the mysterious forest of the Ibarra family.

The boy stumbled several times and fell, but he would pick himself up, not feeling the pain: all his being was focused on his eyes which followed the beloved figure.

They passed the brook which was murmuring softly. The bamboo thorns fallen on the muddy bank pierced his bare feet, but Basilio did not stop to pluck them out.

To his great surprise he saw his mother penetrate deeper into the thickets, entering through the wooden door which closes the tomb of the old Spaniard at the foot of the *balete* tree.

Basilio tried to do the same, but found the door closed. The mad woman guarded the entrance with her thin arms and dishevelled head, keeping it closed with all her strength.

"Mother! It is I, it is I; I am Basilio, your son!" cried the exhausted son falling to the ground.

But the mad woman did not give way; planting her feet firmly on the ground she offered energetic resistance.

Basilio beat against the door with his fists, his head bathed in blood. He sobbed in vain. Painfully he raised himself, gazed at the wall, thought of scaling it but could not find any foothold. He went around and saw a branch of the ill-omened *balete* tree crossing the branch of another tree. He climbed. His filial love worked miracles, and from branch to branch he passed through the *balete* tree and saw his mother still with her head against the panels of the door.

The sound coming from the branches called Sisa's attention. She turned and wanted to flee but her son, letting himself fall from the tree, embraced his mother and covered her with kisses before losing his senses.

Sisa saw his forehead bathed in blood, bent down towards him, her eyes almost popping out of their sockets. She gazed at his face: and those pale features awakened the long dormant cells of her brains; something like a spark was kindled in her mind, and she recognized her son. Letting loose a cry she fell on the unconscious boy, embracing and kissing him.

Mother and son remained motionless...

When Basilio recovered consciousness, he found his mother lifeless. He called her, lavished on her the most tender names, and seeing that she neither breathed nor awakened, he stood up, went to the stream to fetch some water in a cone of banana leaves and sprinkled it over his mother's pale face. But the mad woman made not the slightest movement; her eyes remained closed.

Basilio regarded his mother, stricken with horror. He pressed his ears against her heart, but the thin and withered bosom was cold and the heart did not beat. He put his lips over hers and did not perceive any breath. The hapless boy embraced the corpse and wept.

The moon shone in the majestic sky; the breeze wandered, sighing, and under the grass the crickets chirped.

The night of light and happiness for so many children, who in the warm bosoms of the family celebrate the feast of the sweetest memories, the feast that commemorates the first glance of love sent by heaven to earth; that night when all the Christian families eat, drink, dance, sing, laugh, play, love, kiss each other...this night, which in cold countries is magic for children with its traditional pine tree loaded with lights, dolls, sweetmeats and tinsel, whose round eyes reflecting innocence look dazzled; that night had nothing to offer Basilio more than orphancy. Who knows? Perhaps in the home of the taciturn Padre Salvi, children are playing too, and perhaps singing:

> *Christmas is coming*
> *Christmas is gone...*

The boy wept and moaned intensely, and when he lifted his head saw a man standing before him, regarding him in silence. The stranger asked him in a low voice:

"Are you her son?"

The boy affirmed this with a nod.

"What are you planning to do?"

"Bury her!"

"In the cemetery?"

"I have no money, and besides the priest will not allow it."

"So?"

"If you could help me...?"

"I am very weak," answered the stranger, who was gradually sinking to the ground, leaning with both hands on the earth...I am wounded...It has been two days since I have eaten or slept....Has someone come tonight?"

The man remained thoughtful, contemplating the boy's interesting features.

"Listen!" he continued in a weakening voice. "I shall have died too before the break of day...Twenty paces from here, by the other bank of the creek there is a big pile of firewood. Bring it over, make a pyre, put our bodies on it, cover us and set it afire, a huge fire, until we are turned to ashes..."

Basilio listened.

"Afterwards, if no one else comes...you will dig here, you will find much gold...and all of it will be yours. Study!"

The stranger's voice was becoming more and more unintelligible.

"Go, fetch the firewood...I want to help you."

Basilio moved away. The stranger turned his face towards the east and murmured as though praying:

"I die without seeing the dawn break on my country... You who are about to see it, greet her...do not forget those who have fallen during the night!"

He raised his eyes to heaven, his lips moved as if murmuring a prayer, then he lowered his head and fell gradually to the ground....

Two hours later, Sister Rufa was in the *batalan*[1] of her house doing her morning ablutions before going to mass. The pious woman gazed towards the nearby forest and saw a thick column of smoke rising. She frowned and, filled with holy indignation, exclaimed:

"Who could the heretic be who, on a day of celebration, would make a *kaingin?*[2] That is why many misfortunes come! Let him try to get into Purgatory and he will see if I take him out of there, the savage!"

Epilogue

Many of our characters being still alive, and having lost sight of the others, a true epilogue is not possible. For the good of the public we would gladly kill all our personages starting with Padre Salvi and finishing with Doña Victorina, but that is not possible...let them live: the country, and not we, will in the end have to feed them...

Since Maria Clara entered the cloister, Padre Damaso left the town to live in Manila; likewise Padre Salvi who, while waiting for a vacant mitre, preaches many times in the church of Sta. Clara, in which convent he holds an important post. After a few months Padre Damaso received orders from the Very Reverend Father Provincial to take charge of a parish in a very distant province. It is said that he took this so badly that the next day he was found dead in his room. Some say he died of apoplexy, others, from a nightmare, but the doctor dispelled all doubts by declaring that he died suddenly.

Not one of our readers now would recognize Capitan Tiago if they saw him. Weeks before Maria Clara took her vows, he already fell into a state of total depression such that he began to lose weight and became morose and brooding and as suspicious as his ex-friend, the unhappy Capitan Tinong. As soon as the convent had closed its gates, he ordered his disconsolate cousin, Tía Isabel, to pack up everything that had belonged to his deceased wife and to his daughter, and to go to Malabon or San Diego, because from now on he wanted to live alone. He took to playing *liampo* and to cockfighting with such frenzy that he began to smoke opium. He no longer goes to Antipolo, nor does he order masses said. Doña Patrocinio, his old rival, celebrates her triumph with piety, by snoring during the sermons. If at any time, when afternoon comes, and you pass the first street of Santo Cristo you will see seated in a Chinese store a smallish jaundiced man, thin and bent, with sunken sleepy eyes and muddied lips and nails, staring at people as if he does not see them. At nightfall you will see him rise painfully, and, leaning on a cane, head for a narrow alley to enter a filthy hut at the entrance of which there is a sign in big red letters: The Anfion Public Smoking Den.[1] This is that famous Capitan Tiago, now totally forgotten even by the *sacristan mayor*.

Doña Victorina has added to her artificial ringlets and her Andalucian accent—the words escape us—the new hobby of wanting to drive the horses of the carriage, herself, obliging Don Tiburcio to be quiet and stay put. Because of her weak vision many accidents occurred, so she now wears a pair of pince-nez, giving her a singular look. The doctor is no longer called to treat anybody; the servants see him during many days of the week without dentures, which, as our readers already know, is an evil omen.

Linares, the only defender of this hapless man, has long been in repose in the Paco cemetery, a victim of dysentery and of his cousin's ill treatment.

The victorious *Alferez* went to Spain as a *Teniente* with the grade of commandant, leaving his amiable wife in her flannel blouse of a now undistinguishable color. The poor Ariadne, thus abandoned, dedicated herself as did Minos' daughter, to the cult of Bacchus and to the culture of tobacco, drinking and smoking with such passion that she is feared not only by the maidens but also by old women and children.

Our acquaintances in San Diego are probably still alive, that is if they did not perish in the explosion of the steamship Lipa which commutes between the provinces.[2] Since no one took the trouble to find out who the hapless victims were who perished in that catastrophe; to whom belonged the legs and arms scattered in the Convalescencia Island[3] and on the river banks, we are completely ignorant as to whether anyone among them was an acquaintance of our readers. We are satisfied, as were the Government and the Press of that time, with the knowledge that the only friar who was in that boat was saved, and that is enough for us. What is important to us is the life of the virtuous priests, whose reign in the Philippines may God preserve for the good of our souls.

Nothing of Maria Clara has been heard again, except that the sepulchre apparently keeps her in its bosom. We have asked various persons of much influence in the holy Convent of Santa Clara, but no one was willing to say a single word, not even the talkative devotees who are the favored recipients of the famous dish of fried chicken livers with the still more famous sauce called *de las monjas,* prepared by the clever cook of the virgins of the Lord.

One night in September, however, a hurricane raged and pummeled with its gigantic wings the buildings in Manila; thunder reverberated at every moment; lightning and flashes illuminated at times the ravages of the storm, plunging the inhabitants into fearful terror. Rains fell in torrents. In the brilliance of the lightning flash or of the bolt that zig-zagged, one could see a piece of the roof, a shutter fly through the air and fall with a terrifying crash. There was not a single carriage nor person wandering the streets. When a loud clap of thunder a hundred times repeated, was lost in the distance; then the wind was heard to sigh, which churned the rain, producing a repeated *trac trac* against the shell panes of the closed window....

Two sentries were taking shelter in a building under construction near the cloister: they were a soldier and a *distinguido.*[4]

"What do we do now?" said the soldier. "There is no one walking in the street...we should go into a house. My mistress lives on Arzobispo street."

"From here to there, is a great distance. We will get wet," said the *distinguido.*

"It does not matter as long as we are not killed by lightning."

"Bah! Don't worry. The nuns must have a lightning rod for their safety."

"Yes!" said the soldier, "but of what use is that on a dark night like this?"

And he raised his eyes above to look into the darkness. At that moment there was a flash of lightning followed by a formidable thunderclap.

"*Naku! Sus mariosep!*"[5] exclaimed the soldier, making

the sign of the cross, and pulling at his companion. "Let us leave this place!"

"What is the matter with you?"

"Come on! Let us leave," he repeated, his teeth chattering in fright.

"What did you see?"

"A ghost!" he murmured, all shaken up.

"A ghost?"

"Up there on the roof...it must be the nun who gathers firewood during the night."

The *distinguido* stuck his head out; he wanted to look.

There was another flash of lightning and a vein of fire surged through the sky, leaving the sound of a horrible explosion.

"Jesus!" he exclaimed crossing himself. As a matter of fact, in the brilliant light of the lightning he had seen a white figure standing, almost on the ridge of the roof, its arms and face stretched towards heaven as if imploring. The heavens answered with lightning and thunder!

After the thunder was heard a doleful moaning.

"It is not the wind; it is the ghost," murmured the soldier in answer as it were to the pressure of the hand of his companion.

"Ay! ay!" was floating in the air, drowning the noise made by the rain. The wind could not cover with its whistling that sweet and plaintive voice, full of hopelessness.

Another ray of lightning flashed with blinding intensity.

"No, it is no ghost!" exclaimed the *distinguido*. "I saw her again. She is beautiful as the Virgin...Let us leave this place and report this."

The soldier did not wait for the invitation to be

repeated, and both disappeared.

Who is it who moans in the middle of the night, despite the wind, the rain and the tempest? Who is the timid virgin, the spouse of Christ, who defies the unchained elements and chooses this dreadful night, and the open sky, to voice from that perilous height her complaints to God? Has the Lord abandoned His temple in the convent? Does He no longer listen to prayers? Will the cloister vaults not allow, perhaps, the aspiration of the soul to soar to the throne of the Most Merciful?

The tempest raged furiously almost throughout the night. In that darkness not a single star shone. The desperate laments mingling with the sighing of the wind continued but they came across soundless to Nature and to men. God had shrouded Himself and did not hear.

The following day, when the skies had been cleared of dark clouds and the sun shone anew in the purified atmosphere, a carriage stopped at the door of the cloister of Santa Clara. A man alighted; he introduced himself as the representative of the official authorities, and asked to speak immediately with the abbess, and demanded to meet all the nuns.

It is said that one of these appeared with her habit soaking wet and torn to shreds; weeping, she asked for the man's protection against the violence of hypocrisy, and revealed other horrors. It is said that she was very beautiful, that she had the loveliest and most expressive eyes that were ever seen.

The representative of the authorities ignored her. He conferred with the abbess and abandoned the nun despite her pleas and tears. The young nun saw the gates close behind the man as the damned might see the gates of Heaven close against them, if Heaven had become as cruel and unfeeling as man. The abbess said she was out of her mind.

The man perhaps did not know that in Manila there is a home for the demented, or perhaps he thought that the convent of nuns was only a house of refuge for the demented, although it was alleged that the man was somewhat ignorant, particularly in the matter of judging when persons are in their right minds or not.

It is also said that the Governor General Señor J.[6] thought otherwise when the matter was brought to his attention. He wanted to protect the mad woman and asked for her.

But this time no beautiful and forlorn young woman appeared, and the abbess forbade visits to the nunnery, invoking on that score the authority of the Church and the Holy Rules of the Order.

Nothing more was said about this nor of the hapless Maria Clara.

End of the Narrative

Notes

The title, **Noli Me Tangere**, is the Latin for *"Touch me not,"* and comes from the Gospel of St. John, XX:17, where Jesus says to Mary Magdalene: "Touch me not, for I am not yet ascended to my Father..." The author relates this to a social cancer "of a breed so malignant that the least contact exacerbates it and stirs in it the sharpest of pains" in his dedication: "To My Motherland (A mi patria). On 5 March 1887, Rizal wrote to the painter Resurreccion Hidalgo: "The book (Noli) has matters which no one among ourselves has spoken of until now—so delicate that they cannot be touched by anybody..."

Chapter 1

1. **Capitan Tiago:** The *gobernadorcillos*, or what were then the equivalent of town mayors, were also commonly called the Captains of the town. Capitan Tiago in the novel is the personification of various Filipinos, some friends and acquaintances of the author who enjoyed the respect of

Manila society. It is believed that Rizal particularly had in mind two men from Manila, Don M.B. and Don T.C., and one from Malabon.

2. **Intramuros:** Literally "inside walls," the Walled City, Old Manila. It was the primary district of the City of Manila in Spanish times, for here were the offices of the Spanish Government, the Cuartel de España and Fort Santiago. Intramuros was then encircled by thick wide walls ringed by a moat; access to it was through five solid gates, among them La Puerta de Isabel II, La Puerta del Parian, and Puerta Real, making it one of the best fortified Oriental cities.

3. **Calle Anloague:** It was named after the Tagalog *anluwagi*, or carpenter, "because many carpenters lived there who were dedicated to the construction of buildings of wood, bamboo and nipa." (Retana, *Diccionario de Filipinismos*). Today it is that portion of Juan Luna St. from Plaza Calderon de la Barca up to Plaza Cervantes.

   Binondo: When the Noli was written, Binondo (from *minundoc*), north of the Pasig River and close to Santa Cruz and Tondo, was, according to Bowring, "the most important and wealthy town of the Philippines, and her true commercial capital." Most of the Chinese in Manila lived in Binondo. Its main commercial street was Rosario (from Plaza Moraga to the Binondo Church).

4. **The House on Anloague Street**: The house described here was the property of Don Balbino Mauricio, which during the first years of the American regime housed the Office of Internal Revenue. It was a large house located on a piece of land between Juan Luna and Rentas and Ingreso Streets behind the *estero*, or Binondo Creek.

5. **Ria de Binondo:** Today it is called the *estero*, a small creek

no longer used as described by Rizal by reason of its being dirty and undredged. It has been the canal of Binondo since 1861, when its banks were paved.

6. **Pearl of the Orient:** Metaphor for Manila, and on a larger scale, for the archipelago. Rizal used it in his last poem, "Mi ultimo adios": "*Adios, patria adorada, region del sol querida | Perla del Mar de Oriente, nuestro perdido eden...* (Farewell my adored motherland, region of the sun beloved, / Pearl of the Orient seas, our lost paradise...").

7. *Caida:* The spacious living room in houses of strong materials, which one encounters immediately at the top of the stairs.

8. **Arevalo:** Jose and Bonifacio Arevalo, father and son, were both sculptors, engravers and dentists, and Rizal may have referred to either of them. Both figure in M. Artigas y Cuerva's *Galeria de Filipinos Ilustres*; Jose taught many promising young men who later became prominent sculptors, and had a shop in Quiapo for religious works; Bonifiacio modelled artistic images.

9. **Nuestra Senora de la Paz y Buenviaje:** Our Lady of Peace and Good Voyage, the Virgin of Antipolo. The image was brought to the country in 1626 from Acapulco, Mexico, by Governor-General Juan Niño de Tabora. Yearly, in May, thousands of devotees flock to the shrine in Antipolo, Rizal, to pay homage to the Virgin.

10. **Capitana Ines:** A Filipina, almost legendary in her great devotion and generous donations to the church and to religious feasts; stories link her with many miracles.

11. *Buyo:* A small wrapped chewing wad of betel nut leaves, slaked lime and *bonga* (*Arecha catechu*).

12. *Teniente*: Lieutenant.

    Guardia Civil: A semi-military body tasked to go after criminals, maintain the security of the highways and order in the towns. Formed in 1869 with some 4000 Filipino privates under Spanish officers, it was patterned after a similar body in Spain. Its main functions were military and police, which it performed well for a time, but like most institutions it slid into corruption and came to be noted for misdemeanors and brutality.

    Duke of Alba: Fernando Alvarez de Toledo, duke of Alba, was a celebrated Spanish general during the reigns of Charles V and Philip II (1508-1582) who distinguished himself for his vigorous repression of Protestantism, and for being so bloodthirsty and cruel that his name was used as a bogey to frighten children.

13. **Young Dominican, parish priest of Binondo:** Rizal is said to have perhaps been referring to a Fr. J.H.C.

    Colegio de San Juan de Letran: first known as the Colegio de los niños huerfanos de San Pedro y San Pablo, then renamed in 1706 and converted into a school for primary and secondary education.

    B. de Luna: Don Benedicto de Luna of Tanauan, Batangas, who graduated in Philosophy and Law from the University of Santo Tomas, and was considered one of the best debaters of that epoch, as well as an educator. He established a famous private school in Santa Cruz, Manila.

14. **Three monks in Heine's "Gods in Exile":** Bacchus, the Roman god of wine and fertility, and two of his proteges, who were all attired as Franciscan friars.

Hijos de Guzman: the Dominican friars, belonging to the religious order founded in 1215 by St. Dominic de Guzman (1170-1221).

15. **Mendieta:** A well-known person in Manila at that time, doorkeeper to the mayoralty, manager of childrens' theaters, manager of a merry go round, etc. (Notes, Maucci edition).

16. *Indio*: "The Malays of the Philippines were called Indios by the Spaniards," noted Professor Blumentritt (Retana, *Vida y Escritos del Dr. J. Rizal*). That was a pejorative name in a time when "Filipino" referred to the Spaniard or Spanish mestizo born in the Philippines, and "Peninsular" to the Spaniard born in Spain.

17. **Tertiary Sisters:** Members of the Tertiary Order of St. Francis of Assissi. The three orders under Franciscan rule are: the first, for young priests; the second, for nuns; and the third for the laity.

18. **Tobacco Monopoly:** This reserved for the government the right to regulate the cultivation, manufacture and sale to the public of tobacco, and was imposed in 1782. It soon became a source of graft and corruption. It was abolished in 1881.

19. **"The reforms of the ministries are irrational":** The reactionary elements in the Philippines had always opposed all liberal reforms that some ministers intended to introduce.

20. **"The *Indio* is so indolent":** To denigrate the native he was branded as indolent, so much so that Rizal wrote an essay entitled *"Sobre la indolencia de los Filipinos* (On the Indolence of the Filipinos)".

21. *Bailujan*: a "Tagalized" word referring to dances (*bailes*).

22. **San Diego:** A fictitious town. It is believed that Rizal had in mind the towns of Biñan, Calamba and Malabon.

23. **Camiling:** A town then in the province of Pangasinan, and now in Tarlac; hometown of Leonor Rivera, Rizal's betrothed.

24. **Calamity of a little general:** An allusion to General Emilio Terrero y Perinat, for his adverse attitude against the monastic orders, or for his distressing campaign at the Rio Grande of Mindanao against Datu Uto. Terrero was the Governor General of the Philippines when Rizal returned from Europe in 1887, and governed from 1885-1887. It was he who designated a lieutenant of the Guardia Civil, Don Jose Taviel de Andrade, to be at the side of Rizal during his stay in the Philippines.

25. **Vice-Royal Patron:** The highest representative of the King in the Philippines was the Governor-General, to whom the monarch delegated his powers and who was next to him in authority. He carried the title of Vice-Royal Patron.

26. **Governor General Bustamante:** Certain radical elements of Manila rose against this Governor General, assassinating him in October of 1719 in his own palace.

27. **"No other King but the legitimate":** The decree issued by Ferdinand VII naming his daughter Isabela as his heir instead of his nearest male heir, Don Carlos de Borbon, resulted in the Carlist movement, followed by a civil war which lasted more than 40 years (1833-1876). The majority of the members of the religious orders did not recognize Isabela II as the real monarch. For the Spanish Carlist political party, the legitimate king was the pretender to the throne.

28. **Padre Damaso:** Rizal apparently did not wish to picture any specific person, and this seems to have been confirmed

by Antonio Ma. Regidor, who, speaking of the characters of the Noli said: "Who does not know Padre Damaso? Ah! I have dealt with him; and even in his brilliant fictional personification, he carries the trappings of the dirty Franciscan, always gross, always tyrannical and constantly corrupted. I in real Filipino life have dealt with and studied him, clothed sometimes in the white habit of the Augustinian, sometimes the Franciscan as you have pictured him, and others with their bare feet and the habit of the all-knowing Recollect." (Letter to Rizal, May 3, 1887).

29. **The Doctora Doña Victorina:** In the Philippines, the wife of a dignitary or of a professional is often addressed with the title of her husband: thus the wife of the governor is called the *gobernadora*, that of the *capitan*, *capitana*, etc. In Doña Victorina, Rizal is said to have pictured a real-life matron, Doctora Agustina Medel, well known in Manila society, and married to a Spaniard surnamed Coca, who is said to have helped in some way the landowners of Calamba in their litigation against the land grants.

30. **Berthold Schwartz:** A German Franciscan monk of the 14th century who is credited with the invention of gunpowder.

    Savalls or Chevas: A play on words. Savalls was a famous Carlist head (Notes, Maucci edition).

31. **Padre Sibyla:** Taking into account the picture that Rizal detailed of this personage in both the Noli and the Fili, it appears that he had in mind the Dominican Father B.N.

Chapter 2

1. **"The cub of the lion was a lion":** A slogan spread by the supporters and sympathizers of the Spanish republicans in

the Philippines, "The cubs of the lions are also lions."

2. **Tondo:** The ancient town bordering Manila, ultimately a suburb of the capital. It was in Tondo that Rizal's La Liga Filipina was organized. It was the parish priest of this district who received in the confessional the news of the existence of the Katipunan.

3. **La Campana:** An old restaurant situated on the Escolta, at #35 corner San Jacinto St., today called T. Pinpin. Like its namesake in Seville, it was then the mecca of high society.

Chapter 3

1. ***"Jele jele bago quiere"***: Pidgin Spanish-Tagalog saying, meaning that one pretends not to desire a thing which in reality one wants. Here it refers to both Padre Damaso and Padre Sibyla wanting to sit at the head of the dining table, a place usually given to the most esteemed guest.

2. **"Age, dignity and rulership":** More completely: "To the elders in age, dignity, knowledge and rulership" is the formula with respect to ceding primacy over whatever act to the person one wishes to honor as superior to one in any of these concepts.

3. ***"Cedant arma togae"***: Latin words meaning that arms should give way to the toga, and that right is might; used figuratively to signify the superiority of the civil government. *Cedant arma cottae* means that arms should give way to the surplice, or military to religious power.

4. **Lucullus did not dine in the house of Lucullus:** Lucullus was the Roman General who acquired fame for his

gastronomic appetites and banquets of luxury and splendor. Once given an ordinary meal when there were no guests, he indignantly replied that day "Lucullus dined in the house of Lucullus." Rizal reverses it here since Capitan Tiago had no seat at his own table.

5. *Tinola*: A dish of chicken stewed with white squash or upo (Lagenaria siceraria), potatoes or green papaya, often served as the first dish at dinner, like soup. It was generally said then that no European could pass eight days in the Philippines without tasting *tinola*.

6. *Benedicite*: The first word, meaning "to bless," with which a prayer in Latin begins, was said before meals. Prayers to bless the meal were said at the moment of sitting at table, following the custom of religious communities. Prayers giving thanks for the meal were said at the end of the meal. The *Benedicite* was said by the superior or head, and answered by the community.

7. *Peñinsula*: Unlettered Filipinos believed that they were hispanizing it by pronouncing the n as ñ (Notes, the Sempau-Maucci edition of the Noli).

8. **Exodus:** In the figurative sense, the peregrination of the emigrants of a nation, their vicissitudes, evolution, history.

Chapter 4

1. *Calesa*: a horse-drawn chaise or buggy.

2. **Binondo Plaza:** The plaza in front of the Binondo Church, officially called the Plaza Calderon de la Barca.

3. **Sacristia Street:** Thus called because it begins in front of the

windows of the sacristy of the Binondo Church. Today it forms part of Ongpin St., from Rosario St. to the first bridge over the Reina estero.

Jacinto Street: Today that portion of Pinpin St. from Ongpin St. to the Escolta.

4. **Our prestige:** A kind of *noblesse oblige*. Among other things Spanish prestige, which had to be preserved at all costs, consisted of not lowering oneself to manual labor. It was a good and dignified principle that was much abused.

5. **Ba-be-bi-bo-bu:** These syllables are part of the Spanish phonetics included in the primary reader called the *Cartilla*, one of the books used for teaching Spanish in the primary grades in the Philippines at that time.

6. **Subversive:** One who worked for reforms in the colonial government, or the Filipino with liberal ideas, who did not conform to the monastic-military ruling regime. Any Filipino who protested injustice and abuses, or sought freedom and reforms, was called a *filibustero*, and ran the risk of exile and other punishments.

7. *El Correo de Ultramar: The Overseas Mail*, a newspaper of liberal character published in Madrid, which sympathized with the aspirations of the Filipinos for autonomy. Many of those exiled after 1872 were subscribers of this paper, which was banned for Filipinos by the Spanish Government.

8. **The priest sentenced to death:** One of the three executed in Bagumbayan in 1872, Fathers Gomez, Burgos and Zamora.

9. *Camisa*: A shirt worn outside, untucked, the attire of the well-to-do Filipino, now known as the barong tagalog. It is made of different materials, of Canton, of piña, embroidered, fretworked or plain.

10. **Young Filipino lawyer:** It is thought that he was alluding to the legal consultant Don Cayetano Arellano.

11. **Sr. M.:** Don Francisco Marcaida or Don Manuel Marzano, famous practicing lawyers.

12. **Fonda de Lala:** A hotel owned by Lala Ari, a British Indian famous then for the bounty of his kitchen. It was also known as Fonda del Conde, and was located at No. 37 Barraca St., now Plaza del Conde. It had accommodations for 35 guests with a reading room, billiard hall, baths and a school for horseback riding.

Chapter 5

1. **River:** The estero de Binondo.

2. **Piña:** Very fine, transparent fabric woven in the Philippines from the filaments of the leaves of the pineapple plant.

3. **Bagumbayan Field:** The field, now part of the Luneta, between San Luis and P. Burgos Streets, where Rizal was executed by firing squad on 30 December 1896. It is mentioned throughout the *Noli*, seemingly hounding Rizal like an inexorable fate. Was he clairvoyant? Russel and Rodriguez tell the story that once when crossing the field, Rizal said to his companion: "In this place I will one day be shot."

Chapter 6

1. **Zacate:** A grass also called talango; forage of diverse grassy plants, especially of the *Russelia junccum*. Zacate is an American term (Note, Maucci edition).

2. **House gods:** The protective gods of the Roman family. The Tagalogs had *anitos*, deities of mountains, fields, waters and home. Ancestors were also worshipped as household gods.

3. **Masterpieces of the sculpture of Santa Cruz:** Santa Cruz district has been called the cradle of the first Manila artists, for here were born jewelers, sculptors, engravers, painters, and musicians, also goldsmiths, aesthetes and lyricists. Furthermore, "the first images of saints that were brought and paraded in the provinces...came from the sculpture shops of Sta. Cruz, and were famed for the majesty as well as beauty of their saints and virgins, cherubs and angels." (Florentino Torres, *El Debate*, 19 October 1924).

4. **Artists of Paco and Ermita:** In Paco and Ermita were found the studios of the painters of that epoch, whose work was predominantly religious in theme.

5. *Talibon, Talibong:* A sword synonymous to the Muslim *kampilan* and the *bolo*. The *bolo* is a large blade used for domestic tasks, work in the field, and as an offensive weapon.

6. **Joloan** *kris:* A blade smaller than the *kampilan*, usually double-edged and serpent-shaped.

7. **Malchus:** When Jesus Christ was taken by the Jews, St. Peter cut off the right ear of Malchus, a servant of the high priest. Jesus "touched his ear, and healed him" (John xviii:10-11).

8. **Carpentry shops of Paete:** The cabinet makers of Paete and Pakil, towns along the Laguna lake, are still known for fine work and carving.

9. *Sinigang:* A stew of fish and vegetables soured with tamarind or other sour fruits or leaves.

Dalag: A species of fresh-water mudfish or murrel (*Ophicephalus striatus*); found in rivers, lakes, rain dams, ricefields and inundated fields.

Butterfly leaves: *Alibangbang* (*Bauhinia tomentosa*), the leaf of a flowering plant of the legume family, which is sour and used as a condiment in *sinigang*.

10. **Guardian of a brotherhood:** The person designated as watchman for a congregation or fraternity formed by devotees for the purpose of undertaking works of piety.

11. **Official of the fifth rank:** Line officials of the Spanish administration were divided into five categories: 1) Superior heads of administration; 2) Heads of administration; 3) Heads of trade affairs; 4) Officials; 5) Candidates for officialdom.

12. *Sangley:* A Chinese peddler or merchant. The words comes from the Chinese *xiang-lay* or merchant.

13. *Gobernadorcillo:* A native official exercising control over a town, somewhat like a mayor or municipal judge, discharging at the same time the functions of a magistrate and even of notaries with certain powers.

14. *Ayuntamiento:* A city corporation or governing council, or the building housing members of the city corporation and all its officials and employees. The Ayuntamiento in Manila was located in Intramuros, between Postigo and Aduana Streets, with entrance at Cabildo Street.

15. **The silversmith Gaudinez:** A Filipino who had his shop in the Quiapo district.

16. **La Naval:** The October feast of the Holy Rosary celebrating the Spanish naval victory against the Dutch in 1646, credited to the intercession of the Virgin of the Holy Rosary. Also commemorated on this occasion is the victory obtained by Don Juan of Austria over the moors in Lepanto.

17. *Audiencia Real*: The highest court of justice in the Philippines, established in Manila, a court of appeals and consultative body to the Governor General.

18. **Virgin of Caysasay:** The image of Mary venerated in Taal, Batangas. It stands in the middle of the main altar, within a carved eagle's belly which serves as a tabernacle for Our Lady.

    Virgin of Turumba: The patron saint of the town of Pakil, Laguna; actually Our Lady of Sorrows, but popularly called Turumba or "jump for joy" because of a ritual procession.

19. **Saint Pascual Baylon:** The patron saint of women who want to have children, and the patron of Obando, Bulacan, whose feast on May 17 is the occasion for dancing to ask for a child.

20. **The Amat:** A treatise on scholastic philosophy written by Felix Torres Amat, archbishop of Tarragona, Spain; also his translation of the Bible into Spanish.

21. **Nunnery of St. Catherine:** A college for girls founded by Padre Juan de Sto. Domingo, Dominican provincial, in 1696. It used to be on Anda Street in Intramuros.

22. **Mother Eavesdropper:** The religious sisters in the convents or girls' schools, had the duty to chaperone those who received visitors, and to keep watch over them.

Chapter 7

1. **Song of Songs:** A poem (*Cantar de los Cantares; Cantica Cantorum*) in one of the books of the Old Testament, written by King Solomon, and referring to the love of husband and wife.

2. **Lotus of forgetfulness:** The metaphor is based on the legend that foreigners who eat of the fruit forget their country (see Homer's *Odyssey*).

3. *Sigueyes:* Shells (*Cyprea moneta*) which in ancient times served as money, and were also used as counters in a game.

   Siklot: A children's game involving seeds, shells or small stones placed on the palm and thrown upward, to be caught on the back of the hand.

   Sintak: A children's game consisting of seven small pebbles or shells and a large one called the "home."

   Bantil: A penalty applied to the loser, consisting of finger-flick strokes on the back of the hand.

   Chonka: A Filipino game played on a piece of wood about a meter long and six inches deep, shaped like a banca, with seven small hollows on each side and a main hole at each end called home. The player who gathers the most pebbles or shells into his "home" wins.

4. **Ateneo:** Now the Ateneo de Manila University, this educational institution, originally called the Ateneo Municipal de Manila, was on Arzobispo Street between Real and Anda Streets in Intramuros. It was established by the Jesuits in 1859, and educated Filipinos, employing the most advanced methods of instruction then known in Europe.

Rizal graduated from the Ateneo on March 14, 1877, with high honors and the degree of Bachelor of Arts.

5. *Gogo: Entada purseta,* tree bark that is wet, beaten and used as a shampoo.

6. **Baltazar:** Francisco Baltazar, also called Balagtas, known as the prince of Tagalog poets, especially for his masterpiece, the metrical romance (*awit*) *Florante at Laura*.

7. **Plaza de San Gabriel:** The plaza or square located between Rosario and Juan Luna Streets, near the Pasig River, and eventually known as Plaza Cervantes.

Chapter 8

1. *Carromata:* The ancestor of the calesa, a two-wheeled, horse-drawn vehicle with a tarpaulin-covered top.

2. *Salakot:* A round, wide-brimmed hat made out of thinned and woven bamboo strips layered with palm leaves.

3. **Escolta:** In the first half of the 20th century, the busiest and most important commercial street in Manila, where financial houses and the most elegant stores were located.

4. **Puente de España (The Bridge of Spain):** The bridge stretching from the Puerta Parian to Nueva Street, and spanning the Pasig River between Jones Bridge and MacArthur Bridge.

5. **Isla de Romero:** Romero's Island, which no longer exists since one of the canals ringing it (now called Estero Cegado) was blocked.

6. *Banca:* A small canoe or wooden dugout.

7. **Ermita:** That district of Manila located between the Luneta and Malate; formerly famous for embroidery on piña cloth.

   Malate: The district adjoining Ermita, in which many Filipino elite families resided.

Chapter 9

1. **Rivera:** Jose Rivera, also known as Lo Spagnoletto (1588-1656), a Spanish painter identified with the Neapolitan school of painting, a disciple of Caravaggio who produced paintings admired for their technical perfection and known for their frightening themes.

2. **Malacañang Palace:** The residence of the Governor General, now the offices and residence of the Philippine President.

Chapter 10

1. *Cabonegro: Borassus gomutus,* the sugar palm, which produces fruits (*kaong*) and a strong and incorruptible black thread.

2. *Balete: Ficus indica,* a tree that grows large, with sturdy spreading roots, for which many Filipinos hold religious beliefs and respect.

Chapter 11

1. *Fulanito:* The Spanish expression meaning "Little Mr. So-and-so."

Chapter 12

1. **INRI:** *Iesu Nazarenum Rex Iudaeorum*, Latin for Jesus of Nazareth, King of the Jews, the acronym usually found on top of a crucifix.

2. ***Tarambulo, Pandakaki:*** *Solanum zeilanicum* and *Tabernaemontana laurifolia*, respectively, shrubs that grow profusely in native cemeteries.

Chapter 13

1. **Padre Garrote:** A name referring to Padre Damaso, and to the instrument of torture often used on natives.

2. ***Ilang-ilang:*** *Canaga odorata* or *Uvaria aromatica, Anonacea*, a tree with intensely fragrant flowers, the oil of which is used in perfumery.

3. ***Palasan:*** A species of climbing root of great strength (*Calamus Maximus*), noted for its hardness and valued for use as canes.

Chapter 14

1. **San Jose College:** Set up by the first bishop of the Philippines, Fr. Domingo de Salazar, it was placed under the control and supervision of the Jesuits and inaugurated in 1601 as the Colegio de San Jose. It was later placed under the Dominican Order. One of its most distinguished alumni was Fr. Jose Burgos.

2. **Santa Barbara:** The patron saint against lightning, especially invoked during thunderstorms.

3. *Teniente Mayor*: Chief lieutenant, not a military officer but a municipal official, second in authority to the gobernadorcillo or the mayor of a town or municipality during the Spanish regime. He was the senior member of the town council, and took over the duties of the *gobernadorcillo* or *Capitan* if the latter was incapacitated or had passed away.

Chapter 15

1. *Cuarto*: Smallest monetary denomination then used in Manila. Eight *cuartos* were equivalent to five centavos, two *cuartos* to 1.25 centavos.

2. *Sacristan Mayor*: The head of the altar boys, who was in charge of all of the employees of the sacristy.

Chapter 16

1. *Oremus*: Latin for "Let us Pray."

2. *Timsim*: A Chinese word to describe the pith of the reed which served as a wick for small coconut oil lamps. *Timsim* is a plant (*Aegilops fluviatilis*) which grows in humid places; from its pith were made hats like *salakots*.

3. *Sahig*: Flooring made of strips of bamboo.

   Palupu: The ridge of the roof.

   Tunko: Tripod of stones over which the pot or cooking dish is placed.

4. *Kalao*: The Philippine hornbill, a large bird.

5. *Kundiman*: A native song of a particular rhythmic pattern, generally interpreting sentiments of love, pain, or suffering, but occasionally also humor or patriotism.

Chapter 17

1. *Tinhoy, tinghoy*: An oil lamp used by the poor, with a wick of *timsim* and coconut oil as fuel.

2. *Alpay*: A medium-sized tree which bears small, juicy and sour fruits, of the genre *Nephelium*.

Chapter 18

1. *Pako: Athyrium esculentum,* an edible fern which grows along the banks of creeks; fiddlehead fern.

2. *Patola*: The sponge gourd, or *Momordica charantia*.

Chapter 19

1. *Ciruela*: A teacher who, although he did not know how to read, put up and taught in a school in one of the towns of Badajoz, Spain.

2. *Cartilla*: A small printed folder which contained the alphabet and was used to teach the first steps of reading.

3. **Father Astete:** Author of the Catechism of Christian Doctrine which was adopted as a textbook in the primary schools according to the provisions of a royal decree dated 20 December 1863.

Chapter 20

1. *Tribunal*: The Maucci edition of the *Noli* defines this as equivalent to the Spanish Ayuntamiento; it also refers to a municipal building or town hall.

2. *Cuadrilleros*: The police agents of the tribunal, whose duty was to maintain peace in the towns by pursuing outlaws and guarding the prison and town hall. They used old guns and swords and went barefoot.

3. *Cabeza de Barangay*: Village chief, a municipal official serving the town under the *gobernadorcillo* or *capitan*, with charge over 50-60 families in a *barangay* or *barrio* (village) of the town.

4. *Capitan*: The *gobernadorcillo*, the recognized chief civil authority in a town, the equivalent of today's mayor.

5. **San Juan de Letran**: Established in 1640 for primary education, it offered secondary education in 1871. (Cf. Chapter I, note 13).

6. *Patres Conscripti*: When Rome became a republic, the character of its senate was altered by the enrollment of plebeian members, known as *conscripti*, and hence the official designation of the senators thereafter was *patres conscripti* (conscript fathers).

7. *Hermano mayor*: Literally "older brother", being a respected man, generally wealthy and religious, who takes charge of and bears the greater part of the expenses of a fiesta.

8. *Capones rellenos*: Capons stuffed with meat, mushrooms, olives, sausages, etc.; a traditional Spanish Christmas dish.

9. **Sulla:** Lucius Cornelius Sulla, a celebrated Roman dictator (138-78 B.C.), said to be a good friend but a bad enemy.

10. *Liampo:* A Chinese game of chance much played by both Chinese and Filipinos during the Spanish era.

11. *Tikbalang:* A creature of lower Philippine mythology, said to assume the form of an old man, or a horse, or a monster.

12. **Mariang Makiling:** A legendary enchantress said to dwell on Mt. Makiling, and to be a benefactress of the poor of Laguna. Rizal was born in Calamba, at the foot of Mt. Makiling.

Chapter 23

1. *Kalaway:* A little egret.

2. *Baklad:* Bamboo fish pen.

3. *Kamias: Averrhoa bijimbi*, an acidic fruit used for souring.

   Paayap: Cowpea; a species of stringbean.

4. *El Canto de Maria Clara:* The song Maria Clara sings at the picnic, the three main verses of which have assumed a life outside the novel as "The Song of Maria Clara."

5. *Ayungin:* Silver perch (*Datnia plumbea*).
   Bia, biya: Flathead goby (*Gobius juris*)
   Buan-buan: Tarpon (*Megalops cyprinoides*)
   Banak: Mullet (Family *Mugilidae*)
   Dalag: Fresh-water mudfish, murrel (*Ophicephalus striatus*)
   Pesa: A dish of fish cooked in water with ginger, peppercorns, onions, and often served with soybean mash.

Chapter 24

1. **Actaeon:** A hunter who, according to Greek mythology, watched Artemis bathing, and was transformed into a stag whom his own hunting dogs devoured.

Chapter 25

1. *Pangingi, Panguingue:* A game of cards

Chapter 26

1. *Kupang:* A large tree (*Parkia javanica*) reaching 25-40 meters in height, and found in La Union, Laguna and Palawan.

Chapter 27

1. *Kaluskus:* Bamboo whose outer skin is superficially scraped, with the scrapings left to adhere and serve as adornments in the making of bowers and arches.

2. **Chananay, Ratia, Carvajal, Yeyeng:** Filipino actors in the 19th century zarzuelas, comedias and dramas, some of whom had Spanish blood. Chananay was Valeriana Mauricio, and Yeyeng Praxedes Fernandez, one of the most famous of her era. Nemesio Ratia and Jose Carvajal were actors, the latter often playing comic roles. Rizal does not mention the Spanish performers who had preceded and trained them (Elisea Raguer, Alejandro Cubero, etc.), perhaps because they may not generally have gone to perform in the provinces, or because he wanted to feature Filipinos.

3. **S.P. de T.:** The town of San Pedro de Tunasan, Laguna.

4. *Kasama*: Tenant, who works the land of a proprietor on a crop-sharing basis.

5. *Biga*: A plant (*Alocacia macorrhiza*) used as adornment.
   Tikas-tikas: A native plant with lance-like leaves (*Canna indica*)

6. *Baino*: An aquatic plant with large beautiful flowers (*Nymphaea nelumbo*).

Chapter 28

1. *Tabi*: **"Move aside,"** which coachmen shouted to open the way and warn pedestrians that their carriages were passing.

2. **House of *giring-giring*:** A tumbledown house in near ruin, giving no protection against sun, rain and wind; the huts of the poor.

Chapter 29

1. **The town of B.:** Biñan, Laguna

2. **La Galvez:** Doña Buenaventura Galvez y Mijares de Reyes, graduate of the Madrid Conservatory, a distinguished pianist who, with her indisputable merits, monopolized the teaching of piano in Manila.

3. *Mestiza* **dress:** Formal wear for Filipinas, consisting of a blouse of jusi, sinamay or piña with butterfly sleeves, a *panuelo or neckpiede*, and a *saya* or skirt with a long train, and often a *tapis* or overskirt.

Chapter 30

1. **Bossuet:** Jacques Benigne Bossuet, a French preacher who earned fame in Paris for his eloquent sermons.

Chapter 31

1. **Galen had reason:** Father Salvi is likened to Galen's passing smoke through the nostrils to the head with the incense. The expression means that the air goes to one's head, or that one is arrogant. Galen was a Greek doctor (130-200).

2. **Segismundo:** The protagonist of Calderon de la Barca's play, *La Vida es Sueno*, a work that was translated into Tagalog and performed in Manila.

Chapter 32

1. *Errarle es hominum*: A misspelling and a reversal of the words and grammatical construction of the Latin phrase *Errare humanum est* (To err is human).

2. **Sinibaldo de Mas:** "A man of rare talent and very extensive culture; he was minister of Spain in China, and for reasons of health was obliged to spend long periods in the Philippines, where he wrote his well known Informe sobre el estado de las Islas Filipinas in 1842..." (Retana, *Aparato II*, 588).

Chapter 33

1. **Juan Palomo:** A man of great skill with an inordinate love of self, who would not seek the assistance of his fellowmen in his labors.

2. *Directorcillo*: An unofficial functionary, the only one of his kind and indispensable in the municipal bureaucracy; a sort of municipal official, right-hand man of the gobernadorcillo or capitan and his interpreter (in Spanish) with Europeans.

Chapter 34

1. **Tagalog**: The language of the Tagalogs (*taga-ilog* or river people) of the central region of Luzon.

Chapter 35

1. *Kalikut*: "An instrument used to mince the buyo nut, made up of a container with a lining of horn, and a blade like a chisel with its corresponding handle." (Serrano, *Diccionario*, 434).

2. *Dikines*: Plural of the Tagalog term *dikin*, a coiled pad of climbing vines or bamboo on which to seat cooking pots.

3. *Nito*: Filaments of a Philippine fern (*Ligodium circinnatum*), used for weaving wallets and native hats.

4. *Cumare, Cumpare*: From *comadre, compadre*, the godmother/ godfather of one's children, with whom one shares a spiritual parenthood. It is also used to address friends and acquaintances familiarly.

5. *Deminos pabiscum*: A corruption of the Latin *Dominus vobiscum*, or The Lord be with you.

Chapter 36

1. *Plibastiero*: A corruption of *filibustero*, filibusterer or subversive.

2. *Tarantado y saragate*: From *atarantado*, a Spanish vulgarism meaning thoughtless, reckless; and *zargate*, a Mexican word meaning trouble-maker, respectively.

3. *Betelapora*: A corruption of *Vete la porra*, a vulgar Spanish expression used to drive one away; the equivalent of "go to hell."

4. *Ispichoso*: A corruption of *sospechoso*, or suspicious. In the Philippines then this was equivalent to being branded as not supportive of those handling the situation.

5. **Villa-Abrille**: Don Faustino Villa-Abrille, a Spanish army major commissioned to conduct a campaign against outlaws in the Philippines, and noted for his aggressiveness and unusual physical strength.

6. *Santusdeus*: From *Santo Dios* or Holy God.

   Requimeternam: A corruption of *Requiem aeternam* or Rest in Eternity.

Chapter 39

1. *Loa*: A short dramatic poem in praise of an illustrious person or deed, and usually recited in processions, or before the image of a saint, or before a dramatic presentation.

2. **Giovanni Bernardone:** The name of Saint Francis of Assissi, founder of the Franciscan Order.

3. **Elias of Cortona and Cesario of Speyer:** Senior friars of the Order, contemporaries of the founder.

4. *Sampaga*: *Sampaguita (Nicantes sambac)*, the fragrant jasmine-like white flowers strung into necklaces.

Chapter 40

1. **Don Francisco de Canamaque:** A Spanish government official who wrote several books about the Philippines, in which he criticized the character and conduct of both Spaniards and natives, and the wrongdoings of the government and the friars. At least one book was banned by the Spanish authorities in the Philippines.

2. *Mankukulam:* Witch doctor; someone with the capability of harming someone or making him ill by sticking pins into an effigy.

3. *Orofea:* Mispronunciation of *Europea*, or European.

4. **Volapuk:** A universal business language invented by the Swiss professor J. M. Schleyer in 1885, which fell into disuse when replaced by Esperanto.

5. *Pala:* An expression meaning "Ah, so!"

6. **Ulango:** A barrio in Tanauan, Batangas, known for the fabrication of whips.

Chapter 41

1. *Monte:* a game of cards in which huge bets are placed on two cards crossing each other.

2. *Crispin and Comare:* The title of an operetta from Spain, popular in Manila in the last quarter of the 19th century.

3. *La Calandria:* (The Lark) A Spanish zarzuela by Ruperto Chapi which was popular in Manila.

4. *Himno de Riego:* A march identified with the Spanish liberal

movement, and popular in the Philippines for *komedya*.

Chapter 43

1. **Agustina de Zaragoza:** The heroine of Zaragoza, who by her courageous defense of the headquarters of Pilar against the French invader became the symbol of Spanish patriotism in 1808-09.

2. **Salvadora:** The name of the ship on which Rizal embarked the first time he left the Philippines.

3. **Samaniego:** Felix Maria de Samaniego, a Spanish writer of fables in verse.

4. **Malecon:** In the Spanish times, the dike which stopped the banks from caving in from the rush of waves; today it is known as Bonifacio Drive in Port Area.

5. **Peninsular:** A peninsula-born Spaniard resident in the Philippines.

6. *Kamagon, kamagong:* A species of ebony tree (*Diospyaros pilosantera*).

Chapter 44

1. **"I will go down to the plains and extinguish the fires of my vengeance and my own existence! And that day will come, or there is no God!":** The author's note in the Berlin edition identifies the place where the incident happened as either Tanauan, Batangas or Pateros, Rizal.

2. **Corte:** The Spanish parliament.

Chapter 47

1. *Soltada*: The term used in cockfighting for the letting loose of the two fighting cocks with their sharp metal gaffs. The way a cock is let loose can mean victory or defeat.

2. *Pare*: Short for *compare, compadre*.

3. *Mama*: A term used to address a stranger; equivalent to Mister.

Chapter 48

1. *Puput*: A pejorative term given a female European, or one who passes herself off as one.

2. **Juan Lanas**: One who is weak-minded and who does all that is asked of him; a coward or ne'er-do-well.

Chapter 49

1. **"The dark swallows will return"**: The opening line of a well-known poem by the Spanish poet Gustavo Adolfo Becquer:

Volveran las oscuras golondrinas
En tu balcon sus nidos a colgar,
Y otra vez con el ala a sus cristales
Jugando llamaran...

(The dark swallows will return
To your balcony, their nests to hang,
And once more, with a wing at your windows
Playing, they will call...)

2. *Molave, dungon, ipil, tindalo, narra*: First class Philippine woods used for fine constructions.

Chapter 50

1. **Capitan-General de la Torre:** Carlos Maria de la Torre y Navancerrada was the first Governor-General sent to the Philippines (1869-1871) after the fall of the monarchial government. He issued an amnesty to the outlaws, and established the Guardia Civil out of the men given amnesty.

2. *Encomenderos*: The Spanish soldiers who had distinguished themselves in their services and were rewarded with land grants called *encomiendas*, from the inhabitants of which they exacted tribute.

Chapter 51

1. **Padre Gaspar de San Agustin:** A Spanish missionary who came to the Philippines in 1668 and died in Manila in 1724. He wrote an account of the conquest of the Philippines, and a famous letter (1720) detailing derogatory criticism of the Filipinos, and commenting on their vices and customs. Later it was discovered that his observations were based mainly on the behavior of the servants in the convents of the friars and the residences of the Spaniards.

2. **Concordia**: The College of the Immaculate Conception or Colegio de la Concordia on Herran St., Sta. Ana, Manila, established in 1868 as a school for girls.

Chapter 52

1. **Los Baños:** A town in the province of Laguna at the foot of Mt. Makiling, known for its many hot springs.

Chapter 54

1. Rizal gave this chapter an Italian title: *IL BUON DI SI CONOSCE DA MATTINA*.

2. **University of Santo Tomas:** Established in 1611 as a college, and made a university on November 20, 1645 by a Papal Bull by Innocent X.

3. *Claudite jam rivos, pueri!*: Taken from Virgil's Third Eclogue, meaning "Lower the curtain, children!" or enough of this.

Chapter 56

1. **Argus:** According to Greek mythology, Argus, son of Jupiter and Niobe, had a hundred eyes, 50 of which were always awake, so he was made to guard Io by the jealous goddess Hera.

2. *Tulisan:* Bandit or highwayman; in those times it also referred to the fugitive from the law, or those persecuted by the law for crimes they did not commit.

Chapter 58

1. **My joy in the well:** *Mi gozo en un pozo*, a Spanish saying referring to frustration, i.e. when one fails to attain what he wanted to do.

2. *Timbain*: Literally, to take water from a well with a pail (*timba*). Here it is taken in the context of the torture described in the text, a forerunner of the water torture during the American occupation.

Chapter 60

1. **Marianas:** Las Islas Marianas or Islas de los Ladrones, a group of islands in the Pacific not far from the Philippines. Among the islands in this group are Guam and Saipan.

2. **General Bad Omen:** General Mal-Aguero, a nickname derogatorily given to General Joaquin Jovellar, Captain-General of the Philippines from 1883 to 1885. He attempted to introduce some reforms during his term, to the displeasure of the friars.

3. **Father Secchi:** Angel Secchi, S.J., Italian astronomer who by his own merit was retained by King Victor Emmanuel to run the Italian observatory even after the Jesuit Order was expelled.

4. **Virgin of the Girdle:** The patroness of the Augustinian Order, venerated in the Church of San Agustin in Intramuros, Manila.

5. **Virgin of Carmel:** Nuestra Senora del Carmen, an image from Mexico and now the patroness of the Church of San Sebastian in Manila.

6. *El Diario de Manila*: The oldest as well as the most reactionary newspaper published in Manila at the time of the writing of the *Noli*.

7. **Those of 72:** This refers to the Cavite Mutiny of 1872, in which the Fathers Burgos, Gomez and Zamora were implicated, and for which they were executed in

Bagumbayan. It is considered to be the first spark of the Revolution against Spain.

Chapter 62

1. **Those of Pandacan:** In those times, most of the zacate used for horse fodder in the capital came in bancas from Pandacan.

2. *Malapad-na-bato:* "Wide rock" in Tagalog; a rock that jutted out into the river where the streams from Laguna de Bay joined the Marikina River to form the Pasig River. This was a post for collecting revenue on goods brought over the river. Customs guards were stationed here to collect duties.

3. **Talim Island:** An island in Laguna de Bay northwest of Los Baños, seen as soon as one enters the lake coming from the Pasig River. It is a fishermen's barrio, and in its center is the mountain called Susong Dalaga, or Maiden's Breast.

Chapter 64

1. *Batalan:* That part of a house of light materials which is equivalent to a balcony in a house of strong materials.

2. *Kaingin:* Raw land prepared for planting through the slash and burn method—chopping down the forest, burning it, and planting.

Epilogue

1. **Anfion Public Smoking Den:** In the Philippines then, Anfion was the name given to opium compounded and prepared for smoking. Opium was controlled by the government,

which derived revenues from it. Only Chinese were permitted to smoke opium in licensed public smoking rooms.

2. **The explosion of the steamship Lipa:** This happened on 2 January 1883, according to Rizal.

3. **Convalescencia Island:** An island in the Pasig River known to many because of the hospital established there under the friars of San Juan de Dios. Here convalescent patients of the hospital in Manila were sent to speed their recovery.

4. *Distinguido:* A military rank between that of the ordinary soldier and that of a corporal in the Spanish Army.

5. *Naku! Sus Mariosep!:* A contraction of *Ina ko!* (Mother mine) and *Jesus, Maria y Jose!* (Jesus, Mary and Joseph); an expression of surprise, admiration or terror.

6. **Governor General Senor J.:** A reference to Captain-General Joaquin Jovellar y Soler who was Philippine Governor-General from 1883-1885.